OPEN HEARTS

BENNETT SISTERS, BOOK #2

EVE DANGERFIELD

First published by Eve Dangerfield Books in 2018
Copyright © 2018 by Eve Dangerfield
All rights reserved. No part of this publication may be reproduced, stored or transmitted in any form or by any means, electronic, mechanical, photocopying, recording, scanning, or otherwise without written permission from the publisher. It is illegal to copy this book, post it to a website, or distribute it by any other means without permission.
This novel is entirely a work of fiction. The names, characters and incidents portrayed in it are the work of the author's imagination. Any resemblance to actual persons, living or dead, events or localities is entirely coincidental.
Second edition

ACKNOWLEDGEMENT OF COUNTRY

This novel was written on the unceded ground of the indigenous people of Australia, specifically the Wurundjeri Woi-wurrung people of the Kulin Nation. I honour the traditional custodians of the lands and waterways and pay my respects to Elders, past, present and emerging.
Always was, always will be Aboriginal land.

DEDICATION

For my girls. By which I mean the women I know and love and not my boobs. But also, my boobs.

1

Fifteen minutes until I can smoke, Ashley Bennett reminded herself as she drummed her chipped purple fingernails on her chair. *Just fifteen tiny little minutes...*

For the millionth time that night, she scanned the room, checking the babies and making sure no parents or visitors were attempting to sneak into the nursery. Technically it was the 'Specialist Infant Care Room,' but she and all the other midwives at Southern Star Hospital called it the nursery.

It was nine at night, and all the preemies were in their little chambers, the jaundice babies dozing fitfully under UV lamps. Tiny humans, born not quite ready.

Ash stared at the closest baby, a purplish walnut of a thing, wriggling on its back. The little girl was probably confused as hell. Eight hours ago she was tucked inside her mother, warm and safe. Wholly connected to someone she loved without needing to do a thing. Now she was here, pinned by gravity, surrounded by light and noise. Ash couldn't imagine how confused she must be. As she watched, the baby let out a tiny hiccuping squeak, a prelude to the scream Ash could feel coming. She stood and walked over to the crib, running her hands over the warm plastic. "Everything will be okay, baby. Everything will be all right."

Ash wasn't if sure if what she was saying was true. In her experience, things started out beautiful, then turned to shit. Lovely promises bled into bland reality. High hopes crumbled into mundane disappointment. Still, that wasn't something you told a baby, especially one that wasn't yours.

As she performed another spot check, Ash's stomach gave a low rumbling growl. Her breakfast had been vending machine chips washed down with Diet Vanilla Coke. Usually, she ate a big meal before a shift, but Zach had woken up, and Ash had eaten a forty-minute argument instead.

Her boyfriend's gripes were always the same; she was ignoring him, she didn't love him, she 'judged him' for not making as much money as she did. Today he'd followed her around the house, refusing to give her her car keys, insisting she needed to ditch work so they could 'talk it out.'

In her heart, Ash knew there was nothing else to say. She and Zach hadn't been happy for months, they weren't in love anymore, but she couldn't handle another half-baked breakup. It was just easier to snatch her keys and run out the door, to turn off her phone and come to work.

Work, where everything had its place. Work, where there were rules and order, and lots of other women to talk to. Ash loved being a nurse, but she also loved who she was when she was a nurse; her hair tied back in a ponytail, her scrubs neat and clean. At work she had all the answers, she could solve people's problems, deliver their children. At work, no one knew about her grubby past as a welfare baby turned wild child or her shitty present tied to a man who felt more and more like a ten-kilo bag of cement around her neck.

So go, her mind whispered for the hundredth time. *You know it's not right, so go.*

Ash stared at the sleeping baby, all Zen-like and still with her little UV blindfold on. A baby for whom all the world was still a lovely promise.

Open Hearts

"It's not that I'm scared of him," she whispered. "It's just every time I tell Zach I want to break up, he says he won't leave until he finds another place to stay, which he never does because he's not really looking. And then he's so nice, I forget why I tried to dump him in the first place, which is crazy because the things he's called me…"

She shook her head, unwilling to say the words out loud. She left them in the haze of three am arguments when he was drunk, and she was crying and a small part of her whispered, *is this the time? Is this the time he picks up the ashtray and throws it at me instead of the wall?*

Ash stroked the baby girl's crib with her finger. "My sister hates Zach. Her name's Julia. She designs video games."

The baby made a soft cooing noise that Ash chose to interpret as a sign to keep talking.

"Julia and I are really close. People say we look the same but she's way smarter than me. And taller. She thinks Zach is a complete," Ash glanced around to make sure no one was watching, "fuck-knuckle. She won't come home if he's there; she goes to her boyfriend's place instead."

Ash wasn't being honest with the preemie. Two weeks ago Julia had come home to find the PlayStation broken, her new Fallout game lying on the filthy carpet and the bottle of gold vodka in her room empty. She'd confronted Zach who claimed Julia owed him money and the PlayStation was broken when he got there.

Ash could only watch as her favourite human in the world packed a bag and left. Before she got in her car Julia told Ash that she loved her but she wasn't coming back until she 'dumped that toxic tyre-fire shitheel fuckface on his arse.'

All their lives she and Julia had been practically joined at the hip. Their mum was a train wreck, and their dad took off when they were young. Ash, three years older, had basically raised her baby sister, but she and Jules were more than family, they were best friends. They lived together, knew every detail of each other's lives, and exchanged roughly ten million texts a day. Except now for the first time since Valeria Zolnerowich told Ash she had a sister, there was silence between them. And all because of an ex-Nitro Circus stuntman who refused to do the washing or get a proper job but still had a hold on Ashley's heart.

"Do you have any brothers and sisters?" Ash asked the baby. "No, I think you're mummy's first. Well, let me tell you something. I hope she has another baby, and I hope it's a little girl. Sisters are the best thing in the entire world. Much better than boys."

The baby made another cooing sound, like a baby pigeon.

Ash lay along the preemie's tank, a hard lump welling in her throat. "Julia used to be the reason I dumped guys. No matter how bad it got, when she sat in front of the TV and refused to move, that's when I knew it had to end."

The baby frowned, its tiny mouth puckering. To Ash's weary brain it seemed like disapproval. "You don't need to tell me I'm pathetic. Julia already did that."

"I'm so sick of you letting guys treat you like this," her sister had yelled as they stood in the front garden. "You deserve so much better!"

"That's easy for you to say!" Ash had yelled back. "Not all of us get to be tall and hot."

"Are you fucking *kidding me?* You used to be a model!"

"Yeah, used to be! And it was only ever print work!"

Julia had screamed with hysterical laughter. "Moving past the fact that guys still Facebook friend me to ask if you're single, and there is a subreddit thread full of your old modelling pictures called *'I would ten out of ten smash Ashley Bennett,'* what are you doing with this dirtbag?" She pointed towards the window where Zach was sulking. "He makes all your other boyfriends look like Jesus."

Ash had rolled her eyes. "I'm sorry about the game and the vodka. It was an accident, and I'll replace them as soon as I get paid."

"I don't give a fuck about that!" Julia's face was scarlet with rage. "I give a fuck about you. That man is scum and I know he's abusive. I heard him call you an ugly bitch last night and I don't care how fucking drunk he was, he wasn't joking."

Ash's skin had gone tight and hot. She hated Julia for saying what he said out loud, for making it real in a way she didn't want it to be real. "Grow up," she told her sister. "Relationships aren't all sunshine and rainbows. Not all of us get locked in a cupboard with their perfect narc boyfriend like you did."

"Max is not a narc!"

"Yes, he is."

"He's a cop! And even if he was a narc—"

"He is a narc."

"Yeah, well at least he treats me well!" Julia pointed a finger in Ash's face. "Why can't you find someone who treats you well and just be with them instead of all these fuckheads?"

Ash had laughed in her sister's face. "Like who? I'm almost thirty, I've had a million boyfriends and I can tell you there is no one better out there."

"So why don't you *be single*?" Jules had screamed. "Are you that scared of being without a man that you'd let someone abuse you rather than be alone?"

Ash, without thinking, had said yes.

That was the last straw. Julia had gotten in her car and driven away without looking back. But in the days that followed, Ash realised she was wrong; she wasn't afraid of being alone, she was afraid of something else. A future that was impossible without a man in it.

Ash smiled at the newborn girl. While all babies were precious, there was no denying the fact some of them came out looking like gnomes. This one, however, was perfect. She had a cupid bow mouth, smooth skin, and a surprisingly thick head of chestnut hair. Get rid of the yellowish tint of jaundice, and she'd be one of the prettiest babies Ash had ever seen. She clutched her belly and imagined the newborn in front of her was her own. That she'd grown inside her body, feeding off her blood, her life, until it was time for her to come into the world.

Ash wasn't afraid of being alone, but she was so, so afraid of never becoming a mother.

She'd always thought it would happen in her mid-twenties, but here she was almost twenty-nine and baby-less. Julia didn't understand, she and Max were years away from considering kids, caught up in their relationship and professional lives, but for Ash, the dream had always been a family. A family in the most Disneyfied sense of the word: a father, dependable and strong, a mother full of affection and love. Cute kids in pretty clothes who didn't flinch when someone knocked at the door or stand on chairs to microwave their tinned spaghetti dinners.

She wanted the fairy tale, everything she and Julia never had, and that picture wasn't complete without a man.

It was embarrassing, really. With her past, she was as far from a Disney princess as a blonde woman could be and Zach was more Mel Gibson than Prince Charming, but at least he was there. He was a handsome guy who was open to the idea of having a baby. If she dumped him, what next? Start again? Go out on the hunt for another guy and pray that he wanted kids? And what if Zach was right? *He* was mostly okay with her past, but a lot of guys didn't want to marry the girl whose bedpost was more notches than wood and who paid for her nursing degree doing nipple-heavy bikini photoshoots. They preferred to have terrible sex with her, then brag to all their friends and never call again.

What if Zach was her last chance to have a baby? She knew there were other options, but she just couldn't reconcile herself to them. It was painful to admit you wanted a fairy tale family, but it would be even more painful to admit you'd never have it. To go to a fertility clinic in search of a sperm donor, a stranger who would never love their child, or her, the way she'd always dreamed the father of her children would.

But she was almost twenty-nine with a family history of early menopause and a boyfriend who was meaner than a cut snake. The fairy tale option was starting to look like exactly that; a hideously unrealistic fantasy that she should never have believed in the first place.

Ash traced a finger over the plastic above the sleeping baby's cheek. "What do you think about me dumping my terrible boyfriend and having a baby on my own?"

Maybe Ash was only seeing what she wanted to see, but it looked like the tiny newborn smiled.

"People would talk," Ash warned. "They'll say I'm selfish. They'll say my kid needs a dad, even if he's rude and prematurely bald, and on Snapchat the entire time Mummy pushes a human out of her vagina."

The baby let out a gentle crooning noise.

"You're crazy," Ash whispered. "It would never work."

She kissed the top of the incubator lid and walked away. After looking over the other babies, she sat back on her plastic chair and resumed drumming her fingernails against the arms. The *Winnie the Pooh* clock on the wall told her she had five minutes of her shift to go. It seemed an unbearable stretch of time, like the minutes you spent waiting for a pregnancy test to flash one line or two. But where was she going to go once work was over? Zach would be waiting at home full of beer and fresh accusations and she couldn't pretend anymore. She couldn't keep hoping that maybe he would turn out to be different in every possible way. Julia was right, she needed to end things, but that meant putting her hope of having a baby on the back burner, leaving it to chance that she would meet someone before it was too late for her to become a biological mother. Except...

"What if I did it?" she said, testing the words in the open air. "What if I just... Had a baby by myself? I'd love them more than my mum ever loved me, I'd give them everything I had. Would that be enough?"

The room was silent. The babies, dreaming under the UV lamps, were quiet, but Ash's guts fizzled, and she knew it wasn't from hunger. It was the realisation that maybe, just maybe, things *could* be different.

"It won't look the way I wanted it to look," she told the room. "But nothing about my life looks the way I wanted it to look. What if I quit smoking and bad men and fantasising about something that might never happen and just... Have a baby? On my own?"

The idea seemed to hang in the air like a glowing apparition. Ash felt a huge surge inside herself, as though she'd just been struck by lightning. Suddenly she wasn't tired. Not even a little bit and she knew exactly what she had to do.

The second her shift was over Ash power-walked to the car park. As she passed the outdoor bin, she reached into her bag for her cigarettes and threw them in, *swish*! Then she dug out her phone and called Julia. It went to voicemail.

Ash took a deep breath. "Hey, Jules! I'm so sorry I yelled at you. You were right and I was wrong and I'm going to dump Zach. Do you think you could send Max around to the house tomorrow, so he'll leave with a minimal amount of wall punching? I can't be bothered dealing with him tonight so I'm going to stay at a motel. I've missed you so much by the way, let's never fight ever again. I'm sorry for not listening to you and I'm sorry I called your boyfriend a narc. He's alright, I guess. For a divorced bag of man-pain. Also, I'm going to have a kid!"

She smiled at the night sky, then realised what that sentence would sound like to Julia. "Shit! I didn't mean it like that, I'm not pregnant and I'm not going to have a baby with Zach, I'm thinking a sperm donor. You know, someone smart and hot with good bone density, if that's a thing sperm donors have to prove before they're allowed to wank into a tub. I'm not sure. I'm gonna go look it up. Call me back! Love you! Bye!"

2

Eight months later

Ash waved away the bacon-wrapped prawns for what felt like the hundredth time. "No thanks."

"Are you sure?" The green-haired server was visibly straining under the weight of her silver platter. "They're really superb!"

"I'm sure they are, but unless you want to be giving me the *Pulp Fiction* treatment in fifteen minutes, I should pass. I'm allergic to shellfish."

The server gave her a pained glare and shuffled away, her mountain of pork-swaddled crustaceans held high in front of her. To Ash's amazement, she moved through the crowd of beautifully dressed nerds without anyone so much as glancing at the prawns.

"Free food going uneaten?" she muttered. "What kind of party is this?"

A ridiculously overpriced one, that was for sure. Because her sister was a scrappy hipster, Ash had expected the launch of her video game, Scarlet Woman, to be the same. She'd arrived at the party thinking she'd see paper lanterns and buckets of fake blood and bad sangria.

But the launch was being thrown by Julia's parent company, DMX Industries. As an organisation worth billions of dollars, Ash guessed they could afford to splash out on fancy uneaten shellfish and a twelve-piece jazz band. Still, it wasn't in keeping with Julia's gore-filled feminist video game. If it weren't for the cut-outs of characters, Ash would have thought she was at a rich couple's engagement party. Which was why she felt utterly out of place.

Ash moved over to the window and pulled out her phone, trying to look like she wasn't perusing high-end lipsticks on Pinterest. More than anything, she wanted to head out to the balcony and smoke her ass off, but that wasn't an option. She was due to see a fertility doctor next week, and 'haven't smoked in eight months' sounded a lot better than 'had a cheeky few on Friday because I felt socially awkward at a nerd party.'

"Naked pistachio croquette?" a server with a septum ring asked.

"Sure." Ash picked up one of the greenish balls and tossed it back like it was the vodka shot she wanted. "Cheers."

"Yeah, no problem. Cute shoes, very conformist Barbie."

Ash beamed. "Thanks! Wait, hang on…"

Unfortunately, the man who burned her had already vanished. Ash groaned to herself. She knew she looked overdressed. The décor in the three-level art gallery might be 'stuffy one-percenters renew their wedding vows to general disgust' but the crowd had an edge. She'd yet to see a single person not rocking a shaved head, surface piercings, tattoos, theatrical makeup, and androgynous footwear. But Julia had failed to tell her about the dress code so she was wearing a silver slip dress, neutral make-up, and pink pumps. In a sea of cool, she looked like exactly what she was: white trash. Still, she supposed someone had to remind Julia where they came from. She was just contemplating the open bar when a warm hand grasped her arm. "Hey, Ashley."

For the first time in her life, Ash was relieved to see Max hovering behind her. "Hey man! How are you?"

"Pretty good."

Despite his words, her sister's boyfriend looked distinctly uncomfortable. His black hair was on end, and his equally dark eyes kept darting around the room as though he expected someone to leap out from behind a water feature and declare themselves a terrorist. As a big-time cop that might have been part of his shtick, but Ash knew from experience Max was pretty hard to rattle. She figured his unease was either because of his incredibly fitted Armani shirt (he was a notorious fashion whore) or because of the cut-outs.

Eli, the handsome male lead of Julia's game, was based on Max, which meant several of the life-size cut-outs closely resembled the police officer. While Max was flattered to be included in Julia's game, he seemed profoundly scared someone would recognise him. Ash understood that. She wouldn't be caught dead next to a life-size cut-out of herself.

Max tugged at the sleeve of his shirt. "How are you finding things?"

"Yeah, great." Ash mentally crossed her fingers. "Wish I got a memo about the dress code."

"You look fine."

They stood in silence for a moment, eyeing each other up. Ash's relationship with Max had always been a little tense. He was a cop, and a childhood riddled with cops dragging your mum away for selling Valium in the Woolies car park wasn't easy to forget. He'd also hurt Julia, a crime usually punishable by pain and/or lifelong snubbing.

In fairness, Max hadn't hurt Jules intentionally, he'd just had a lot of blokey conflicted feelings about dating her sister. He was older than Julia was, thirty-three to her twenty-four when they began their whirlwind romance, and he had been married, though legally separated.

When Ash was introduced to Max for the first time, he was moping around their front door trying to get Julia to talk to him again. She'd assumed he was an arrogant, beefed-up dickhead trying to unload his post-divorce man-feels on her sister and threatened to do him an injury. It hadn't gotten their relationship off to a great start. After almost two years together, Max had well and truly proved he loved Jules, but Ash was still inclined to keep him on his toes, make sure he knew he was being monitored for signs he was fucking up.

"How did Julia seem before the party?" she asked.

"Pretty nervous. You know how she gets about being the centre of attention. She was shaking all over, like a hairless cat."

"You should give her vodka. That's what I used to do before she had to give an English presentation at school."

"Good to know, usually when Jules is shaken up I…"

Max's cheeks turned ruddy, and Ash had the misfortune of knowing exactly what he had done to relax her sister instead. *Gross.*

She looked around for a distraction, any distraction, and snagged a glass of sparkling wine from a passing server. She was supposed to be staying off alcohol, but this was an emergency. Max seemed to be thinking along the same lines. He took two, downing a glass in one go. "Sorry," he said thickly. "This whole night has been pretty weird for me."

"I can't imagine why…" Ash pointed to an Eli cut-out. "Hey, do you have a twin brother?"

Max groaned. "I love Jules, but some of the people I work with threatened to come tonight, and if they see the cut-outs…" He shuddered, draining his other glass of wine.

Ash, figuring she'd do as the Romans did, tipped her own glass up.

"Helps when it's good stuff doesn't it?" Max took their empty glasses and put them on a side table. "So, have you had any trouble with your ex lately?"

Ash glanced around as though someone she knew might be listening. Seeing no one but unidentified hipsters, she figured she could risk it. "No, I think Zach's finally given up his attention quest."

"Good to hear. Anytime that guy needs a knee in the back, just call me."

"Oh, I will."

Max and Julia drove to Brenthill the day after her nursery

epiphany. They'd waited in Max's car as Ash told Zach it was over. Her ex-boyfriend had refused to go quietly. First, he'd cried, then he'd begged, then he'd thrown her stuff around and shouted that he had a right to be there (he didn't) and she couldn't just dump him (she could). Then Max had rushed in and pinned him to her dining room floor, while Julia called Brenthill Police Station.

Their former colleagues arrived in record time, and Ash watched, half-laughing, half-crying as another one of her ex-boyfriends got piled into the back of a divvy van.

She'd had a whole day of relief before Zach launched his campaign to win her back. It wasn't a great campaign by any means; he drove past her house at all hours blaring the horn, left used condoms on her doorstep, and harassed her on Facebook. In the end, she'd had to take out an intervention order. She hadn't wanted to. She'd been convinced the cops would laugh at her behind her back, *'Ash Bennett? That footy slut? Of course, she's got some loser doing laps around her house. She'll be back with him in a month,'* but Julia had convinced her it was the right thing to do, and to her surprise, it worked. Zach stayed away, and the ugliness of dealing with him killed whatever remained of her fairy tale romance dream dead.

She'd spent the last eight months alone, discovering who she was when she wasn't dating, pursuing, or being pursued by men. Turned out she could read a detective novel in two days, make gnocchi by hand, and after several weeks of intensive yoga, do the splits. She cleaned out her wardrobe, ate whole strawberry cheesecakes, and stayed off cigarettes and booze until it felt natural, or at least more natural. At times it was painfully boring, especially on weekends, but it was worth it. There were no cocaine highs when the only steady man in your life was the bin guy, but there were no gutter lows either. While electronic buzzing was hardly a gratifying substitute for sex, a vibrator never asked you for money or puked on your couch and tried to blame it on the dog. If you didn't like a vibrator, you chucked it in the bin. No cops necessary.

It had taken almost a year, but she finally had a life outside of Southern Star Hospital that was together, and she passed the necessary health checks and counselling sessions to become applicable for donor sperm with flying colours. It seemed too good to be true but she was on the fast track to having a baby by the end of the year.

"Greek feta pastizzi with truffle oil and fresh chives?" The girl with bright green hair was back, once again overburdened with hors d'oeuvres.

Ash took two. "What is it with rich people and nibbly things stuffed into other nibbly things?"

"No idea, but I'd kill for an actual meal." Max scanned the crowd. "Have you seen Jules anywhere?"

"Last I saw, she and Tiff were talking to a group of people who looked like elves."

"Shit. I don't know whether I should be hovering behind her, doing the whole supportive boyfriend thing, or leave her alone to network."

"Don't look at me, I'm thinking the same thing, except sister instead of boyfriend."

Ash spotted a guy with a faux hawk pointing at Max, then to the cut-out of Eli, then back to Max. Everyone in his group turned to gawp at them.

Ash nudged Max's side. "Hey, you're a celebrity, Connor."

Max gave the group a feeble wave. "That's all I need. If the guys at work find out about this, I'm *done*."

"You'd think they'd be impressed you're an action star."

"No, they'll just laugh their asses off. Then they'll get their hands on one of the cut-outs and keep it in the office forever."

"That's amazing."

Max scowled. "Would you want a cut-out of yourself at the hospital?"

"If it could supervise routine childbirths while I took a nap, yes."

"I guess mine could stand by a window and intimidate bad guys. Like those cut-outs in *Home Alone*. Come on, let's move before one of them comes over and tries to get a picture."

As they walked away they crossed paths with a willowy blonde waitress bearing a tray of pale pink cocktails. "Strawberry gin and micro-basil martini?"

She and Max looked at one another, then took one each.

Max held up his glass. "To Julia being so fucking talented."

Ash tapped it with hers. "Agreed. Also, free drinks."

When she and Max were done with their martinis, they tried ginger and orange vodka sours, then whiskey and cherry somethings, then tequila and coconut something-elses and within an hour they were both fairly loose. The alcohol greased over their usual tension until Ash found herself enjoying talking to Max, about football, then work, until finally…

"You still thinking about having a baby?" Max asked, gnawing at a lime he'd plucked from his lavender gin cup.

"Yeah. I've had all the tests done. Apparently, my eggs are good, and my uterus is raring to go."

It was a testament to how drunk they were that Max smiled. "That's great."

"Thanks. I'm due to see the doctor about going through some donor lists this week."

"Wow. Big move."

"I guess, but I'm excited, too."

Max downed the last of his lilac cocktail. "Glad to hear it. I'm sure you'll be a great mum."

Ash smiled, not really paying attention. She'd caught sight of a hot young couple making out in the corner and realised something. She was horny. Not for Max. *Gross*. Even if he wasn't Julia's boyfriend, authoritarian men did nothing for her. While that meant she'd dated more than her share of stoners, losers, and the chronically unemployed, at least she and Jules rarely found the same men hot. Except for Liam Hemsworth, but come on, everyone wanted to fuck that guy. Zach wanted to fuck that guy.

No, she was just horny in general. Especially now she was dressed up and drunk for the first time in ages. She could stand to flirt with someone, feel that prickle of mutual interest, of 'what are you like in the sack?' She scanned the room, seeing nothing but hipsters and couples and hipster couples. She supposed it was for the best. Besides, even if there were single guys checking her out, none would risk approaching with Max 'ask me about my license to carry a concealed firearm' Connor standing beside her like the world's biggest cockblock. An evil part of Ash's brain wandered to her phone, to the men she could text if she wanted a quick tumble. Eight months she'd endured celibacy, was tonight going to be the night she finally cracked?

Max's face loomed close to hers. "Hey, um, Ash? Can I ask you something?"

Ash stepped backward, alarmed by the intensity of Max's expression in contrast with her dirty thoughts. "Don't put your head that close to my head ever again."

Max quickly backed off. "Sorry. But can I ask you something about Julia? It's pretty serious actual—"

"Maxie!"

A man's voice cut through the room, so inappropriately loud everyone stopped what they were doing to look around for the source of the noise.

"Christ." Max pinched the bridge of his nose with his thumb and forefinger. "I forgot Jules invited him. Sorry in advance."

Ash, who'd been distracted by her phone buzzing in her purse, said 'Huh?' but Max was already addressing whoever it was behind her. "You found the place okay?"

"Sure did," the guy said in the same too-loud voice. "Sorry I'm late, I ordered a taxi, then I forgot I hadn't brushed my teeth, and by the time I was done doing that, the taxi had bailed, so I ordered another taxi..."

Ash, who knew a pointless story when she heard one, checked her phone. She had a text from Julia.

I hope you're having fun. Sorry, I can't talk, there are so many industry d-bags I need to chat up and not enough time xxx.

She smiled and tapped a quick message back.

You do your thing, Max and I are getting smashed on level two. Join us when you're free. I'm so proud of you xoxoxo

Ash tucked her phone back into her bag, smiling to herself.

"… And then I ordered *another* taxi, but the guy was dropping someone off in Preston, and it took him ages to get to Coburg…"

Fucking hell, was this guy still talking? About how he failed to catch multiple taxis? What a der-brain. Ash turned around to rescue Max and then everything went sort of slow and fuzzy like someone had rubbed Vaseline on her eyeballs. Max's dipshit friend was… Gorgeous.

Ash was no stranger to beautiful men. Her back catalog contained three AFL footballers, an Oscar nominee, and one of the guys from The Kings of Leon, back when The Kings of Leon were a big deal. But whether it was because of her stint in the no-fuck-zone, or because she was surrounded by elvish nerds and her sister's boyfriend, this man seemed almost unreasonably hot. He was tall, even taller than Max, with shoulders like the Bolte Bridge and a smile that could kill an old lady. He wasn't a pretty boy, his nose was crooked and his grin lopsided, but he had that square-jawed, salt-of-the-earth handsome look that made a girl think of loose-hipped cowboys and demanding Scottish Lairds. And speaking of Scottish Lairds, old mate was a redhead. Usually, gingers weren't her scene but this guy's hair was the rich coppery-auburn of a fox's pelt. It gleamed like rose gold under the floodlights, his short beard the exact colour as the stuff on his head. It was beautiful. Big Red was doing it for her. Big time. And apparently, the feeling was mutual.

"Whoa," he said, taking a step backward. "Who *are* you?"

Max whapped his friend in the stomach. "Dean, that's not something you say to people."

"It's fine." Ash straightened her spine so Red could see the extent of her cleavage. "I'm Ash. Ash Bennett."

"You're stunning," he said, eyeing her up and down. His irises weren't watery blue like most redheads, but a warm caramel brown. Ash's lady areas tingled, as though they too craved a cigarette. "Thanks."

"Anytime." Red grinned at her. "Seriously, are you single?"

"Dean," Max barked. "This is Julia's *sister,* Ashley."

Red flashed him a mischievous smile. "I know. They look heaps alike. And she said her name was Bennett."

Ash was torn from visions of dragging Red into the nearest cupboard and sitting on him, to ask, "How do you know Jules?"

"Dean's my housemate," Max said, in the tone of someone who very much did not like what they were seeing. "He moved in four years ago when his girlfriend dumped him for killing her rabbit."

"I'm sorry, what?"

"It was an accident," Red said earnestly. "I just got back from the gym, and I thought Bugsy—that was the rabbit's name—looked like he wanted to go outside, which is fair enough. Who wants to sit in a cage all day, chewing little bits of wood? So I walked over and I thought, 'should I be doing this?' And that's when I noticed…"

As Big Red launched into another story with no discernible plot or purpose, Ash and her drunk brain measured him with her eyes. He had to be six-four or five, lean, but beefy everywhere it counted. How would all that weight feel bearing down on her? She imagined his handsome face screwed up in pleasure as he pounded away at her practically revirginised pussy. Everything below her belly button tightened.

She couldn't, could she? And what of red-gold pubic hair? Did the carpet match the drapes? Was it beautiful? She bet it was beautiful.

"… Random ears and little bits of fur everywhere," Red concluded. "So yeah, I had to move in with Max. It's been an absolute ball though, wouldn't want to live anywhere else."

"Something you've made abundantly clear." Max gave them a pained smile. "How about we all go find Jules and hang out together?"

"She's busy," Ash said. "Red, what do you do, work-wise?"

"Until about three months ago, I did weekends at The Penny Black."

"Bartender?"

"Yeah." Another flash of that boyish 'who me?' smile. "I wasn't great at it, but the pay was good. Plus free drinks."

"Except he got fired," Max chipped in. "He was sleeping with the manager and the sales rep for Strongbow cider at the same time, and they found out about each other and started a cat fight in the smokers' area. The police had to attend, didn't they, Dean?"

Dean shot his friend a look. "It wasn't like that."

"It sure was." Max turned to Ash. "One of the girls scratched his eyebrow, he had to get stitches."

"Seriously?"

"Yeah."

Dean's expression was apologetic. "He's making it sound worse than it was. I still don't fully understand what happened, but I think one of the girls went through my phone when I was in the bathroom and—"

Scared he was about to launch into another long, rambling story, Ash jumped in. "So, no more bartending. What do you do now?"

"Roofing," Dean said cheerfully, completely unperturbed by being cut off. "I did it for a while after I first left uni. I love being outdoors because..."

As he talked, Ash scanned him for further information. The lines around his eyes told her he was around thirty-four or so. Check. Massive shoulders, hands, and feet. Check. Full head of hair. Check. No wedding ring. Check. Ash tried to remember what else Julia had told her about Max's housemate. A nice guy? Bit messy, maybe? She felt like she was forgetting something. Something important...

The green-haired server girl popped up, this time bearing another motherload of bacon-wrapped prawns. "*Please*," she begged. "*Please* just take one?"

"Seriously?" Red looked like someone had just offered him a free Lamborghini. "Are they...? Can I just... Eat them? Or am I meant to start some kind of prawn TAB or something?"

The server beamed at Dean as if he was the messiah. "No, they're free! Please, take as many as you want!"

"Well, alright then."

Considering his hands were the size of small dogs, it was no surprise Red put a serious dent in the plate of prawns. Though he had previously claimed to be full, Max also took a handful, as though bound by man code to prove he too could eat an unreasonable amount of prawns.

As they talked and gnawed on pink shellfish, Ash racked her brain for the thing Julia had told her about Dean. She struggled for a few minutes, then it hit her: Dean was the guy who'd gotten arrested in New Zealand. Jules had told her the story ages ago. How Max's housemate had gone to Queenstown on a snowboarding trip, gotten maggotted on Bacardi 151, and done a run down the slopes, butt naked. Unless she was mistaken, Dean had wound up getting arrested and thrown in the drunk tank for two days. For a while, it looked like Max might have had to fly over to New Zealand to straighten everything out. As she told the story Julia had been rolling on the floor, holding her sides.

"I don't get it," Ash had said. "How is your narc boyfriend mates with someone so dumb?"

"You don't know Dean, but trust me, if you did, you'd think this was hilarious, too. And don't call Max a narc."

Now that she'd met Dean and felt his energy, Ash got what Julia had meant. Red was a genuine Aussie larrikin. The kind of careless, fun-loving guy who was useless at anything other than stupid dares and drinking forty-two cans of beer without dying. The kind of rogue that could carry off a man's wife and have the bloke say, *'Oh, go on then, scamp!'* Larrikins were fun at parties and bad at life; they also made terrible, terrible boyfriends. As Max and Dean snarfed prawns, Ash allowed herself a small moment of despair. Red was gorgeous. Why was the universe always making gorgeous men and giving them the brains of iguanas? Or were tall, handsome, white guys just encouraged to atrophy at the age of seventeen by a society that held them up as rulers of the world, regardless of what they actually accomplished? Either way, it was a fucking shame.

"... Isn't that right, Ash?" Max turned toward her with a 'c'mon, let's have a nice chat and forget all about fucking my hot dumb friend' smile.

"Yeah, of course," Ash said, not missing a beat. She spent the majority of her shifts at the hospital pretending to listen to doctors' whine about their nannies while she inwardly planned her dinner. She was the David Beckham of feigning interest.

"Oh yeah?" The skin around Dean's bright brown eyes crinkled. "What was your favourite part?"

"I liked all of it."

"But if you had to choose?"

"I wouldn't choose."

"But if you *had* to—"

"Dean," Max said, a warning note in his voice. "Ash doesn't have to tell you shit about Sergeant Fitzgerald."

Ash let out an inward sigh of relief. They were talking about movies, specifically the movie she and Julia had seen last week. "My favourite part was when the Sergeant took his shirt off. That, and any and all scenes where his back was exposed."

Dean chuckled as he helped himself to another large handful of shellfish, the waitress giving him a giddy thumbs up. "You like super-hero movies?"

Ash almost reflexively lied. It was her go-to move with men—agree, agree, agree—but eight months of singledom had her catching herself just in time. "I hate them."

"Why?" Dean looked intrigued.

"They're all the same. Every movie ends with that countdown clock, sky laser bullcrap."

"Then why'd you pay to see it?"

Max rubbed a hand over his face. "Mate..."

"It's fine. Julia picks the movie. That's how we do it. I just go for the Frozen Raspberry Coke."

Dean made a face. "Seriously?"

"Yup, I'd sit through paint drying if I got to drink that stuff. And Jules knows it, so she always gets to pick the movie."

Big Red plucked half a dozen chicken skewers from a passing plate and began ripping the meat off with his teeth. "Sounds fair. You look beautiful in that dress, by the way."

Ash distracted herself from Max's disapproving glare by

collecting another cocktail from a passing waiter. "Thanks. It's my year eleven formal dress."

"Wow, you must have been a pretty teenager. Not that you're not pretty now, 'cos you're really pretty now."

Ash was shocked to see a blush working its way across Red's cheeks. God, he was something else. A big dumb sweetheart. Ash just wanted to take his hand, tell him everything was going to be okay, gently steer him towards a quiet room, and fuck the shit out of him. She sipped her drink. It tasted of butterscotch and rum, as mellow and appealing as the sexual interest percolating inside her. "Thanks, Red. It's nice of you to say that."

He shoved his hands in his pockets. "It's nice of you to be so pretty. I've wanted to meet you for ages."

Ash looked up from beneath her lashes, unable to stop herself from giving him The Sex Eyes. "Well, you've met me now."

"I uh, guess I have."

His gaze fell to her mouth and the heat between them was suddenly as tangible as the scent of bacon and warm sugar. Max cleared his throat. "I think I'll... Go see where Julia's at. Dean, wanna come?"

"No." Dean's gaze didn't move from hers. "Think I'll stay here."

"Right." Max shot them both a nervous look. It was clear he wanted no part of what was brewing between them. "I'm out of here."

"See ya, Maxwell," Dean said. "Say hi to Julia, tell her the food is awesome, and that I picked up that model TARDIS from the post office for her. It's on the kitchen bench."

"Right, I'll do that." Behind Dean's back, Max pointed to Ash and mouthed *'don't do it.'*

Ash twinkled her fingers at him. "Bye, Senior Constable Max Connor. Try not to get locked in any rooms with my sister."

Max flushed burgundy, and glared at her before disappearing into the crowd.

Dean chuckled. "So cool how your sister and my best friend are together. Makes us like... Well, I was gonna say in-laws, but that's not right."

"I hope not." Ash licked some sugar from the rim of her martini glass. Dean's gaze followed her tongue, and his cheeks and ears darkened. *Oh, he wants it, all right.*

Ash pictured him stiffening behind his jeans, blood flowing down, getting him ready so that he could do what men did to women. In the same way, she could feel her thong dampening, her body preparing itself for him even without her full consent. Big Red moved a little closer. "Ashley, are you, um, single?"

She took another small sip of her drink. "I am."

"How?" Dean asked a faint note of wonder in his voice.

I want to have a baby and in my experience, the men I'm attracted to are about as useful as a kick in the teeth. "Maybe I haven't met the right guy?"

Dean grinned and placed his half-gnawed chicken skewers on a side table. "I'm a guy."

Ash forced herself to stop looking at the way the chicken was coating the fancy table with peanut sauce and concentrate on the hot doofus who had her soaking her underwear. "Yeah, you are."

Dean stepped forward, and his scent sealed the deal. He had that sweet, musky man smell. The one you wanted all over your pillows and sheets. That smell that made you steal t-shirts so you could try to hold that scent on nights when he wasn't there.

Ash made her mind then and there to do this. It couldn't be serious, and it couldn't go beyond tonight, but if Red's mouth had half the enthusiasm for pussy as it did for bacon-wrapped crustaceans, she'd be a happy girl. The problem was how. And where.

No way in hell was she going back to his place, AKA Max's place. No way could they drive all the way back to Brenthill, even if she wanted him to see her shitty, broken-down house. She didn't have the cash for a hotel, and she couldn't just stand around making small talk, eating a dozen more mini-foods until Jules showed up.

She put her cocktail down next to Dean's discarded chicken. "Are *you* single, Red?"

His face lit up. "I am."

"Great, well maybe we should do something about that?"

"Do you want to get a drink and talk?"

"I've already had a lot of drinks. And we're already talking."

He flushed as red as his beard. "Oh, okay, um... Never mind, then. Sorry if that sounded dumb, by the way. I have a habit of saying dumb things, like once I went into a bakery and asked the girl behind the counter if they had any bread and she thought I was joking so..."

Ash stared dreamily at the rambling redhead in front of her. It so wasn't her style to be turned on by cluelessness, but god, she just wanted to bury her hands in Dean's hair and *tell him what to do.* Force him to stop talking and do something useful with his mouth.

So why don't you, her drunk brain suggested. *Have a filthy one-night stand, teach ginger a trick or two, and then move on with your life, baby mama. What do you have to lose?*

"Nothing," Ash whispered. She moved closer to Red, pressing her boobs against his plaid shirt.

Dean froze. "Ash, are you...? Um, is everything okay?"

"Yes," she said, rubbing her nipples against him slightly. "I was thinking me and you could go somewhere private and explore how single we both are?"

Dean's mouth fell open. "You're serious? With me? Like right now? With me?"

"Yes."

Dean blinked. "Oh, okay, wow. So, uh, do you mean back to mine or...?"

Under the illusion of straightening his collar, Ash ran a light fingertip over his throat, loving the way his eyes closed in what looked like sheer ecstasy. "I was thinking more the bathroom on the bottom floor."

He swallowed. Hard. "Uh, yeah. That sounds good. Do you wanna go there now or—"

"Yes," Ash said, grabbing his hand. "God, yes."

3

"God, Red. I just want to *eat* you." Ashley's surprisingly strong hands steered him toward the bathroom sink, her lips nuzzling against his throat. *Holy shit, how is this happening?* How, within minutes of meeting such a ridiculously hot chick was she making out with him in a bathroom?

She's Julia's sister, his brain reminded him. *Should you be doing this?*

To be honest, he wasn't sure. As soon as he'd seen Ash, golden and perfect in her tight little dress, everything had gotten hazy. Though to be fair, where his brain was concerned, everything was always kind of hazy. He wasn't intentionally dopey, he just kind of forgot what people told him, usually while they were telling it. He began things, got halfway through, then couldn't remember why he'd started. He wasn't dumb, at school, he could read and write and do maths as well as anyone... For about twenty minutes. Then he just kind of stared blankly into space, thinking about dinosaurs or horses or cars or girls. They'd tried to diagnose him but there was no apparent medical explanation for his behaviour. He was just what his mum called 'away with the fairies' and Max called 'a bit of a lost cunt.'

At thirty-five he'd mostly come to terms with it. Having a smartphone that let you set a lot of alerts and alarms and reminders helped. So did being big and okay looking, if you weren't prejudiced against gingers. He usually did pretty well for himself with women, but Ash Bennett was so far out of his league it wasn't funny. Julia had told him about her, how she was a nurse, owned a Kingswood, had been all over Europe and America, and once got expelled for making out with her girlfriend during assembly after her principal said a bunch of homophobic bullshit in front of the school.

He knew she'd be beautiful; Julia had told him she used to be a model, but he hadn't been prepared for just how beautiful. She had that glossy, tanned popular girl quality that made Dean's palms sweat. It reminded him of Violeta Cummins and her gang of terrifyingly hot girls. How they'd stalked the halls of Hanley Grammar with their short dresses and sugary perfume inspiring unwelcome erections wherever they went. Violeta had been Dean's first crush. She'd also been the first girl who made it clear that while he was good for the occasional finger-banging session, she had smarter, less gingery boyfriend material to choose from.

That had made sense. What didn't make sense was why, twenty years later, a girl even prettier than Violeta was trying to hook up with him in a ladies bathroom at a fancy party. He was used to being picked up, especially when he worked behind a bar, but there was at least some chatting first, a few drinks, a little 'where are you from?' This had gone from zero to a hundred in less than ten minutes flat. Was she hooking up with him as a joke? If so, who would have put her up to it? Jules? Max? "Um, Ashley?"

Julia's sister stopped running her hands all over his body and looked up. "Yeah, mate?"

"Are we…? Do you…? Are you doing this because you feel sorry for me?"

Ash laughed. "Why would I feel sorry for you, Red? Lift me up?"

Without thinking, he reached down and hoisted her into the air.

"God, that's sexy." Ash hooked her thighs around his hips. "How tall are you?"

"Uh, six-four."

"Thought so. Put me on the sink, Red."

He did what he was asked and Ash, her back against the bathroom mirror, continued running her hands across his chest, as though sizing him up for a job she wanted done. Dean swallowed, tasting blood from where he'd chewed his cheeks. "Ash, you're super-hot and this is great, but it kinda feels like we skipped a few steps here. Maybe we should talk for a bit?"

Ash smirked at him. "About what? Our star signs?"

"No..." Dean cast his mind around for a suitable topic. "What about... You're a nurse, right?"

Ash slid a hand from under his shirt and cupped the front of his jeans. "Yeah. Need me to take your pulse?"

She stroked him lightly through his jeans and Dean's vision went misty. Okay, this was not a drill. A hot blonde stranger did want his dick, and she wanted it *now*. "Ash, do you promise you're not too drunk to do this?"

She paused, her hand still cupping his most favourite of body parts. "You're a nice boy aren't you? You try and do the right thing? You have good intentions?"

"Uh, yeah?"

Ash kissed him lightly on the cheek. "That's sweet. I promise I'm not too drunk to make this the best video game launch of your life."

"Well, that shouldn't be hard, it's the only—"

Ash yanked on his shirt collar and brought his mouth to hers. The minute their lips touched, Dean knew he was fucked. It was like being a fifteen-year-old virgin again. His whole body thrumming, excitement and terror chasing each other around inside his head.

It was happening.

It might stop happening.

She was kissing him.

She might stop kissing him.

Ash's lips were soft and small, and Dean felt like he was going to shatter her if he moved too fast.

He kept his mouth firm but light until Ashley's nails dragged down the back of his shirt, and he knew she wanted more. He slid his tongue against hers, groaning at the way her legs tightened around his hips. It was bizarre how good this felt, and not because he was kissing a girl (though that was always nice). Having Ash in his arms felt like a seat belt had clicked around his middle like something was holding him fast. Safe. It was fucking weird.

Dean cupped Ashley's smooth cheek and tried to kiss all the dopey feelings away. It might have worked because they stayed making out that way for ages until Ash pulled back breathing hard. "That was intense. You're a good kisser, Red."

"Thanks," Dean said, still trying to get his head around what was happening.

Ash smiled. She had a gorgeous smile, sly like a cat that knew exactly how to manipulate her owner. Her narrowed eyes were a deep blue-green, the colour of the seawater at Noosa Bay. She was frankly, the prettiest person who'd ever kissed him. What was he doing with her in the ladies bathroom? He should be taking her out to dinner or like, carrying her across the beach at sunset while someone played the violin. He took a deep breath. "Ash, I'm not sure if we're just gonna kiss—"

"Oh, we're gonna do more than that, Red."

"Well, uh, not that I'm not happy to hook up here, but there are a lot of tampon dispensers around us. Maybe we could, um, head back to my place?"

Ash shook her head. "Julia can't know about this."

"Okay, right. Then why don't we get a room somewhere?"

"I can't afford it."

"I'll pay!" Dean fumbled for his phone. "I have an app that tells me about discounts all over the city and—"

"No," Ash said. "No hotels."

"Okay, but I still think we should go somewhere else," Dean said, with increasing desperation. "I mean this is a *bathroom*, a pretty nice bathroom, but still. You deserve better than this."

"I don't." Ash tucked her fingers through the loops of his jeans and tugged him closer. "Can you take off your shirt?"

Dean's brain stabbed a warning, but he was powerless to resist. He tugged off the plaid shirt Max had given him, hoping Ash wouldn't mind his skin. His Lebanese granddad meant he wasn't ghost-white like most redheads, but he still had about fifty bajillion freckles. Thankfully Ash seemed too preoccupied with his upper arms to notice. Dean resisted the urge to flex as he stood there and let her look her fill.

"Ooh, what's this?" Ash grabbed his wrist and turned it over, examining the tattoo on his forearm.

"It's a horse," Dean said as if it weren't fucking obvious.

"It's beautiful. You like horses, Red?"

"Yeah. My uncle owns a riding ranch and I always helped him on school holidays. This is Delilah." He tapped his tattoo. "She was my favourite when I was a kid."

A sly smile played around the corners of Ash's mouth. "Was she an Arabian or a thoroughbred?"

"A thoroughbred."

"Interesting." Ash's hand stroked along his thigh, making his skin prickle beneath the denim. "You ride her?"

"Yeah. Um, not until I was big enough, but yeah."

Ash's fingers brushed along the crease of his thigh, dangerously close to his throbbing dick. "You're big enough now, Red."

"I... Yeah," he panted. "I guess I am."

"You want to ride me like you used to ride your pony?"

The idea of mounting this slender, beautiful girl and riding her as roughly as he used to ride Delilah, his thighs straining, his hips working hard to control her... It made all the blood in Dean's body rush south. "I... Yeah, if that's what you want."

"And what do you want?"

Dean thought about lying in a stable, hay at his back, his cock red and wet and hard across his stomach. He pictured Ashley clutching his dick, straddling it without even looking at him. *'Hurry up and do me, Red. I don't have long.'* "Whatever you want I want."

Ash let out a little huff of laughter. "You're adorable, Red. Makes me wish we had more time."

Before Dean could process what she'd said, she was kissing him, this time with an urgent quality that said chit-chat was over. Her hand slid over his cock once more and Dean grunted in her ear. "Are you sure...?"

"Yes. Stop asking." Ash leaned forward and nibbled on his neck, causing goosebumps to break out all over his body.

How is this happening again? Dean thought as she sucked his tongue. All through high school, he'd wished he had brown hair and a functioning memory so Violeta would go on a date with him, instead of just letting him eat her out against the side of her parents' pool. And now he was once again being used for sex by an insanely hot blonde. Well, if it was going to go down here, in a toilet, Dean supposed he'd better get to work. He slid his hands over Ash's breasts. "Is this okay?"

"God, yes."

She wasn't wearing a bra, and Dean could feel her nipples through the thin material of her dress. He circled them, not applying pressure or pinching, just stroking. Ash quivered, her thighs tightening around his hips. "Oh. That feels nice."

"Good."

Dean loved a woman with sensitive nipples. Give him a girl who sobbed while he was suckling her over big cans any day. He had a sudden flash of Ashley in his lap, riding him hard as he licked her breasts. His cock throbbed painfully against his thigh.

Just wait a while, he promised it. *Let's make her like us first.*

For a few minutes, Ash let him play with her nipples, but then she jerked away, shaking her head as though she disagreed with what he was doing. "That's some nice petting, Red, but it's not going to get me off—"

He gently tugged on her nipple, making her gasp. "I'll make this good for you, I promise, just lie back."

"But..."

He put his mouth on hers, effectively cutting off her response. She seemed eager to rush him, but Dean knew a slow build paid off. If he was going to be the guy she fucked in a toilet, he was going to make this good. So good she'd consider calling him afterward.

He'd been a bit of a late bloomer, nineteen when he finally lost his virginity and so terrified about being bad at sex that he lapped up anything that might help him. *Cosmo* Magazine, *The Joy of Sex,* a woman old enough to be his mother who was pretty unflinching with her criticism...

After some trial and error (drizzling honey over bare skin was adhesive and not a sexy way to spend an afternoon. Especially if you had chest hair) he could safely say he knew how to give women pleasure. Sex, it turned out, was the one area of his life where he rarely lost focus. He could stay concentrated on a girl's pussy for hours and the feedback, fuck-wise, had always been positive. Now, if he was lucky, those skills were going to make Ash Bennett come all over him.

As they kissed Ash's hips rocked against the seat of his jeans and as the minutes passed she began moaning into his mouth. "Red?"

"Yes?"

"Don't you want to fuck me?"

Dean let out a pained laugh. "I can't even tell you how much."

"Then do it to me. Now?"

Dean shook his head. "We have to take it slow first, babe."

"Why?"

He slipped a hand between Ashley's legs, parting them slowly. "Because it's only gonna be the first time once. I wanna do it right."

"You're a tease."

"Not at all." Dean felt the panel of her thong and was relieved and a little smug to find it saturated. He moved the strip of silk to one side and stroked the wetness beneath it. "Does this feel like teasing?"

Ashley moaned, loud and long. *"Yes."*

"But it's good, right? Makes you want it more?"

"I already want it enough."

"No, you don't. Close your eyes and feel me."

To his amazement, she did what he asked. He pressed a fingertip inside her, toying with the slippery hole, his breath coming hard through his nose. Ashley's nails dug into the skin of his neck. "Oh my god. How am I so *ready*?"

"Because we're taking our time. If you like it now, imagine what it'll be like when I'm inside you. I'll go so fuckin' slow, you'll be able to feel every inch of my cock sliding in and out. I'll make you so hot you think you're gonna explode."

"So what are you waiting for, Red?" Ash's hands moved to his belt, but Dean kept his hips pressed close, cutting off her access. "Easy there, not yet."

Ashley dragged her nails down his thighs, as though trying to mark him as punishment. "Tease."

"You women, always trying to rush straight to sex. Whatever happened to romance?"

Something about that rubbed Ash the wrong way. She went stiff and flashed him a roulette dealer's smile. "Not my scene Red. Although I could give you a nice, romantic blowjob if you like?"

Dean gritted his teeth. *Be strong, mate, if she puts her mouth anywhere near you it'll be over.*

"I think I'd rather do this for a while." He dipped his finger back inside her, relishing her soft whimper. "Is that good?"

"Yes, but I like it hard." She moved her hips forward, enclosing his finger in wet heat "I like it hard and fast and deep."

Dean groaned. "Yeah, it feels like it."

Ash pulled away, her forehead furrowed. "What?"

With a stab of horror, Dean realised he'd accidentally implied her beautiful, heavenly, magical pussy was overworked. "Fuck! Oh fuck, I'm a moron. You remember how I said I say dumb things? This is that. This is exactly that. Your pussy is so nice, it feels amazing. Please don't be mad at me."

To his relief, Ash laughed. "You're something else, aren't you, Red?"

There was a loud rap on the bathroom door. "Hello? Is anyone in there?"

It was a woman and she sounded pissed off.

"Fuck!" Dean moved to pull out of Ash's pussy but she gripped his wrist and held him in place. "I'll take care of this, you just do your job."

"Which is?"

She flexed around him.

"Oh shit." Dean resumed stroking in and out of her, his thumb pressed hard against her clit.

Her head rolled back in catlike pleasure. "Hi, who's there?" she called out, almost lazily.

"Someone who needs the fuckin' bathroom! I've been waiting for, like, ten minutes."

Ash's thighs convulsed around Dean's hands. He pressed harder and was rewarded with a tiny moan.

"Um excuse me?" The angry woman seemed to be growing angrier by the second. "I need to pee!"

"So. Go. Upstairs," Ash panted.

"The line's super long. Can't I just come in there with you?"

Ash raised an eyebrow at him. "What do you think Red?" she whispered. "Should she come in here with us?"

"No," Dean said resolutely. "I want you all to myself."

"Then it's time to pull out the big guns. Sorry about this."

Before Dean could ask what she meant, Ash made a loud, gagging noise.

"Oh god," she gasped, her voice dripping with nausea. "I would let you in, I just... I don't feel good. Maybe try the other bathroom again?"

"Ugh, yeah, I'll do that." Loud high-heeled footsteps clacked away from the door.

Dean smiled at Ash. "You a nurse or an actress?"

"Trust me, when you spend as much time in hospitals as I do, you know what being sick sounds like. And how to make people leave a room."

"I'm impressed. And a bit scared."

Ash smoothed her hands over his shoulders. "Thanks, Red. Keep going?"

It was on the tip of Dean's tongue to suggest a hotel again, but he didn't want to push too hard. "Can I try and make you come?"

"And how are you planning on doing that?"

"I can show you if you like?"

She smiled. "Go on, then."

Dean gently withdrew from her pussy and knelt on the floor, slinging her thighs over his shoulders. He was tall enough that his head was exactly where it needed to be. Ashley's thong was still pulled to one side beneath her dress, and for a moment Dean just stared between her legs. Her cunt was as gorgeous as the rest of her, small and pink and gleaming. He wasn't the most hung guy in the world (or even in the house where he lived), but it didn't seem possible he would ever fit inside her. God, he wanted to try. Maybe if he ate her out for long enough, got her soaking wet...

Ash wove her hands through his hair. "Red?"

He tore his eyes away from her pussy to glance up. "You don't want me to? I know some girls don't like it, but honestly, if you turn me down I might die."

Ash smiled. "I want you to, it's just this is very... Intimate, what with you staring directly at my vagina."

"I know." He blew out a slow, steady stream of air and watched her shiver. He could see her clit, swollen and slightly distended, as though reaching out for him.

"Red..."

"Sorry, I'll get going in just one sec," he lied, still staring between her legs. "And don't worry about my beard, it's not as rough as it looks." He rubbed his chin against her thigh demonstrably.

Ash shuddered. "It's like cashmere."

"I use balm on it. It has grape-seed oil. And apricot oil. And some other oil. I'm not sure Argan maybe? Or macadamia?" Dean could hear himself rambling but he was too preoccupied with the pussy in front of him to stop. "Peanut oil? Or is that just for cooking? Coconut oil?"

"Okay, that's enough of that." Ash yanked on his hair, pulling him face-first into her twat. "Red?"

"Mmmf?"

"Lick my clit already."

Dean was glad his mouth was where it was. Firstly because it tasted and smelled awesome, secondly because Ash couldn't see the way he was smiling. He rubbed his lips up and down her before nuzzling deeper, unearthing the small pebble of her clit and sucking it lightly. It felt bizarrely like another first kiss. Which he guessed in a way, it was.

The fist in his hair tightened. "Faster, Red. Now."

"Uh-uh." He needed more time to explore, more time to play. He'd never tasted anything like her before. Hot and exotic and kind of flowery at the same time. Like his granddad's garden after a storm. The way it was making his head spin, it felt like this was his first time again.

Let's hope it isn't, a voice in his head warned. *Remember how shit it was to walk home after coming in your pants? Multiply that by a hundred million and that's how it'll feel to do it in the bathroom at a flash party, aged thirty-five.*

He kept his pace slow and steady, running his tongue between her lips, toying with the place where he longed to put his cock. She was incredibly wet, more of that tangy juice spilling onto his tongue with every swipe. Again he imagined his cock sliding inside her, stretching her wide and seeing her eyes roll back in her head.

He swore, as his dick jammed against his thigh-burning with unspent pressure. He'd always loved eating pussy, but for the first time since Violeta Cummins, he was at genuine risk of coming against his briefs. He kept his hands clamped around Ash's thighs, so he wasn't tempted to touch himself as he worked and tried to think about something else. What were the flowers that smelled like Ash's pussy called? He was pretty sure they were small and white. He could always ask his granddad, but then he knew he'd forget to invent a lie and tell his granddad he was asking about the flowers because they smelled like the most amazing pussy he'd ever eaten and his granddad would freak out. Or be incredibly jealous, God knew his days of eating pussy were over. At least Dean fucking hoped they were.

There was a sharp tug on his hair. "Red?"

"Yeah?"

Ash's eyebrows were raised. "You just made a face. What are you thinking about?"

She looked so stern he couldn't help but blurt out the truth. "My granddad."

"What the fuck!" Ash pushed his head away from her. "Ew!"

"Sorry! I mean because he has these flowers that smell kinda like your pussy and I was wondering what they were called, but I can't ask my granddad because he might be jealous and then I was thinking about him eating pussy. And then I kind of grossed myself out, but I was only thinking about other things because I was trying not to bust in my—"

Ash snapped her fingers in his face. "Look, Red, it's clear you have some concentration problems—"

"Not usually! It was only because I couldn't—"

She snapped her fingers again. "I genuinely don't care, because here's the deal. I am horny, like insanely horny. So I need you to put your mouth on my cunt and leave it there until I come. And you can't be thinking about old people and making funny faces and changing up the pace while I'm trying to do that, are we clear?"

"Yes," Dean said. "But you should know I might jizz in my—"

"I don't care." Ash re-gripped his hair hard enough that it hurt. "I'm sorry, Red, but I've waited too long and you're too good at giving head for me to care."

"Okay. Happy to help. And to make you feel like that."

"I'm glad but seriously, man. Lick my pussy."

Dean, who'd spent a year as a naval cadet, gave her a right-handed salute.

As he went down on her this time he kept his mind one hundred percent on the job. It was torture, within seconds even the pressure of his pants felt like a sucking mouth, but he held on as Ash ground herself all over his face. He held on as she whimpered his name and swore and said he felt amazing. He held on as her thighs squeezed his head and her taste flooded his mouth. He didn't count sheep and he didn't think about old people, even as he edged closer to the point of inevitable pants-ejaculation.

"Red... Red..." Ash tugged on his hair as she humped his mouth and chin. "Oh, fuck, don't stop, for the love of God, don't stop. I'm so close."

Dean fought the urge to go faster with excitement. He kept his tongue moving consistently, floating up and down her slit, and after a few seconds, she screamed his name, high and sharp.

As wetness spilled onto his tongue, Dean couldn't restrain himself anymore; he grabbed his cock, shifting his hand against the bulge. He didn't need sex, he just needed to taste her while he came. He could untuck his shirt afterward or something.

Unfortunately, Ash had other ideas. She squirmed away crying, "Too much! Too much!" and Dean was forced to withdraw from his new favourite place in the world and adjust himself as best he could. "How was that? For you?"

Ash pushed her head against the flecked bathroom mirror and smiled. There was no PR in that smile. It was all joy, all pleasure. It also exposed a tiny gap between her front teeth. Dean stared at it, transfixed. It made her look different. Older, and younger, and a little more human—all at once. "I fucking loved it."

She's perfect, Dean thought, and then, clear as a bell, came another, crazier, thought. *I want to marry her.*

He closed his eyes. He had a habit of falling way too hard too fast with girls but this was bad. Clearly, his agonisingly hard shaft was driving him toward the brink of insanity. If Ash wasn't keen to keep messing around, he was going to have to jack off in one of the stalls. Although if another woman came in that would probably get him on some kind of sex offender registry—

"God," Ash gave another happy sigh. "You know, I almost never come when I'm with people for the first time?"

"Really?" Dean said, shocked that anyone would ever touch her and not literally kill themselves trying to get her off.

"Yeah, you're incredible."

He pictured the sun's rays breaking through the clouds, showering him, the chosen one, in its bright white light. "Does that mean you're gonna come home with me?"

Her smile dimmed, the gap in her teeth vanishing. "Red, I told you. No."

Dean bit the inside of his cheeks. "I... Sorry."

"No. I'm sorry, I don't mean to be a dick." She spread her legs, beckoning him closer, and because Dean was a sucker for punishment, he stood and moved between her thighs.

"Kiss me," Ash said, and he did. It was bliss, soft and warm until he felt her smirk against his lips. "What?"

"You're kind of *into* bossy women aren't you?"

Dean felt a flush rise up his neck. "Yeah."

"Is that why you're such a good little pussy eater?"

"P-probably."

"So if I said I wanted you to use your hands on me again...?"

Dean pressed a palm against her right thigh and slid it up until he reached her soaking folds. "I'd say 'yes ma'am. Whatever you want from me you can have.'"

That satisfied catlike smile grew wider and she gripped his belt. "That's interesting, Red. I like it."

He liked it too, almost as much as he liked the feeling that she was tethering him to her. Holding him in place while she took what she wanted from his body.

"Put your fingers inside me." Dean did exactly what he was told. "Very good. Now I want you to—"

There was another loud rap on the bathroom door. "Um, hello? Me again. I just wanna know—are you for real vomiting, or are you in there with a guy?"

Dean stared at Ash in panic.

"Don't worry, I've got this." Ash made another disgusting heaving noise. "I told you before woman, I'm sick."

"Then why can I hear sex noises? And I know I can hear them because I've been listening for the last two minutes."

"Shit!" Ash glared at the bathroom door. "What is this bitch's problem?"

"She wants to use the toilet?"

"I know, but can't she just go somewhere else? Or hold it?"

"Not sure, but I think we might be busted."

"Right." Ash shot the locked door another filthy look. "Okay, well done, Agatha Christie. You solved the mystery of the occupied bathroom."

The girl said something angry in response, Dean wasn't entirely sure what. Most of his attention was honed on the pussy clenching around his fingers. He curled his hand slightly and Ash let out a moan of pleasure.

"Hey! Are you still fucking?" The angry woman demanded.

Ashley's teeth gently traced Dean's neck. "If we say yes, will you go away?"

"No!"

"Then we're not."

The urge to laugh butted up against his arousal and Dean choked on his own spit. Ash gripped his shoulders and shook him. "Red? Are you okay?"

"Yeah, but laughing when you're super hard is... Super hard."

The woman let out a loud frustrated scream. "Stop talking to each other!"

"God, this hook-up is going really well for me, can't you just give us ten more minutes?" Ash shouted back.

"No! I'm going to get security. If you're smart, you'll pull up your underwear and get out of there before I come back!" The woman's footsteps clopped angrily away.

Ash giggled softly. "I guess our fun's over. We should get out of here."

Dean's heart leapt. "You wanna come back to mine? Or, as I said, I'm more than happy to get a hotel room. Or I could drive us out to yours. I haven't had anything to drink yet. You're from the country, yeah?"

Ash made a face. "Um, yeah but no, when I said we should get out of here I meant, um…"

His heart sank. She meant she wanted this to be over. She was ditching him, right by the liquid soap dispenser and while his fingers were still in her pussy. *Fucking hell.*

"Okay, well I'd better…" Dean eased his fingers out of Ashley, half hoping she'd attempt to stop him. She didn't. He resisted the urge to suck his fingers clean, shoving them in his pocket and trying to subtly wipe them on his pants.

"Thanks, Red." Ash adjusted her thong so it covered the place he'd just been licking and tugged her dress down her thighs. "This was great, though."

"Cool, can I, uh, get your number?"

The length of time it took her to respond was all the answer he needed but he waited for her to explain anyway. Ash closed her eyes. "Look, Red, you seem like a nice guy, and you clearly know your way around a vagina—"

"I try."

"—But I am not going on a date with you. I can't."

Dean had a sudden, violent flashback; Violeta Cummins laughing as she pulled on her bikini bottoms, having just come on his face. 'Oh my god, Dean, we can't *go out*. That would be *so weird.*'

Before he knew what he was saying he asked, "Is this because I have red hair?"

"*What?*" Ash looked at him like he was insane. "No, you dork. Your hair's lovely."

"Then why don't you want to hang out with me? Are you worried about Julia? I promise she likes me. We play COD every time Max is in the shower. Which is most of the time."

Ash slid off the bathroom counter and began digging through her handbag. "This is not about my sister, Red."

"Then what? Please just tell me?"

Ash produced lipstick and began carefully painting her mouth in the mirror, avoiding his gaze. "I don't want a casual, fuck-buddy thing. If I *were* going to see someone it would have to be… Serious."

Dean laughed in pure relief. "That's *great*."

"Excuse me?"

"I'd love something serious!"

Ash's brow wrinkled. "Huh?"

"I'd love to have something serious! Especially with a girl like you. I know we rushed it with all the..." he waved his hand around. "Bathroom pussy-eating stuff, but I promise I can do serious. Let's go out. Have a proper date. What about next weekend? There's an Indian place by my house, it looks dodgy, but it's the best korma in the whole world. Unless you don't like Indian, in which case—"

"Red! Listen to what I'm saying to you!" Ash put the cap back on her lipstick and turned to face him. "You're hot and sweet, but I just can't see it working between us."

"Why? I mean, we get along, and clearly, you're attracted to me—"

"That's not enough. It's never enough when it comes to guys like you. No offence."

Dean thought anyone would be hard-pressed not to get offended by that. "Okay, please, just tell me what's wrong with me. Specifically. I'll go crazy thinking about it otherwise."

Ash chewed her lower lip, scraping away some of the bright pink gloss. "Fine. I'm almost thirty, and I finally know who I am and what I want. I have... Plans. Big plans, and they're already in motion and I can't throw them away to start something with another guy like you."

"Guy like me?"

"Yes."

Though he was sure he didn't want to know Dean asked, "And guys like me are...?"

"Immature."

Dean winced. He'd been called immature many, many times in his life. Mostly by his family and ex-girlfriends, but Max still busted it out a few times a year, usually when Dean found himself living on instant noodles and walking everywhere because a forgotten bill had come due with interest. Still, Ashley couldn't possibly know what a birdbrain he could be. At least not yet.

"I'm not *that* immature," he protested.

"Naked snowboarding ringing any bells?"

"Oh fuck." Dean held up his hands. "About that, what you need to know is—"

"Red, stop. I get it. You don't *mean* to be immature. Guys like you never do. But I'm done with men who order a taxi and can't get their shit together in time to sit in it. Who don't cook or clean or take out the bins, and forget your birthday and your anniversary and draw dicks on their ballot paper at election time."

Dean refused to think about the penis he'd drawn on his last voting slip. "How do you know I can't cook? I could be a great cook."

Ash raised a blonde brow. "Are you?"

"I can make..." Dean cast his mind around for something that wasn't toast. "Bacon and eggs."

"Yeah, I'm not falling for that one anymore." Ash slung her bag over her shoulder. "I've been with guys like you, Red. You're not bad people; as far as fuck-buddies go, you're a lot of fun. But you never grow up. You're seventeen forever. Like that Zac Efron movie, without the abs."

"I have abs." He raised his shirt to show her.

Ash's gaze snapped to his stomach and then she looked away. "Abs aren't everything."

"They are pretty good, though." Dean tensed. "See?"

Ash licked her lips. "That is not fair, Red."

"Sure it is. Come on, let's just go out to dinner. Do you know I can bench press a hundred and thirty kilos? And I once ate pussy for like, an hour and forty-eight minutes?"

For a moment Ash look tempted then she shook her head. "No. No dates. No hook-ups, no prolonging whatever this is—"

"We like each other."

"We want to fuck each other," Ash corrected. "That's not good enough. I need to be with someone who's got the grown up thing handled. Otherwise, I'm better off alone. Now, we should bail before security shows up."

"Uh-huh." Dean ran a hand over his beard, the smell of her arousal striking him hard across the face. His cock, in spite of the depressing conversation, was still optimistically rock-hard. "I, uh, might need a minute."

Ash glanced at the bulge in his jeans. "Oh shit, I forgot. That's kind of bitchy of me. Do you want me to like, give you a hand?"

"No thanks." Dean would rather let his dick drop off than accept another pity wank like the ones Violeta Cummins had given him when he was fifteen. He was better than that. At least he hoped he was. Surely, he was? Yeah, no, surely he was?

Before he could make up his mind Ash gave him a smile that didn't show any teeth, let alone the cute little gap, and said, "Okay, well I'm gonna go. Nice meeting you, Red."

"Ah yeah, you too, I just—"

Bang. The bathroom door slammed shut, and Ashley Bennett vanished.

"Fucking hell," Dean said to the empty bathroom. "What a night."

He stayed in the room for longer than necessary, smoothing his hair, hoping Ash might come back. Finally, when a security guard arrived and politely asked him to get the fuck out of the girls' toilets, he went to find Max.

His best friend was staring out a first-floor window with what looked like a Cosmopolitan in hand. Even drunk, holding a pink drink and gaping into the darkness like a Batman-style poser, Dean couldn't help but be jealous. Max was so many things he wasn't; charming, conventionally handsome, hung like a bull, and could successfully match shirts and ties without thinking about it. If Dean didn't love the guy, he'd hate him. He clapped his best friend on the shoulder. "Hey, Maxwell."

"Deano." Max eyed him over. "Where's Ashley?"

"No idea," Dean said, hoping he'd washed all of her out of his beard.

Max glared at him. "Do I want to know?"

"You really don't."

"Want to go see if the bar does shots?"

"I really do."

4

The Dark Elf gazed at the horizon, his pixilated face staring blankly out at nothing. On Max's couch Dean was doing the same thing. It was Friday night, and instead of celebrating the weekend's arrival, he was sitting in his boxers playing PS4.

There *was* less pathetic stuff he could be doing. A few gigs he wouldn't mind seeing and one of the footy boys was having a 'Crocs and Socks' themed birthday party, but Dean wasn't in the mood for music and if he was the oldest non-parent at the party it would bum him out. The past week everything had bummed him out. He reached for his bourbon and knocked it over. "Fuck!"

He pulled his shirt off and used it to mop up the liquid, feeling like a clown. Omorilo didn't do this shit. The guy could drink his weight in mead and still bag a man with a crossbow from six hundred meters away. If only he were a Dragonborn warrior, trekking the countryside, proposing to priestesses who accepted straight away because they saw him as a hero and not just a tongue stapled onto some abs...

"Stop it," he mumbled to himself. "*Stop.*"

It wasn't like him to be so down about a girl. When he caught his ex webcamming her old science teacher, naked except for the tie he'd worn to her sister's wedding, he was annoyed for like, three hours. He didn't know what it was about Ash Bennett that was driving him so crazy, only that she was all he could think about: her body, her laugh, her lips. She said she had big plans. What were they, and were they other guys, and did these other guys have their tongues in the softest, sweetest pussy Dean had ever tasted? It shouldn't matter, since they'd hooked up less than once, but it did. She was stuck all through his brain like raspberry ripple.

He'd tried everything to get her out again. Well, he'd tried flirting with the hot spin instructor from his gym, but that only made him feel guilty. He'd also tried alcohol, which was slightly more effective. The trick was drinking the right amount. Too little and he got all horny thinking about the way Ash had ridden his face, too much and he got all sulky and found it hard to sleep.

That was probably going to happen tonight, considering he'd killed half a bottle of Wild Turkey on his own, but Dean didn't care. He poured himself a fresh glass and returned to his game, or returned to watching Omorilo look at the ocean. In a minute he'd continue his quest for the old wizard's fire necklace. He would. Any minute now. Annnyyyy. Minuuuutttee—

"Dean?"

Max was home. Once upon a time, Dean would have tried to look like he was doing something important, or at least put a shirt on. Tonight he couldn't be fucked. "Yeah?"

"Mate?"

"Yeah?"

"What are you doing?"

"Nothing."

"You're right about that." A soft weight hit Dean in the back of the head, making him mash his PS4 controller and accidentally barbecue a herd of passing goats. "Shit! What was that for?"

He turned to see Max holding another couch cushion. "Stop chucking shit at me!"

"Answer my question. What are you doing?"

Dean held up his controller. "I'm playing Skyrim! See?"

"Are you playing Skyrim though, or are you sitting here, getting drunk and staring into space like a dickhead?"

"I just killed a dragon."

"Sure you did."

"I did. It was a big white one. Got all his bones. Gonna turn them into armour if I have enough iron ingots. I think I do. Maybe I don't, though. I had to ditch some stuff in a tree log before, I was way too heavy—" a couch cushion bounced off his face. "Hey! What the fuck?"

"You tell me. Why are you doing the rambling, pain-in-the-arse thing?"

"I'm not…"

"Yeah, that's convincing." Max slung himself over the couch and sat beside him. "I didn't want to know what happened between you and Ash and I've tried to ignore this sulk you've been on, but seriously, I think we should talk."

"You don't wanna know."

"No, I don't, but Julia's at work 'til nine, and I'm scared if I don't ask, you're gonna do something stupid. Like show up at Ash's hospital and play Husky songs through your Bluetooth speakers until she agrees to talk to you."

If Dean hadn't considered doing that, he might have been insulted. "Husky makes me feel things."

"They make all of us feel things, but that's no excuse for stalking."

"I can't stalk Ash. I don't know where she works."

"Southern Star Hospital," Max said automatically, like the big know-it-all he was.

"And what does she drive?"

"A 1978 Kingswood. A nice orange one."

"Uh-huh, sure, and what's her number?"

His best friend gave him a sharp look. "Stop trying to stooge me into giving you information and tell me what happened at the game launch."

"No." Dean refocused on the TV screen to find that Omorilo was being attacked by a mountain lion. "Fuck!"

Another couch cushion hit him in the side of the head. "Dean, tell me what happened with Ash, or you and I have a serious problem. Swear to Earl."

Dean paused the game at once, setting his controller aside.

When he and Max were thirteen, Dean's Kelpie had been run over while he was taking him for a walk. His parents thought he hadn't put the leash on properly and no matter how much he told them Earl's collar snapped no one believed him. No one except Max. Max had ridden his bike to the park and spent hours looking for the collar. The look on his old man's face when Max showed him the frayed piece of rope had changed Dean's life. In that moment he knew his dad wasn't always right, he, though still a dopey ginger, wasn't always wrong, and that Max was the best mate he'd ever had. Three for three as far as revelations went.

For Max, Earl's death marked the day he decided he wanted to be a cop like his mum and dad. It was also the day he lost a nice big chunk of his innocence. He'd crouched in the garden after he gave Dean's old man the collar and watched as Gerald Sherwood belted his son in the mouth. Dean's fat lip had lasted days, Max's shock that a man could do that to his own son lasted months, years, maybe forever. That was why they swore on Earl. Earl was the day everything changed. Earl was serious business.

"I'll tell you whatever you want to know," Dean said. "But first you have to promise not to tell Jules."

Max gave a strained laugh. "Trust me, if this story is half as bad as I think it is, I'm *never* telling Jules."

"Great 'cos it's worse."

"Yeah, fantastic." Max made a circular motion with his finger. "Talk. Where'd you go after I left?"

"The girls' toilets on the bottom floor."

Max gave him a pained look. "Please tell me she needed you to help her, I dunno, fish a ring out of the bowl or something?"

"I ate her out."

"Shit." Max rubbed a hand over his forehead. "Did you guys at least hang out for a while?"

"No. She dragged me in there, like, seconds after you were gone."

"Fucking hell. That was Julia's party!"

Dean threw up his hands. "It wasn't my idea so, don't get mad at me. I told Ash we should go to a hotel, but she wanted me right then and there."

Max raked a hand through his short black hair. "Okay, what happened next?"

"She came on my face and we got busted by a chick who threatened to get security, so we stopped—"

"Thank fuck."

"— And I asked Ash out on a date but she said she wasn't interested because I'm a loser. Then she left, and I washed my beard under the sink and came and found you."

"Right." Max stared blankly at the TV. "Sure."

"Are you okay?"

Max bent his neck from side to side, Dean could hear his spinal cord cracking. "I'm guessing that's a no?"

"You're damn right, it's a no. Do you have a bottle with you?"

Dean lifted the Wild Turkey in the air. "You mean this?"

Max silently held out a hand.

"I thought you swore off alcohol after you got poisoned by all those new-age cocktails?"

"Don't remind me. I haven't been that shit-faced since uni."

"I know. It was great."

"Glad you and Jules thought so."

After Max had passed out on the couch, Dean and Jules had drawn on his face, just a little. Max with a sharpie Tom Selleck moustache was the only thing that had made him laugh since Ashley called him immature.

"Dean," Max snarled. "Wild Turkey. Now."

"Maybe you should stay sober? You're not a young buck anymore, Connor. You've got a twenty-six year old girlfriend to keep up with."

"Fuck you." Max made a grab for the bottle and Dean, more out of habit than anything, held it out of his reach. "What's the magic word?"

"I'll tell Jules what you did to her sister?"

Dean almost dropped the bourbon. "Please don't do that. I love Jules. I don't want her to think I'm a sleaze-bag."

"Then let me get drunk."

Dean handed Max the bottle and his friend took a long swallow and scowled. "Hate Wild Turkey."

"Then give it back, you're backwashing."

"Fuck you." Max tipped the bottle up, draining at least two shots.

"Maybe you should slow down?"

"Dean?" Max re-capped the bottle, his cheeks flushed. "You, my best friend, performed oral sex on a woman I hope will be my sister-in-law, in a *toilet*."

"It wasn't *in* a toilet," Dean protested.

"But a toilet *was* there?"

"There were *some* toilets nearby, yes."

Max took another swig. "Right. So, what happened after you tongued my girlfriend's sister?"

"I told you. She said I was a loser and it wouldn't work, then she left."

A smile tugged at Max's lips. "You do it wrong?"

Dean scoffed. "I never do it wrong. I eat pussy like it's birthday cake. She came all over me. Like... *All over me.*"

"Yeah, okay." Max's brow wrinkled in disgust. "Then what's all this about her calling you a loser? No, wait, first explain to me how you wound up in the toilets so fast. When I left you were trying to eat your body weight in prawns. How'd you go from stuffing your face to—"

"Stuffing my face?"

Max clearly didn't want to laugh, but it rumbled out of him anyway. "Yeah, that."

"Like I said, she uh... Just kind of asked for it. Straight up."

"She propositioned you?"

Dean rolled his eyes. "Don't be such a cop. She asked me if I wanted to hang out with her."

"In a toilet?"

"In a *bathroom*."

"So, she did proposition you. She invited you to the bathroom under the explicit assumption you were going to have sex."

Dean picked up a cushion and threw it at Max. "If you don't stop making Ash sound like a sex predator I'm gonna leave."

"Sorry, it's just... What do you actually know about the girl?"

"I know she's beautiful and smart and funny and she has an awesome pussy."

"I mean, what do you know *about* her?"

Dean snatched back the bourbon and took a swig. "Just bits and pieces from what you and Jules have told me. She used to be a model, now she's a nurse, she lives in Brenthill..."

A thought hit him like a stray bird. A few months ago Max had to go around to Julia's house to help her sister get rid of her boyfriend. He remembered Julia saying the guy had turned nasty, and Ash ended up taking out a restraining order against him.

"Holy shit. How did I forget that?"

"Forget what?" Max asked.

"Her ex was the guy you had to chuck out! That lazy bastard who wouldn't leave."

Max's face darkened. "A lazy *stalking* bastard who treated her like shit."

Panic burst in Dean's gut. "He didn't—"

"No, I swear. Just verbal stuff, nasty but not on that level."

Dean breathed a sigh of relief. "That's good, I guess. If I ever meet that guy, I'm gonna shoulder-check him into the nearest wall. How anyone can treat a woman like that blows my mind, but Ash? Was this cockhead like, ridiculously good looking or rich or something?"

"No..."

"But?"

Max seemed to choose his next words carefully. "Ash doesn't have the best track record with men. Her boyfriends' were on Brenthill Uniforms' radar all the time."

"Shit, that sucks. Do you think I should have talked to her about it?"

"No. Ash never talks about that shit. Not even with Jules. This is just stuff I've pieced together on my own and from working at the station."

"Then what does it have to do with me?" Panic bloomed inside him. "You know I'm not like that right? No matter what my old man was like I'd never ever—"

"Dean," Max said sharply. "I know. I promise I know that. I was just surprised when you said things went down between you two. According to Jules, Ash swore off guys. Hasn't been with anyone since I helped her chuck out her ex. Not one hookup."

Warmth radiated through Dean's body. "Maybe she saw me and was like 'there's a guy worth breaking a vow of celibacy for.'"

"Yeah... Maybe."

"Cheers for the vote of confidence."

"No, it's not about you, it's just..." Max shifted in his seat. "I shouldn't say anything."

"What?"

"It's none of your business. Or my business. It's between Ash and her... We shouldn't talk about it."

Dean honed in on the magic word, *shouldn't*. "Okay, so maybe we shouldn't, but on the other hand, maybe we should? I mean, if it stops me from pining over her, and trust me, I'm pining, then all's fair in love and war, isn't it?"

"Maybe, it's just... I dunno..."

"I drove to Brenthill and walked around the supermarket hoping to run into Ash while she was doing her shopping," Dean confessed. "And I went down her whole Instagram feed and screen-shotted the pictures where she's smiling. And where you can see cleavage."

"Jesus H. Christ."

"Yup. So if you're holding onto any information, now would be a good time to hand it over."

Max's expression was strained. "Fuck, fine I'll tell you."

Dean handed him the bourbon. "Liquid courage?"

"I don't need any more courage." But Max took the bottle and drank all the same. "Okay, this stays between you and me, or you'll be put on the terror watch-list, you hear?"

Dean nodded eagerly.

"Ash wants to have a baby."

Most of the time Dean's head was foggier than London in Jack the Ripper times, but every now and then, the mist cleared, and he felt a surging sensation, like he was being hurtled through a train tunnel at top speed, everything hot and sharp and certain. As Max told him Ash wanted a baby it happened, stronger than Dean had ever felt it before. "That's incredible! I want to have a baby! Multiple babies!"

Max slapped his arm. "Don't even... Look, Ash wants a baby *now*. As in, she's going to a clinic this week to look at a big folder full of sperm donors."

Dean's eyes expanded. "Shit. Seriously?"

"Yeah, she got tired of waiting for the right guy. So, as you can see, there's no chance—"

Dean shoved Max in his side. "But she doesn't know I like kids! What if I tell her and she wants to have a kid with me!"

"She won't."

"You don't know that!"

The idea was like a rainbow bursting in Dean's brain. He had always wanted to be a dad and lately he'd been wondering if it was ever going to happen. Then Ash had come along; hot, funny, her pussy smelled like nice flowers *and* she wanted kids ASAP. It had to be fate.

"I'm calling her." Dean reached for his phone but Max kicked it away. "Hey! You know my screen's already cracked!"

"That's not the only thing that's cracked, you can't seriously think Ash would want to have your kids?"

"Why not? I'm bringing a *lot* of genetic stuff to the table; I'm tall, my resting heart rate is sixty-one beats per minute, I know how to make margaritas—"

"Dean!"

"—I *am* ginger but if she doesn't have ginger in her family, she could be in the clear. Do you know if Jules has any aunties or uncles who are redheads?"

"Are you fucking kidding me? Ash is seeing a doctor about a sperm donor *this week*."

"So, she's not pregnant yet. There's still time for me to do the job."

"You gave her head once! In a toilet! That doesn't make you a contender to give her your children. That makes you the *opposite* of that."

But Dean wasn't listening. He was lost in visions of little girls and boys with great big blue eyes and strawberry blonde hair, of him and Ashley snuggled up on the couch and family trips to the beach.

Max snapped his fingers in his face. "*Sherwood*! Look at me."

Dean blinked hard at his best friend. "Why do people keep doing that?"

"Because you're a dipshit. Now, I told you Ash wanted a baby to snap you out of your mope-quest, not make you fixate on having a modern family with a girl you don't know. No, *worse than that*, a girl who's the sister of the woman I'm in love with!"

"Why not?" Dean demanded. "Maybe if Ash knew I was into the idea of having a kid she'd—"

Max stood up so fast he sent the spare PS4 controller flying. "Say one more dumbarse thing and I'm going to backhand you."

"What? You don't think I'd be a good dad? I think I'd be a good dad!"

"This isn't about you being a good dad! You can't just volunteer to give Ashley your sperm. That's not something people do."

"Who cares what people do? You fell in love with Julia the night you met. Maybe it's a Bennett thing. You kiss one, and you're done."

Max buried his hands in his hair and pulled so hard Dean was legitimately concerned. "Why are you so stressed out?"

"Because whenever you get like this you're impossible to talk to." Max fixed him with a glare that was one hundred percent cop. "*Listen to me.* You and Ashley aren't anything. She let you eat her out in a bathroom because she clearly wanted a fling before she got pregnant. Your head was just in the right place at the right time."

Dean stood as well. Max might be a cop but he was taller, and the footy season *just* ended. If he had to beat him into submission, he could. "Are you saying she used me?"

"Not maliciously. But there's a reason she left, and there's a reason you're circling the drain right now, and I'm thinking it has little to do with Ashley, and everything to do with Violeta Cummins."

The two words hit Dean like a slap in the face. "What?"

"Violeta. Cummins," Max repeated. "I don't want to talk about her any more than you do, but fucking hell, mate, Ash looks just like her."

"Not exactly!"

"Exactly. Same hair. Same face. Same body. Why do you think you haven't met Ash until now?"

"Because you made her sister cry and she threatened to hire someone to bash you?"

"No." Max's black eyes were full of anger. "It was because I did everything I could to keep you two apart."

"Why would you—"

"Because, I know how you are about mean blondes who are out of your league. I watched you turn yourself inside out over Violeta Cummins for *years*. I didn't want a repeat of that shit-show."

"It wasn't *that* bad."

"No, it was worse. Violeta Cummins could have kicked you square in the balls, and you would have thanked her for touching you. You saved your virginity for her, remember?"

"Yeah." Dean scratched his beard. "I didn't know girls don't want your virginity. You could have said something."

"I DID! *You're* the dickhead who wouldn't listen. Who went running whenever she needed a shoulder to cry on or a face to sit on. God, it used to drive me crazy, watching you sneak around to her house, having to talk you down whenever she hooked up with another guy, which was all the fucking time because Violeta Cummins is a skinwalker and a demon witch who was put on this earth to try and suck the good parts out of men's souls. Remember that?"

Dean did. He remembered Max begging him not to give in

whenever Violeta called him after weeks of silence wanting to hook up. He remembered never listening. Until the day she moved to Sydney for university, he'd always done exactly what Violeta Cummins wanted. "I'm sorry I was such a pain in the arse back then."

Max's shoulders slumped. "It's fine. You were just a kid, but Jesus, I don't wanna watch you get used like that again."

Dean stared at his friend. "You really think Ashley's that much like Violeta?"

"No, but I don't want you to read too much into one hook-up. I know how you get when it comes to…"

"Mean blondes who are out of my league?"

Max looked sheepish. "I don't mean… It's just… I'm sorry."

"It's cool." Dean reached around for his forgotten glass of bourbon and knocked it back in one. "For the record, I like her. Ashley. And not because she reminds me of Violeta. I dunno, she made me laugh. She's interesting and cool. It felt *different* with her. I was hoping she'd text me or something."

Max gave him a considering look. "Does she have your number?"

"She could get it from Jules. Or find me on Facebook." He sounded pathetic, even to his own ears. "She's never gonna text me, is she?"

Max patted him on the arm. "If she doesn't, it's not you, mate. She's not dating anyone right now, she's trying to have a baby."

"I know, and I know it sounds crazy, but I think if I told her I wanted kids—"

Max shoved the bourbon bottle against his mouth and took an almost violent swig. "Enough. You don't want to impregnate Ashley Bennett via a petri dish so she can fulfil her dream of becoming a mum. You want to do it with your dick because she gives you a hard-on. That's a terrible reason to have kids."

Dean's magical certainty died. "Yeah, maybe."

Max patted his shoulder. "Cheer up, mate. She still picked you, didn't she? She must have liked what she saw, even if she didn't wanna rent it out."

"Please don't give me a pep talk after smashing my hopes and dreams."

"I'm not! I'm just saying you should stop sitting around in your underwear like a sad clown and get back on Tinder or something?"

Dean harrumphed his disapproval.

"You could ask that chick from the gym out?" Max wheedled. "You like her legs."

"Not as much as I liked Ash's."

Max smacked him on the back of the head. "I'm going to do that every single time you mention Ash. Now, are you gonna stop sulking and ask out the gym chick or what?"

Dean threw his hands in the air "Fine, I'll ask the gym chick out. And I'll stop bringing up Ash."

"And thinking about her."

"And thinking about her," he repeated dutifully. *I won't think about her pretty hair and her pretty pink mouth, and the gap between her front teeth and her tight little pussy, and how I want to give her my babies. Even though I obviously will do that and you can't stop me.*

Max, oblivious to Dean's internal monologue, looked happier. "Good, get out of the house, enjoy being single, live life to the fullest, experience every day like it's your last, stop drinking alone in your underwear. All that inspirational shit."

Dean made an affirming noise, his head full of a pregnant Ashley curled up in his arms. God, how could something that felt this good to imagine be wrong? Surely it was a sign?

"Dean you can't be..." Max shook his head and sighed. "Fuck, man, what do I know? It's not like I have my relationship shit together."

Dean snorted. "Are you kidding me? You and Jules are like the best couple ever. You make single people want to kill themselves."

Max perked up a bit. "We do?"

"Fuck yeah. I've never seen you happier, and I once saw you pat a dolphin while you were on ecstasy."

"Yeah, I guess." Max took another swallow of Wild Turkey. "It's just complicated, isn't it? Relationships?"

Dean's heart sank. "Don't tell me you and Jules are having problems? If you guys break up I'll cry. I'm not joking, I *will* cry."

"No, it's not that, it's just..." Max's expression was pleading. "Promise you won't laugh?"

"Sure." Dean clamped his jaw shut, just in case.

"I want to ask Jules to marry me."

Dean was glad he'd pressed his teeth together. Not because he wanted to laugh, but because he wanted to shout '*what the fuck is wrong with you, you moron?*' One quick-draw proposal was a mistake. Two might be a coincidence. But Max asking a third girlfriend to marry him so fast was officially A Pattern.

"What?" Max asked. "What do you think?"

Dean weighed his options. Max already seemed on edge. Telling him he had no right to be dishing out relationship advice because he was clearly the craziest cunt alive might push him over. "Congratulations?"

"Don't give me that shit, what do you really think?"

Truthfully, Dean was thinking about Max sitting on Jerry Springer's couch, while the voiceover guy said, '*Meet the man who just can't stop getting engaged! Max Connor doesn't know how to save the ring. Hopeless romantic or massive dickhead?*' Then the camera would cut to Max, shaking his head. "I thought it was going to work out this time!"

Real-life Max punched him in the arm. "Dean? If you don't say something I'm going to go get my OC spray."

Dean tried. He tried to say something encouraging, or constructive, or sensible. Instead what came out was, "Are you some kind of chronic proposer? Like, do you have a problem with proposing that you should talk to a medical professional about?"

Max's face crumpled. "Everyone's gonna think that, aren't they?"

"Yes, they will."

"You're sure?"

"Yes."

Max's expression was pleading. "But maybe—"

It was his turn to slap Max in the arm. "Yes! Yes, yes, yes! I can't believe you were giving me shit for licking Ashley's beaver in a public toilet when you're the one who keeps proposing to chicks left, right, and centre."

"Hey!"

"I mean it, Max, everyone's gonna think you're scared of dying alone or some shit."

"Really?"

"Like I keep telling you, *yes*. What's your hurry? You and Jules are cruising along fine. Why propose?"

His buddy's face fell. "Because I love her. I want us to be a family. I want to make her my wife."

"I get that, but you've only been together… I can't remember, but not long enough. Just wait another year. Or like five years."

"I don't know if I can. I can't stop bringing it up."

"What? Marriage?"

"Yeah, the other night we were watching *Love Actually* and Jules said 'that guy who stalked Keira Knightly at her wedding is a fucking weirdo' and I said 'we won't have any weirdos at our wedding,' and she freaked out. I spent the next five hours trying to convince her it was a joke."

"Terrible fucking joke."

"Yeah, that's what Jules thought." Max sank his fists into his hair. "How can I convince her this is different for me? That, yeah, I've been married, but I've never loved anyone as much as I love her? I mean, for fuck's sake, I was thinking about her when I married Bonnie. I almost sweated out of my skin."

"I know, I thought you were going to pass out and hit your head on that big church table."

"It's called an altar."

"Whatever, you were shitting yourself. I swear your face was *green*."

"That's because I knew I was making a huge mistake." Max took another slug of bourbon. "Never tell Bonnie that, by the way."

Dean shrugged. Max's ex-wife Bonnie had cheated on him in his own bed. He didn't feel like he owed her a single thing.

"*Dean?*"

"Fine! I won't tell her. I never see her anyway."

And everyone knew your marriage was gonna be a bust.

Max chugged a long line of amber liquid out of the Wild Turkey bottle. "For years, I thought I'd ruined everything. I used to look at Julia and think 'there she is, the one who got away' but now I'm with her. I'm with the girl who got away. And all I want to do is propose to her, but how can it mean anything when I've already proposed to Bonnie?"

Dean couldn't help himself. "And Mel Honeycook."

"What?"

"You proposed to Mel Honeycook. At Funfields Water Park when we were at Uni. Remember?"

"Fuck! *Mel Honeycook!*" Max gripped his hair again, and this time he seemed determined to tear it up by the roots.

"Hey, let go," Dean said, smacking his friend's hands.

Max's eyes were wild. "Jules can *never* find out I proposed to Mel Honeycook!"

"Okay," Dean said. "She won't. Not from me, anyway."

"Fucking hell. Mel Honeycook? What was I even thinking?"

"You were thinking she liked motorbikes and gave good head," Dean reminded him. "I was there, remember? You got that ring from the pawnshop, and before she could put it on I took it and threw it in the typhoon waterslide?"

"Shit!"

"You know Mel Honeycook has two kids now?" Dean said, thinking of Ash. "I saw it on Facey. They're pretty cute. All blonde and little."

Max glared at him. "Can we try and stay on point here?"

"Sorry." Dean racked his brain for something reassuring to say. "You know Jules loves you. If you have to propose, then propose. Just buy a ring that looks nothing like the ones you got for Bonnie or Mel Honeycook—"

"Oh my fucking God!"

"— And take her on a helicopter ride."

"Julia's afraid of heights."

"— Or maybe a hot air balloon ride."

"What did I *just* say?"

Dean threw his hands up. "Whatever! Just propose already. Fuck what other people think. Get engaged and have a massive party."

Max eyed him suspiciously. "Are you just saying that so you can see Ashley again?"

"No," Dean lied. "I think you and Jules should get married. Like right now."

"Really?"

"Yeah, I've ironed all the kinks out of my best man speech."

Dean wasn't surprised when Max punched him in the stomach. It had been a big night.

Fifteen minutes and a few aching ribs later, he and Max called their alcohol-and-romantic-failure-fuelled wrestling match a draw. They sat back on the couch and examined their injuries between swigs of victory and/or consolation bourbon.

"How the fuck am I gonna propose to Julia?" Max said, studying a scratch on his arm. "Cut your fucking nails, by the way. You've got cat claws."

"They're not long, they're just jagged because I bite them."

"Stop biting your nails, you thirty-five-year-old baby."

"Shut up. Anyway, how did this become about you? This whole conversation was meant to be about me going to town on Ash's pussy then getting ditched."

Max shrugged. "I had my own stuff to say."

"Typical." Dean sat bolt upright. "Maxwell, get this: if I marry Ash and you marry Jules, we'd be brothers. Officially."

For a moment Max looked excited, then he slumped back into the couch. "From where I'm sitting, that's about as likely as a double wedding on the moon."

"Hey, speak for yours—"

They both froze as the front door swung open. "Hey dudes," Julia called out. "What's up?"

Max stood so fast he might have been powered by magic. "Hey gorgeous, we're in the lounge."

He turned to Dean and slashed a finger across his throat. "*Not a fucking word.*"

Dean mimed opening a ring box and screaming with excitement. Max kicked him in the thigh.

"How's it hanging, party people?" Julia appeared in the doorway, tall and slender, her long brown hair falling into her eyes as usual. "Hey, man-fight! What's happening here?"

"Nothing." Max moved toward her. "How was your night, babe? I missed you."

"I missed you too..." Julia examined the lounge room, which looked a lot worse for wear after his and Max's tussle. "Are you sure nothing happened?"

"Yes. And stop standing there asking questions, because you and I have unfinished business, little girl."

Julia bit her lip, her cheeks darkening. "Is that right?"

That was Dean's cue to look away but he could still hear Max tossing his girlfriend over his shoulder, hear Julia's delighted squeals as he carried her up the hall.

The lounge room seemed even quieter in Max's absence and more than a little lonely. He'd been single for the last year and a half, and while he'd had some fun, particularly where The Penny Black was concerned, he was over it. Meeting Ash had given him some dumb hope that true love finally had him in its crosshairs, but everything pointed to that being a complete fucking pipe dream. Maybe Max had a point, maybe he needed to put in some effort.

He picked up his phone and opened Tinder. His vision wasn't so great now that he was drunk and Max had put him in a thirty-second chokehold, but he knew after a couple of swipes he wasn't going to find what he was looking for. He closed the app and, resigning himself to what a loser he was, went into his saved photos. He scrolled through Instagram snaps of Ashley in her scrubs at work, Ashley at barbecues, Ashley in front of the Eiffel Tower until he reached his favourite; Ashley arm-in-arm with Julia at a music festival. It wasn't a perfect snap, Julia was yelling at someone out of frame and Ash was laughing, her head thrown back into the sunlight. There were sexier photos in her feed, but he liked this one best because you could see the gap between her front teeth. All Ash's other pictures were half-smiles, her head angled to show off her killer cheekbones, but in this one, you could tell she was really happy. He stared at her, weighing up whether to bite the bullet and message her. Then he thought about Violeta Cummins and the look on Ash's face when he suggested they get a hotel room.

It's nothing, he told himself. *She doesn't want you and you don't know her. You just imprinted on her like one of those baby birds that thinks a cat is their mum, then gets eaten.*

He put his phone down, picked up the PS4 controller, and resumed play.

5

After her little tête-à-tête in the bathroom, Ash had said a hasty goodbye to Julia, feigned cystitis, and fled the Scarlet Woman launch like demons were after her. Which, in a way, they were. The demons of reckless sex with useless men.

Not that Dean Whatever-His-Last-Name-Was wasn't *nice*, that was part of the problem. He was nice and hot and amazing at sex. She'd almost have preferred if he'd been *bad* at sex. Then she could have put random hook-ups right back in their box. But the way he licked her, soft and slow while making noises that sounded like *he* was the one being sucked off? Yeah, that was a fucking game changer. If they hadn't gotten busted, she'd probably still be sitting on the bathroom sink, refusing to let go of his hair.

Still, she told herself the next morning when she was hungover and realised she'd spent two hundred bucks on an Uber home, it wasn't worth it.

"I'd love something serious," Dean had said, but he had no idea what serious meant to her.

If he knew she wanted a baby, he'd have ran like the wind, scared she'd bag the condom and use his unsuspecting jizz to impregnate herself. Besides, guys like him didn't know the meaning of the word serious. Their lives were a series of narrow scrapes and big jokes and what no one ever saw was the long suffering women, be they mother or wife, in the background. The woman forever driving them around when they lost their license, helping them find new jobs when they got fired for their latest tragically misunderstood prank, spotting them cash when they couldn't make rent, *again*. Ash had grown up around and been that woman. No more. Never again.

Yet later that morning when she was lying in the bath, it was Dean she pictured as she stroked herself under the water. Then in the afternoon when she was theoretically taking a nap but actually using her vibrator, it was his tongue she imagined between her legs. And then later that night when she was riding Eric, her emergency dildo, her brain was fucking that inconvenient redhead senseless.

Eric was an emergency dildo, because Ash didn't like penetrating herself while masturbating. She only used Eric (named after the Disney prince and her first crush) when she was at dire risk of slipping up and screwing someone. In her eight months of celibacy, she'd used Eric four times. What did it say about Dean that she'd busted Eric out less than twelve hours after they'd hooked up? Ash was sure she didn't want to know.

"It's a coincidence," she told herself. "I must be ovulating."

She wasn't. Ash knew her cycle like the back of her hand, especially now she was considering IVF, but it was a comforting lie. Unfortunately, as the next nine days passed and she remained in a state of constant horniness, it wasn't a lie that held any water. Memories of Dean standing in front of her, his erection straining through his jeans, begging her for a date *haunted her*.

She could take or leave the sight of actual penises—they felt good, but they looked like gross floppy sea cucumbers with hair at the bottom. But seeing hard cocks through a guy's jeans? Knowing they were trapped, needy and aching? It gave her serious tingles. And it was hard to think about babies or being responsible or anything, when you had serious tingles. So on Monday night Ash did something wrong. She looked Dean up on Facebook. She'd had some vague idea about finding out more about him, maybe stashing some pictures for Eric-related purposes, but as soon as she saw his stupid handsome profile photo that looked like it was chosen just to get women moist, she typed a message into his inbox.

Hey Dean, sorry for freaking out on Saturday. I'm sure you could tell, I had a great time, but if not, I had a great time. Hope you're having a good week so far, Ash.

It was a terrible message; too short and too long, ridiculous in every way, but she hit send before she could stop herself. She spent the next forty minutes with her head buried under a pillow, wishing she could go back in time and stop herself. She didn't know what she was more afraid of, a response or no response at all.

Then she got his response and it was even worse than she imagined. She'd been expecting something like, 'LOL kk, wana get eatn out agɪn?!?' Or maybe she'd been *hoping* because a message that silly would have been easy to ignore. But Red was more charming, and grammatically correct, than Ash could have ever anticipated.

The pleasure was all mine, I'm glad we met. Also, I keep thinking about what you told the lady who interrupted us and laughing. I am having a good week and I hope you are too, Dean.

She read the message. She drank a glass of wine. She considered that he might just be being polite for Julia's sake. She re-read the message. Then she drank another glass of wine and sent one back,

Glad to hear it, Red, but please tell me that me yelling at some lady wasn't the highlight of your evening?

The fifteen minutes it took Dean to respond were like exquisitely beautiful nails scraping down a blackboard.

No. But if I think about the real highlight anymore I'll go blind. It should be illegal to replay memories as many times as I have.

When Ash read that she squirmed between her sheets. She'd forgotten this, the anticipation and reward of an online flirtation, the tension and blessed release. She couldn't stop smiling.

Glad I made a good impression, and I give you permission to think about that encounter as much as you like, Red.

The dots doing the worm appeared below her message almost instantly.

Very kind of you, Ms. Bennett. What are you up to tonight?

Ash's flirty shit-eating smile slid off her face. It sounded like Dean was edging back toward asking her on a date, and why wouldn't he? She'd contacted him and brought up their hook-up. Why wouldn't he be getting the wrong idea? She was such a shitty human. She wrote back right away.

I'm watching TV and now I'm just about to go to sleep! I'm switching off my phone now, have a good night!

She put her phone on flight mode and then, sheets pulled over her head, she scrolled through Dean's pictures. There were snaps of beautiful sunsets and Dean on top of half-finished houses. There were pictures of him on the footy field, his muscles bulging, his easy-going face drawn into a macho snarl as he lunged for the ball. A little digging revealed he played seniors for the Bundoora Bulls. That was a big deal. They were a feeder club for the AFL and had won their league premiership this year. If Dean played for them, he had to be good. It certainly explained his drool-worthy body.

He was tagged in a lot of group shots at club functions. Despite her early shift in the morning Ash couldn't stop scrolling through them and the deeper she got, the less sleepy she felt. Alongside the traditional 'men giving each other overly touchy hugs, but not in a gay way' shots, there were dozens of pictures of Dean with hot girls.

They were touching him, too: kissing his cheeks and slinging themselves all over his shoulders. When she and Dean first met there had been some relief in knowing he was competent with other women, but all this proof was inspiring nothing but jealousy. Jealousy and a weird nostalgia. She'd been the women in these photos once when she modelled and dated football players with semi-regularity. Strange how easy it was to forget how she used to live, even though the parties, club politics, and low-functioning notoriety used to mean the world to her. Strange that Dean was still there, a minor celebrity in his own little way.

"All the more reason to stop talking to him," she told herself, before shutting her phone off for real. But the pictures, especially the ones of the pretty girls, seemed to have burned themselves into her brain. She didn't sleep well that night.

The next morning she drove into work without turning her phone on. She didn't want to see if Dean had texted, and with a cesarean scheduled first thing that day, she was looking forward to being so busy she couldn't spare a thought for technology.

Of course, because Murphy's Law was Murphy's Law, it was an unnaturally slow day in the antenatal clinic. The scheduled birth was canceled, with the woman electing to proceed naturally, and three couples didn't show up for their consultations. Ash had never had such a boring morning. In a hospital, that was always good news, but when she was relegated to the backroom to work through a backlog of paperwork she knew avoiding her phone was going to be hard.

Sure enough, she only lasted ten minutes before seizing it in a mad, undignified scramble and switching it on. To her relief, a text popped up right away.

Now that you've messaged me, how could I not have a good night? Also, because I have to show someone, here's a picture I took at work. I can't believe how good it came out. Dean xx

He'd attached a snap of a fairy-wren, its pale blue wings caught in mid-flutter, its dark eyes peering into the camera as though curious as to what it was. Ash caught herself grinning at the screen and slammed her phone onto the desk.

This is wrong, she thought. *I shouldn't be talking to him. Why am I talking to him?*

She picked up her phone and read the message again. So sweet. So nice. Such a pretty picture of a bird... How had he taken it? Was he some kind of bird as well as pussy charmer?

She became aware she was, once again, grinning like a moron at her phone, but thankfully no one was watching. Well, no one except the mold of a dilating cervix. It glared accusingly at her, its plastic slit narrowed in derision.

"Oh, shut up," she said. "Like you know anything about men."

"Ashley?"

She jumped almost sending her phone flying.

"Sorry, love." Jocelyn, the maternity ward's unit manager, had poked her head into the room. "I just need a word. I didn't mean to scare you."

"Yeah sure," Ash said, feeling stupid. Of course, her boss would look in when she was talking to a vaginal mold. Murphy's fucking Law. "Sorry about the phone. It's uh... a bit quiet."

"Not a problem. Makes a nice change, doesn't it?" Jocelyn strode into the room. A solid woman with a friendly face, Ash had met dozens of nurses like her. They were pragmatic, kind-hearted, and if you crossed them, fucking scary. They were the mothers she and Julia would have had if life was more compassionate.

"Now, what I need to talk to you about..." Jocelyn pursed her lips. This was a look Ash knew well, it showed up when a couple said they didn't want to attend prenatal birthing classes because they'd seen a lot of *ER*. "Is something wrong?"

Jocelyn folded her arms over her ample bosom. "I couldn't tell you, but Doctor Huxley wants to see you in his office before you hand-off for the arvo."

"Doctor Huxley? You mean Doctor Huxley in orthopaedics?"

Jocelyn raised a sparse eyebrow. "Is there another Doctor Huxley?"

It was a pretty unique name, but Ash had a good reason for being confused. In a big hospital like Southern Star, there was little crossover between midwifery and orthopaedics. She had no idea why Huxley, AKA Resident DILF (doctor I'd like to fuck) wanted to see her in his office, except that it sounded bad.

"I'm not in trouble, am I?"

"I don't think so. Apparently, he thinks you have 'personal business,' to discuss. I told him to send you an email but he insisted on me delivering the message myself." Jocelyn's nostrils flared.

"What personal business?" Ash said. "I've barely ever talked to him!"

Although she *had* been the one to coin the phrase Resident DILF. Had he traced it back to her? Could she get fired for that? God, if she got fired she'd have to put all her baby plans on hold—

Jocelyn patted her on the back. "I don't think it's anything too serious, love. You were excellent during that last breach. Maybe he wants to headhunt you. Get you working in orthopaedics."

"Fuck that for a joke."

Jocelyn laughed. "You never know love, you might like it. That's where all the talent is after all."

"True."

Midwifery was a female-dominated field, orthopaedics was the exact opposite. Bone doctors had a reputation for being cocky sluts and Doctor Nate Huxley fit the bill perfectly. In his forties with clear blue eyes and a head of thick, sandy hair he had the entire gay and female population of the hospital in his thrall. He and his wife divorced last year and the gossip mills churned with stories as to why. They'd split because Monique walked in on Nate having a three-way with his chef and her personal trainer. They'd broken up because he poked an enrolled nurse half his age. They'd separated because Nate was hosting *Eyes Wide Shut* orgies in the basement. All the usual garbage. Still, there was no denying the fact that he'd slept with a fair few hospital staff members. They were constantly feuding over who was ultimately going to win his heart and become the second Mrs. Nathanial Huxley II. Ash wasn't one of them. She might have coined the term Resident DILF, but that was for shits and giggles. At forty-four the man was out of her age bracket, besides he was rich and successful and her ovaries had always helpfully pointed her towards penniless dropkicks like Zach.

And Dean, her mind added nastily.

Jocelyn waved a post-it pad in her face. "Earth to Ashley. Come in, Ashley."

"Shit, sorry." Ash straightened her spine. "I'm so out of it today."

Jocelyn's eyebrow went up again. "New boyfriend?"

Ash laughed thinking of her night spent under her covers jealously looking at pictures. "No, not a chance."

"Hmm. Well, keep looking, won't you? Plenty of men out there."

Ash bit the inside of her cheeks so she wouldn't be tempted to say anything.

Jocelyn was part of that older generation who believed a baby needed to be smashed up during lovemaking or not conceived at all. When word spread that she was thinking about using a sperm donor, Jocelyn and two other nurses mounted a campaign to set her up with as many eligible Daddy-ready men as they could find. Inevitably all of them were divorcees with entitlement issues and bald spots. A hard pass as far as Ash was concerned. She might not be a twenty-two-year-old model anymore, but she didn't need some accountant called Paul acting like he was a hero for letting her gestate his spawn. Although, if she got fired for making up a hilarious nickname she might have to rethink that stance.

"I've only got twenty minutes until lunch and it's slow," she told Jocelyn. "Would you mind if I went and found out what Huxley wants now?"

"Sure. Get your perky arse out of here. Be sure and tell us all what he says later, won't you?"

"Will do."

Curiosity burning in her stomach, Ash gathered her bag and paperwork and sped up the ward to orthopaedics, checking the signage to make sure she was in the right place (asking another nurse for directions was embarrassing.) Eventually, she found Huxley's name embossed in a gold placard on his door. *Dr. Nathanial Huxley II, Orthopaedic Consultant.*

"And Resident DILF," Ash muttered, rubbing her sweaty palms on her scrubs.

For some unknown reason, she was nervous. She'd have compared meeting Nate to being sent to the principal's office, but she'd had a special 'Batman and Joker' relationship with the principal of Brenthill Secondary. This felt more like going to see your GP after you noticed a weird rash on your undercarriage. She pulled out her lipstick (NARS, Pink Chocolate) and applied a thin coat. Feeling braver, she knocked as loudly as she could. "Hello? It's Ash Bennett."

"Come in," a man's voice called.

Ash opened the door to find Huxley reclining in his office chair, his tie loosened, his white coat slung over his desk. Maybe it was because she'd been internally dramatising his appearance out of nerves, but he wasn't as supernaturally beautiful as he usually seemed. Instead, he was blandly handsome, like an English teacher you imagined boning while he taught you *Hedda Gabler* and instantly forgot when class was over.

"Hi Doctor Huxley, you wanted to see me?"

Resident DILF sat up straighter. "I did, thanks for coming, Ashley — do you mind if I call you Ashley?"

"Yeah, whatever y'want's fine."

Ash mentally cursed herself. When she got nervous, she slipped into what Jules called the *'Yeah, nah, farken graaate cunt'* accent, a working-class bastardisation of Australian English that made a's and h's last an eternity. It had been one of her trademarks when she was a model, the whole 'hot bogan' thing and she never liked it. It made photographers dress her in flannel. She'd spent most of her adult life trying to tone her accent way the fuck down. Luckily, Resident DILF didn't seem to notice; he gestured to his guest chair. "Ashley it is, then. Feel free to call me Nate."

"Not a problem." Ash made sure to keep her voice clipped and suburban. "What did you want to see me about?"

"It's a bit of a long story." Nate pointed at his fancy pod machine. "Would you like a coffee?"

Ash wrinkled her brow. She'd already had two, another would tip her into insomnia, but it would be rude to say no. "Yeah, alright. I mean, yes, please."

As Huxley busied himself with the coffee machine, Ash stared around his office. It was well decorated as far as the space allowed, dark wooden shelves, an oil painting of Port Fairy Bay, and a framed picture of Nate arm-in-arm with Hugh Jackman.

Bit wanky, Ash mused. *But if I met Hugh Jackman, I'd make everyone look at the evidence too.*

Nate handed her a warm latte glass. "Here you go. It's a new coffee machine, so let me know what you think."

Was he nervous? He looked nervous, all sweaty and pale. God, what if she *was* about to be accused of sexual harassment for the Resident DILF thing?

She sipped her coffee. "It's good. Nice and... Warm."

In truth, she barely tasted it; her mind was focused on running 'what if' algorithms over and over. What if Nate was going to try to blackmail her into wanking him off? What if he wanted an alibi for murdering a homeless person? Rich people were into that shit, right?

"Glad to hear." Nate downed a gulp of coffee, his Adam's apple bobbing. "Now, why I asked you to come here... There's, uh, no smooth way to say this, but you know how gossip is in a hospital..."

Ash's coffee suddenly tasted like melted crayons. Jesus-fuck this was about the Resident DILF thing, what the hell was she going to say?

"... And forgive me if you think this is inappropriate, but..."

He was going to ask her to jerk him off. Ash stared helplessly at her handbag, why hadn't she thought to record this conversation while she had the chance?

"... The word on the street is you're thinking about having a baby?"

Ash was so relieved, she laughed. "Oh my god, yes, I do. I am."

"Oh, excellent!" Nate looked as relieved as she felt. "Glad I wasn't listening to the wrong people. I also heard that you're thinking of using a donor?"

"Yeah, I am! Hang on... Why do you care if I want to have a donor baby? It won't violate my contract or anything."

Nate's pale blue eyes went wide. "No, of course not. This isn't about your job, I promise."

"Then what?"

"It's a little... *Complicated,* Ashley." Nate gave her a look like he was about to suggest they skip town and fly straight to Paris. Ash had a feeling this facial arrangement had gotten him a lot of pussy in the past. "What's complicated about it?"

"Well, it's just hearsay at this point, but rumour is you had concerns about the material you were offered at Glendale?"

Jesus, the gossip mill really was working overtime. She'd only just told Marianne Muller about her trip to the clinic, but if Orthopaedics knew, then all of Southern Star knew. "Um yeah, that's right."

"Can I ask what your concerns were?"

Ash recalled sitting on the edge of a hard-backed clinic chair, scanning the files of sperm donors and wondering who the hell these strangers were and why they'd decided to jack themselves into cups so that she could have a baby. "I was just a little... Overwhelmed. I didn't think it would be so impersonal, so...clinical."

She felt stupid saying that, Glendale was a fucking clinic after all, so she added, "I felt like the consultant was trying to pressure me into picking someone before I was ready. I don't know if Glendale is the right fit for me."

Nate beamed. "Well, maybe I can help you with that."

Ash bit back a groan; she should have seen this coming. Doctors loved giving medical recommendations. If you so much as coughed in front of them, they pulled out their pads and directed you to the otolaryngologist they dormed with at uni.

"Do you know a good clinic?" she asked, trying to sound enthusiastic.

"Not exactly."

Huh? Ash stared at Nate. "What do you mean?"

Nate tugged at his tie. "You've, uh, might have heard I got divorced last year?"

Are you fucking kidding me? The chicks around here acted like Julia when she found out they were making more Star Wars movies.

"Um yeah, I think someone mentioned something."

"Well my ex and I wanted kids, but it never happened, and I'd still love to be a father..."

Ash felt like all the air had just been sucked out of the room. Surely he wasn't implying what she thought he was implying?

"... I know it's an unconventional idea, but I'm forty-four, I'm not seeing anyone, and I guess what I'm trying to say to you is..."

Nate gave her a beseeching look, as though begging her to join the dots herself.

"You want to be my... Donor?" Ash ventured.

"Yes," Nate said, looking utterly relieved. "If you're open to the idea, I'm interested."

Ash blinked at him, unsure if this was real or if she'd fallen asleep in front of the TV after eating a lot of Kraft cheese. "You. And me. A baby?"

"Is that so hard to fathom?"

"Well *yeah*."

"How come?"

Ash considered the question. For one thing, it was a pretty ballsy move, calling her in here at work, literally while she was working a shift, to ask if she wanted his sperm. For another, Doctor Nathanial Huxley II was a man with a Mercedes and shoes worth more than her entire wardrobe. Ash wasn't entirely ashamed of who she was, but her and Nate blending their DNA together? It would be like a purebred pointer mating with the bitch who lived behind KFC.

"I guess I just wasn't expecting you to make me an offer," Ash said. "What makes you think it's a good idea?"

Nate looked mildly taken aback. "Well... I've only ever heard good things about you."

"That's because you don't know anyone from my hometown."

He laughed.

"That's not a joke. But, seriously, we work together. I don't know what the HR stance on getting sperm from your co-workers is, but I don't think Vera and her minions would be very impressed."

Actually, it wasn't the pointy-heads in Human Resources who had her worried, it was every female employee who had a crush on or had slept with Nate. If they knew he wanted to give her his baby, she was a dead woman walking.

Immune to his own problematic attractiveness, Nate grinned. "We wouldn't have to worry about me working here. I just accepted a consultancy position at the Royal Children's Hospital."

"Oh, congratulations. When do you leave?"

"In a couple of months. I've already put in my notice. I like Southern Star, but I think it's time for a change of scenery."

Plus you banged too many nurses and shit's getting awkward, Ash thought. "Well, a lot of people are going to be disappointed to see you go." *And by people, I mean 'chicks.'*

"Thanks, I'll be disappointed to leave this old place behind too, but on the plus side, that frees up your concern about us working together. What's next?"

"Er..." Ash's brain was so crammed full of information she could barely anticipate another question. "I don't know, this is a lot to take in."

"I understand," Nate said in his buttery doctor's voice. "All I wanted to do today was lay my cards on the table."

"Well, you've definitely done that."

Nate's smile was a patented 'everything is going to be all right' grin, honed to a high gloss on a thousand anxious patients. "I'm sorry if I've overstepped the mark. It wasn't my intention to upset you."

"It's okay. It's just a bit full on."

"I can see that." Nate's toothy grin grew wider, and Ash found herself thinking about Dean. Dean and his bright, boyish, painfully sincere smile. She'd only spent an hour with him, and she knew his happiness lived right on the surface. He'd never fake a smile, or use a phrase like 'it wasn't my intention to upset you.' But then Dean wasn't a doctor or a homeowner, and he wasn't suggesting they fulfil her greatest wish and have a baby together. So why the fuck was she thinking about him? Truth be told, Nate was an ideal donor, handsome, professional, and accomplished. Why wasn't she being more positive about this?

"I'm not *opposed* to the idea of you being my donor," she told Nate. "I'm just a little taken aback."

Nate's face lit up. "That's excellent! About you not being opposed, I mean. I wouldn't necessarily want dual custody. Just weekends or fortnightly visits, whatever you're interested in arranging. And I'll have myself screened so you can get a better look at my genetic history. I think there's a mild case of anaemia in my family, but that shouldn't be a—"

"Um, Nate?"

He stopped talking at once. "Sorry, I'm getting ahead of myself, aren't I? I'm just so bloody excited."

Ash smiled. "It's fine. It's good you're excited, but maybe I should go away and give this some thought?"

"Of course! Whatever you need! Here's my number if you want to call and have a chat." He slid a cream card across the table and Ash slipped it into her scrubs pocket. "Thank you."

"No problem. There's just one more thing I'll add before you go. If we did decide to embark on this... I guess we could call it a journey of creation?"

Ash laughed. "Sure, why not?"

"Well, if you did decide to accept my offer, I'd have my lawyer draw up a contract promising you an initial payment of four hundred thousand dollars and, once the baby was born, two thousand dollars a week in child support."

Fireworks went off behind Ashley's eyes. "I'm sorry, *what*?"

Nate repeated his offer, a slightly patronising smile tugging at the corners of his mouth. Ash was too overwhelmed to care. "God, why would you give me that much doss to have a kid I already want?"

Nate laughed. "Well, you'd be taking the physical risks during the pregnancy, but also, I'd want my baby to have the best possible life. I know you make decent money, but if we did proceed, I'd want to ensure you and my child were taken care of to the best of my ability."

Ash stared at Hugh Jackman's glorious inanimate face and tried to absorb what Nate was proposing. That kind of money would change *everything*. She and Jules could finally knock down the crappy pink house they'd inherited from their grandma and rebuild. Or better yet, she could ditch it and live in an inner-city suburb and become one of those ultra-glamorous young mothers you saw in cafes. The ones who did nothing except puree carrots and post adorable Instagram photos.

For a moment she revelled in the idea, then her bullshit detectors started firing. "You're a rich, hot doctor. Why would you want to have a baby with me?"

Nate looked taken aback. "I suppose because you're an intelligent and hardworking—"

"No, I mean, why donate your sperm? You only *just* got divorced, and it's not like you're on a deadline the way women are. Are you sure this is a commitment you want to be making?"

Nate laughed, but the sound was strained. "You're straightforward, I like it."

Ash sat silently, waiting for an answer.

"I suppose I'm a little burnt out on women and relationships," Nate explained. "I've been married, and I don't think it's for me. I have no plans to settle down again, and I have a lot more faith in mutually agreeable business arrangements than I do love."

Somewhere inside Ash registered a little ping of wrongness, but she shoved it away. "So you're sure you'd like to have a baby?"

"Oh, yes," Nate said at once. "That kind of love is different. I've always been able to see myself as a father. The idea of making my parents grandparents, of passing along our family name—it's important to me. And you're right, I'm not on a deadline the way women are but, I would like to become a father before I risk breaking a hip every time I go down the stairs."

"Right." Ash didn't love the whole 'my progeny' thing, but it was a relief to see Nate had legitimate motives for wanting to become a dad.

"I guess that makes sense. That's kind of what I was getting at by looking for a sperm donor. I got sick of watching the years go by, hoping the right guy would just come along, marry me, and then give me a kid."

Nate nodded. "The fact you were planning to have a child alone spoke volumes to me about the kind of woman you are. It's admirable, Ashley."

Ash relaxed a little into her chair. "Thanks. It's nice to meet someone who gets where I'm coming from. People can be a little... judgemental about parenthood."

Nate chuckled. "Isn't that the truth? Well, I'm glad we're on the same page. I hoped we would be. Throw in the fact that you're the most beautiful nurse I've ever seen, and I knew I just had to risk making an idiot of myself today."

Ash stiffened. The subtle ping of wrongness had become an almighty gong. Was Resident DILF *hitting* on her? At work? Right after he asked if she wanted to harvest his jizz? God, if he didn't stop throwing situational wood on the fire, her head was going to explode. "Thanks?"

Nate seemed to know he'd dropped the ball. "You being beautiful is only relevant because we might have a baby together! Good genes and all that."

Ash felt her cheeks heat up. "Sure, well, um, I guess I should go. My lunch break will be over soon, and I haven't eaten."

She got to her feet, and Nate stood up too. "Ashley, let me take you to dinner this Saturday? I don't know about you, but I'd feel a lot more comfortable discussing this over a bottle of wine."

Ash stared at him. Standing up, she could see how trim and muscular Nate was, all handsome like an actor in a movie, but this was all too much to take in right now. "Um, can I get back to you?"

Nate plastered his doctor's smile over his obvious disappointment. "Sure."

He walked around his desk and held the door open for her. "Thanks for meeting with me, Ashley. I hope we speak soon."

"Okay, thanks." Ash tore out of Nate's office like a hurricane. Resident DILF wanted to give her a baby. A baby, a whole new life, and possibly his penis as well. It was official. Her Cinderella moment had finally come. Sure, it wasn't Prince Eric, proposing on bended knee, but it was a hot doctor promising her a small fortune to fulfil her heart's desire. Ash ran back to the antenatal ward, her handbag slapping her side and she knew she should have been thrilled, or at least excited.

Instead, her hands were shaking, and she was craving a cigarette more than she had in months.

She went to the lunchroom but was too wound up to eat her leftover risotto. She made herself a cup of tea and sat at one of the empty tables. Thankfully, none of the nurses in the room seemed to be aware of her meeting with Nate; the last thing she wanted was a rehash. Her bag buzzed, and she pulled out her phone, half-convinced Nate had sent her a text. The relief she felt when Dean's name popped up on her screen was ridiculous. He'd sent her a picture of the sunrise, accompanied by the caption: *made me think of you. Because it's so pretty, not because you're orange or anything.*

Ash stared at the picture and felt the ridiculous urge to cry. He wasn't asking her for a date, or a chance to finish what they started in the bathroom at Julia's game launch. He'd just sent her a picture because...

"Because he likes me," she whispered. "He likes me."

With a shaky thumb, she pressed the phone icon next to Dean's name.

He answered after a single ring. "Ash! You called! I mean... How are you?"

How was she? Well, the mere sound of his voice had relaxed her from head to foot, and she swore she could *see* him smiling, all bright and hopeful, but other than that she was pretty damn shitty. Something she was hoping he could help her with. "I'm good, Red. What are you doing this afternoon?"

6

As she drove to the address Dean texted her, Ash was barely aware of her surroundings. She stuck to the speed limit, registered the cars in front of her, but for the most part her brain was fully occupied by Dean. His smile, his texts, the way he made her laugh.

The roofing company he worked for was finishing off a three bedroom house in a suburb not far from Brenthill. Ash had offered to meet Dean there so they could go to a nearby cafe and have *one* hot beverage together. At least that's what she'd said on the phone. If she was being honest with herself, there was probably a lot more on the table.

A roofer makes plenty of money, she thought, as she exited a roundabout. *Does Red like kids?*

Um, hello? Another, snarkier voice said. *Naked snowboarding. Naked snowboarding. Arrested in New Zealand for naked snowboarding.*

"Shut up," she told herself. "This isn't about that. About either of those things. We're just going to hang out."

She found the neighbourhood without any difficulty. It was a freshly built outer suburb. A ghost town waiting to be filled with middle-class couples and middle-class families. The kind of place she had grown up idolising and would never be able to afford.

Unless you take Nate's offer, the snarky voice reminded her. *Four hundred thousand dollars is one hell of a deposit...*

"Again, shut up," she warned herself. "No thoughts, no future, just now."

She pulled up in the driveway of the house Dean had directed her to. She could see a macho-looking Ute, but no Dean, on the roof or otherwise. She braked and used the free time to check herself out in the rear-view mirror. She didn't look her best. A lack of mascara meant her lashes were fair. Her hair was slightly oily, and then there was the matter of her boob-and-ass flattening scrubs. For a moment she considered leaving before he saw her, then she thought *'fuck it,'* and kicked her car door open. Southern Star's best looking doctor had just asked her to carry his child. She couldn't be *that* repulsive.

"Ashley?"

She turned toward the sound of Dean's voice and words just... failed her. What had she been expecting? A smaller man? A slighter man? A man whose hair didn't blaze like polished copper in the light of the dying sun? Dean wore typical tradie gear: a fluoro shirt with the company's name on it, boots, and thick navy drill pants, the kind she'd washed for a hundred ex-boyfriends. He had something black smeared on the side of his face and his hair was curly with sweat, but he looked—there was no other word for it—lovely.

When their eyes met his face broke into the biggest, nicest smile she'd ever seen. "Hey, it is you! How's it going, gorgeous?"

For the second time that day, Ash felt stupidly close to tears. Then, before she knew what she was doing, before she'd even answered his question, she ran toward him. Dean didn't miss a trick. He bent his knees and scooped her up, pulling her tight against his chest. As soon as Ash felt those thick arms lock around her, her whole body relaxed. The tension she didn't even know she was carrying just melted away. "Hey Red, it's good to see you."

"You, too." He pressed his face against her neck and inhaled. "You smell nice."

Ash smoothed her hands over his broad shoulders. "So do you."

"You're joking, right?"

She wasn't. He didn't smell like cologne, but then no cologne could capture fresh sawdust mixed with sweat, sunshine, and Dean. If they could, society would collapse because everyone would be too busy fucking all the time. Ash cupped his cheek, his short beard soft against her palm. "I don't know if I came here to have coffee with you, Red."

She felt, rather than heard Dean swallow. "Whatever you want, Ash, I promise I'm game. I can't stop thinking about you."

"About what we did?"

Dean nodded.

"Have you, you know... While you thought about it?"

"Yeah." He gave her a guilty smile. "I can't stop. I'm thirty-fuckin'-five and I might as well be sixteen for all the jacking off I'm doing."

"Sorry, Red."

"Don't be. I like it. It feels good to be this crazy about someone, even if it's making me even dopier than usual—"

Ash couldn't help herself. She kissed Dean, no, she *attacked Dean*, sinking her fingers deep into his hair and claiming him like she was a Viking warrior and he, a helpless English milkmaid. They'd kissed before, but without a litre of alcohol numbing Ash's senses, it was even more electric. Their mouths moved in harmony, hands gripping each other with equal fervour. Ash forgot they were outside, forgot she wasn't meant to be doing this, forgot everything but Dean's tongue. She ground against his hips, rubbing herself against his thick pants.

Dean chuckled. "Are you horny, Ash?"

"Um, maybe just a little."

His hands slid to her arse and squeezed, pressing her flush against his hard-on. "That why you brought yourself to me, huh? You wanted me to take care of you?"

No. Sex hadn't been on her mind when she called him. She'd just wanted to be soothed by whatever codeine-heavy air syrup he exuded along with his scent. But once the soothing was done, approximately one second after he hugged her, yeah, screwing was suddenly at the top of her list of priorities. "Would you hate me if I did? If the only reason I came here was to get laid?"

Dean buried his face in her throat, kissing and rubbing. "I wouldn't give a single fuck, Ashley. I've been hurting for you for days. All I want is to make you come again. And I promise it'll be good, so good you won't be able to think about me without getting wet."

"Cocky."

"Confident," he corrected. "It's been days, and all I can think about is you riding my face, making me taste you. The way you rubbed yourself against my mouth... I smelled you on me for hours afterward. I swear to fuckin' God I never wanted to wash you off. If I get another shot at your pussy there's no way I'm screwing it up."

Ash felt the last of her self-restraint bleed away. "You can go down on me anytime you like, Red. Like right now, for example."

"Where?"

Ash considered the half-built house, its wooden framework poking out like a piney rib cage, and winced at the many twat splinters it promised. "Hood of my car?"

Dean didn't need to be told twice. He began carrying her back toward Tangerine, her beloved Kingswood, then paused. "Whoa, I know I was kinda distracted by you and how beautiful you are, but this is an awesome car."

"Thanks." Ash chewed her lower lip, half-convinced he was going to ask if Tangerine belonged to her dad or her ex-boyfriend, or if she had any idea how rare or expensive her car was. Dean did none of those things. Instead, he placed her gently on the still-warm hood and smiled. "Now that's a fuckin' picture."

"I'm wearing scrubs."

"And you look gorgeous in them." Dean stepped backward, his hands positioned like a camera frame. "Awesome car. Smoking hot girl. Half-built McMansion in the background. It all fits."

Ash laughed. "You ain't seen nothin' yet."

She cocked her head and gave him her best Playboy pout. Dean pressed a palm to his chest. "You're killing me."

Ash giggled, feeling ridiculously light and pretty. "I guess I should stop, then?"

"Only if you want me to live." Dean walked toward her, hands in his pockets. "Where'd you get the car from?"

"A private dealer from Carlton. I worked my arse off to buy her. Took every single modelling gig my agency offered, even gross stock photos."

"Why'd you want her so badly?"

"It's kind of... Stupid."

"I bet it isn't," he said, sincerity blazing out of his every pore.

Ash felt a hot stab of guilt. She had used this beautiful man as a vagina-pacifier and now come back for seconds and all he could do was stare at her like she was some kind of lady-Jesus. She owed him the truth. "I was trash, Red. At school, in Brenthill, everywhere, really. I don't know what Julia told you, but we had a rough time growing up. We lived in government housing, everyone knew our mum was a drunk, everyone thought we were Centrelink scum. When it came time for me to grow up, I did not change that image."

Dean chuckled. "You were a rebel."

"I think the proper term is 'feral bogan rat-child.'"

Dean stepped between her legs. "I don't believe you, but where does the car come in?"

"The car was about being as showy and obnoxious as possible. I wanted to tell everyone who judged me, everyone in Brenthill, that no matter what they thought about my family or me, I wasn't trying to fade away or fit in. That I was better than them in every possible way."

"I'd say it worked." Dean bent down, so their faces were inches apart. "From what Julia told me you had a pretty intense past..."

Ashley's heart stopped; for all her big words, hearing that Red thought she was a skank would hurt like hellfire.

But then he said, "You were a model! You've been all over the world—"

"Just Europe and America."

"And now you're a nurse who gives people the gift of life—"

"I help deliver babies."

"Same difference," Dean pressed his forehead against hers. "You're beautiful and smart and funny and you smell like bottled cupcakes, plus I heard you once got suspended for a little girl-on-girl activism?"

Ash sucked her lips into her mouth, trying to hold in the smirk threatening to emerge. "Oh, you heard that, huh?"

"I did. Very brave and cool of you. Did anyone like, take pictures or...?"

She laughed and seized the collar of Dean's polo shirt. "Enough about my past, Red, are we going to hook up? Or are you just going to linger over me, being charming?"

"I can do both." Dean reached down and untied her right shoelace.

"Don't bother." Ash dug the right toe of her trainer against the left and kicked her shoe off.

He tutted. "You ruin 'em doing that."

"Meh." Ash kicked off her other shoe, hoisted her hips and began tugging off her scrubs pants.

"So, we're just jumping right in, then?" Dean's voice was warm with laughter but Ash blushed. "I'm just trying to get the awkward undressing phase over with. We don't have to do anything you don't want to."

"Oh, I want to." Dean helped her ease her scrubs pants down her legs. "Hey, cute socks."

He picked up her left foot and pressed a thumb into her strawberry-covered arch. Ash gave a piteous moan of pleasure. "Seriously, Red, eww."

"Why?" he asked, massaging her gently. "I like feet. I mean, not like that, but I do like touching them and I thought it would feel good. Do you like it?"

"I do but I was just wearing runners on an eight hour shift," Ash pointed out. "Besides, we're in public."

"I know, but I kinda like the wild factor. Besides, the sun's going down, and there's no one around to traumatise."

"True, I guess…"

"What's the matter, rebel?" Dean teased. "Lost your nerve?"

Ash remembered her conversation with Nate, his decent, or possibly indecent proposal. Would he have made it if he knew the kind of person she used to be? If he heard the way she really talked? The thought made her twitchy. She glared up at Dean. "Not on your fucking life. You like the wild factor Red? Watch this."

Before she could lose her nerve, Ash removed her foot from Dean's grasp and tugged her panties down, kicking them on the ground. Then she spread her legs nice and wide. Dean made a sound like a wounded animal. "God-*damn.*"

Ash slid a hand down her stomach, gently toying with her landing strip and the soft lips below. She was slick to the touch and even the lightest caresses made her legs quake. Ten days and she and Eric hadn't managed to fuck away the hot, aching feeling Dean Sherwood had left inside her. She met his gaze directly. "You like this?"

Dean ran a hand over his mouth. "How is this happening?"

"How is what happening?"

"How was I going home to microwave lasagna and my right hand and now I'm watching a model touch herself on the hood of the coolest car I've ever seen up close."

Ash smirked. "If you like that, you're gonna love this."

She slowly sank a finger between her legs, sighing as nerves that had been primed since their kiss buzzed and tingled. "Hmm, that feels nice. Does it look nice?"

Dean bent down, his forearms on the hood of Tangerine, and stared between her legs. "God, yes."

"You like my pussy?" Ash slid in another finger, reveling in Dean's slack-jawed arousal.

"Yeah," he muttered, his voice seven decibels lower. "God I fucking love it, Ash."

Ash was secretly hoping he'd lunge forward and take over but he just stared intently, breathing hard through his nose. She continued toying with herself, sliding her fingers gently in and out of her needy pussy. As the minutes passed she found her arousal reaching a peak almost inevitably, like an electric kettle bringing water to boiling point. And yet while she was clearly a woman in need of a hand, Dean didn't make a single move to assist her.

What is his problem? She thought, frigging herself irritably. *One minute he couldn't stop raving about my pussy and now he's just staring at it like it's repeats of Law and Order. What the hell is happening?*

Then Ash noticed the *way* Dean was staring at her, his expression drawn and needy, his shoulders shaking. She couldn't see his cock, but from the way his bicep was flexing, he was gripping it pretty damn hard. He was watching, not because he couldn't be bothered getting her off, but because...

"He wants me to tell him what to do," Ash whispered. Of course, he did. The night they met all she did was drunkenly boss him around and he loved it. At least she *thought* he did, she was ten drinks in at the time. Ash decided to road test her theory sober. "Red?"

"Huh?" Dean glanced up at her face. "Did you, um, need something, Ashley?"

The way he stammered her name, like a nervous employee calling their boss 'sir,' sold her on her theory. She gave him her sweetest smile. "If you don't start eating my pussy in the next nine seconds, I'm going to drive away and you can go home to sad lasagna and your right hand and think about how you wasted my time."

For a terrifying moment, he didn't react and she was sure, utterly convinced, she'd fucked up. Then Dean's face went slack. "I'm sorry, Ash."

Bennett, you fucking genius.

Ash assumed her bitchiest expression. "Tick tock, Red. Get to it."

And then big hands were shoving her thighs apart and a wet mouth was descending on her with such enthusiasm she could only gasp.

"Christ, I've missed this," Dean muttered after a few frenzied laps.

Ash let out an unintelligible moan of encouragement.

"I mean it," he said, as though she'd accused him of lying. "It's all I can think about. You making me do this."

He bent forward and tasted her, a quick flick of his tongue, like an attempt to sample her flavor. "It tastes even better than I remember. Like flowers and sex and rainbows and fuck, I just want to do it forever."

He licked her again, slower this time, making every muscle in her legs tense. His rough palms found her thighs, stroking them slowly, the calluses in direct contrast with his soft tongue. Ash found herself acutely aware of the open sky, the myna birds and magpies calling as they nestled in for the night. This was far, far too familiar.

She sat up a little. "Red, my twat isn't a vegan gelato truck, I don't give out infinite samples because I sell a dubious product no one likes."

Dean gave a soft snort of laughter. "Glad to hear it."

"You shouldn't be glad to hear it, ginger, because what I'm trying to say is *hurry the fuck up*."

Again she felt a stab of fear that she'd taken it too far, snapping at Dean like he was some kind of under-performing fast-food employee, but he only let out a pained groan and bent back to his task. This time he slid his tongue inside her and, through some act of sorcery, proceeded to *writhe* the wet muscle inside her in a way that made her scream with pleasure.

Dean's brown eyes gleamed up at her. "Something wrong?"

"What is *up* with your tongue, man?"

"Oh, just a little trick I picked up from a lesbian I used to bartend with. Shall I...?"

He ducked his head, and Ash slapped a palm to his forehead. "Not a chance. You keep doing that and I'm gonna scream so loud every cop in Victoria comes running. Including our buddy, Max."

Dean gave her a filthy smile. "Then what should I do?"

She grabbed herself a fistful of Dean's hair. "Suck my clit like you did in the bathroom."

"Yes, ma'am."

His mouth descended and holy fucking Jesus... Most guys had a particular style of doing this, a carpet bombing, slap-their-tongues-over-everything-and-hope-for-the-best kind of style. Dean didn't do that. As far as cunnilingus went, he was in a league of his own. With his lips sucking her most sensitive zone, he pressed the tip of his tongue directly against her clit and repeated the snakelike writhing motion he'd used inside her, never removing himself from the tender bundle of nerves. She cried out, and without thinking yanked the fuck out of Dean's hair. He grunted into her pussy and Ash let go at once. "Shit! Sorry!"

Dean looked up at her, his eyes glazed. "Do it again. Go as hard as you want. You won't hurt me."

Ash seized two tight fistfuls of hair. "Like this?"

"Fuck yeah." Dean's mouth returned to her pussy and… Bliss.

Ash didn't consider herself a chilled-out person. Unlike Julia, who could sit motionless in a beanbag for hours playing games about wizards, she needed to be moving, doing things. The only time she felt relaxed was when she was drunk or asleep. But lying on the hood of her car with Dean's beard tickling her inner thighs, unbelievable pleasure radiating from her pussy, the sky fading to a velvety blackish-blue above her, she felt so damn relaxed she wanted to laugh out loud. She'd always liked sex but it was so often a performance, she found herself playing the part of the model, the hot girl, the trophy, seeing herself through the eyes of the man she was with, sucking in her stomach and wondering if he'd noticed one of her nipples was slightly larger than the other. When you were an object, you couldn't feel the sensations in your body. You couldn't relax and when you couldn't relax, you could rarely come. It was usually only boyfriends who could get her off and after weeks of careful, *'I don't want to hurt your feelings, but…'* tutoring.

With Dean it was different. She knew he wasn't licking her because he wanted to tell his mates about it later. He laughed at her jokes. He sent her a picture of a fairy-wren. He liked her. And even if it couldn't last, he felt so damn good. All of a sudden Ash wanted to know what it would be like to have everything this man had to offer, right on the hood of her car. Suspecting it was how he'd prefer to be interrupted, she yanked on Dean's hair. He stopped what he was doing at once. "Help you with something, Ash?"

"You can. Fuck me, Red. Fuck me right now."

Dean ran his tongue over his glossy lips. "Right now?"

"Right now, I want to come with you inside me." *I want to know what it's like to have you, even if it's only once.*

"You want me like that, huh?"

Ash's pussy, missing the attention it had so recently been treated to, throbbed. "Yes. So badly."

"Good." Dean stood up and swiped a heavy-knuckled hand over his mouth. "There's something you need to know about my dick—"

"I don't care if it's got a weird curve or anything, just take it out already."

Dean laughed. "No my dick's normal. Better than normal, some have said."

Ash pressed her fingertips into the hood of her car, trying to exorcise her short burst of jealousy. "Glad to hear it. So, what's the hold-up?"

Dean shoved his hands into his pockets. "Well, before you showed up tonight, my dick and I had a little talk, and we came to a decision about you."

"And that is?"

"You want my cock? You wanna know how I fuck? You want me to ride your tight little body like I used to ride Delilah?"

Yes, Ash's cunt snarled. *Yes, you fool. Ride me.* "I do want that."

"... Then you'll have to go on a date with me first."

Ash stared at him, her heart sinking, her pussy deflating like a punctured tire. "Red..."

"It'll be good," Dean promised. "Worth it. I'll even let you pick the place we eat in before I fuck you senseless."

Ash groaned. It was so naive of her not to have seen this coming. She collapsed back onto the car, her head banging on the metal. "What is it with men making demands on me today?"

Dean's expression hardened. "What other man's making demands on you?"

Ash wondered what he'd say if she told him the truth; '*A doctor at work. He wants me to give me his baby. Possibly via a turkey baster, possibly via his actual penis.*'

She shook her head. "Never mind. And we can't go on a date."

"Sure we can. It wouldn't have to be a big one. Pizza? Movie?"

"I just... I can't." Feeling like utter scum, Ash sat up. "I'm sorry, I shouldn't have come here."

Dean pressed a warm hand into her thigh. "It's fine, I'm glad you came. It'll sound a bit intense, but I missed you."

His sincerity burned like acid in her belly. Why couldn't he just be a prick? Screw up? Say something mean? Call her a bitch? Why did he have to be so fucking *nice*?

"So, then I guess that's that," she said, trying to think of a not-awkward way of asking Dean to hand her her pants.

She didn't need to bother, Dean bent down, tugged her hips back toward him, and resumed sucking on her aching clit.

Ash tugged his hair. "Hey there! What are you doing?"

Dean grinned. "I never said I wasn't going to finish you off. I still wanna make you come so hard you see stars."

He glanced at the sky. "Well, more stars."

"But—"

"But nothing. Hold onto my hair again, that was fucking hot."

Ash wanted to protest but found she couldn't do anything but laugh. "Go on then, you generous, sexy pain in the ass."

It was different from before. Before Dean was driving her towards climax like a sheepdog drove cattle. Now he was playing, teasing. Giving her little flickering laps that made her arch her back and cry out his name. She took it, well aware she deserved a little torture, but finally, she could take no more. She yanked on his hair. "Fuck me with your fingers."

Dean unsuctioned himself from her clit. "Won't feel half as good as what I've got between my legs."

Ash moaned at the thought. "How big are you?"

"Big," he said without ego. "Big enough I worry I won't fit inside you. I'm gonna have to get you real wet first, baby. Eat you a couple times I reckon. Use my fingers or a toy."

Ash let out a moan of frustration. "I'm wet now, why can't we—"

"You know why," Dean said lightly. "You have any toys, Ash?"

She thought about Eric, lying on her bedside table next to the lube. "Yes."

"You ever use them while you think about me?"

Only about a two dozen times in nine days... "Yes."

Dean's tongue fluttered like butterfly wings over her pussy. "That's a job I'd like. Living in your bedside drawer, getting pulled out whenever you wanted to fuck, then put right back in again. Would you like that, Ash? Do you want me to be your toy?"

Ash's hands sought her breasts, tugging at her nipples. "Be inside me, Red. Please?"

He obeyed, sort of, lightly tracing her opening with blunt, rough fingertips. "What's the magic word?"

He was enjoying this, Ash knew, stealing a little of her power back, but she wasn't built for surrender. She gripped his hair hard enough to tear it up from the roots. "Now."

Dean dipped a rough fingertip into her pussy and Ash groaned. She hadn't known how much she needed the penetration until he was pressing her sodden walls apart. She was so swollen she felt like a split peach.

After a few seconds, Dean withdrew and resumed his lazy stroking. "Last time we saw each other you called me immature."

"Yeah, yeah, sorry," Ash moaned. "Deeper? Again?"

"Immature people are selfish," Dean continued, as though he hadn't heard her. "They don't think about anyone except themselves. I'm a lot of things, Ash, but I'm not selfish."

"No." She rocked her hips toward him. "No, you're not. You're so... You're very..."

He gave her a couple of slow laps, and instead of protesting Ash pressed her thighs against his ears and tried to press him closer. He chuckled. "Not so fast, greedy girl."

Ash scowled at him. How did she ever think she had anything over this guy? He was leading her around by the clit like some kind of clit-farmer. "I know you're not selfish, you're a..." Dean gave her clit a particularly firm suck. "*Oh my god.* You're a... Great guy... But like, seriously, be inside me? Please?"

"I *am* a great guy." Dean eased a long, work-roughened finger back into the place where she needed it most. "I know you don't believe that right now, but I'm gonna prove it to you, Ash."

Before she could question this dubious course of action, Dean bent down and his tongue did the snake thing again, writhing against her as his finger worked in and out of her pussy. Ash clung to his hair for dear life. "Red. Red!"

He kept sucking, drawing the shocking sensation out to breaking point until everything inside her exploded. Ash cried out as she came, rocking so hard against her car she could hear Tangerine creaking. Thankfully, she managed to release Dean's hair before she made him partially bald. He gave her a couple of gentle laps then slid his finger from her and sucked it. "Feel good?"

Ash let out a piteous moan.

"Good. That's what I wanted."

"When I... Can breathe... Let me... Do something for you?"

Dean pulled away, yanking down his zipper and adjusting his cock before zipping up again. "Nope."

"But—"

"But nothing. You're not getting any more from me unless we go on a date. I'm classy that way. Now do you still wanna go get coffee or should you head home? It's getting late."

Ash sat up. "Are you mad at me?"

Dean looked surprised. "No, I think you're awesome. I'm gonna message you as soon as I get home. Actually, I'm gonna crank one out, then I'll message you."

Ash slid off Tangerine's hood. "Why don't you just let me suck you instead?"

Dean backed away like she was a starved tiger. "Not now. You know the rules."

"*Your* rules." Ash advanced, eyes locked on the bulge at the front of his pants. "I think third base can go both ways. Picture it, you watching your big hard cock disappear into my little mouth, feeling my tongue wetting you down so I can try and take you deeper..."

Dean's eyes drifted closed, and Ash lunged. Quick as a flash Dean turned to the side, avoiding her. "Uh-uh. Hands off the merch, missy."

Ash hissed like an angry cat. "Why are you being such a... *Shitbag*?"

Dean angled his body away from her. "Because I know you like me and I know you want to fuck me, and I think I can get at least one little date out of that. It's all about compromise, Ash."

"I will never compromise," she vowed. "I'll die of horniness first."

"There's no need for that. You've got my number. You get too pent up, call me. I'll come lick your pussy whenever you want. Finger you, too, if you like."

Ash stared at him, not entirely convinced she'd heard him properly. "Are you serious?"

"As the fucking grave. I said I wouldn't mind being your toy. I'd take the job very seriously."

"Is this like, a service you provide in exchange for money? Like you tongue-fuck busy women who don't have time to date?"

"More of a hobby." Dean picked up her underwear and handed it to her. "But if you wanna slip me a twenty every now and then, I won't try and give it back."

Ash didn't laugh. "I can't treat you like some kind of whore."

Dean paused in the process of picking up her scrub pants. "Why not? If it's what I want, where's the harm?"

The harm was that they would catch an even worse case of feelings for one another, but Ash wasn't going to point that out. Instead, she pointed at his still-visible erection. "Are you sure you don't want to...?"

"Very sure. Not without a date. Happy to take care of you, though."

"Like I said, you're a tease." Ash slid into her ground-undies, trying not to think about the potential debris inside them. As sexy as the idea of texting Dean in the middle of the night and having him drive all the way to her house to satisfy her was, she wasn't evil. She wouldn't be texting or calling or Facebook-stalking or especially *dating* Dean Sherwood. Tonight was the end.

Ash pulled on her scrub bottoms then shuffled around, trying to find her shoes while avoiding the loose gravel on the driveway. Dean snorted. "Here..."

He hoisted her onto Tangerine's hood, then with seeming night-vision he located her runners and began easing them onto her feet.

"You don't have to do this," she protested. "I know my shoes don't exactly smell like fresh bread."

"It's already happening, just go with it."

"Well, thanks, Red."

"No worries." He laced her left trainer up tight then tapped her foot. "Done."

"Great." Ash slid off her car once more. "Have a good night."

"Oh, I will." Dean cupped her jaw and planted a hard, fast kiss on her mouth. Ash could smell her pussy mixed in with his muskiness, a thrilling twist on an already amazing scent.

"Think about it," Dean said.

"Think about what?"

"Calling me when you want to get eaten out." Dean pulled away and walked around her car, opening her driver's side door. "Anywhere, anytime, after work, before work, I'll come give it to you."

Ash laughed, though she knew he wasn't joking. "Sure thing, Red. Next time I need a service you're my man."

"I am," he said, without any irony. "Drive safe."

7

"So, you signed up to be Ashley's scratching post?"

Dean scowled, partly from what Max said, partly because tiny bits of mince were flying up out of the saucepan and adhering to his arms. "No."

"You are, though. You're like one of those carpet things that cats..." Max made scrabbling motions in the air "... Do that on."

"Piss off."

Dean knew it was a weak response, but he didn't have the time or energy to think of a better one. All his focus was on making enchiladas. He'd arranged all the ingredients on the bench, fine. He'd cut up the onions and capsicums, sure. Now actual cooking was taking place, and shit was unravelling fast. The rice, though still hard, was running out of water, and the mince was trying to give him third-degree burns. Max was allegedly 'supervising,' but all he was really doing in Dean's opinion was pounding beers and being a pain in his ass.

"I can't believe you thought you could get away with not telling me." Max shook his bottle of Prickly Moses in Dean's face. "I *knew* something was up. You were walking around whistling John Mayer and asking me where to buy a mop."

"Yeah, yeah, you're a fuckin' genius," Dean muttered, as he tried to keep more mince from leaping out of the pan.

Max had been highly suspicious of his attempts to cook dinner and figure out how to use the washing machine. Two hours ago, he'd come home with a bag of groceries and scratch marks on his upper arms from his latest rendezvous with Ashley and Max had deduced, correctly, that they were still hooking up. Now he wouldn't stop gnawing at him like Earl used to gnaw at raw chicken wings.

"I can't believe you've offered yourself up as a human sex doll. Whatever happened to playing it cool?"

Dean prodded the rapidly congesting rice with a wooden spoon. "I did play it cool. That's what got Ash to message me in the first place. Then I played it cool a little more and, waddaya know, she showed up at my worksite."

"To get laid."

"No. To see me."

"To see you laying her." Max glanced at the rice. "Boil the kettle and put more hot water in or it'll burn."

"Here's an idea—you could do it?"

"Then how will you ever learn?"

Swearing, Dean hit the tab on the kettle.

"How many times have you and Ash met up now?" Max asked.

"Four. Five if you count Julia's game launch."

"I *don't* count Julia's game launch. I don't count any of these encounters because you're not dating, you're not even fuck-buddies. You're just replacing whatever sex toy Ash was using before you came along."

Dean's face grew hot as he remembered what he'd said to Ash on the hood of her car, how he'd volunteered to take over the role of her vibrator. But they were just playing around, right? She wasn't *really* using him as a substitute sex toy? "You don't understand—"

"I understand everything," Max interrupted. "You're whoring yourself out in the hope that it'll make Ash fall for you. It's not hard to follow."

"Then why won't you shut up about it?"

"Because it's a stupid fuckin' idea. And if Jules finds out about you two sneaking around, she'll be livid."

"I know, but Ash made me promise not to tell anyone we're meeting up."

"Another encouraging sign your non-relationship is headed in the right direction." Max drained his beer and headed back toward the fridge. "You need to get real here man; unless she agrees to go on a date with you, and soon, she's using you. This is Violeta Cummins part two."

"She isn't, and it's not," Dean called over his shoulder. "We talk every day. She likes me, I know she does. Soon we'll—"

"Share a meal that isn't her pussy? Have sex that involves your dick?"

"Exactly—*ow!*" A chunk of mince welded itself to Dean's forearm and he flicked it off, rubbing the red patch that it left behind. "Why the fuck does that keep happening?"

"It's the way you're stirring. Stop flinging your hands around like a dickhead."

"Yeah, cheers." Dean abandoned his wooden spoon to pour boiling water into the rice. "Cooking is such bullshit."

"Everyone makes a mess when they're starting out. You'll clean it up."

Dean groaned at the idea of yet *another* job once this was over. "We could have ordered Indian *and* picked it up by now. Why do people do this? Why even bother?"

"Well, it depends, Deano. Do you think if Ashley stops using your face like a drive-by vibrator and decides to be your girlfriend she wants to live on an endless supply of takeaway korma? Or do you think vegetables might have to enter the equation at some point?"

"Korma has potatoes in it," Dean muttered, but cognisant of Max's point, he re-dedicated himself to the enchiladas. If he wanted to be husband material, he needed to be able to cook at least five things that weren't bacon.

"I don't get it." Max picked up a spare capsicum and tossed it into the air. "I've been trying to get you to cook for two decades, and you wouldn't have a bar of it. You go down on Ash a couple times and suddenly you're Donna Hay."

"Who's that?" Dean asked, eating a bit of mince off the wooden spoon.

Max threw the capsicum at him. "Don't eat raw meat, and don't fucking lick stuff we all have to put in our mouths later."

Dean returned the wooden spoon to the pan. "So many rules."

"There are *not* that many rules." Max picked up three brown onions and began juggling them. "So what's your plan here, anyway? You text Ash a picture of the enchiladas, she realises you're good dad material and then it's all..." he whistled the opening bars of, *'Isn't She Lovely'* by Stevie Wonder.

"Ha-ha-ha. I don't have a plan, but this is gonna work out. I can feel it."

Max took his eyes off his airborne vegetables long enough to shoot Dean an incredulous look. "Seriously, not that I'm not excited to eat food I didn't make, but you might be putting the cart before the horse here."

"Maybe. But you can't feel what I'm feeling. You don't know what it's like when we're together and Ash is touching me and talking to me."

"You're right," Max conceded. "But you're texting and muff diving in her car, not picking out plates, or God-fuckin'-forbid, baby furniture. You can take the meat off now, man, it's cooked."

Dean moved the frying pan away from the burner. "This isn't like Julia's game launch. Ash knows who I am now. She knows I'm a bit dopey and a roofer and a ginger and she's still talking to me. She still wants to meet up all the time. That has to count for something."

"I guess. What about..." Max hesitated.

"What?"

His friend resumed juggling, and Dean knew it was so he didn't have to look at him. "Does she know about your video?"

"Oh *shit*." Dean pressed his palms into his eye sockets, accidentally poking himself in the face with the wooden spoon. "That fucking *video*. It's going to haunt me for the rest of my life."

"So, I'm guessing Ash *doesn't* know about it?"

"No. She knows about the naked snowboarding situation but not… you know…"

"That the whole thing is up on YouTube with a hundred thousand views?" Max suggested.

"Yeah, that. And it's closer to one fifty now."

"Fucking hell, that's bad."

"You're telling me?"

When the clip of him snowboarding naked down the mountain in Queenstown had been first uploaded to Facebook, Dean figured it was better to laugh it off than try to browbeat his mate into taking it down. But that was before the video, entitled *'Ginger Giants' Snowboard Fail,'* had been posted to Imgur where it got upvoted about a bazillion times. Strangers rarely recognised him from the video, but everyone who knew him knew it was there and they tended to bring it up. A lot. His chances of ever working in public service were pretty much nil and his chances of convincing a beautiful blonde nurse he was mature enough to be a dad didn't look much better.

"Do you think I should tell Ash?" he asked Max.

"Yes. This kind of thing doesn't age well, mate. The longer you keep it a secret, the more she'll feel you led her up the garden path."

"But what if she doesn't believe me when I tell her I didn't know anyone was filming?"

Max made a face. "You've gotta admit it's not a classy story either way, going snowboarding with your dick out because you're too drunk to know better. Trust me man, just tell her. You don't want her to find out on her own. Especially if she sees the bit where the chick comes in at the end."

Dean groaned. "There is no way she'll ever want to have my babies. I'm doomed."

"No, you're not. Everyone's got naked shit floating around on the internet these days."

"Not you."

"That's just luck. Remember the time I streaked across O'Grady oval? If people had iPhones fifteen years ago, my dick would be all over the internet too."

"That was exactly Ash's point about me being immature," Dean said. "You went streaking when you were twenty. I was thirty-four."

Max opened his mouth then closed it again. "I don't know what to say to that, mate, except you can't change the past."

Dean's mood sank even lower. "I'm never gonna get Ash to be my girlfriend. All I'm bringing to the table is red hair and public nudity. Who wants to have kids with the naked snowboarding guy?"

"Well, I mean..." Max broke off shaking his head.

"What?"

His friend looked slightly uncomfortable. "Well you know Ash is no angel, right? Not sure what she's told you, but she was pretty wild when she was younger. Hell, she was pretty wild until not that long ago."

Dean glared at him. "Are you saying she's damaged goods?"

Max's mouth fell open. "No! Fuck no! But she's dated a fair few guys and she got into a bit of shit with the cops, nothing too serious, but you know..."

"It's on her record?"

"Yeah. Plus, there's a lot of pictures of her online. They're modelling pictures but still, they're pretty, you know, *sexual*. And I'm fully aware I'm a jealous prick, but I'd struggle if guys were jerking off to pictures of Julia."

Dean decided not to tell Max anyone could go on Instagram and jerk off to pictures of Julia and judging from some of the comments, did. "These 'sexual pictures', where are they online?"

"If you google 'Ashley Bennett' and 'model' they should come up. Jules reckons she's on a few Reddit threads. She has kind of a cult following from an ad she did where she sucked on a lollipop and a bunch of internet nerds came in their pants."

"Sure." Dean googled Max's suggestion and his phone was suddenly full of Ashleys, all tanned skin and tousled blonde hair, pouting in low-rise jeans, straddling chairs and kneeling on the beach in tiny bikinis. Some pictures were sexier than others; the lollipop one Max mentioned was a GIF. Dean clicked on it and watched Ash suck a long stripy piece of candy. What struck him was that she wasn't making a sexy face while she did it. She looked bored, almost mean, as though whoever was filming her was wasting her time. It was the exact expression she'd worn when she ordered him to go down on her on the hood of her car. Dean's dick twitched against his thigh. *I can't believe I've eaten that girl out.*

"What do you think?"

Dean somehow managed to tear his eyes away from the GIF. "I think I'm gonna look at this stuff later. When I'm alone."

Max laughed. "So it doesn't bother you?"

"No, it's cool. I can't believe I have a shot at a girl this beautiful."

Max didn't reply, but his eyes said things Dean didn't want to acknowledge. Things about how he might not have a shot after all.

"Modelling's not on par with my video," Dean said loudly. "She's not even topless, and even if she was, she's not falling off a snowboard, showing the whole world what ginger pubes look like."

"I guess." Max leaned against the kitchen counter. "Maybe I'm just a piece-of-shit pig."

"Nah, if Jules were a model you'd be okay with it. You'd just walk around with your hand in the back pocket of her jeans, glaring at everyone even more than you do now."

"True." Max grinned at him. "You're better at this stuff than I give you credit for."

"Thanks, Mum. Am I also the handsomest boy in school?"

"I'm giving you a compliment, dickhead."

"And I said thanks. Wait, what was the compliment?"

Max rolled his eyes. "I was trying to say even though you're spacey as fuck, and you're letting the rice burn again, you kind of get relationships."

"Thanks, I mean, shit!" Dean rushed over to the rice which was indeed glugging at the bottom of the pot, the water having all been absorbed. "Is it ready? Should I take it off?"

"Taste it, you spud. If it's soft, then it's done."

It was done. Dean scraped what he could into a sieve and then put the pot and the rest of the congealed rice in the sink to soak. "What now?"

"Crank the oven up to one-eighty. I'll give you a hand with the actual enchiladas or we'll be here until midnight."

They stood shoulder to shoulder, filling the wraps with mince and cheese, placing them in a Pyrex baking tray, covering them with sauce and sliding them into the oven. As they baked, Max got another beer and Dean commenced the long, painful task of cleaning up. As he attempted to unstick the overcooked rice from the bottom of the pot, he noticed Max staring at him with something even worse than serious face: sympathy face. "What?"

"When are you seeing Ash next?"

Dean scrubbed the rice pot as hard as he could, ignoring the question.

"Dean?"

"I'm not sure. She messages me when she wants to meet up."

Max's brows pulled in. "Seriously?"

"Yeah."

"Well you know, if you're really into her, I could always talk to Jules, ask her to invite Ash over for dinner?"

Dean dropped the pot into the sink, making soapy water splash all over his front. "No way in hell! The second last thing I need is for Jules to think I'm using her to bang her sister."

"Okay, okay, I won't ask her." Max frowned. "What's the last thing you need?"

"For Ash to think I'm using Jules. We haven't talked about it a whole lot, but I'm pretty sure she'd rip my throat out if I, like, gave Jules a nasty cold, let alone used her."

"She would. It's amazing I'm alive and un-castrated." Max patted his crotch absently, as though making sure his tackle was still safe. "You're right, we should keep your secret on lock for now. You being a scratching post aside, Jules always hates Ash's boyfriends."

"Hey, she likes me!"

"She likes you as *my mate*. Trust me, she's as protective of Ash as

Ash is of her. Who knows how she'll feel when she finds out you two have been humping each other all over the eastern suburbs?"

Dean's guts knotted. "Jesus. I never even thought about that. If Jules doesn't want us together, I'm fucked."

"Exactly. You need to tread fucking lightly."

"Trust me I'm treading so lightly I couldn't bend a blade of grass. By the way, where is Jules tonight?"

"Working on promo stuff for her game." Max suddenly resembled a kid whose football had been booted over a fence. "I've barely seen her lately. Her commute's shocking and we're too busy to go out and look for a new place."

Though he knew it was selfish, Dean was quietly relieved. He'd lived with Max for the better part of four years and he loved it. He loved coming home to a friendly face (unless he'd broken something or forgotten to pay a bill or left his footy boots in the hallway). He loved sharing mid-week beers and playing PS4 with his best friend. When Jules came along things got even better, the three of them had dinner most nights and laughed and chatted about everyone's day. It was like having a family. A family that wasn't shit. If Max and Jules moved out, he'd either have to find a share house or move in somewhere on his own and the thought of that was just... Not cool. He decided to change the subject. "How's the ring hunt coming along?"

"Shithouse."

Over the past couple of weeks, Max had sent him around three million pictures of engagement rings, asking his inept opinion on black opals and square cut rubies. Max was a pedantic nutcase about fashion, but Dean suspected his best mate's struggle to find a flawless one-of-a-kind ring was down to the fact that he hoped a perfect ring might convince Julia to overlook any reasons she had for saying no to his proposal. Like his previous two proposals.

"Keep looking," Dean advised. "The right one will show up."

"Hopefully. I don't know when I'm supposed to ask her to marry me, anyway. She's been so busy we only see each other at night, and then all we do is fuck and then fall asleep."

"Cry me a river. I've been going down on the sexiest girl in the world and wanking in my car afterward."

Max made a disgusted face. "In public?"

"Don't be such a cop."

"Mate, please tell me you haven't actually been pulling your dick in public?"

Dean picked up the kitchen sponge. "I make sure there are no people around."

"Jesus! Dean, we were *just* talking about you having a naked video on the internet and…" Max let out a furious breath. "I'm not discussing this with you, my point is if Jules and I are barely spending time together, how the fuck can I be like 'let's get married?' She'll think I'm crazy."

Dean swept his sponge in a wide arc across the kitchen counter. "You're forgetting Julia already thinks you're crazy. You have like, four different kinds of hair wax."

"You need different ones depending on the weather!"

"Sure you do."

Max glared at him. "Stop dumping cheese on the floor! Catch the bench crap in your hand and put it in the bin!"

"Why?"

"Because what you're doing is beyond putrid."

"At least the bench's clean."

"Yeah, but the floor's dirty and then we'll step on it and track it all through the house and get fucking bubonic plague and die, you nong!"

With an over-exaggerated sigh, Dean did what Max asked. "Cleaning is bullshit too."

"I don't care. Fucking do it."

"Taskmaster. And you know what? Just bite the bullet and propose. If Jules says yes, great. If she says no, she says no. Either way you have your answer."

"Either way I have my…?" Max shook his head. "I take back what I said before, you are an absolute baked potato when it comes to relationships and I am never listening to your advice ever again."

"I know stuff!"

Max snorted. "Yeah, how to be Ash Bennett's human dildo."

"You wait, we're gonna be together."

"You're gonna be a dildo."

The timer on the oven beeped. Dean switched it off and grabbed a tea-towel so he could safely extract the baking tray. Despite looking kind of sloppy and amateurish, the enchiladas smelled pretty good. He hefted them onto the counter. "See? Could a man who was nothing but a dildo make this?"

"Yes."

Dean glowered at his friend. "You know, I bet you'd be Julia's dildo if that was the only thing she wanted from you."

"Probably." Max picked up his beer. "Except it isn't."

"How do you know?"

"Hmm let's see…" He began checking reasons off on his fingers. "Julia sleeps in my bed every night, she tells me she loves me, all her friends know who I am, she made a video game character about me, her screen-saver is a picture of me, we put one of those love lock things on a bridge in Paris… Is that enough reasons, or do you want me to keep going?"

Dean gave him the finger. "Shut up."

Max pretended to catch his one-fingered salute and pressed it to his heart. "Awww, spoken like a man who's nothing but Ash Bennett's dildo."

Dean lifted his tea-towel, intending to throw it at Max, but he never got the chance.

"The fuck did you just say, Connor?"

Max jolted as though someone had shoved a cattle prod up his arse; Dean dropped the tea-towel. *No way, she couldn't be—*

He turned to see yes, Julia Bennett *was* standing in the doorway, having clearly just heard everything they'd said. He gestured wildly toward the Pyrex dish. "Oh hey, Jules! Can I, uh, interest you in an enchilada?"

Julia's hazel eyes crackled with fury. "No you fucking can't, Redbeard."

Though they shared physical similarities, Dean never thought of Ash when he saw Julia. Ash was blonde, of average height and smoking hot, whereas Julia was like a big, pretty giraffe. Her dark hair was always covering a third of her face, and she expressed most of her non-Max emotions through snark. Right now, however, with her hair pulled back and her expression livid, her resemblance to her older sister was uncanny. "Jules, I—"

"Shut up." She snapped her fingers at Max. "You. Buttfuck. What did you just say about Ash?"

Max shot him a look of sheer panic. "Um, nothing?"

"Don't you play dumb with me! What did you mean when you said Dean is Ash's dildo? Why are you even talking about Ash's... No. No *way*. It can't be."

Dean's guts churned. This was bad. This was very bad. Before he could consider running away, Julia had pointed straight at him. "Did you fuck my sister?"

He gave her a weak smile. "Not with my dick?"

"I knew it! I knew she was screwing someone!" She turned to Max. "And you knew it, too!"

"Um, kind of? I mean I found out when it first happened—"

"Which was?"

"At your game launch."

Julia let out a small but ear-splitting scream. "What the fuck!?"

Max held up his palms, as though to show his girlfriend he wasn't carrying a gun. "Jules, I swear I didn't know they started seeing each other again until tonight—"

"*Traitor!*" Julia stepped backward, fumbling for something in her bag. Dean sincerely hoped it wasn't the military-grade OC spray Max made her carry. That shit burned. "Jules, I swear me and your sister just kind of *happened*."

Julia pulled out her phone. "Rain just kind of happens! You banging my sister is not like the fucking weather."

For a second Dean was relieved that she wasn't going to mace him, then he realised what she was going to do instead. He stepped forward, his own palms raised. "Jules, I get it, I fucked up but please don't call Ash. *Please?*"

"No."

"What can I do to change your mind?"

"Go back in time and unfiddle with my sister."

Dean looked to Max. "A little help, please?"

"Gorgeous, could you maybe…?"

Julia silenced her boyfriend with a look and unlocked her phone.

Dean shook his fists in the air. "Please, Jules; I can explain everything, just gimme twenty minutes?"

"Don't tell me what to do, sister-fucker."

"I haven't fucked—"

Julia made a hissing noise.

"—I haven't *had sex with* your sister. We've just done, y'know, mouth stuff…"

Max groaned.

"Mouth stuff aside…" Dean began.

Julia pointed her phone at him. "Shut up. I invited you to my game launch so you could eat free prawns, not use my sister for quote-unquote 'mouth stuff.'"

Dean figured now was neither the time nor place to say Ash was the one using him for mouth stuff. "I like her, I promis—"

"Can it, ginger." Jules began scrolling through her phone contacts. "Hiding stuff from me? Lying to me? You and Connor can both eat an entire dick."

She located Ash's number and hit dial. Dean had a vision of his not-relationship going up in flames and he sprinted around the kitchen counter and snatched Julia's phone away.

"Oi!" Julia chased him around the kitchen. "Give that back!"

"No." Dean hung up the phone then held it high over his head. "Not until you hear me out. It's a matter of life and death."

"Life and death?"

"Well, it's a matter of life anyway." He dropped to his knees, cradling the phone against his chest so she couldn't snatch it back. "Please, Jules, for the love of *Legends of Zelda* just hear me out?"

At first, it looked like Julia was going to tell him to go fuck himself, then she sighed. "Five minutes, Dean, that's all you get, and give me back my fucking phone."

Dean handed it over.

"Thank you. And Connor?"

"Yeah?" Max said hopefully.

"You are in the doghouse. There will be no coming near my labia for a month. It's total labial recall."

Max let out a howl of misery.

8

Julia was hiding something. Ash knew the signs. Too-wide eyes, constant fidgeting. References to the weather and other suspicious topics of conversation. In the past it meant her sister was hiding an empty Nutella jar or a hickey from a boy she knew Ash wouldn't like (the bar for Julia's 'special friends' was set far higher than Ash ever set her own) but Julia was twenty-six now, and Ash was sure she was hiding a much bigger secret than overindulging in chocolate spread or nerds from shitty alt-rock bands.

When she knocked over her water glass in a fit of awkward hand gestures, Ash she'd seen enough. "Okay, why are you acting like you're hiding something?"

Julia blinked six times in quick succession. "I'm not hiding anything."

"You are, though. You clearly invited me around to Max's house for dinner as a part of a scheme."

"It's not a scheme! I was lonely. Max is at his conference all weekend and Dean—"

Ash's heart lurched into her throat.

"—is on his end of season retreat until tomorrow. Plus, there's a rat around and you know how I feel about rats."

"I do." Ash took a swallow of cheap wine. "I also know they're almost always mice."

"Not always. Have you done something with your hair?"

"No. What aren't you telling me?"

"Nothing!" Julia gave an unconvincing laugh. "What do you think of the place? I know it's kind of wrong that Max's ex-wife designed it and then she cheated on Max and now I kind of live here, but hey—decent bathrooms!"

"I guess."

Julia looked hurt. "You do think it's wrong, don't you?"

Ash stayed silent. The house wasn't wrong because Max's marriage had died in it, it was wrong because Dean lived here, ate breakfast at the counter, washed in the big, not plastic-curtained shower, slept in one of the bedrooms. She hadn't worked up the courage to peek at said bedroom yet, she was too scared it would be decked out with nudie posters and beer can hats. Yet in spite of these very real possibilities, she couldn't stop thinking about the man.

Dean was the only word rattling around her brain these days, like a pop hook so catchy you sang it even as you watched someone's perineum tear. Ash had tried to do what she always did when a song got stuck in her head, listen to it over and over until she couldn't stand to hear a single bar. Only it wasn't working. The more she kissed Dean, came on him, messaged him, called him, and stroked his red-gold beard, the more she *wanted* to do it. Meanwhile, everything else in her life was falling apart. The bathroom in her grandma's house was leaking, everyone at work was suspicious of her dizzy *'I met someone and am now getting my clitoris sucked like it's hard candy'* smile, Dean was still refusing to put out, Nate was trying to pressure her into making a decision about his sperm and her favourite lipstick was missing (MAC, Please Me).

Also, Dean's on a footy trip, no doubt getting shitfaced on piss-water beer and having sex with topless waitresses, her brain chipped in. *Or maybe he's just snowboarding naked again.*

Stupid brain.

"Ash? Are you okay?" Julia asked.

Ash took another swallow of wine and attempted to smile. "I'm fine. This *is* a nice house. Way less dog hair than ours."

"You're right. I do miss our dogs, though."

"They miss you. Hey, did you invite me around to tell me you're officially moving out of our place and into the narc hut?"

"No. I don't want to move out yet."

Ash breathed a quiet sigh of relief. It was selfish but she couldn't get her head around the idea of living in her grandma's house without Julia. Even though her sister spent most of her time at Max's, Ash could take comfort in the knowledge that all of her wizard statues and retro Sega games were still where they should be. "Are you two still thinking about getting a flat closer to your studio?"

Julia toyed with a leftover piece of spaghetti. "I don't know. I was thinking about it, but Max has been kinda off lately. Distracted or something. In his own head."

Ash stared at Julia, liquid suspicion flooding her veins. She knew firsthand that when a man grew distant and distracted it was because another woman had wandered onto the scene. She and Captain Cowboy-Dick had a deal: he agreed he was going to treat Julia better than any man on earth, or she was going to slice open his nut sack and throw its contents into the sea. And if that oversized copper had gone back on their arrangement... Ash clenched her teeth. "Have you found anything suspicious? Lipstick stains? New perfume smell? Is he working late? Going to the gym more than usual?"

"No! I mean, I don't think so!" Julia looked so terrified, Ash instantly regretted putting the thought into her head. "Sorry, forget I said that. Max wouldn't cheat. He loves you."

Julia didn't look reassured.

"And he's too much of a total fucking square," Ash reminded her. "Remember when that chick at Bunnings Warehouse undercharged him for gardening stakes and he drove all the way back to the store just to give her nine bucks? That is *not* someone who could live with cheating."

Julia's face relaxed. "You make a valid point. Still, I dunno, he's just being odd. Maybe he's having a hard time at work or something."

"Yeah, maybe," Ash said, unconcerned with the inner workings of Max Connor's mind. "So that's the secret you're hiding? Max being off?"

Julia frowned. "I don't have a secret."

"Fine then, I guess we'll just sit here and enjoy this delicious pasta in silence."

"I guess we will."

Five minutes passed before Julia put her fork down. "There may have been another reason why I invited you to Chez Connor. Aside from my entirely legitimate rat-fears."

Ash slapped both hands to her cheeks, à la Macaulay Culkin. "No way!"

"There's no need to be mean about it."

"Sorry, but you're useless at keeping secrets. Always have been."

Her sister scowled. "I can keep secrets!"

"You mean like the time you used my cocoa butter to give Jamie Langham a handy and confessed a full *twenty minutes* later?"

Julia flushed. "You don't know. I could be holding onto a massive, life-changing secret and one day, when the timing is right, I'll drop it on your head like ka-blowww." She mimed a mushroom cloud explosion.

Ash forced herself to laugh, her hands tingling with nerves. "You *don't* have a massive secret, do you?"

Julia tilted her head to the side. "What if I do? What if I know something that will blow your mind?"

Oh shit. "What is it?" she asked, though she was suddenly sure she knew the answer.

Ever since Ash was sixteen she'd suspected she and Jules didn't have the same dad. That might not have surprised anyone who'd ever met their loose cannon, multiple-boyfriend-having mother, but she and Jules looked so alike Ash had never even considered the possibility. At least not until their paternal grandmother, the one whose shitty pink house they'd inherited, pointed out not a single member of her family had hazel eyes like Julia.

"She must get them from mum's side," Ash had said, not understanding why her grandma was whispering.

"But your *mother*," Lana Bennett gave a customary sniff of disapproval, "has blue eyes as well. So does her sister, Leda, and you know I'm sure I've seen a picture of her parents and they had blue eyes, too."

"So?" Ash asked, nonplussed.

"So your sister might not be a Bennett, Ashley. In fact I'm sure—"

At that moment Julia had poked her head in the door and asked if they were still going to the Milk Bar for ice cream. Grandma had jumped to her feet, said 'yes, of course' and then rushed out of the room. She never raised the subject again, but the seed of doubt had well and truly been planted in Ash's mind.

It was true she and Jules both looked like their mum, but Julia had a uniqueness that seemed less a dice-roll difference between siblings and more like genetic gifts bestowed from someone other than sloppy, lazy-ass Martin Bennett. There was her height, her tech savviness, her freckles, her lack of a shellfish allergy, her inability to curl her tongue into a hot dog bun, the way her earlobes were connected to her head while Ash's weren't—a thousand little quirks which added up to a big question mark.

At sixteen, Ash had decided not to investigate or question Julia's shadowy paternity. Their so-called dad wasn't around to stake a claim, neither was their bullshit mum. Who was there, was Jules—being tall and awkward, smashing every boy she met at video games and loving Ash unconditionally, day in and day out. That, Ash decided, was what mattered, not if a guy other than Martin Bennett had donated his DNA toward the best, funniest, most essentially perfect human in the world. She and Jules were family and that's all there was to it.

It was one of the reasons she had considered having a sperm donor baby. It was the people you grew up with that mattered, not the dude who had an orgasm inside you. Or a cup in a doctor's office.

Still, she had prayed this day wouldn't come, that Jules would never discover who her father was or wasn't. Some petty part of her was convinced her sister wouldn't love her the same way if she knew they were only half-siblings.

Julia cleared her throat. "My secret is I know about Dean."

"You *what*?"

"I know you're face-humping Dean? You know, the guy who lives here?"

Ash's relief at Jules not bringing up her paternity was short lived. "I, uh... We haven't..."

Julia shook her head. "Don't. Don't start with that shit. I know and I've made my fucking peace with it. I'm just kind of hurt you didn't tell me."

Ash sighed. "I'm sorry Julesie, it's just after everything with Zach I didn't want you to think I'd gone backward. I've been so good about men for ages and then I just... Slipped up."

Julia stretched a hand over the table and placed her long, cool fingers on top of Ash's. "I'm not going to judge you, I know you and Dean are grownups, but I'm confused about the baby situation, and also I didn't think you were into gingers."

"I'm not! Dean is just a beautiful specimen of ginger."

Jules scrunched up her nose. "You reckon? I think he looks like a big reddish bear."

"Seriously?"

"Oh God, yeah. And he's kind of goofy looking, like someone stapled a kid's face onto a man's body."

"He's boyish!" Ash protested. "It's cute. You seriously don't think he's good looking?"

"I mean, maybe I can see it objectively, but I don't feel the..." Julia gestured to the area between her hips. "You know?"

Ash laughed. "I do know. I guess it's for the best, but I was into Dean the second I saw him. I felt it right in the..." she gestured to her own pelvic area.

"Is this when you met him at the game launch?"

She nodded guiltily. "He was shoving forty prawns into his

mouth, and I still wanted to fuck him. I figured it would be a one-time thing. You know, dip my toe into the sex ocean before returning to dry land forever? But it didn't turn out like that."

Julia groaned theatrically. "Of course it didn't. When you tell yourself you can't have something, you only want it more."

"I know. And once I opened the sex dam it was... *Intense*."

Julia sighed. "As your friend, I will allow you to describe the sex. As your sister, let's try and stay away from descriptions of Dean's penis. I already see way too much when he wears white underwear."

So Ash told Julia about their encounters, about Dean's enthusiasm, his penchant for her to be downright rude to him, the way he never failed to make her come.

But she left out the way he held her afterward, laughing and batting her hands away from his cock. She left out that he called her every night. She said nothing about the warm kisses or the jokes or the way he called her 'missy' and 'babe' and 'rebel.' She didn't tell Julia about the photos he sent her of himself naked in bed, a sheet draped over his waist and the captions some variation on *'go on a date with me and I'll show you the rest.'*

No, she just told Julia about the fucking.

"So you don't have sex-sex," Julia said with a frown. "You're just doing one-sided oral. Max was right."

Ash almost spat out a mouthful of Sauvignon Blanc. "The narc knows about Dean and me?"

"Yeah man, that's how I know. I walked in on them talking about you. Something about Dean being your dildo?"

"What? Dean isn't my dildo, Eric is."

Julia groaned in disgust. "You named it after *The Little Mermaid* guy, didn't you? You know what, don't tell me, my point is Max knows about you letting Dean go down on you in cars."

"Jesus." Ash rubbed her forehead. "Well, I guess Dean has a right to say what we've been doing to his mates."

"Dean didn't tell him," Julia scoffed. "As if he'd ever betray *you*. Max worked it out. Dean's been doing all this domestic stuff—cooking food, trying to wash his own clothes, he fucking *ruined* a pair of my good undies, by the way—and Max figured he was trying to impress you."

Ash could hear her pulse in her ears, *bah bum, bah bum, bah bum*. "Why would he be trying to impress me?"

"Because he thinks the two of you have some kind of amazing connection! He thinks if he just keeps eating you out, you'll come around eventually and marry him."

"No. He *can't* think that."

Julia's expression was foreboding. "Well, he does, and Ash? He knows you want a kid."

Ash's throat closed over. "No. He can't. How could he know that?"

"Max told him after my game launch. He thought it would help him to understand it wasn't meant to be. Instead Dean got all excited and now he thinks he could, you know... Instead of a donor?"

Goosebumps popped up across Ash's arms and legs. Dean was open to the idea of kids? Right now? Dean wanted to be a father? Ash tried to picture it and with laughable ease saw Dean tossing a little girl into the air and catching her again. She shivered all over. "That... Wow. That kind of fucking changes things."

"It can't!" The panic in Jules' voice was worse than when Ash had suggested Max might be cheating on her.

"Why not?" Ash wanted to laugh out loud. "Jules, he's handsome, so sweet, he makes me laugh and I know he's a bit of a dead-shit, but if he wants to be a dad—"

"You need to know something," Jules interrupted. "Something that doesn't make me look good, but you need to know it before you go any further down this line of reasoning."

"What?"

Her sister balled herself up in her dining chair, hugging her knees. All she needed was a Garbage t-shirt and a shitload of eyeliner, and she'd look like her sixteen-year-old self again. "I thought about introducing you and Dean a long time ago. When Max and I first got together. I thought you'd like each other."

Ash stared at her sister. She could have met Dean eighteen

months ago? Before Zach, before she started planning to have a baby on her own? "Why didn't you introduce us?"

Julia mumbled something unintelligible.

"What?"

"I said 'I realized Dean's a potato.'"

"What do you mean he's a *potato*?"

Julia closed her eyes. "He's the nicest guy on earth, but he's useless. You have no idea of the extent to which he's useless. He thought jaywalking was crossing the road diagonally. He thought he was making porridge by putting cold water in rolled oats and eating it raw."

"Jesus."

"I could go on for hours; Dean is like if *Clifford the Big Red Dog* was a person and also bad with directions and time and talking and being alive."

Ash couldn't help but laugh. "I know Jules, I've been hanging out with him for ages and I get that he's kind of—"

"A space cadet?"

"— a bit unfocused," Ash finished. "But I like him. I know it's fast and I know he's a bit of a ditz, but I haven't felt like this about anyone for ages."

Now she'd said it out loud, she knew it was true. She'd never expected to fall for a guy like Dean, but she was falling. The tingling in her stomach, the endless energy, the need to see him all day every day—she clearly had a crush. The kind that had every chance of turning into the most famous of L-words. And he wanted kids? Ash could hear her pulse in her ears again, this time echoing her excitement. "This is amazing."

There was a low clunk as Julia banged her forehead on Max's dining table. "No this is a nightmare. I should have talked to you before now. I should have warned you."

Ash felt her mood grey around the edges. "Warned me about what?"

"Dean! You're in the la-la stage of the relationship and you think you can handle him, but there's so much that's gonna be a problem, especially if you want to have a kid."

"You keep saying that, what do you mean?"

Jules looked up, her eyes dark and round as olives. "Dean is appalling with... You know..."

There was only one thing Julia had that much difficulty talking about. Their shitty childhood had left her near-incapable of discussing the thing that had been the source of all of their mum's problems, the thing that threatened every sense of safety and comfort they had. "Money?" Ash offered.

"Yeah. He's fucking terrible with... That stuff."

Ash was nowhere near as conflicted about cash as Jules, but her heart still sank like a stone. "How bad is he with money?"

"So freaking bad. He has no savings and he's constantly broke and has to eat toast until he gets paid again. He's not a gambler or a drinker or anything," she added quickly. "He's just the kind of guy who never has any fucking... You know..."

"Money. But how does that happen?"

"He's always buying drinks for everyone, or going to places on the spur of the moment and drying up his whole paycheck. He buys games and consoles and cars, too. Fixes them up for fun. If Max didn't make him sell them, I'm pretty sure they'd just be lying around here."

Ash pictured the ugly government houses of her childhood, awash with tire-less vehicles propped up on concrete blocks. "Christ."

"Yeah. And here's the thing, he should have savings. Hell, he should have a fucking *house*, he's always worked, and during footy season he makes five hundred bucks a game."

Ash gasped. "Five hundred bucks a game? The only way I'd make that much cash in two and a half hours is giving out BJs!"

"I know, right? But again, the man is broke. Flat broke."

"But *how?* Where the hell does cash like that go?"

"No idea. Even Max doesn't know. I think he's just one of those people who is a bad mix of generous and irresponsible."

As horrible as this conversation was, Ash wasn't the least bit surprised. She could just picture Dean pulling out his wallet with the same eager benevolence with which he went down on her. And she knew from dealing with a dozen cash-strapped exes that trying to cure a man of 'The Spendsies' was a bleak, head-ruining exercise in futility. She buried her face in her hands.

"That's not even the worst part," Julia warned.

"There's *more*?"

"Yep. And trust me, I don't want to shit all over your dreams here, but with the baby situation being what it is…"

"I understand. Hit me."

Her sister took a deep breath. "Dean's not qualified to be a roofer."

"What? But I've visited him at worksites. He has a fluoro top!"

"That doesn't mean he's qualified. He hasn't done an apprenticeship. He's not technically meant to be working there."

Ash's head was spinning. "But he told me he did roofing right after uni."

"Yeah, along with about a million other things." Julia rolled her eyes. "He doesn't have any qualifications. A friend of his owns the company, and he lets him work full time as a casual because—"

"It pays better," Ash groaned. She'd had more than a few boyfriends run that racket. "So, he's not on a contract?"

"No. He's got no sick leave, no long term service leave, no superannuation, and no certifications. If he hurt himself, or the company went bust, he'd be screwed."

"Jesus wept."

Julia sucked her lower lip into her mouth. "I'm sorry Ash, I didn't want to be an asshole but I don't think Dean's ready for a kid. At least not the way you are."

Ash stared at her hands. "I… Yeah."

Dean having a steady job had been a shining beacon of hope. A promise that while goofy and insanely forgetful (he constantly called Southern Star Hospital the Northern Cross Hospital) he might have his shit together. And he didn't, not by a long shot.

Julia gave her a sad smile. "I'm sorry Ash, but Max knows him better than anyone and he doesn't think Dean's ready to be a dad, either."

Ash stayed quiet, thinking hard. She'd always known Dean was a hot loveable doofus. If she was being honest she *liked* that about him. It would be terrible to resent him for being who he was, but who he was was incompatible with the life she wanted for herself. She didn't want the disappointment and heartache of trying to change another man, banging her head on a brick wall and blaming it for her migraine. If she was going to look after a semi-helpless individual, it was going to be a baby.

"You're right. I need to end it."

Her sister breathed an audible sigh of relief. "Good, well, that kind of brings me to the second reason why I invited you over. Dean is coming home from his trip tomorrow, and I think you should sort this whole situation out. You know, end things."

Ash's gut reaction was *no*. She needed more time. Another week. One more hook up. She wanted to keep Dean tucked away in her purse a little longer, like a burner phone or a stolen ring. Her guilty pleasure, her dirty little secret.

Then reality tapped her on the shoulder, reminding her of all the deferred calls from the donor clinic, all the dodged dates with Resident DILF, all the lies she'd told, chores she'd neglected, and fast food dinners she'd eaten in her car, all so she could spin out a doomed romance with a beautiful, broke, dangerously under qualified ginger.

Ash's eyes prickled, the wine and emotional overload lending itself to tears. "You're right. I have to end it. I haven't been honest with Dean. I've been such a selfish bitch."

"Hey, don't talk like that." Jules got to her feet and came around the table, wrapping her arms around Ash's middle. "You were just having some fun. No one died. Dean will be okay. He got to have sort-of sex with FHM's 2012 runner-up model of the year. Besides, he'll move on. Ladies can't get enough of that ginger mug. Who knows, maybe one of them will be rich enough to keep him as a boytoy and let him have all the busted cars and PS4 games he wants."

The thought of Dean with another woman stabbed at Ash's guts, but she ignored it. "Sorry for not telling you about all this sooner."

Jules kissed her head. "I understand. I hid Max from you for ages. Well, a few days, but it felt like ages. Either way, no harm done. Maybe checking out some other donor clinics will help you focus on the baby?"

"No, I just—fuck!"

"What? Is everything okay?"

"Yeah, I just remembered I haven't told you about Nate! You remember Nate, the hot bone doctor I work with?"

"Resident DILF?"

Ash had to smile. She and Jules had always had a good working knowledge of the hot guys who operated in each other's work/life vicinity. "Yeah, he approached me about being a donor."

"*What?*" Julia moved around the table and looked Ash in the face. "That is next-level intense. How? Why? Actually, hang on. I need visuals."

She snatched up her nearby tablet. "What's his full name?"

"Nathaniel Huxley II."

"*Ooh là là,*" Jules said, tapping away.

"I know, he's from Prahran." Ash pronounced it the way the locals did, '*Pahraaahaaan.*'

"Gak." Julia's fingers drummed her device at roughly the speed of light. "Does he know we come from feral bogan wino stock?"

"He knows I'm from the country but no, I couldn't see an opening to tell him our life history."

"Fair enough. So how did Resident DILF pop the question about being your baby daddy?"

"It was just *bizarre*. He invited me into his office for coffee because he heard a rumour I was thinking about having a kid with a donor."

"And he was all '*free sperm, get it while it's hot?*'"

"No, he said he wants to be a dad before he's too old and he no longer believes in the power of love to make it happen."

Julia snorted. "Nice. He say anything else?"

"Just that he wants me to consider the idea and he'd be willing to pay child support."

"Duh, goes without saying. How much child support?"

"A decent amount." Ash didn't want to bring up the four hundred thousand dollars, plus a weekly two grand. She didn't want Julia's head to explode.

"Well, that's a massive advantage over..." The look of pure guilt on her sister's face told Ash she was planning to say Dean. "It would be a massive advantage," she agreed.

"Yeah, right." Julia cleared her throat. "How old is Resident DILF again?"

"Forty-four."

Julia made a face.

"I know, but he's good looking and in shape. Besides, we wouldn't be a couple—"

Jules let out a tiny gasp. "Why not? That is one seriously hot dude."

She held up her tablet and displayed a photo of Nate, shirtless at what looked like a rich person barbecue on a yacht. "He is buff as."

"That's why we call him Resident DILF."

Julia whistled. "You're dead on, he *is* a doctor I'd like to fuck. If you had a kid with this guy, it would, no joke, be a supermodel. A supermodel who cures cancer."

Ash laughed. "Wait, how'd you get onto his Facebook profile? All the girls at work say its super private and they would know."

Julia put her tablet back on the table. "Never mind."

"You hacked him, didn't you?"

"You know I don't like that word, Ashley."

"That's not the point though, is it? I can't believe you hacked Resident DILF."

"I can't believe he offered to fill you with his sperm! Are you really considering taking him up on the offer?"

Ash thought about Nate's beautifully symmetrical face. "I don't know. He's nice-ish, and I like the idea of going with someone I know from real life, but there's something about him that just seems a bit strange..."

Julia's eyes narrowed. "Could it be that he's not a gigantic redhead called Dean?"

Ash squirmed in her chair. "I guess. I've been a bit blindsided by that whole situation."

"But now you've conclusively decided Dean's not ready to become a dad, are you going to go with Resident DILF?"

"I don't know. I've been blowing him off a bit lately. He keeps saying he wants to 'go out to dinner with me' to discuss it."

Julia caught what she was implying at once. "You reckon he wants to make this baby the old fashioned way?"

"I'm not sure. All I know is I was single for eight months and as soon as I decided to have a kid by myself, I met two men. What the fuck, universe?"

"When it rains it pours," Julia agreed. "Well, you don't have to accept this guy's jizz just because it's there, but seriously…"

She raised her tablet, showing Ash the picture of Nate once more. "Would you be opposed to having sex with this rich handsome doctor? Or creating a subsequent life with this rich handsome doctor?"

Ash thought about Dean, and her heart plummeted. "I don't know."

She and Julia stared at each other for a long, painful moment.

"Let's stop talking about it," Julia suggested. "We'll just do the dishes and watch a movie."

Ash breathed a sigh of relief. "Sounds good. *The Craft* then *Practical Magic* then *Sleepy Hollow*?"

"The Witch Trilogy? Fuck yes. And while we watch, we can look through Resident DILF's Facebook profile and see if any chicks have commented on anything."

Even though her head was full of Dean and dashed hopes, Ash laughed. "Sure, why not?"

For the next few hours, she and Julia turned Max's house into their own, eating popcorn on the couch, taking silly pictures, and chatting all through the movies, which they'd seen at least a dozen times before. They both put away a few big glasses of wine and by the time they decided to go to bed, Ash was drunk. She wasn't out of it, just tipsy enough that when she passed Dean's bedroom door, she paused. Before you could say 'invasion of privacy,' she'd slipped inside his room.

As with all things Dean, Ash had been expecting one thing and gotten something else. There were no framed footy jumpers on the walls, no nudie posters or tacky paraphernalia. His room was tidy and clean, filled mostly by a huge king sized bed with dark sheets. There was an old acoustic guitar in the corner and photos all over the walls. Best of all, it smelled like him, all warm and peppery and *Dean*.

Figuring she was already going to hell, Ash snooped in his wardrobe. That was where he appeared to store all his crap—tools, novelty mugs, bags and bags of receipts. She paused to shudder at what his tax returns must look like, then remembered she wasn't supposed to care. She closed the wardrobe door and looked over the photos. They told the story of a man with a lot of friends and a lot of former jobs—navy cadet, mechanic, truck driver, bartender. A few images stood out: a round-faced baby Red sitting on an enormous palomino horse, grinning from ear to ear. An under thirteens' football photo, Dean's arms folded over his chest as he glared into the camera, trying to look like the grown man he so clearly wasn't. A teenage Dean arm-in-arm with a teenage Max, both of them insanely good looking, Max's stern face slightly softer, Dean's hair long and curly around his ears. The affection they had for each other was obvious and almost painful. They looked nothing alike, but they could have been brothers. That thought called something to Ash's attention. She re-scanned the wall for pictures of Dean's family and couldn't find a single one. That was odd; she'd always assumed a big sweetheart like Dean would have a couple of doting parents and lots of siblings to distract from his bad behaviour...

A tap turned on down the hall and Ash started. She should get going. She shouldn't stay in here waiting to get busted by Julia. Except... Her gaze fell to Dean's mammoth sized bed, all warm and musky with Dean-ness. Maybe she could just sit on it? See what it felt like?

The instant her butt sank into the bed, Ash knew she had to lie down. Just for a little bit so she could imagine what it would be like to sleep there. She star-fished onto her back, moaning at the softness of the sheets, the warm sponginess of the mattress. Squirming up to the headboard, she discovered Dean had amazing pillows, all firm and snuggly, like the man himself.

She decided she'd get under the covers for a moment, just one, before she went back to the guest room. Of course it would be rude to get under the covers fully dressed, so she tugged off her leggings and pulled her T-shirt over her head. Clad in just her panties, Dean's sheets felt like a warm hug.

"Mmm," she moaned cuddling a pillow. "Just a little nap and then I'll leave. Just the tiniest, little sleep…"

9

Dean refused to get his hopes up. Just because Ashley's car was in the driveway, it didn't mean she was there. Knowing his luck she and Jules had probably decided to hit up a club, have a girl's' night while Max was out of town.

He eased the front door open and crept inside; the house was quiet, deserted. He passed the guest bedroom and noticed the door was ajar. He pulled it open and saw a pink overnight bag sitting on the still-made bed. He'd been right, Ash and Jules had gone out. Hating the way his guts churned with disappointment, Dean shoved off his boots and moved up the hallway, not bothering to make sure his sports bag didn't connect to the walls.

When Max called and told him Ash was visiting Coburg tonight, he'd decided to cut his post-season trip short and drive home after dinner. It wasn't entirely because of Ash, he was worn out from a week of manual labour and bored with watching twenty-three-year-olds throw up on themselves, but the idea of Ash in his house had been a pretty big contributing factor.

He'd spent the past two days checking his phone, wondering if he was pathetic enough to drive two hours to go down on her. In the end he'd done something even more pathetic: come home without any indication she wanted to see him. And all for nothing. He dumped his bag on the dining table and noticed the empty white wine bottles beside the bin. Ash and Jules had clearly pre-drank before they went out. Trying not to think about the woman of his dreams tipsy and getting chatted up by asshole guys in a dank bar, Dean pulled the orange juice out of the fridge and emptied the carton into his mouth.

What the fuck am I doing? he thought as icy juice filtered into his stomach. *Where does this end?*

He and a few of the boys had gotten into a drunk deep and meaningful conversation about women last night and when Dean told the boys he was in a one-sided booty call arrangement, their reaction had been swift and harsh. "Why would you let a woman treat you like that?"

Dean didn't have the balls to say it, but he knew exactly why. *The Princess Bride*. Everything about his obsession with hot bossy blondes could be traced back to *The Princess Bride*.

He'd been fourteen when Max's sister Lisa, rented the movie. Considering the title and the incredibly dorky cover, he and Max had strongly objected to watching it, but Max's mum had overruled them. Clear as anything Dean could remember lying on the carpet of the Connors' family room, a can of Coke in his hand, prepared to be bored out of his mind. That wasn't what happened.

Throughout the movie, Max had done all the right things—groaning at the kissing scenes, getting into the fight scenes, laughing at Inigo Montoya and the 'inconceivable' guy. Dean had just laid there, his Coke going warm in his sweaty fist, so dizzy he thought he was going to pass out.

When the movie was over, Max invited him to play table tennis, but he lied and said he was too tired. He rode his bike back to his parents' house, locked himself in the bathroom and jerked off until he came for the first time. Over *The Princess* fuckin' *Bride*.

Well, not the whole movie. The first ten minutes when Buttercup called Westley 'farm boy' and bossed him around and, instead of complaining, the guy murmured *as you wish* at her, with enough lust in his eyes to burn a hole through the TV.

Dean had never seen men and women interacting like that before. If his mum had *ever* spoken to his dad like that, all hell would have broken loose. Yet in the world of *The Princess Bride*, Westley, the boy, the *hero*, was Buttercup's servant and he was *happy about it*.

Dean didn't know if the movie had re-routed his sexuality, or if he'd always been that way inclined, but he was never the same after that. His vague ideas about girls and sex took root and started growing like weeds.

He'd never told Lisa what she unleashed in making him watch *The Princess Bride*, but he was one hundred percent sure she wouldn't want to know. Hell, his girlfriends didn't want to know. They liked how big he was. They wanted him to be the bossy one; pick them up, throw them around, tell them what to do. Dean was happy to do that for them but anytime he'd mentioned he might want to be in their position, the relationship always changed. It was as though he suddenly shrunk five inches in his girlfriends' eyes.

"There are things straight men just don't want," an ex said when he drunkenly asked if she could order him to fuck her.

Dean still couldn't see anything gay about his request, but he understood where Gillian was coming from. He was kinky and not the good manly kind of kinky. The kind that made people think about dudes in harnesses drinking out of dog bowls.

Dean didn't want to be put in a harness or drink out of a dog bowl, but he did want to be strung along and teased. It was why he'd been so susceptible to Violeta's particular brand of cockteasing, though he could never tell Max that. Something about being deprived and sneered at, but simultaneously lusted after did it for him.

He didn't know if Ash knew that or not. Sometimes it felt like she was deliberately torturing him, other times it seemed like she was just using him for sex and her hot and cold behaviour was down to a lack of commitment not kinkiness. God knew it wouldn't be the first time he confused the two.

Dean threw the empty orange juice carton in the recycling and headed back up the hall. He knew he was in for a shitty night's sleep, lying awake wondering when Jules and Ash would be home. He considered texting Max and telling him the girls were out, but torturing his mate with the same nauseating mental images he kept seeing wasn't going to help. Besides, then Max would know he came home to see Ash and he wasn't ready to be considered that tragic.

He opened his bedroom door and flicked on the light. Instantly he spotted the sheet of bright blonde hair spread across his pillow and he flicked the light off with a yelp.

"Ashley?" he whispered, unwilling to trust his own tired eyes and believe she was really there.

The hair didn't respond.

He crept forward and flicked on his bedside lamp, twisting the bulb away from what he hoped was Ashley's sleeping face. Dean's mouth went dry. It *was* her sleeping face. Ash Bennett was tucked between *his* sheets, snuggling *his* pillow, her bare shoulders gleaming in the glow of *his* lamp.

She wasn't out getting hit on by random guys, she was in his bed. She must have climbed in there and fell asleep waiting for him to come home, hoping he would—

Dean groaned softly. Ash had no way of knowing he'd be home tonight. Whatever reason she had for getting into his bed, it sure as shit wasn't to wait for him. He couldn't be a creep and get in beside her.

"*Jesus.*" Dean gave his nose a hard pinch then released it.

There were some positives here. Ash was home, safe and sound, leaving her sweet Ashley smell all over his sheets. And surely she hadn't just come in here because his bed was nicer than the guest one? Maybe she was a little sleepy and lonely and she just wanted to be close to him? Fuck it, that was what he was going to believe. Especially since he was facing a night in the guest bed by himself.

He crept over to his dresser and pulled out a new t-shirt and fresh boxers, then he crept back over to the lamp. Before he turned it off, he smiled at Ash's sleeping form. She was so fierce when she was awake, it was strange to see her resting. All pale and petite in the low lamplight. Dean tugged the duvet over her shoulders. "Sleep tight, missy. Dream of me. But only good dreams. No Mark Wahlberg in *Fear* shit."

"Mmmf." Ash rolled over, her arms rising over her head in a slow stretch.

"Shit." Dean backed away, not wanting her to think he was watching her sleep or worse, planning on trying to get his dick wet. "Stay asleep."

But it was too late, Ash's aqua blue eyes were already blinking up at him. "Hey Red."

"Hey, don't worry about me, I'm just leaving, you just go back to sleep, okay?"

She smiled a slow, sweet smile that made his chest ache. "I was having a dream about you."

"No Mark Wahlberg in *Fear* shit, right?"

Ash looked slightly confused. "Wh-no, of course not. It was a nice dream. Come in here and I'll show you."

She peeled the duvet back, exposing her body to the night air. Dean moaned like a man in pain. She was naked except for the scrap of purple floss between her legs, her pert breasts pointed at the ceiling, *his ceiling*. Dean drank in the sight of her bare stomach, the shadows where her thighs met her hips, the curve of her clavicle. She was lovelier than he could have imagined and he'd imagined her a lot.

"Do you want me, Red?" Ash asked, sliding her hands up her stomach and cupping her tits.

"Always, but I know you were just asleep and I know you and Jules were drinking, so I can just go into the guest bedroom and…" *'wank myself stupid'* was the truthful end to that sentence and Ash looked like she knew it. She gave him his second favourite smile, wicked like she knew all his secrets, mean like she planned on exploiting them. Jesus Christ, he wanted to be exploited.

"Do you know what I was dreaming about, Red?"

"What?"

She drew her hands across her breasts, gently tugging at her nipples. "Lots of things. Mostly you being a good boy, taking care of me like you always do."

Dean's cock was now aching against his jeans. "Ash..."

She circled her nipples, making them even stiffer in the lamplight. "Do you think maybe you'd like to do it now?"

It took all the willpower in his body not to say *'fuck yes.'* "I always want to make you feel good, gorgeous, but maybe we should talk about this tomorrow?"

"But my pussy hurts, Red."

Dean's whole body throbbed with arousal so urgent it was a step away from pain. "You want me to kiss it better?" His voice was so hoarse he barely recognised it.

Ash shook her head. "It hurts deep inside."

Dean knew what she was getting at and prayed he could be strong. "I can use my hands on you."

"I don't want your hands, Red. I need something better."

"Go on a date with me," he begged. "Just please, say you'll go on a date with me so I can fuck you?"

Ash gave him a playful grin. "Can you come closer for a sec?"

Dean bent down and, quick as a flash, Ash grabbed the collar of his t-shirt like a bad guy in a movie. He felt her impossibly soft lips press into his neck, raising goose bumps on his neck. "Ash, honey, what are you doing?"

"Smelling you. You always smell so good, it gets me wet just thinking about it. Even when I was asleep I wanted to rub up against your pillow and pretend it was you, but now you're here and you can make me better."

"I... Ash."

She kissed him, her mouth hot and hungry, her fist still clutching his t-shirt, collaring him. "You've made me wait for so long. Will you give it to me tonight, Red?"

Dean's heartbeat doubled, trebled, as he imagined finally plunging into the warm heat of Ash's pussy. "I can't."

Ash's fist tightened around his t-shirt. "Why?"

"You know why."

She made a sound like an angry kitten and kissed him again. Dean had never had a kiss with malicious intent before, but this was exactly that. Ash was not fucking around, she meant to screw him tonight, and he couldn't give in. Keeping his dick out of bounds was a 'we don't negotiate with terrorists' tactic. If he held off, Ash would have to meet his demands. If he gave in, he'd lose his last, best, bartering chip. Although, that was kind of hard to remember when Ash's bare tits were pressed against his chest and her tongue was in his mouth. It was easier to remember the condoms in his bedside drawer and the whimpering noises she made when she came, and how it would feel to grind those noises out of her with his dick.

As though reading his mind, Ash slid a hand down to cup his cock. "I need to know how this feels inside me, Red."

"Go on a date with me, then," Dean panted. "Go on a date with me, and I swear you'll find out."

"I want it *now*." Ash's tongue traced the rim of his ear. "It's been so long since I've been with anyone, almost a year. I've forgotten what it feels like to have a man inside me, pressing down on me. I want to feel it with you."

Dean tried not to think about being the guy to put Ash out of her sexless misery. "One date. I promise it'll be worth it."

She seized one of his hands and placed it on her right breast. "It'll be worth it right now if you just come to bed and do me like I know you want to."

Dean felt like he was being pressured into sex by a horny high school senior. Like the virginity Violeta Cummins didn't want was in Ash's sights and she was juking for it like a motherfucker. He closed his eyes. *I am a rock. I am an island. Nothing she says will change my mind.*

Ash re-gripped his collar, yanking it tight. "Red," she hissed. "Fuck me."

Except that. Except orders snarled in an impatient, bossy voice. He flushed as he felt that sweet mix of desire and humiliation. "No," he panted, like a not-reluctant-enough virgin. "Ash, I can't. Lemme go down on you."

"I don't want your tongue or your fingers, I want dick. I've been patient long enough. Either you give me yours or I'll find—"

"You won't find someone else." The words came blaring out of him loud as a truck horn and they both tensed a little, as though taken aback by the fury in his tone.

"I mean it," Dean continued. "You can tease my cock as the fucking day is long, drive me outta my fucking mind with needing you, but if you let another man lay a hand on your body, there will be hell to pay."

"Then fuck me." Ash's aqua eyes locked on his. "If you want to make me yours Dean, if you want to be the only one, fuck me."

It was only until she said his real name that he realised she never used it. Something about the fact that she'd called him Dean now, combined with the intense way she was looking at him, snapped his will to resist. "Okay. Okay, I'll fuck you."

Ashley looked as though she was trying not to punch the air in victory. "You, um, have condoms?"

"Yeah." Dean scrabbled in his sock drawer one handed as he stripped off his t-shirt. In record time he was standing naked in front of her, rolling cold latex down his shaft.

"Very nice." Ash stared at him with rapt interest and Dean remembered she'd never seen him naked before. All of a sudden he was sorry he'd removed his clothes so fast. They'd rushed through the slow, stripping each other off, kissing everything and discovering new sensitive patches of skin as they went stage of making love.

"Stand up straight," Ash demanded and Dean did what she asked. Considering he'd spent the last days eating hot chips and boozing he thought he still looked pretty good. Ash's gaze stroked over his shoulders and thighs, coming to rest on the dark red hair at his groin. "You're so sexy, Red."

"Thanks."

For a moment Dean considered telling her how much she meant to him, but then she spread her legs so he could see the place that had been his nightly obsession hovering a few inches from his bed, covered in purple lace. "Get me ready."

This woman, he thought as he plunged face-first into her pussy, *is going to kill me.*

Ash didn't need getting ready, she was damp with excitement. Still, Dean licked her, tearing at her G-string with his teeth, stroking at her opening with his fingers. Considering she was so eager to fuck, she let him take his time. He ate her until his body was taut, his hips working against the bed. The condom heated so it felt like he was wearing nothing, and he wondered if Ash wanted him to come that way, rutting the mattress, filling up the condom. If she did he'd be able to keep his vow of chastity another night. Then, just when he dared to think he might be safe, Ash fisted his hair and practically dragged his suckling mouth away from her clit. "You want my pussy, Red?"

He nodded, his cock throbbing between his legs.

"Beg me and I'll let you have it."

Dean's body tingled with the realisation that *this was happening*, a girl was treating him how girls treated him in his brain, when he was alone and pumping himself to porn. "Lemme do it, Ashley, I'll fuck you so good."

"Can you go slow? Can you do it so slow that I can come?"

Dean's tongue tripped all over itself trying to tell her it would be no other way. "I... whatever you want... Promise. For you. Whatever you want."

Another flash of that sweet-evil smile. "Then get up here and put it in me."

Dean braced himself above her, cock clasped firmly in his hand. He was glad Ash wasn't too short, he didn't feel like he was swallowing her up like he usually did in missionary. He paused for a moment, enjoying the feel of her skin against his, trying to capture the satisfaction of having Ashley Bennett beneath him in its entirety.

"Red." Ash grasped the nape of his neck. "Don't make me turf you out of your own bed."

His heart pulsed hard against his rib cage. "You'd do that?"

"Of course I would. I'll make you sleep in the cold, cold guest bed by yourself. Or you can lie down on the floor beside me and listen to me play with myself. Would you like that?"

He moaned, a low animal moan. "No."

"Then fuck me, handsome. Don't make me wait."

Dean closed his eyes and pushed inside her. It was unlike anything he'd ever felt before, sliding closer to Ashley as her tight pussy gripped him like it never wanted to let him go. "Christ you feel good."

She raked her hands down his back. "So do you."

He thrust tentatively, trying not to go too deep, too fast. Ash let out a whimper. "I'm gonna come, Red, I can feel it right now, I'm gonna come."

Dean's balls drew up towards his body, throbbing hard. He pictured some of the scary parts of *The Walking Dead* to try to calm down. "What do you need?"

His breath caught as Ash disinclined to answer. Instead, she rolled him onto his back and, straddling him, proceeded to work herself up and down his cock like he was a man-sized sex toy. Dean's lower half exploded in pleasure. "Ashley, fuck!"

"Shut up and take it, Red."

She rode him, her hips adjusting, getting him right where she needed him. Apparently, he hit a good spot because her eyes rolled back in her head. "*Fuck*, I knew you'd be able to get there. You're so big."

The news of his adequate dick rang around Dean's head like the bells at the end of World War II. "Whatever you need to come, just take it from me."

Ash clenched around him. "I need to feel like you could go forever, Red. If I think you won't last, I can't relax enough to finish."

"I can do that."

Whatever his faults, coming too fast wasn't one of them. Whether it was because he was circumcised or his brain was wired so that all he wanted was a woman's pleasure, he could always make it last as long as a girl needed it to. He set a slow, rocking pace that matched hers, making sure his pubic bone ground up against her clit.

Ash's nails bit into his shoulders. "Oh fuck me, Dean, you're so good."

Holy shit, he thought, looking up at her bouncing palm-sized tits, the way her beautiful face was drawn tight with lust. *I'm fucking Ashley Bennett. She used to be in magazines and now she is one hundred percent riding my cock. Imagine if the guys at school could see this? They'd be so fucking jealous. Especially that asshole Antonio. Wonder what he's up to?*

"Red." Ash snapped her fingers in his face. "Concentrate."

"Sorry, babe. I was thinking about—"

"Don't care. Hands on my hips."

Biting back a grin, Dean did what he was told. Ash leaned over him, her pert tits dangling in his face. "I'm gonna have to take a firm hand with you aren't I, Sherwood?"

"I... Probably?"

Ash pumped herself on his cock, the sensation making him grunt. "I'm close, Red. Lick my nipples."

Again, he did what he was told, sucking her as she rode him, turning her pale areoles hot pink and hard. From the way she was clenching around his shaft, Dean guessed she was close.

"Long as you need," he promised, licking her between words. "I'll give you my cock for as long as you need."

Ash moaned, arching back so her gorgeous breasts were pointed at the ceiling. "This is so amazing. You don't hate me for using you, do you?"

With her cunt gripping him so tight he felt like his brain was bleeding, Dean could only tell her the truth. "I like it. I like being the man you come to for dick."

"Good." She rocked against him, her eyes half closed, her mouth open. "I'm gonna come now. Fuck me while it happens."

He did, maintaining the slow, bobbing pace she seemed to enjoy. Her orgasm rose in waves, she got closer then backed off, then got closer again. Finally, when she was riding him hell for leather, when her cunt closed around him like a fist, he knew she was there. It took all of his strength to keep fucking her the way she'd asked, but he did it, forcing her walls apart with his cock. Ash screamed, screamed his name and dug her nails into his upper arms but he kept working, holding onto his load through sheer self-will. After what might have been hours, Ash collapsed beside him. "That was awesome. Best return to sex ever."

Dean smiled but inside he was stupidly hurt. A return to sex? Is that what this was for her? Not their first time, not the start of something beautiful, but a chance to get back on the horse, the horse being him? He breathed hard through his nose, unsure what to do or say next. Ash gently rubbed a little of the sweat from his forehead. "What can I do for you?"

Dean couldn't help but cringe a little. Being asked what he wanted was like dropping a worm into his delicious hot chocolate, but how was Ash to know that? "I... I'm not sure?"

"After what you did to me you can have anything you want," Ash said with an encouraging teacher-trying-to-get-you-to-stop-clinging-to-your-mum's-leg smile.

Be a bitch to me, Dean begged in his mind. *Boss me around, tell me to make you come again.* "I guess I'd like to bend you over?"

Ash laughed. "I'll bet you would, big guy."

She knelt in the middle of the bed, her back arched up. All sleek and golden and gorgeous. "Like this?"

"Yeah, that's great."

Dean shifted so he was propped up behind her, his latex covered cock braced against her pussy. He didn't like this. The view was spectacular, she was amazing, but the way she'd done what he'd told her to... It grated. Ash had always (at least in his mind) understood what he needed. She'd raked lines into his skin, forced him to keep his focus, made him service her however she needed it. Had that just been because he hadn't fucked her yet?

Ask, he screamed at himself. *Tell her.*

But the fear of getting that disappointed fucking look was too strong. With other girls he had tried to understand that kink wasn't for everyone, but if Ash took that line he knew it would bust him up inside.

Man up, he told himself. *Fuck her like you're normal and you like it.*

He gripped his cock and slid back inside her.

Ash moaned. "Fuck, Red that feels so nice."

Tell me to hurry up, Dean thought, through gritted teeth. *Tell me I don't deserve to fuck you.*

But Ash was just whimpering and sighing and rocking back against him. It *was* amazing, seeing and feeling and smelling her but it wasn't enough. He needed the hooks of his kink dug into his sides like spurs. He needed the fantasy.

Without thinking he slipped into his oldest imagining, the way a needle slipped into the grooves of an old worn-out record. He was a dumb-fuck stable boy, panting after the princess. She liked to screw him after her riding lessons, straddling him in the deep soft hay of the stables. She was engaged to a prince and should have known better, but she couldn't stop humping him whenever she got the chance. He was in love with her, and she tolerated him. He was only good for a fuck, never good enough to talk to when she was with her friends. He got to come inside her, but he knew that, to her, there was barely any difference between him and the horses he looked after: big, nice to ride and available at her convenience.

As always the thoughts and images were accompanied with hot bursts of self-loathing, but the pleasure was like a riptide, drawing him deeper and deeper. He fucked Ash, enjoying the slick glide of her pussy in a way he hadn't before. The sensation, combined with the fantasy had climax building in his balls and the base of his spine. He closed his eyes, picturing the princess, who ever since he had met her, looked like Ashley. He imagined her smiling contemptuously up at him as he eased her cravings with his cock. *"Faster, stable boy. I need to finish before anyone notices I'm gone."*

"Red?" Ash had turned to stare at him. "What's happening?"

Dean flushed hot, sweat prickling on the back of his neck. "Is something wrong?"

"No, it feels good, but where'd you go?"

"I... What do you mean?"

"You're thinking about something else, aren't you?"

If there was a mirror handy Dean was sure he'd see his cheeks were beetroot red. "I'm sorry."

"Don't apologise. Tell me what you're thinking about."

"I... Can't"

Ash's eyes narrowed. "You are attracted to me, aren't you?"

Dean laughed at how ridiculous the suggestion was and realised a second later when Ash's face fell, that that wasn't helpful. He reached forward and cuddled along her back. "Oh Ash, baby, of course I'm attracted to you! I think you're the most beautiful girl in the whole world."

"Then what's on your mind? Whatever it is, I can play along."

Dean opened his mouth again, and still the words wouldn't come out.

"Do you want me to pretend I don't want it? Do you want to call me names you think I won't like?"

He shook his head. If only it were that. Women could understand that kind of play. Those urges.

"Then what?" Ash pressed. "You were gagging for it before. You couldn't keep your eyes off me."

"That's because it was for you," he managed to say though his throat felt like it was the size of a bendy straw. "I liked it when it was all for you."

Comprehension seemed to dawn on Ash's face. "You want me to be mean to you, don't you? Like I am when you eat my pussy?"

Fuck yes, hell yes, by all the angels and saints yes. "Uh yeah, maybe."

"That's the only way you want to do things, isn't it?"

Dean licked his lips, tasting the salt of his sweat and the tang of Ashley's cunt. *No turning back, asshole. Tell her.* "Yes."

Her mouth curled into a deliciously evil smirk. "Fine."

She pulled herself off his dick and turned over, spreading her legs wide.

"Uh..." Dean was at a bit of a loss for what was happening. "What's going on?"

"You're gonna fuck me the way I like it, Red. Now stop talking and get inside me."

Dean fought a grin, almost beside himself with happiness. He braced himself over her, aligning his dick with her pussy. Ashley's natural lubrication had dried a little, and as he pressed inside, the condom snagged.

"Spit on your fingers. Wet me down."

Dean obliged, rubbing her down with his saliva, his fingers lingering on her swollen clit.

"Mmm." Ash wrapped her legs around him, her heels digging sharply into the base of his spine. "You have any limits I need to know about Red? Anything you don't like?"

"I… Whatever you like, I'll like."

She smiled, her cheeks becoming gold apples. "That's good to hear. If I hurt you too bad or you want me to stop, what are you going to say?"

Dean's head was so full of excited gratitude he could hardly think. Princess? No there was a good chance he'd fuck up and say that while he was hammering Ash's pussy. Horse? No, he couldn't bring horses into this. "What's a word I never say?" he asked Ashley.

"What about… Serenity?"

"Serenity? Well considering I didn't know that *was* a word until just now, I think that'll work. Serenity. Serenity. Serenity—"

"Red." Ash fisted his hair. "Stop saying 'serenity' and fuck me."

"Yes, ma'am." Dean slipped his cock between her legs and rocked back and forth so that the wetness spread. With Ash gripping his hair, it felt like his scalp was connected to his balls. "God I'm so fucking close already."

"Don't worry about that, just keep fucking me like a good boy."

"I like you calling me that," he panted, thrusting harder.

"I know you do," Ash said. "Now hurry up and come, I'm tired."

Dean did what she said, angling his body so he could plunge deeper inside her, gripping her ass so hard his wrists trembled. There was no finesse to his motions now, he was moving on instinct, taking what he needed from Ashley's body. Within seconds they were both moaning, their bodies slippery with sweat.

"If I'd known you were this good, I'd have fucked you the night we met," Ash whispered in his ear. "I'd have made you take me on the bathroom sink and if that bitch had gone and got security I would have let them watch."

Dean felt his balls contract, knew he was seconds away from coming. "Ash, baby, can I finish?"

"Hmm." She reached down and began toying with her clit. "No. I've changed my mind, I want to come again. Can you do that for me, Red?"

Dean desperately tried to think of zombies, disgusting, half-melted, spilling their guts everywhere, zombies. "Yes. Whatever you want I can do."

"Good." Ash ran a greedy hand over his chest while she played with herself. "Keep pace or you can sleep on the floor."

Dean gritted his teeth. "Whatever... Whatever you want."

Perhaps Ash was worried she'd taken it too far, because she brought her mouth to his ear. "Too much?"

"Fuck no, meaner. More."

For a second Ash smiled, he could see the gap in her teeth, then the bitchy look was back on her face. "You like me don't you, Red? You're always panting after me like a little puppy dog. Shame you're not good for anything but a screw."

Hot excitement burst in Dean's belly and spread down to his swollen balls. "Oh God, Ash."

"Shut up and fuck me."

He obliged, drilling away at her for what felt like forever, his orgasm climbing his shaft with overwhelming pressure, kept at bay only with the knowledge that it was what *she* wanted. When Ashley finally came, rubbing her clit, her face screwed up in pleasure-pain, he thought he might pass out.

"On your back," she demanded when she was done. He rolled over, and she straddled him again, this time making him do all the work as she reached back to toy with his sac. "They're so full. Are you hurting?"

Dean nodded dumbly.

"Do you want to empty them inside me?"

"Yes, yes, please. Please?"

"Then come," Ash said, in an icy whisper. "But the minute you're done, you're leaving."

Dean moaned, his hips slowing as he tried to delay his already too-delayed orgasm. "Please no... Let me stay with you?"

"No. Once you're finished you're gone Red, so hurry up and come in me."

He closed his eyes. He was fucking the princess. Ash was the princess, and the princess was Ash. He hammered inside her, wallowing in the feeling of being a powerless inferior, drowning in it, gasping, thrusting, *pounding* and then he came so hard black spots burned behind his eyes.

When he was done, embarrassment replaced the heat in Dean's blood. He found he couldn't look Ash in the eye as he stripped away the condom, though he forced himself to ask, "How was it for you?"

Fucked up, his brain sneered. *You fucking weirdo.*

"So good." Ash stretched her arms over her head. "You're so kinky. I love it."

Safe in the knowledge she couldn't see him Dean grinned as he wrapped the condom in a tissue and threw it in his wastepaper bin. "Glad to hear it. You were fucking incredible."

"Really?"

The trace of vulnerability in her voice washed all of Dean's self-pitying fears away. He climbed back onto the bed and scooped her into his arms. "Yeah, that was the best sex I've ever had. I'm so happy I came in here and found you. I hope..." he couldn't finish his thought. He wanted to believe Ash had come into his room to snuggle his bedding and wish he was there, just like he wanted to believe he wouldn't regret the sex they just had.

He hugged her tight and noticed she wasn't hugging him back. The silence that followed filled his eyes and nose and mouth like concrete. "Were you... Serious about me leaving? Because I'll go sleep in the guest bed if you want me to?"

After a few seconds of agonising silence, he let go of Ash and stood up. "I'll head off then. Sleep well. I'll uh, see you in the morning."

Ash reached out and touched his shoulder, her hand light but warm. "Don't. I'm sorry, Red. I'm just a little shook up. Please stay with me and keep cuddling me and stuff."

Dean didn't need to be told twice, he climbed back into bed, re-wrapped an arm around her middle and kissed the sides of her neck and her cheeks over and over.

Ash giggled. "Just so you know, I talk in my sleep. And not cute stuff. Weird shit."

Dean continued peppering her cheeks with kisses. "I don't give a fuck."

He tugged Ash closer, amazed at her scent and weight against him. The fantasy was over, and he got to keep the girl by his side. Who'd have fucking thought it was possible?

10

Ash had had a lot of sex. It was fun, free (or at least cheap if you insisted on counting the cost of lube and contraception) and it made her feel powerful the way nothing else did.

She never cared what people thought about her sexual history. Her looks, mother, and housing situation meant she was getting called a slut before she'd so much as kissed a boy. Ash had decided not to bother trying to make anyone see her differently. Instead, she got on the pill, bought the Kama Sutra (the only sex book she'd heard of) and reinvented herself as the David Bowie of fucking.

People waited for her to get pregnant or some nasty STD. Instead, she got her Kingswood, modelling campaigns, a nursing degree, and a collection of knobbish but undeniably attractive ex-boyfriends. Julia saw her struggle with self-doubt and heartache, but to everyone else, she was the unshakable queen of shagging, the best your boyfriend ever had. She learned what positions could make her come, what the best brand of butt plugs were and how to separate sex and love, at least most of the time. She also learned men needed to be coached into doing what you liked and no one was as good at making her come as she was. At least she had thought that, until last night. As she lay trapped under Dean Sherwood's freckly bicep, Ash could barely contain her panic. How could a man—a man who seriously thought sugar came from the ocean—have given her the best sex of her life? Because that's what it had been.

She wasn't exaggerating because of months of self-imposed celibacy, either. She knew what good sex was, and that had been the best by far. She had never come twice during a screw, most of the time she struggled to come *once*. But with the big gingery sweetheart nuzzling into her hair, it had been as easy as blinking; by the time he finished she was almost ready to go again. Clearly this man was her kryptonite, and as Dean snored softly behind her, Ash tried to work out why.

Firstly and most obviously, he smelled great, from his hair to his sweat. Secondly, his body was insane. Thirdly, he had a great boyfriend dick. His long-concealed cock had revealed itself to be the length and thickness of a popular dildo. Super big was nice every now and again, but Julia had to do daily yoga to offset the abrasion of Max's (allegedly) ginormous wang. Dean's was something you could happily ride twice a day without wincing. Fourthly, he made her come twice in one session, something unheard of in Ash-land. Five, he was a champion cuddler, not too clingy, warm or sweaty. Number six, his fantasies were incredibly hot. Well suited to a bossypants like her. The kind of thing you could tease out over weeks or months, incorporate costumes and role play, the bitch boss who wanted him to stay back late, the dirty French maid who wouldn't take no for an answer.

Except, Ash reminded herself as Dean's breath tickled the nape of her neck, they didn't have months to tease out his kinky fantasies. She and the man at her back had irreconcilable differences. Problems like 'unqualified roofer with no money' didn't resolve themselves after a night of sex. They might not resolve themselves in ten years and she didn't have that kind of time. She was on a fast track to motherhood, or at least she wanted to be.

Toxic waves of guilt poured over her like a river of sludge. She should never have come in here last night. She should never have slept with the sweetest, most fuckable, most likely to die in a workplace accident and leave nothing behind but an acoustic guitar, man in the world. She'd have to end things this morning, just like she'd told Julia she would. Of course, Julia would have preferred if she and Dean hadn't shagged each other senseless before she dumped him, but there was nothing she could do about that now. She pulled herself from the warm cradle of Dean's body and prepared to get up. Without a word, Dean reached over and tugged her back into his arms.

"Red! Let go of me!"

"No." He nuzzled her neck, raising goosebumps along her spine. "You're here. Wasn't a dream."

"No, it wasn't a dream. I need to get up."

"Mmm." Dean folded his legs over hers, keeping her close. "Innaminnute."

As Ash felt Dean's semi-hard cock nestle against her ass, a bad thought occurred to her, would it be so bad if they just... Did it again? Just once more, to see if it was a fluke? Dean Sherwood could not be the best sex she'd ever had, he just *couldn't be.* The footballers, the yoga instructors, the pro-surfer who took her to Bali. One of them had to be better.

Ash pressed her ass back against him, and Dean got the message at once. His hand moved down her bare stomach to her pussy. He gently parted her folds and began lightly rasping a big finger against her clit. Within seconds her orgasm was ready to explode like a bullet from a gun. "Okay, how the fuck are you doing this?"

"Mmph?" Dean was clearly half-asleep which made his ability to perform cunt voodoo even worse.

"How are you so good at getting me off?"

"Iunnno." He continued to rub her with his big crooked fingers. "Wanmeoostop?"

Ash clutched his forearm like it was a life raft in the middle of a stormy ocean. "Hell no."

Seconds later she was shuddering against him, biting his wrist because it felt so fucking good. Dean seemed to like that. Turned out the boy had a thing for pain as well as bitchiness. She was just contemplating the ethics of putting the erection stuck between her thighs to good use when a phone jangled loudly. Dean swore and rolled over to retrieve it from his pants. "My alarm," he explained, turning it off.

"Shit! What time is it?"

"Seven thirty, why? Do you have a shift?"

She didn't, but Jules was a notoriously early riser. If she woke up and bore witness to the animalistic humping sounds she and Dean were making, everything would be a hundred times more complicated than they already were. Ash's brain whirred into overtime. "Do you wanna get breakfast? My shout?"

"Yeah, sure." Dean's body wrapped around her, his fingers descending to continue their wet rubbing. "Think you can come again?"

As it turned out, she could. Toward the end of their session Dean slid another condom onto his cock and fucked her as he rubbed. It was an explosion of an orgasm, she had to bite a pillow to keep from screaming, too scared of snapping bone to use Dean's wrist. When he finally pulled away a tidal wave of wetness slid from between her thighs onto the bedding.

"Fuck me," he whispered. "I'm never washing these sheets again. Even though I totally wash them now, even when people don't remind me."

Saturated with equal parts guilt, lust, and fear Ash rolled over to face him. "Did you finish?"

He shook his head.

"Blowjob?"

Dean gave her a shifty sort of smile. "As unbelievable as that sounds I uh, like being a little strung out sometimes. I like waiting. I'm happy to head out and get breakfast now if that's okay with you?"

Ash's heart squeezed inside her chest, and she wanted to tell him that if he didn't take her now, he might be waiting a long, possibly infinite amount of time. But she didn't. "If you're sure, can we be ready to leave in five?"

Dean huffed out a laugh. "You want to be up before Julia, huh?"

"Yeah. Hearing me having sex has always bummed Julia out and unfortunately, it's been a pretty common feature in her life."

"I get that. We can leave soon." Dean yawned, stretching his arms over his head. Ash found the dark red hair in his armpits strangely erotic.

"Where should we eat?" he asked.

"I know a great place in Brunswick, Wide Open Road. It's a bit of a drive, but they have fantastic coffee."

"Sounds great." Dean held his arms open. "Quick snuggle before we get up?"

But Ash, who had anticipated that very question, was already on her feet hunting for her discarded panties.

"Did you sleep okay?" Dean asked and Ash could feel him staring at her tits.

"Yes. Get up, Red."

"In a second." He propped himself up against the headboard, his right hand beneath his sheets. With his tousled hair and heavy eyes he looked like a centrefold from one of her mum's old Cleo magazines. Ash was sure he was gripping his cock, feeling it swell in his palm. She felt a corresponding tingle in her pussy and shut it down. It was a miracle Julia wasn't up already, she didn't need her sister catching her sanding the splinters out of Dean's morning wood. "Can we get a move on?"

"Is there anything else I can do for you first?"

She felt a stab of irritation at how badly she wanted to say yes. "Nope."

Dean grinned, he was definitely holding his cock, she could see it propping up the covers like a tent pole. "You sure?"

Ash bundled up her clothes. "Yes. I'm going back to the guest bedroom to change. Meet you in the hall in three?"

She left before Dean could reply. After the warmth of Dean's bed, the guest room had all the charm of sterile birthing suite. Her clothes felt cold and slightly greasy from the previous day's wear and looking in the small dresser mirror she could see her face was a mess. She wiped away the mascara smudges and re-applied along with a dab of concealer under her eyes and lipstick (Smashbox, Always On). Her hands were shaking as she did this but she told herself she was cold, not shitting herself about what she knew she had to do. Dean appeared in her open doorway, impossibly handsome in a charcoal t-shirt and nice jeans. "You're so beautiful."

Ash couldn't bring herself to meet his gaze. "Thanks. Are you ready to go?"

"Almost. Do you want to take my car or yours?"

"I uh, thought we'd take our own cars?" Ash picked up her bag and dug through it for her keys. "I've gotta work later, so I'll head off straight after we eat."

"Right." There was a short pause. "I guess I'll follow you there, then."

Ash was extra glad she'd suggested separate vehicles as she drove to Wide Open Road. It gave her time to get her game plan together and think carefully about what she was going to tell Dean. She'd never been good with breakups, but force of necessity had given her a lot of experience doing it. She had one and only one break-up trick and it was breakfast ditching. Something about telling men you didn't want to fuck them anymore over bacon and eggs made it stick. Possibly because men liked bacon so much they didn't care about you not fucking them anymore until all the bacon was gone, at which point you'd already extradited yourself to the car park and driven far, far away.

"Please let it go down like that with Red," she mumbled to herself, reaching for her pack of Alpines in the glove box. Then she remembered she didn't smoke anymore and groaned. This was going to be a rough morning. Wide Open Road, like everything else in Brunswick, was hipster to the eyeballs, all exposed brick walls, bizarre art, and trendy tattooed waiters. Still, the food was amazing and the atmosphere more earnest kookiness than *'fuck you, mainstream poser'* so Ash could deal with it.

She and Dean queued by the door for a seat. He angled his body towards hers like he was trying to hold her hand, so she crossed her arms under her boobs and stared out at the café.

The place was full of glamorous mums with strollers and suits having breakfast meetings. She and Dean appeared to be the only post-shag couple in the place. The waiter, who eyed the fuck out of Dean's ass as he showed them to their small table, seemed to know it, too.

"Did you two have a fun night last night?" he asked as he presented their menus with a flourish.

Dean smiled at her with even more puppy dog sweetness than usual. "Yes, so much."

The waiters green eyes sparkled. "Naw, isn't that lovely?"

Ash's stomach curdled. It felt like a bad omen, another human knowing she and Dean had fucked, bearing witness to what she was about to do. "Can I have a latte?" she asked the waiter.

"Of course you can, lovely." He gave her a conspiratorial wink before striding away to clear an adjacent table.

Ash scanned her menu, even though she already knew what she wanted, delaying the moment she knew was coming. When their waiter returned they ordered, Eggs Benedict for her, bacon and apple relish toasties for him. Ash excused herself to go to the bathroom and run cold water on her wrists. When she returned, Dean was chatting with their waiter.

"Hey Ash," he said as she got closer. "Did you know Fletcher and I went to the same school? Different years, though."

Ash's heart pounded at her ribs like a cop demanding entrance. It was like Dean was conspiring to be as adorable as possible, so when she ditched him, she'd feel like an even bigger cockhead. "That's cool."

"Isn't it?" Fletcher purred. "I remembered his hair."

Ash kind of managed to chuckle even though her whole body was shuddering with nerves. "Who wouldn't?"

Fletcher gave her another admiring 'you lucky bitch' look, then departed.

"So what do you have on for today?" Dean asked, fiddling with the jam jar of raw sugar that all hipster places were legally ordered to provide.

"Gotta go home and feed the dogs before work."

"That's right, you and Jules have got about a million dogs, don't you?"

"We used to. Once things got hectic with Jules' game, we gave a few away, and a few died this year as well."

"I'm sorry."

"Don't be, we adopted most of them when they were ancient. We won't adopt any new ones for a while, it was getting insanely messy."

Actually, as much as Ash missed having a herd of dogs running riot through the house, she'd chosen not to adopt anymore because it wasn't a good environment for a baby. Then again, little about their grandma's dilapidated wooden house was. Without a serious injection of cash, the house was doomed to fall into disrepair. She remembered Nate's offer of four hundred grand and her hands and face prickled with guilt.

"What are you thinking about?" Dean asked.

The cop in her chest knocked again. "I... Just how much I'd love to live around here."

Dean raised his eyebrows. "Really?"

"Well not *here* in peak hipsterville, this is Julia's rightful home, but closer to the city, at least. Somewhere closer to work, where the food's better. I had Eggs Benedict at the café in Brenthill once, and they just put straight mayonnaise on poached eggs."

Dean laughed. "Well, I can recommend Coburg if you're thinking of making a switch. Good parks. Nice neighbors." He wiggled his eyebrows at her.

"Did you grow up in Coburg?" Ashley asked, determined to change the subject.

"Essendon. Max and I went to Hanley Grammar."

So he was a private schoolboy, too. Not on Nate's level, but miles closer to the top of the social heap than her. "Did you go to uni?"

Dean nodded. "For a year. Studied geology. I hated it, though."

"Why did you do it?"

For the first time since she'd met him, Dean's face tensed with something that bordered on anger. "My old man wanted me to go."

"But you didn't want to?"

"No."

It was the first single syllable sentence Ash thought she'd ever heard him say. "Are you okay, Red?"

"Yeah, anyway, enough about me. What made you want to study nursing?"

"I don't care about blood, and I knew I could get a job afterward."

"You didn't have, like, a calling?"

Ash shrugged. "No. I like nursing, but I only got my degree because I knew modelling wasn't going to last. The only thing I wanted was enough money to take care of Jules and to…"

"What?" Dean urged.

Be a mother. Have the fairy-tale family I never got to have. Husband, me, and baby makes three.

She couldn't do this anymore. She closed her eyes. "Dean, I need to tell you something."

"What?"

They were interrupted by the arrival of their coffees, perfectly poured into ecologically friendly cups. The waitress tried to place Dean's mocha in front of Ash.

"It's fine," Dean said as he claimed his rightful beverage. "Everyone gives me shit for drinking chocolate coffee, but it's the only way I can get it down."

The waitress laughed, and Dean ran a hand across his scalp ruffling his hair even more. Ash's suspicion that he was trying to be cute purely to mess with her intensified.

She took a hasty gulp of latte, willing the caffeine to give her the energy to proceed. "So, um like I was saying before…?"

"Yes. Yeah. Go right ahead." Dean sipped his mocha. "Hey, that's good as. How's yours?"

"It's good. So about our... *Relationship* I guess you'd say."

Dean grinned. "Sounds promising."

Ash hated herself. Like properly hated herself. Hated herself for fucking him, hated herself for seducing him at Julia's game launch. Just straight up hated herself, but she forced herself to continue. "So you're an amazing guy..."

Dean's face lit up.

"... But we're just not right for each other."

To her amazement, Dean gave her a huge lopsided grin. "Am I allowed to disagree?"

"Huh?"

He reached for the sugar and poured a teaspoon into his mocha. "I can see *why* you think we're not good for each other, but you've kinda said this to me before. I believed you the first time, but then you started texting me and visiting me at work and sitting on my face and you snuck into my bed last night and then you practically begged me to make love to you, so..."

He trailed another stream of glistening brown crystals into what had to already be a disgustingly sweet drink. "I think you like me. And I think we should keep having sex and date and fall in love."

Ash stared at him, the cop in her rib cage bashing harder than ever. '*Fall in love?*' What the fuck was he on about? She needed to break out the heavy artillery fire. "I want to have a baby."

Dean didn't even blink. "I know."

"So then... Can't you understand why I don't want to start a relationship right now?"

"I can." Dean took a swallow of mocha. "But here's the thing—I like you, and I like kids, and I'm thinking you can just cut out the middleman with this whole 'looking for a donor while still wanting to get laid thing' and just have a baby with me. How'd you feel about redheads? Specifically, giving birth to them?"

The cop in Ash's chest was now whacking on the walls with fucking sledgehammer. "Dean, I can't—"

"Excuse me?" It was Fletcher, their original waiter, now bearing two heavy plates of food. "Can I squeeze in here?"

As he unloaded their breakfast, Ash stared at her gooey eggs. She'd never felt less like ingesting calories. Whose asshole idea had it been to come to a café anyway? She picked up her fork and poked it into the rocket sprinkled on top of her meal. Dean, who apparently wasn't suffering any post-confession side effects, picked up one of his sandwiches and hoed in. For a moment Ash just watched him, utterly transfixed by the gargantuan bites he could take. She'd gotten so used to the precise, sumptuous way he ate pussy, she forgot he snarfed down food like it was going out of style.

"What were you saying before?" Dean asked through a mouthful of sandwich.

"Um..." Ash blinked, trying to retrace her mental steps. "So, about us having kids..."

Dean's bright brown eyes gleamed. "I like the way that sounds too."

Fuck you, stop being cute! Ash poked one of her eggs and watched it effortlessly spill its yellow guts, wishing she could do the same.

"Ash." Dean put down his toastie. "Talk to me."

She took a deep breath. "Okay, well I hope you don't mind, but I know a bit about your situation."

His eyebrows went up. "My situation?"

"How you're working casually for your friend's company. That you're not a qualified roofer?"

Dean looked sheepish. "Yeah, I meant to do an apprenticeship after I left uni, but I kept thinking I might join the police like Max, or head up north and work in the mines, or maybe get a management position at one of my mate's hotels..."

Or colonise the lost city of Atlantis, or become the new lead singer of INXS, Ash thought as she stabbed another egg. "It's none of my business what you do with your life, but put yourself in my shoes. If we had a kid, I would go on maternity leave, I wouldn't be working. And if you then fell off a roof and screwed up your back, we'd be fucked.

I'd have to go back to work with a new baby and support three people on a nurse's wage."

Some of the twinkling light in Dean's eyes went out. "I-I get that."

"Plus there's the fact that you live with your mate, you don't own any assets, and apparently you're not so hot with money."

Dean blanched. "I... uh... Yeah. I'm not great with money."

"Well that's the same situation. It's hard for me to see us being able to make it work."

"But I can change," Dean said earnestly. "Now that I've met you, I'll pull my socks up for sure."

Ash tried to smile and failed. "Red, what we have right now is sexy and romantic and fun. But there's nothing sexy about having to run a man's life for him. There's nothing fun about becoming a nag because otherwise stuff never gets done, and there is nothing—" she swallowed hard, the conversation cutting her far deeper than she thought it would. "There is nothing romantic about being poor."

Dean reached across the table and took her hand in his. "Ashley, I would take care of you and our baby, I promise."

Ash slid her hand away. "I believe that *you* believe that, but there is no evidence to back up what you're promising me."

"What if I went to my boss and asked to start an apprenticeship?" Dean's voice was low and urgent. "What if I saved up and got my shit together before the baby came?"

"Dean you're a great guy, but we're in two different places. I just can't see us taking on money troubles, a new baby and a new relationship at the same time."

Dean stared down at the table. "But we like each other."

The backs of Ash's eyes began to prickle with tears. "I know."

"Isn't that... Couldn't it be enough?" Dean looked up at her and she could see his brown eyes were glassy with tears.

Her chest wrenched as though he'd plunged a butter knife into it, but she knew she needed to keep going. "Dean... No, it's not. It can't be."

"Right, okay, sure, makes sense." Dean swiped a hand across his eyes, then picked up another sandwich and began to eat. Following his lead, Ash shovelled a forkful of eggs into her mouth. They tasted like sanitary towels.

Hurry up, she told herself. *Hurry up and you can leave.*

Dean suddenly slammed his palm on the table, upsetting the jar of sugar. "Fine! You're miles out of my league, and I'm in a shitty position to become a dad, but if you went with a donor, he could turn out to be a secret murderer or a One Nation voter."

Ash was slightly alarmed by this powerful rebound in his mood. "Dean, what are you talking about?"

"Your donor. He could be a fucking serial killer for all you know. Or one of those guys who donor-wanks for money, and your kid will have fifty thousand-half siblings and grow up and marry one of them and you'll have deformed, incest grandkids."

"Dean!"

"It's true!" Dean's brown eyes were wide. "Me on the other hand? Never murdered anyone, never voted One Nation, never donated my sperm, at least not to science, anyway. I'm tall, I'm built, yeah, I'm a bit of an idiot, but I read somewhere a kids' brain-power comes from their mum, so we should dodge a bullet there—"

"Dean," Ash repeated. "I can't—"

"Plus, you'll have someone you know by your side to help you with the pregnancy and the birth and the early stage where the kid cries all the time. And if we fall in love, you'll have me forever and I swear I'll go get that apprenticeship, I'll go call my boss right now and—"

"Dean!" Ash practically yelled his name. Several people turned to look at her and Ash gave them all big 'get on with ya fuckin' breakfast' glares.

When she turned back to Dean, he was blushing a little. "Sorry. I got kinda wound up."

"It's fine, but what I was trying to tell you is that I've had another offer about having a kid."

Dean's face went as dark as a storm cloud. "You're seeing someone else?"

Fletcher, who Ash was sure was only pretending to wipe down a nearby table, made a noise of indignation. Ash shot him a dirty look. "No. I mean a potential donor. Not someone I'm sleeping with."

"Who is he?"

Dean was using the voice men used when they were trying to work out if they could beat someone up bare handed or if they might need a crowbar. Ash glared at him. "He's a guy I work with. An orthopaedic consultant."

"What's that?"

"A bone doctor."

"And he's gay?" Dean asked hopefully.

"He's divorced. He's forty-four and single, and he wants to have kids before he's too old."

Dean's nostrils flared. "So he what, came up to you at the hospital and asked if he could get you pregnant?"

Ash didn't like the thinly veiled jealousy in Dean's voice but saw no way to call attention to it without making things worse. "Yes. He made me an incredible offer, and I have to take that into account when I—"

"What d'you mean 'incredible offer?' Do you mean money?"

Ash could feel herself flushing and hated herself even more for it. She had nothing to be ashamed of. "Yes. He said he would be willing to give me four hundred grand. Then two thousand a week in child support once the baby's born."

Dean looked like he was experiencing acute pain in a back molar. "Right so, fuck all this relationship stuff, when it comes to picking a father for your child, money's gonna be the deciding factor, huh?"

Ash lost it. "No, it fucking isn't! But I'm not gonna sit here and act like money doesn't matter."

"Money *doesn't* matter. Not when it comes to stuff like this."

Ash snorted loudly. "Wow, that 'money can't buy me love' spiel means a fuck of a lot coming from a private schoolboy from Essendon."

"What does Essendon have to do with anything?"

"You're middle class. *Upper* middle class. Never gone hungry a day in your life, always someone to bail you out when you're in trouble, when your car doesn't start, when you lose five hundred bucks. You're thirty-five and you live with your mate and work whatever job pops up, and you have the nerve to tell me money doesn't matter? Fuck you."

Dean's face fell. "Ash, I'm sorry I shouldn't have said that—"

"No, you shouldn't have. I grew up shit-poor on Centrelink, and my childhood *sucked*. The power was always getting turned off, Julia and I ate baked beans every day, and had to put sticky tape over the holes in our shoes. Do you know what I would do to make sure my kid didn't grow up like that? Anything. Fucking *anything*. And if that means having a baby with a doctor instead of some unqualified roofer who doesn't have two cents to rub together, then *fine*."

Dean leaned forward so he was practically resting in his bacon sandwich. "Ash, I'm so sorry."

"Good." Ash was embarrassed to find herself tearing up in public like a complete nerd. She dug in her bag for a tissue. "I don't need four hundred grand, Dean, but it's okay to need stability for your baby. Or even for your fucking self."

Dean's usually bright eyes were dull. "Of course it is. I'm sorry, I don't mean what I said, I was just jealous."

"Yeah well, thanks for making me feel like a hooker." Ash stood up, slinging her bag over her shoulder.

"Ash, please just stay, we can talk about this?"

"What else is there to say, Dean? You can't change shit just by talking about it." Ash pulled out her wallet and Dean waved a hand at her. "I've got this."

"No, it's fine. I asked you to come here—"

"Goddammit Ashley, just let me pay."

Ash froze. It was the first time she'd heard Dean display any kind of forcefulness. It was... Odd. She stared into his face, seeing the lines around his mouth, the darkness in his eyes and she remembered the way he'd spooned her last night, kissing all over her cheeks and neck. The memory cut like barbed wire and she knew she needed to leave before she did something stupid, like ask him to kiss her one last time. "Okay, see you later, Red. Or around."

Dean didn't reply, just stared down at his half-eaten food. Ash dillydallied with her bag strap, trying to think of something else to say and when she realised she couldn't, turned her back on him and headed for the exit.

"Not hungry?" Fletcher called from the front counter.

"No."

"Sorry to hear that. Also, I think you should have his baby, honey. I would."

11

Because his situation wasn't already bleak enough, it started raining on Dean's drive home, the thick cloud cover making eleven in the morning feel like nine at night. Dean studied the grey drizzle through his windshield; it perfectly reflected his mood—grey, miserable, pathetic.

Still, there was nothing he could do about it. Just like there was nothing he could do about Ash dumping him over the best bacon and egg sandwich he'd ever had. Not that she'd really dumped him. 'Dumped' implied he'd had a relationship with her, instead of just being her temporary dildo, the way he had been for Violeta Cummins.

That's not true, he reminded himself. *Ash likes you, you're just too much of a useless fuck-up for her to have a kid with you.*

Dean groaned. As far as pep talks went this one wasn't doing a lot for him. He just wanted to go home, turn on the PS4 and lose himself in another reality. Instead, he was stuck in his head while stuck in the rainy purgatory of Sydney Road traffic. As he listened to his outdated windscreen wipers screech over the glass, Dean considered whether it was good he'd come home early from the postseason trip, or if he'd have been better off watching his teammates blow chunks onto the beach.

If he'd stayed on holiday, he might have avoided the worst conversation of his life, but then he'd never have slept with Ashley. But maybe she'd broken it off with him *because* they'd had sex. Maybe she hadn't liked what he'd wanted her to do. The thought made his guts knot. If he'd ruined everything by freaking her out with his dumbshit fantasies...

"She would have dumped me either way," he said aloud. "She made up her mind the night we met. She doesn't think I'm good enough for her and she's right."

The thought made his dick twitch against his thigh. Dean groaned. "Not in a hot way, you idiot. In a 'she's-going-to-have-a-baby-with-a-doctor-and-we're-going-to-die-alone' way."

But cock-eyed optimist that it was, his dick kept right on swelling, reminding him of how Ash had straddled his hips, pumping herself up and down on his cock moaning, *harder, Red, do me harder*. Dean's scalp tingled as though phantom fingers were pulling his hair.

Beeeeeeeeep, the driver behind him let rip on the horn. He was sitting motionless in front of a green light.

"Fuck, sorry!" He waved apologetically as he pressed his foot hard on the accelerator. The guy behind him gave him the finger.

"That's it," Dean told himself. "I'm done thinking about her."

He wasn't. By the next red light, he was remembering how his cock had looked disappearing into Ash's pussy, how he'd ground his hips against hers, mashing his pubic hair into her swollen pink flesh. Her mouth had been open, her nails raking red lines down his back... Dean swore as his erection scraped against his zipper. He'd reached maximum jean capacity and it fucking hurt. Like he needed anything else to hurt right now.

After glancing around for onlookers, he pried his top button open. "This is not sexy," he told his dick. "Being dumped for being a useless, penniless fuckwit *isn't sexy*."

His cock ignored him. That wasn't surprising. One of his most common fantasies was the princess showing up at the stables in her wedding dress to fuck him before the ceremony. A brain that could get horny over something that fucked-up could get turned on by being ditched. It wasn't entirely his dick's fault. He hadn't come when he was fucking Ash this morning because he'd been secretly hoping they'd go back to bed after eating. That wasn't the case and now he was pent up *and* broken hearted. The last thing he wanted to do was go home and have a sad wank. At least not right away. He planned on hitting the PS4 and staying there for at least eight solid hours.

And you wonder why Ash thinks you're not mature enough to be a dad, a voice whispered in his ear. Dean ignored it. Ash was already gone. She was going to have a baby with some rich dickhead, live in a fancy house and remember him as 'that ginger I nailed when I was thinking about whether to have a baby with some rich dickhead. So glad I decided to go with yes.'

"Stop it," Dean muttered, pounding his skull with a closed fist. "Concentrate."

When he pulled up at the house twenty minutes later he noticed his neighbour Mrs. Berry in her front garden, pruning her rose bushes. Mrs. Berry had a major wide-on for Max and was always telling Dean to say hello to him for her. She'd definitely notice if he got out of the car with a hard on.

He shifted around, trying to adjust his cock without looking like a dirty car-wanker and his hand got trapped in his jeans. Dean felt a hot burst of irritation, not at his clothes, neighbour or the traffic, but the person who had done this to him in the first place. Ash had practically begged him to turn her out last night. She'd been sleeping in *his* bed, seduced him, fucked the life out of him, left marks all over his back, neck, and shoulders and had then taken him out for breakfast and told him he was a waste of space. Who did that?

"It doesn't matter," he reminded himself. "It's over now."

He got out of the car trying to ignore the pain in his head, cock and heart.

"Hello, Dean," Mrs. Berry called. "What are you up to this morning?"

Gaming, jacking myself, drinking hard liquor, maybe a little crying depending on how I feel as the day wears on... "Nothing much."

"Well, I hope you enjoy yourself! Don't forget to say hello to Maxwell for me!"

Dean gritted his teeth. "I won't."

He walked up the garden path and tried to unlock the front door. He started off with the wrong key and tried to insert another one, which was also wrong. Then, after he swore for a bit, he found the right key, shoved it into the keyhole, and realised the door had been unlocked and he'd just succeeded in locking it again. "Shit!"

He forced the key back into the lock, flung the door open, stepped into Max's house and slammed the door behind him so hard it shook the foundations of the house.

"Mother of fuck!" Julia yelled from somewhere down the hall. "Why!?"

Dean cringed. "Shit, sorry!"

"Sherwood? What the hell, man?"

Dean swore under his breath, was this day ever going to stop sucking? He decided to go and apologise to Jules in person. He found her right where he planned to be, in front of the living room TV, except she wasn't playing PS4; she wasn't doing anything aside from staring at the floor, her hair hanging in front of her like a damp tea-towel. "Are you okay?"

Jules flinched, as though he'd shouted at the top of his lungs. "No."

"I can see that, no offence. What happened?"

"Ash drinks like an investment banker. That's what happened."

The casual mention of her name lashed him like a whip. Max had warned him that if this ended badly he'd still have to see and hear about Ash because of Jules. The idea made him feel as nauseous as Julia looked. "That... Uh, sucks."

"I should have known better than to try and keep up with her in the first place, she's a fucking machine, gets it from our mum. What about you, how was the trip and the drive home and everything? Are you hungover as well?"

"Hungover…?" Suddenly it clicked. Jules thought he'd just gotten home from his post-season trip. She had no idea he'd spent the night with Ash, or that they'd gone out for breakfast. He cleared his throat. "I'm fine. I'm too old to go apeshit on those trips anymore."

"Makes sense." Julia let out a small moan of despair. "I know people say they're never drinking again but seriously, fuck this, I'm never drinking again."

Dean smiled for the first time since he left Wide Open Road. "Why'd you get so hammered?"

"I had to tell Ash something she didn't want to hear and telling Ash things she doesn't want to hear makes me nervous."

Dean's smile vanished. Someone had told Ashley he was an unqualified roofer and bad with money, and he was damn sure that person wasn't Max.

"Are you okay, dude?" Julia yawned. "You look weird."

Dean stared at Max's girlfriend. He and Jules had always gotten along great, playing COD, eating meat lovers' pizza, giving Max shit about his hair. She was his friend in her own right, or so he'd thought before she sold him down the river. "Why'd you do it?" he demanded.

"Huh?"

"Why'd you tell your sister about me working casually and being shit with money?"

Julia's already pale face turned the colour of bad milk. "I, yeah. I'm sorry, Dean but Ash means everything to me and I could tell…" Julia squinted at him. "Hold up, how do you know I talked to Ash? Did she call you?"

Fuck, he hadn't thought that one through. "Yeah, we uh… She and I… Last night…"

Julia hadn't become one of the youngest game designers in the world because she was dumb. She began flapping her hands in the air like she was trying to fly. "Oh fuck, you came home last night, didn't you? I thought Ash made the bed for once, but she didn't sleep in the guest room, did she? She slept in—*oh my god, you fucked my sister!*"

Dean winced. "I… Yeah."

Julia pressed her face into the beanbag and made a disgusted screaming noise.

"Are you okay?" Dean asked.

After a few long seconds, she lifted herself upright. Big spots of red had blossomed on her freckled cheeks making her look like a creepy horror-movie puppet. "So, despite my advice, Ashley slept with you. Then what? You guys went for a break-up drive or something?"

"We went to Wide Open Road for breakfast."

Amazingly, the corners of Julia's mouth kicked up.

"What?"

"Ash is *always* dumping guys at Wide Open Road. It's like her signature move."

Dean closed his eyes. "Great, well I wasn't sure I could feel worse, but hey, I feel worse."

"Sorry." Julia looked so miserable, Dean immediately felt guilty. "Don't be sorry. You didn't tell her anything that wasn't true. All the stuff she said about me not being ready to be a dad, that's on me not you. I'm sorry for slamming the door and being a jerk. I'm gonna head to my room."

He turned to leave.

"Hang on!" Julia croaked. "Don't you want to talk about it? Or like, maybe I could give you a hug?"

"I never thought I'd say this, but I'm too sad for hugs. I just wanna lie down."

Julia's chin trembled. "Dean, I promise everyone likes you. Everyone thinks you're great. You're still a legend."

"Right. I'm a legend. A legend is what I am." Dean stared at the blank TV. He was beyond tired, beyond depleted. He needed something to take the edge off. Then it came to him. "When does Max get back?"

"Around nine tonight, why?"

"I may or may not be in possession of a joint."

Julia's eyebrows went up. "Are you thinking…?"

"I am."

Fifteen minutes later he and Jules were huddled under the porch trying to light the slightly damp spliff he'd been keeping in his glove box. Like most people on planet earth, he and Jules enjoyed smoking weed, but living with a cop made that complicated. Max wasn't opposed to pot, but his job was what it was, and he couldn't be party to illegal substances in his house. The three of them had adopted a *'don't ask, don't tell'* policy. Dean and Jules only smoked when Max was out, never kept weed in the house, and signed as many petitions calling for legalisation as possible. Max, for his part, overlooked the occasional deck of rolling papers and suspicious smell.

"Shit, this is harder than I remember." Dean clamped the butt between his teeth and fiddled with his lighter. "You're *sure* Max isn't due back until later?"

"Completely sure. God, cereal is amazing." Julia had brought a packet of Rice Bubbles with her and was eating them with slow, methodical crunches.

"Cereal is amazing, you are correct." Dean flicked his lighter open and sucked hard on the joint. For a second he wondered why his lips were so sore, then he remembered Ash had bitten and kissed them half to death. Gloom welled inside him as the joint burst into flame.

"We have lift-off!" Julia threw a fistful of puffed rice into the air like confetti. "Hooray."

Dean took a deep drag and heat blossomed in his throat. It hurt, he didn't smoke enough for it not to hurt, but today he liked it. It felt like it was burning away his misery.

He exhaled and extended the joint toward Jules. They smoked in silence for a while, watching the rain drip off the roof. It wasn't awkward, but the mood was a little melancholy, what with his heart-break and Julia's hangover. He got the feeling Jules was waiting for him to talk and as much as he wanted to spill his guts, he couldn't manage it. At least not until they were halfway down the spliff.

"I don't want what happened with your sister and me to come between us," he said, shouting to be heard over the rain. "I think you're ace, Jules."

"Oh, yay!" Julia coughed out a big cloud of purplish smoke. "I was sitting here feeling like such a tosser thinking I'd ruined things between us."

"Don't think that. You're funny and cool and you make Max so fucking happy. He never pouts around anymore, which is a fuckin' miracle. I get it, you thought Ash and I would be shit together—"

"I didn't."

"What?"

Julia looked down at her knees. "I didn't think you'd be shit together."

Dean's head felt like it was going to explode. "Then why would you try and warn her off me?"

Julia put down the Rice Bubbles, her expression weary. "Because having a kid with a man-baby is what happens to girls where we're from. In Brenthill, half the chicks in my year were knocked up before we could drink. Ash dodged a fucking bullet. She had a couple of boyfriends who wanted a kid, just so they could lock down a hot chick with a steady pay-check and not do anything more strenuous than blow a load. I thank Buffy every day that never happened." Julia took a sharp drag on the joint. "Then when it finally looked like she was gonna have a baby without some clueless dude on the scene, you came alo—"

Julia shot him an apologetic look. "Sorry."

Dean bowed his head. "It's okay."

"It's not. You're miles better than any of Ash's exes, you're not lazy or an arsehole you're just—"

"A bit of a lost cunt?"

Julia gave him a rueful smile. "Well yeah, man. But it's more than that, you're shit with… You know…"

"Money?"

"Yeah. And having a kid is expensive. There's time for you to get your shit together, but Ash wants to have a baby now. Premature menopause runs through our family and if she misses her chance…" Julia shook her head. "I just thought maybe the timing was wrong. I thought if she fell in love with you she might regret it and I love her more than anything. I had to tell her what I knew."

Dean had to give Julia credit for having the balls to say all of this to his face. Plenty of people wouldn't. He held out his hand for the joint. "It's okay. I understand."

Jules turned to face him. "Why *are* you so broke? You work full time and play semi-pro footy. Is it just a carelessness thing? Or is the cash going somewhere? Does it have something to do with your family, which Max told me I'm never allowed to bring up, but I'm realising as I'm saying it that I just did?"

Dean looked out at the rain, his insides churning.

"Fuck, sorry." Julia picked up the Rice Bubbles again and stuffed a handful into her mouth. "I shouldn't have asked. I'm just stoned and probably still drunk. Ignore me."

Dean wished it was that easy. He didn't want to talk about his past and even Max didn't know where so much of his money had gone, but this wasn't about pride or keeping his family's secrets. This was the difference between being misunderstood and being recognised. He was a sucker, no doubt, and an idiot, but a different kind of idiot sucker than everyone assumed he was. If Julia knew the truth, then maybe there was the foggiest chance in hell he could still turn this around. "Hey, Jules, can you look at me?"

She turned to him, her eyes half-closed. "Yeah, mate?"

"My mum's an alcoholic."

"Oh." Julia studied him curiously. "So's mine. She lives in Queensland."

"Mine lives in a rehab place. At least she has for the last couple of months. She went off champagne and got into prescription meds. Shit really hit the fan."

Julia's face contorted with sympathy. "I'm sorry, Dean. That sucks."

"Yeah." His heart raced inside his chest. "It does, but, uh, my dad doesn't think my mum has a problem. He just tells her she needs to get a grip. A few times he's chucked her out of the house with no money."

Julia shook her head. "Take it from someone whose dad is a piece of shit, your dad sounds like a real piece of shit."

"He is. He, um, didn't want to pay for her to go to rehab. Neither did my brother. Though to be fair, he wouldn't pay for a Christmas present for Jesus. We're kind of a messed up family. I never see them. I barely speak to them. I didn't come from a happy home, which is weird because I'm a pretty happy person. Anyway, I'll shut up now."

Julia trickled a fistful of cereal into her mouth and chewed it slowly. "You're paying for your mum's rehab, aren't you?"

Dean nodded, relieved that her bright gamer brain had once again joined the dots.

"And it costs…?"

"The twenty one-week program? Fifteen grand."

Julia released a series of tight hacking coughs, spraying bits of half-masticated Rice Bubbles everywhere. "*What the what?*"

"Yeah, it's expensive. My mum, uh, went to rehab last year as well."

"Fuck! And you paid for that, too?"

Dean dipped his head, unable to say the words out loud.

"Holy smoke, does Max know?"

"He's got some idea. I keep it to myself mostly, I-I don't want to embarrass my mum. Or maybe I don't want to embarrass myself."

Julia frowned. "Why would you be embarrassed?"

"Because before I managed to talk her into rehab, I loaned my mum loads of cash. She'd come find me at work, all sloppy drunk and say my dad had cut her off. I didn't know what else to do. I just gave her whatever money I could, even though I knew she was just gonna get wasted. I just wanted her to go away. I know how this is gonna sound, but I don't like my mum. I don't like anyone in my immediate family. They used to… They're just bad people. Mean, miserable people."

Julia gave him a look that Dean couldn't explain. It was sympathetic without being patronising, it said she understood his situation precisely because she'd lived chest-to-chest with the same beast. She pushed her chair back, walked over and hugged him from behind. "I'm sorry. For what I told Ash. For not understanding."

"Thanks, but I can't put everything on my parents. I've still been a fuckstick. I could have saved plenty of money by now, but I haven't. I could have gotten a job that I liked and climbed the ladder or bought a house or not paid for my ex to go to Ireland without me, but I didn't."

"Yeah, but you had to go through all this bullshit. It's so fucking unfair."

"There are people who have it worse," Dean said. "That's what I always used to tell myself. I always had Max and his family. I never felt like I didn't have a place to go."

"That's so sweet." Jules sounded on the verge of tears. "I know it's kinda soon after Ash dumped you, but what do you think you're gonna do now?"

"I'm gonna call my boss and ask if I can do an apprenticeship."

"Dean!" Julia pulled away from their hug. "You shouldn't make any big decisions when you're stoned. Or when you just got dropped."

"It's not about either of those things."

"Then what...?"

"I'm done aiming low. Even if it never brings Ash back, I'm done. All my friends are married or have kids or houses or *something*. I'm sick of just waiting for that to happen to me. If I want to be a proper grown up, I can at least start by making sure I have a job that I can do long term."

"But are you sure you want to be a full-time roofer?"

Dean shrugged. "More than I want to be anything else. I love being outside and there's awesome views from multi-stories."

Julia shuddered. "Better you than me, I guess... Do you promise you're not just doing this for Ash?"

Dean hesitated, but he couldn't lie right to Julia's face. "I'm one hundred percent doing it for Ash."

"You shouldn't—"

"I know it's too late. I know she might go with that doctor donor." He swallowed, his chest and throat throbbing at the thought. "But even if she does, that doesn't mean she might not come back around. Maybe in a couple of years she'll look me up and I'll have money and a place of my own and she'll see that I'm ready for her. For us…"

Dean, realizing he was only a few more sad thoughts away from tears, stopped talking and stared out at the rain again.

Julia walked over to her deckchair and sat down, an odd expression on her face.

"What?" Dean asked.

"If Ash did have a baby with the doctor, you would be okay with that?"

Dean stared down at his feet. "It would hurt, but I know how much Ash wants to be a mum. I could see it when she was talking about having a baby in the café. If she doesn't have long, I want her to go for it."

Julia's odd expression intensified. "You mean that, don't you?"

"Yeah. Ash deserves to be happy, even if I'm not the one who can make it happen." He ducked his head so that Julia wouldn't see the way his eyes had gone all wet. There was a long, stretched out silence and then Julia began tapping her foot on the floor, hard and fast. "Dean, would you hate me if I did a complete one-eighty and said that I might be in favour of you and Ash being together?"

Dean looked up. With his vision as blurry as it was all he could see of Julia was a brownish smudge. "Are you serious?"

The smudge pointed at him. "Do you promise to stop aiming low? To get a proper job and save money?"

Dean's heart pounded in double time. "I promise."

"And do you vow to be as responsible and mature as you can be? Even if it's hard?"

"Yes."

"And you promise to never forget the kid in the backseat of your car and leave it there all day so it bakes like a meatloaf?"

"Of course I won't do that! I'll be the best, most responsible dad ever!" Dean got to his feet, then upon discovering he was well and truly stoned, sat down again. "Okay I'm high right now, but I swear to you Jules, if Ash will have me, I'll be the most amazing boyfriend and dad in the world. I'll change nappies, I'll give the baby milk from one of those little bottles. I'll put up *shitloads* of IKEA furniture without complaining once—"

"Okay." Julia held up a hand. "I've heard enough. I'm gonna help you win Ash over."

Dean punched the air.

"The only problem is the doctor... Now that he's on the scene being all smug and wealthy, shit is complicated."

Dean's good mood deflated slightly. "You think she'll agree to have him donate?"

"I don't know. Ash is kind of famous for making rash decisions, especially when she's upset. I'm worried she'll go all 'spur of the moment' and agree to have his baby."

"So what should I do?" Dean asked.

"Don't panic, ginger, I have a plan. Or at least, I will."

He watched as Julia pulled her tablet from nowhere and tapped frantically at the screen.

"What are you doing?"

"Compiling a strategy. What do you know about *Wuthering Heights*?"

"Is that a skyscraper?"

Julia grimaced. "We have some work to do, Dean. Sit tight."

12

Ash smiled at herself in the full-length mirror. Despite a solid hour of hair and makeup, she looked lacklustre, not to mention insincere as hell. She let her lips fall back to their resting place and saw a well-dressed miserable woman sulking back at her.

"It's not a date," she reminded her sorry reflection. "It's just a meeting about a baby. That is not a euphemism. Just relax."

After weeks of avoiding him, Nate had finally pinned her in one of the hallways at work and demanded to know if she was free to sit down and discuss his possible donorhood. Fully aware she had no plans, and panicky that another staff member would flash the gossip bat-signal, Ash agreed to have dinner with him on Saturday—just to discuss the potential baby and nowhere too expensive.

That evening Nate had texted her and told her he'd booked a table at Rockpool. Michelin starred, caviar, and champagne for days Rockpool. Ash wasn't born yesterday, she knew when a slutty man took you to an expensive as fuck restaurant, getting his dick damp was almost always a motivating factor. She didn't want to berate Nate over text but she would be making it clear over dinner that they had no romantic future. She also planned on bringing up vaginal tearing a lot. Nothing made men's boners go away like vaginal tearing.

Ash's phone buzzed and she checked it, her heart pounding with the hope that Nate had been called into work and needed to cancel their date.

Julia had messaged her.

Good luck with Resident DILF. I'd love to be on standby for cringe-worthy text updates, but Max is taking me to some restaurant where you cook your own tapas, so I may be too busy putting out fires to reply. Order the most expensive thing on the menu. Love you, Jules xxx.

Ash tucked her phone back into her bag. She was insanely jealous of her sister's plans. She didn't want to pay to cook her own food (what the fuck was that about?) but she'd have loved to have been the one about to enjoy a nice evening with a man she didn't suspect was trying to con her into bed under the guise of donating his sperm.

Her thoughts, as always, strayed back to a certain oversized redhead and she forcibly steered them away. She hadn't heard from Dean for almost a week. That made sense, seeing as she'd dumped him, but she couldn't get her head around the idea he was really gone. Some vain part of her was convinced that he'd come back, beg for another chance.

"Fat chance, narcissist," she told the mirror. "Now smile."

Her attempt was as bleak as it had been before. Giving it up as a bad job Ash checked her lipstick (MAC, Dark Deed), her clothes, and made sure she had her keys, wallet, and a spray deodorant that doubled as mace. She added a packet of tissues to her purse and yanked out the emergency condoms because fuck that. Her relationship with Nate's semen was always going to be strictly negotiated with a turkey baster. She straightened her shoulders and headed for the side door. She was just pressing it open when a noise on the other side of the house stopped her in her tracks. Someone was knocking on the front door. No one they knew knocked on their front door at her and Julia's requests. There was even a sign that said '*ring doorbell or be attacked by dogs.*' It was a little irrational but she and Jules had grown up with too many cops, social workers, and their mum's scumbag boyfriends visiting to respond to the sound of knuckles on wood with anything but panic. There was another loud knock and Ash's pulse spiked. She pulled out her car keys and held them in the universal grip like a knife. "I'm coming," she called

"Good."

It was a man at her door, his voice deep and stern. Ash's heart beat faster. She walked towards the front door, her heels clicking loudly against the floorboards. "If you're here to do any weird shit, you should know that my boyfriend's asleep in the other room and he's a…" she racked her brain for something scary "… Convicted sex offender."

Grimacing at her terrible lie, she swung the door open. Dean held out a brown paper bag and a small bunch of white flowers. "For you. By the way, I'm not a convicted sex offender."

Ash's memories hadn't done the man justice. She'd dreamed about him every night since Wide Open Road and yet she'd forgotten the contrast between his cheeky face and his beefed up body. Forgotten the bright brown of his eyes and the deep red of his hair, and the way his face was so fucking mischievous she wanted to shove it into a bucket of sand. Or her pussy.

Ash dropped her keys. "Dean? What are you doing here?"

"I was in the neighbourhood." He leaned in the doorjamb. "Is that what you're wearing on your date with the doctor? The same dress you wore when I first made you come?"

Ash looked down at her silver dress, then back at the man filling her doorway with his ridiculous torso. "What the—! Fuck off, Red!"

"No." Dean stepped into her house, closing the door behind him. "I can't believe you're wearing that same dress. I don't know who to feel sorry for, the doctor or me. Actually I feel sorrier for him. No one's gonna follow my act with anything but a worse performance."

Ash looked behind herself, half expecting to see a film crew eagerly recording her reaction. There was nothing there except ugly peach-coloured walls and a battered hatstand.

Jesus, he's going to see how gross this house is. This needs to end ASAP. She pulled herself up to her full height. "What are you doing here?"

Dean placed his flowers and his paper bag full of whatever-the-fuck on the floor then straightened up. "Are you wearing the same panties you wore the night we met too? That tiny little G-string I sucked on before I went down on you?"

"No—I mean, shut up!" Ash shoved Dean in the chest, ignoring the warmth that zapped up her wrists, ignoring her excitement and relief. "Seriously, I'm going to be late for dinner."

Dean's face hardened, the way it had in Wide Open Road. It was just as unexpectedly attractive as it had been that morning, transforming him from handsome to downright striking. "You still planning on going on your date with that prick doctor then?"

"What!? How do you even know about that?"

"Intuition. You know those flowers are jasmine. I finally figured out what your pussy smells like. Jasmine."

Ash slapped Dean in his stupidly buff chest. "*Your* pussy smells like jasmine. And where I go tonight is none of your business! We broke up, and it's not a date, it's a meeting about a baby, and what Nate and I decide—"

Dean gently seized her upper arms. "Don't say his name in front of me."

"Why not?"

"Because you're my girl." Dean's expression was deadly serious. "You've been my girl since I ate you out in that bathroom and I don't want you saying another man's name in front of me until you admit that."

Ash struggled to get out of his grip. "I am not your girl, Sherwood, you hysterical ginger psychopath, now go away."

"You know you don't want me to leave."

"Yes, I do," she sputtered.

"No, you don't." Dean stroked a thumb along her cheek. "You

want me to stay, don't you? You want me to kiss you. You want me to take you to bed and do all the things you like again."

"No," she lied.

"So if you hand me your phone I won't find the pictures I sent you? I won't find the texts? You'll be able to look me in the eye and tell me you haven't fucked yourself thinking about me? Haven't thought about the two of us having a cute little baby together?"

"I..."

Dean pulled her into his arms, surrounding her with his peppery warmth. "That's what I thought. Well, you're in luck. You don't have to deny it anymore. I'm here. I fucking missed you. I'd fucking do anything to make you feel good. Let me make love to you again and I'll show you we're meant to be together."

Ash's traitorous body quivered. "Dean, I can't. This isn't right. I didn't ask you to come here."

"You didn't ask me because you were scared of how much you like me. And you know what? You had every right to be scared." Dean bent his mouth to her ear. "But you don't have to be scared anymore, baby, I promise. You don't have to worry about whether or not I'm good enough for you. I am, and I plan on staying that way."

"But—"

He reached down and pressed a wrist across her ass, lifting her as easily as if she was a child. "I started my apprenticeship this week. I sold my Kawasaki and now I have seven grand in the bank. I know how to make carbonara. I burned it a bit on the bottom, but Julia said it was still pretty good."

"Red, what the hell is going on here?"

Dean pressed her against the hallway wall, the plaster cool against her skin. "I'm seducing you so you don't go on your date. Thought that was kind of obvious."

"But—"

"I missed you so bad, Ash." Dean nuzzled her neck. "I've missed the way your skin smells. I've been hurting every single day thinking about you. Nothing makes it better, not pictures, not memories, not alcohol, not porn. I've been fucking *aching* for you, day and night."

I've been aching too, Ash thought. *I've been so fucking lonely.* "You shouldn't be here."

"I should." Dean pressed his hips against hers, letting her feel what was waiting between his legs.

Before she could stop herself, Ash let out an embarrassing moan. "And just what do you think you're gonna do with that?"

He smirked. "Well, I was thinking I'd let you ride it. Lie back with my hands behind my head and watch you work your little pussy on me."

Ash's mouth fell open. "Oh you were, *were you?*"

"Yeah." Dean angled his hips so that the thick denim of his jeans was firm against her hips. "If you ask me nicely. And you promise to suck me clean afterwards."

"And why the hell would I do that?"

"Because I'm in the mood to be taken care of, Ashley. I drove all the way down here knowing you were getting ready to go on a date with another man. Imagine if you knew I was getting ready to go on a date with some other woman?"

Ash couldn't stop her eyes from narrowing.

"Exactly. Now that I'm here, the least you can do is suck my cock."

Ash swallowed. When she pictured Dean returning to her, and she was woman enough to admit she'd pictured it, he'd always been begging on bended knee. Yet the whole 'me-Tarzan, you-Jane' thing, it was kind of making her hot. Which was not cool. "You don't just get to barge back into my life and demand a blowjob, Red. I don't want to fuck you right now."

Dean let out a pained chuckle. "I know you're proud, babe, but don't lie to me and say you don't want it. You've been grinding against my jeans ever since I put you on this wall."

Ash stopped moving at once. Instantly her body burned with suppressed arousal. "I hate how horny you make me."

Dean grinned. "No, you don't."

He bent forward, his mouth millimetres from hers. "Kiss me. If you want me to leave I will. But if you can feel it, if you want this, too, then fucking kiss me and put us both out of our misery."

Ash paused, each second scraping over her skin like an uncut diamond, and then she remembered how it used to feel to be worshiped and taken and pleasured by this man, remembered how easy her days were when she had him to talk to and she kissed him.

Dean's lips were hot and firm, spreading warmth through her as surely as if they were made of whiskey. He pressed his body flush against her and kissed her back, sliding his tongue, wet and firm against her own. Arousal exploded in the pit of Ash's belly. She hooked her legs around Dean's hips and rubbed against him in earnest. She'd refused to touch Eric in the days that followed Wide Open Road, refused to do so much as play with herself, not wanting the memories of Dean and with them, the pain, to resurface. Now her deprivation was making itself known.

Dean chuckled into her neck. "Yeah, you've been missing me, haven't you? Missing what I can do to your body?"

Ash moaned her agreement.

"Good girl. Well, don't worry, babe, we're gonna get you taken care of."

Dean slid his tongue back into her mouth as his hands inspected the state of her braless tits. Ash was ashamed to say she didn't put up so much as one second worth of resistance. They made out until her head was spinning and her underwear was damp. Until all she could think about was having Dean's boyfriend cock again. "Red, I need you."

His responding grin was unbearably smug. "I know, beautiful, but before we get down to it, you're gonna call your doctor and tell him you're not going out to dinner, you're going to stay here and sit on my cock instead."

Goosebumps raced down Ashley's spine. "I can't do that."

"Call your doctor or sit on my cock?"

"Either."

"Oh, don't be like that." Dean took her earlobe between his teeth, his hands gently massaging her breasts. "Do you want me to call your doctor and tell him he's never gonna lay a hand on your tight little body? I don't think that's a good idea, but I'll do it."

"Nate... Didn't want to sleep with me..."

"He did." Dean stroked his thumbs across her nipples. "But that's fine, Ashley, because he never will. Maybe you can suck my cock while I call him and tell him that fact? Would you like that?"

Ash imagined herself on her knees, sucking Dean as he talked to Nate.

"You hear that?" She imagined Dean saying, as he held his phone to his groin. *"That's why she's not coming to dinner, fuckhead. She's got better things to take care of."*

"You thinking bad thoughts?" Dean asked as he applied slow, sucking kisses to her collarbones. "You picturing me calling him while you lick my cock?"

She flushed, embarrassed to be found out so easily. "No."

Dean chuckled. "Liar. What do you say? I'll call him if you want me to, tell him you belong to me and that any babies you have are gonna get fucked into you by me."

Ash shivered. "What's with the He-Man act? I thought you were a sub."

She felt him smile into her collarbone.

"I am. But tonight I feel like being a fucking pig." He squeezed her breasts as though willing her to believe it. "Now are you gonna call the doctor or just let him sit by himself in Rockpool all night?"

Julia must have told him about her date, but had she done it because she'd reconsidered her position on Dean or had he swindled the information out of her? She licked her dry lips. "What's in the bag you brought?"

Dean smiled. Not a shit-eating smirk but his usual smile, so sweet it damn near gave her heart diabetes. "Salt and vinegar chips, Stone's Ginger Wine, and a massive bag of Skittles."

She couldn't help but laugh. "Julia."

"Julia," Dean confirmed. "She uh, changed her mind about me. Thinks we'd be pretty great together, apparently. As long as I promise to stop being such a clown about money."

Before Ash could process what this meant on any level, a familiar humming noise reached her ears. Her phone was vibrating, and she knew without a doubt who was calling. Apparently, Dean knew it, too, because he put her down, scooped up her bag and fished out her phone. Ash was instantly light-headed with fear. "No!"

"Don't worry, I'm not going to answer it." He got down on his knees in front of her. "You are."

"Huh?"

Dean held up the phone and she saw '*Nate Huxley*' flashing on the screen. "Go on, rebel, tell him you're not coming to dinner."

Unsure what else to do Ash took the phone and answered it. "Hello?"

"*Hello, Ashley. Getting ready to come meet me?*"

Dean's reason for handing her the phone instantly became clear. He shuffled forward and seized the hem of her skirt. His gaze was fixed on hers and he raised an eyebrow as if to say 'wanna stop me?'

Ash gave him the finger. "Um, Nate about tonight—"

"*Excited? You should be, I heard the new chef is amazing. Anyway, I was calling because—*"

"Are you fucking kidding me?" Dean snarled.

Ash felt a thrill—not quite fear, but close—rattle through her. She knew exactly what had shocked him. Her hem was level with her hips and Dean was eye-to-eye with her very bare pussy. She muted her phone. "It's not what you think—"

"No panties. You were gonna wear no fucking panties to dinner with that asshole?" Dean's jaw was so tight Ash was amazed he could talk.

"It wasn't—"

He leaned forward and licked a long wet line through her labia. She cried out in shock and unexpected pleasure. "Red!"

Her lovers' eyes glowed hot as coals. "It's Dean, Ashley. You call me Red like I'm your fucking teddy bear and there is nothing cuddly about how I feel right now." He licked her again, penetrating her lips and flicking his tongue over her clit. "You better get back on that phone and tell Doctor Fuckface you're not going to dinner or I'm going to get angry."

"I'm sorry, but—"

"Fuck sorry. You're gonna cancel that date and then I'm gonna put you on your back and fuck your pussy until I don't feel pissed off anymore. I can tell you, it's gonna take a good long fucking time. Now hurry up and tell him you're not coming before I do something totally fucking uncalled for."

Before Ash knew what she was doing, she'd hit the answer button and brought her phone to her ear. "Um, hello, again?"

"Ashley? Why did you do that? Is something wrong?"

"Ah, no."

Dean bent forward and applied a sharp suckling pressure on her clit. Pleasure blared through her pussy like a punk song played at high volume. Ash clenched her teeth to keep from screaming, but evidently she made some kind of noise because Nate barked, *"I mean it, are you okay?"*

"I'm, uh, fine." Ash stammered. "What's up with you?"

"I'm calling about tonight. You remember our date?"

Dean unglued his tongue from her pussy. "Yeah Ashley, you know, the date that isn't a date because it was just a meeting about a baby?"

"Shut up," she hissed.

"Did you just tell me to shut up?" Nate sounded indignant, borderline angry.

"No! I just—wait, why did you call me?"

"Because he wants what I've got." Dean muttered, tongue laving at her clit. "Because he wants to be where I am right now. Tasting your pussy, smelling it, rubbing it all over his face."

Ash bit back another moan before realising Nate was talking. "Sorry, uh what was that?"

"I said I called because you're driving into Melbourne tonight, aren't you?"

"Yes," Ash said dreamily. Dean was rolling his tongue around her clit with such precision he could have been a groupie for the Rolling Stones. He was so fucking good at this. How had she forgotten how good he was at this?

"You have that flash car, don't you?" Nate inquired.

"Oh. Oh yes."

"Well, I thought you wouldn't want to park it on the street where it could get stolen and the paid towers are so expensive. I think you should drop your car off at my place, and we'll head into Rockpool together in a cab. Is that okay with you?"

Dimly, Ash understood what Nate was trying to do. He was trying to impound her car in his building so they'd have to go back to his house after dinner where no doubt offers of nightcaps and kisses would be made. She'd be put in the unpleasant option of either making out with a colleague or rejecting him and risking losing the donor sperm, not to mention the money Nate was promising. Ash knew she should be angry, but it was hard to get angry when Dean's mouth was between her legs sucking her orgasm to the surface like a long-submerged treasure chest.

"Ashley?" Nate snapped. *"Are you listening to me?"*

Shit, she needed to abort mission *'orgasm standing up'* and address mission *'refusing to be trapped in a cab with Nate.'* "Sorry… Uh, I can't make it tonight."

There was a long, tense moment of silence, punctuated only by soft sucking noises Ash prayed to God Nate couldn't hear.

"You can't make it. I see. Are you going to tell me why?"

If Nate had sounded disappointed, Ashley would have felt awful, but his voice was tight and authoritative, as though she were cancelling a shift at work when he really needed her on staff. "I'm not feeling well," she told him.

"And after I went to all the trouble of getting a reservation at Rockpool, you couldn't have told me sooner?"

"I didn't ask you to get a reservation at Rockpool. In fact, I specifically requested you not book somewhere expensive for us to talk."

She could practically hear Nate rolling his eyes. *"You know I would have paid."*

"Well, that's not the—"

Dean's tongue slipped back inside her, curling upward in that uncanny ability he had to seek out her sweet spots. Ash bit her cheeks so hard she tasted blood.

"Yes?"

"I'm sorry. About cancelling."

"It's fine," Nate said in his lofty doctor-knows-best voice. *"I just would have expected better from you, Ashley."*

Dean's mouth left her pussy. "Same here, *Ashley*. Now, your pussy's nice and prepped, how would you like to get started on something else?"

"I...?"

"Great, glad to hear it." Dean stood up, easing his hefty cock out of his unzipped jeans with a groan. "That feels good. Not as good as it's gonna feel though. Bend over. Hands against the wall."

"No!" Ash held her phone at arm's length, as far from her mouth as possible. "We can't!"

Dean pulled a condom from his pocket. "Oh, we can and we will, Little Miss No Panties. Now bend. The fuck. Over."

And maybe Ash was high on some airborne bath salts because she found herself moving to the hallway wall pressing a palm against it and bending over.

"That's nice," Dean growled behind her. "Keep that phone up to your ear though. I don't want you to miss a thing the good doctor's telling you."

Ash raised the phone back up to her ear. She was sure Nate would have hung up but to her amazement, he was still yammering away. *"...I'm beginning to think you're not serious about becoming a mother. When we first spoke, you were all ears, but then you started avoiding me at work and now you're ditching me three hours before our date..."*

Dean's work-roughened hands gripped her hips, yanking her back into the cradle of his groin. "You ready for me?"

Ash cupped her hand over her phone speaker. "We can't do this!"

"Yeah, we can." Dean tugged the hem of her skirt up, exposing her pussy to the cool air. "Scream if you want. I don't care if the doctor can hear. Fuck it, he can come down and watch. Closest he'll ever come to ever getting his hands on you."

"But—"

"Ashley, are you listening to me?" Nate snapped.

"Um yeah. Yes. Please, keep going."

"Well, it seems to me that if you ever want to have a baby..."

The broad head of Dean's cock pressed against her. "Last chance, Ash. Tell me to stop, or I'm gonna fuck you while this prick listens."

Ash hesitated. Talking to Nate while Dean banged her from behind was wrong. Except, well... Was it so wrong? It didn't feel wrong, it felt like vindication. It felt fucking hot. She kept her mouth closed, knowing Dean, with his seemingly infinite understanding of her feelings, would know what that meant.

"Okay," he muttered. "Here we fuckin' go."

She bit back a whimper as he pressed the head of his boyfriend cock inside her.

"Fuck," he groaned. "You're even tighter than I fuckin' remember."

She heard him spit in his hand, felt him wet them both down with his saliva and the obscenity of it made the damp flesh between her legs clench. He eased his way inside her slowly, gentle in spite of his rough words, and began thrusting into her at a slow, delicious pace.

"Ashley, are you there?"

"Talk to him." Dean slid forked fingers over her pussy, pressing a finger on either side of her clit and plumping up the sensitive tissues between. "Talk, or he'll know you're not paying attention. I want him to think you're paying attention, *Ashley*."

Ash obligingly returned the phone to her ear. "I'm—I'm listening, Nate."

"Good, because I know that you work as hard as I do but I don't think you understand the hours you have to put in so that you can..."

"Imagine having to listen to that all night," Dean crooned in her ear. "Me, me, me, me, me. Aren't you glad I'm here? Taking care of you? Stopping you from going on that date?"

Ashley chewed her cheeks, trying to keep herself making a sound. This was so hot. This was so *wrong*.

"That doctor can't take care of you," Dean muttered as his prick worked in and out of her most intimate place. "You're just some woman he can get something out of. Pussy tonight, a baby down the road, it's all the fucking same to him."

He rubbed the fingers straddling her clit in a way that made her legs shake. "Feel that? I know what you like. I know who you are. Admit you're mine and I'll spend the rest of my life pleasuring the fuck out of you."

In the tiny part of her brain that wasn't stoned on sex, Ash knew Dean wasn't just talking dirty, he was petitioning her to choose him over Nate while he fucked her. "Dean—"

"Shh," he whispered. "Be quiet and feel me. Feel how good I am for you, Ash."

She moaned in protest but was entirely too close to orgasm to do anything of substance. A dirty, vain part of her didn't want it to end and Dean knew it. He fucked her harder, his balls slapping against her sensitive flesh. This wasn't making love or even sex; this was fucking, pure animalistic possession. A man claiming a woman with his flesh.

Ash pictured Dean doing this without a condom, filling her with his bare cock and her inevitable climax swirled between her legs.

"... *The owner's a friend of mine,*" Nate burbled in her ear. "*That's how I got the table. He won't be happy when he hears you're not coming...*"

"But you *are* coming, aren't you, Ash?" Dean's fingers pressed harder against her cunt, making pleasure whorl like fire. "You're coming all over my cock."

Ash bit the inside of her arm as Dean thrust deep inside her. Her legs were spasming, she could feel sweat beading all over her back.

"Yeah, there it is," Dean muttered. "There's your fucking orgasm. Come on me, sweetheart. Let go, right now."

"*Ashley.*" Nate snapped. "*Is there a man there with you?*"

"It's just... A labourer," she whimpered, barely conscious of what she was saying. "I needed some... Stuff done around the house."

Dean strummed her like a stringless guitar, his cock pumping hard. "You mean like your pussy? Is that what you needed a man for, *Ashley*?"

Nate sniffed in her ear. "*You have a labourer at your house on a Saturday night?*"

"He works late," Ash breathed. "All hours."

"Fuck yeah, I do." Dean ground his hips into her ass. "Come on honey, feel me. Come on my big fat cock."

She closed her eyes, feeling him, feeling herself. She was so close; she was so close.

"Ashley." Nate's voice was high. *Strained. "Are you... Are you having sex?"*

Everything seemed to stop. Ash became acutely, horribly aware of her hands, one splayed against the wall, the other holding the phone a few inches from her mouth. She was conscious of the sweat beading on her neck and lower back, and most of all, the feel of Dean's cock dragging in and out of her, the sound of his hips slamming into her ass. Mortification flared inside her like a nuclear explosion and she hung up without another word. She turned to look at Dean for the first time since he'd started fucking her. Her lover's cheeks were as red as his hair but from exertion, not embarrassment. He smirked. "Guess that's that, then?"

Ash glared at him. "You think you're pretty smart, huh?"

Dean pretended to consider the question as he rolled his hips against her ass. "I guess I am inside you right now and I ruined your little fucking date, so yeah I do think I'm pretty smart baby. Now, how about that fucking orgasm?"

"You..." Ash was so furious and happy and embarrassed and horny she couldn't even spit out his name. "Are a cockhead of the highest caliber."

Dean shook his head. "If I was a cockhead of the highest caliber I'd fuck you bare right now."

Ash's heart all but stopped. "You would?"

"Yep. Fill you up with my come, put my baby between your legs. Make sure that doctor never has a chance." Dean fixed her with a mean, unblinking stare. "That what you want? Don't tempt me if it isn't, because I've been picturing riding you bareback for weeks now and if you keep looking at me like that, I'll fucking do it."

Ash swallowed, her throat thick and sore. "How-how am I looking at you?"

"Like you want my come." Dean began pumping into her so hard

Ash had to cushion her forehead with her wrist. "Do you, Ash? Do you want my bare dick inside you? You want me to get you pregnant?"

Ash moaned. "I-I don't know."

"Then stop looking at me. Turn back and face the wall. I've laid awake nights thinking about riding you raw, coming inside you, giving you my baby. Don't look at me and say you don't know if you want it."

Ash closed her eyes, but she could still see Dean's cock buried between her legs, she imagined it without the condom, imagined him grunting then pulling away, leaving a rivulet of white running down her thighs. Her body prickled with sweat and suddenly all she could feel was the latex sheath that separated them. "Take the condom off."

"You don't mean that, right?" It was the first sign of hesitance Dean had shown since he'd rocked up on her doorstep with flowers, Skittles, and a condom.

"I do mean it," Ash said.

"But... Are you sure?"

Ash gave a strangled laugh. "You showed up at my house and screwed me while I was on the phone with another man. Don't check your moral compass now Dean, I was having so much fun."

Dean paused, then slipped out of her. There was a snap and then Ash heard the condom hit the floor.

"Ash, baby..." Dean braced his hands on her hips. "I want to be your good time. I wanna make you come, but before we do this, you gotta know how I feel, what I want—"

Ash reached back and looked him in the eyes. "I already know, Red. And so do you. Now fuck me."

Dean's smile was a thing of beauty, sweet mischief fading back into the furious cruelty of the man who'd told her Nate could watch him fuck her for all he cared. He pressed his bare cock to her pussy and the sensation was startling. Hot and slick and raw. It shouldn't have made so much of a difference but it did. Ash threw her head back, resting it along Dean's shoulder. "Yes. More."

When he returned to where he was they both groaned. Dean set a brutal pace, one neither of them could sustain for long. His hand returned to her clit and this time he didn't stroke, just pressed hard against the tender nub, making her cunt feel like it was full of starbursts.

"Gonna give you my baby," he vowed. "Big redhead like me. See how your doctor likes that."

"Dean," Ash said, almost terrified that she wasn't going to finish in time. "Dean!"

"Yeah, I feel it, too. Don't worry, I'm gonna hold out till you come then I'm gonna unload inside you. I'm gonna get you pregnant. Let the world see you're mine, that I fucked you and gave you the thing you wanted most."

It was the taboo of it. When he came, when his wet heat filled her, Ash came as well, scrabbling her nails against the wall, thinking of nothing. Numb to all but the pleasure racking through her body.

Boyfriend cock, she thought dumbly. *Old faithful. Dear God, I hope I'm pregnant.*

13

The sun was rising through the bedroom window and Ash was splayed all over him, toes hooked around his calves, face pressed against his chest, as though determined to take his body heat as well as all of his energy. He'd woken up to find her like that, and though he was a little warm and uncomfortable, he never wanted her to move.

I love you, he thought, trailing a finger down her spine. *You can take anything you want from me.* The night before had passed in the best kind of blur: manic bouts of sex interspersed with fistfuls of Skittles, chips and pillow talk. They'd kept the ginger wine by the bed, taking swallows as they changed positions. In the early hours of the morning, he'd gone down on her with a small amount in his mouth, letting the alcohol trickle into her folds as he licked. Ash grew squirmier and squirmier, before screaming so loudly Dean asked if he should stop. Her response had been to wrap her legs around his neck and demand he keep going.

"We just sort of did figging," she said once they were done.

"What the hell is that?"

Ash giggled. "When you shove a lump of raw ginger up your butt and it kind of burns and feels good at the same time."

"That's a thing?"

She nodded. "The trick is not to go too small. I found out about it when a guy came into the emergency ward at Fern Creek Hospital screaming his head off. He'd lost a piece inside himself, and he was convinced his butt was going to be on fire forever."

They'd both laughed hysterically, then Ash had sucked his cock back to life and rode him. As he came for what felt like the millionth time, it seemed to Dean that he was stoned. Stoned on pussy and wine and pure, uncut joy. They'd fallen asleep at God knew what hour, exhausted and sticky, covered in bodily fluids and crumbs. He loved that she hadn't wanted to shower afterward like she thought their reunion orgy was too good to wash away, too.

Dean studied Ashley in the morning light. She had reddish marks on her neck, shoulders, and chest where he'd sucked and scraped her skin until it bruised. He was sure she had the same marks between her legs. It made him wince a little to see it. He wasn't usually the hickey type, but last night the need to mark Ash in some tangible, physical way had been undeniable.

With a throb of arousal, he remembered that hickeys weren't the only mark he'd left on her. He'd taken her bareback all night, come inside her more times than he could remember, and the experience had been... Something else. He'd had condomless sex with exes and a couple of stupid incidents when he was younger, but never with the possibility, no *the hope*, of a baby hanging in mid-air.

Dean had never thought the idea of getting someone pregnant could be a turn on. He'd kind of always thought that would be the worst thing that could come out of him getting laid, but it had well and truly fired him up to think that he might be putting his child inside the most beautiful woman he'd ever known. It was sexy in a caveman kind of way. In fact, when you thought about it, the whole baby thing was kind of wild. He and Ashley, blending their genetic material together to create a whole other person. A half-Ash half-Dean hybrid. It was almost like magic.

"Dean..." Ash mumbled into his chest. "Dean?"

"Right here, babe, being your pillow. And blanket. And sex toy."

Ash raised her head and smiled. "Hey."

"Do you need anything?"

She shook her head in adorable lethargy. "Are you staying?"

"'Course." He stroked her upper arm. "Go on, fall back asleep on me. I've got nowhere to be."

Instead, her eyes fluttered open, and even in the semi-darkness, Dean could see they were full of uncertainty. "Is everything okay, babe?"

"Why?" Ash whispered. "Why did you come here last night?"

Dean swallowed. He could cop out, say he'd just been jealous or make up some dumb lie but the truth was he'd been planning his return to her life since that day on the porch with Julia. He didn't want to lie. "I missed you, Ashy. I came because you're all I want. Ever since I first saw you, you're all I want. And I had a feeling maybe you wanted me too."

"Hmm." Ash snuggled back into his body. "Your chest hair is really soft."

Dean cupped her head with his palm. "Thanks."

"And I do want you. I always wanted you. I just... I don't know."

Dean stroked her hair, loving the way her eyes slid shut like she was a cat exalting in her owner's touch. "Sleep, babe. We'll talk after."

"Mmmfkay."

It had been Julia's idea for him to turn up at the house and stop Ash from going on her date. He'd thought showing up unannounced was weird, borderline stalker behaviour but Julia, pacing the deck of Max's house like an admiral, disagreed.

"Ash likes the fuck out of you, but she's stubborn. If you call she won't answer. If you text, she won't reply. You need to give her a few days to stew in how much she fucked up and then *pow*, you're right in front of her, a manifestation of ginger beauty."

"Ginger beauty?"

"That's what she said about you. I feel bad for fucking up your relationship so I'm throwing you a compliment bone."

"Oh." Dean blinked. "Thanks, I guess."

"So, you show up at our house, I'll give you the address, BTdubs, and then you look her dead in the face and say *'You're my woman, Ash! Get used to it!'* She pointed at Dean like an Uncle Sam poster.

"Um, are you sure that's a good idea? To show up and be a dick?"

Julia rolled her eyes. "Dean, do you know anything about women? Romance? The male-female dynamic?"

"Are you asking me if I know how to fuck?"

Julia made a gagging sound. "Eww, shut up. No. I mean that if you go to Ash with the same, babyish 'please like me' crap you're currently selling, it will go down like a ton of bricks. There is nothing sexy about men pouting. Unless they're holding puppies. And I don't know anyone we can borrow a puppy from."

"Then what—"

"You need to be bold." Julia touched her thumb and forefinger together and shook the circle in his direction. "You need to be assertive. You need to show up at our house and *demand* Ash admit she likes you and wants to have your baby."

Dean raised an eyebrow. "I'm not the sharpest guy in the world, but I kinda think Ash isn't a woman you approach that way. Not if you want a functioning set of family jewels. Which I do, because of the whole baby thing."

"Normally you'd be right, but Ash likes you, so you coming at her and being all bossy is different."

"How?"

"This brings us to *Wuthering Heights*, the Tom Hardy version of which we will be watching later. For now, you just need to know that Heathcliff, the main guy, is a cockhead. Just a massive dick. He's rude, super jealous, and ridiculously possessive. He's basically evil. His only redeeming factor is that he's in love with Cathy, she's the main chick."

"And what does that have to do with me?" Dean asked, concerned Julia was going to draw some parallel between him being a dimwit whose only redeeming factor was being in love with Ash.

"Women, my sister included, have been swooning over Heathcliff for hundreds of years. Not because they want to be controlled by some insane guy who's eventually going to dig up your skeleton and make out with it—"

"What!?"

Jules flapped a hand at him. "Sorry, spoiler alert. My point is that sometimes women find men being bossy bastards sexy. You know how I like romance novels?"

"Uh..." Dean had heard Max talk about Julia liking romance novels, mostly in the context of *'they get her so fucking wet, I want to PayPal Tessa Bailey a hundred bucks to say thank you'* sort of thing. Mentioning that didn't seem appropriate, especially now he was trying to convince her sister to fall in love with and be impregnated by him. "Kind of."

"Well, I like them," Julia continued. "And here's the interesting thing. Most of the heroes are like tortured bikers or millionaires who are convinced they're gonna die alone despite the swathes of pussy they're wading through. They're just the whole gauntlet of brooding assholes, like Heathcliff. And women clearly like that because they're pretty much the only ones writing and reading this stuff."

Dean raised his eyebrows. "That *is* interesting."

"Right? Even though a girl with a shred of self-preservation wouldn't want to be with a brooding ultra-jealous asshole IRL, it's a fun fantasy, being obsessed over, being a possession, having a guy take control of you and tell you that you belong to him. Most people find a way to incorporate the fantasy into their chilled out, normal everyday relationships."

"They do?"

"Sure. It's like when Max got jealous of the guy who kept drawing pictures of me at work, and he showed up at my office one day and dragged me into—" She broke off, blushing furiously.

Dean cleared his throat. "I uh, get what you're saying. Ash would like me being a jerk in this one, specific way."

Julia looked relieved. "Right. That's what I'm saying. Ash is a capable, assertive woman, and she doesn't take shit from anyone, but that's not what showing up and being all commanding is about."

Dean had squinted out at the rainy backyard. "I don't know, Jules.

I'm not a confrontation kinda guy. Unless people try to cut in front of me at Maccas, and even then I just ask them to go to the back of the line."

"Oh yeah?" Julia seized her tablet and began tapping away. "You think you're non-confrontational, huh? We'll see about that."

Dean waited nervously as Julia found whatever she wanted to find. "You're not gonna show me anything fucked up, are you?"

"Yes, but it's for your own good. This—" she held up her tablet, "—is the doctor who wants to help Ashley have a baby."

Dean saw a shirtless guy standing on a yacht. His hair was an enviable light brown and he was perfectly tanned with a grin whiter than the full moon. Jealousy pumped through his blood like lava. Until he saw the picture, he'd been quietly imagining the doctor as some saggy old man who couldn't convince anyone to have kids with him. "That's the fucking guy?"

"It sure is, and if you ask me, he's interested in a lot more than being Ash's donor." Julia swiped through the pictures, showing the doctor with his arm wrapped around a series of beautiful blondes. "She is entirely his type, my man, and from what I've been reading, he wants to fuck her. He messaged a mate of his saying Ash was a 'mint bitch' who is 'gagging for his spoof.'"

Dean ground his teeth hard enough to make a noise. "Hang on, how do you know what he's been telling his mates?"

The tablet vanished beneath Julia's hoodie. "Never you mind."

"Jules…"

"It's not technically illegal."

"Jules!"

She made a face. "Don't say anything to Max. Look, focus up here Sherwood. Imagine Ash going on a romantic candlelit dinner with this doctor pervert followed by some light humping, in which he takes off the condom and tries to get her pregnant the old fashioned way. What does that make you want to do?"

Dean's fists balled against his sides. *Kill him. Kick his pretty boy face in, then fuck Ashley on his unconscious body.*

Julia cocked her head at him. "That's what I thought. Just show up at our house looking like that and all will be well."

With some effort Dean managed to uncurl his fists. "You mean it? Ash will like it? Me being all jealous and pissed off?"

"Oh, she'll like it. Just do what comes naturally. Now let's go watch *Wuthering Heights*. Talking about you and Ash that way makes me feel all wrong inside."

As he lay tangled in Ashley's sheets, Dean knew Jules had been right. The instant he'd seen Ash standing in her hallway in the silver dress she'd worn the night they met, every rational thought had flown out of his head. He hadn't tried to be a bossy dick, he just kind of *became one* for a little while and she had liked it. Though he hoped he'd never have to convince Ash to be with him the way he had last night, he wouldn't mind busting out the alpha bastard act again. Considering he'd always thought of himself as belonging on the other end of the BDSM spectrum, it was surprising how easy it had been.

Then again, the man he was in his fantasies wasn't a pushover. He was a sucker for the hot princess, obliging and a bit pathetic, but he was mostly getting off on fucking some other man's woman. Whether he liked it or not Ash's doctor had been roped into their games last night. He'd played the idiot prince, unaware his girl was fucking a lowlife because she couldn't get what she needed from him. Maybe Dean was an asshole and a pig, but he'd enjoyed every last second of making that prick listen to him fuck Ash.

Shit, Dean thought as he tucked his hands under his head. *My jerk-off fantasies are kinda fuckin' obnoxious.*

Suddenly Ash rolled off his chest, curling into her side. "Give it back, Amanda. I told you to fuck off."

Dean smiled. To be fair, she had warned him she talked in her sleep. He rubbed her shoulders until she quieted down and her breathing returned to normal. This was exactly what he wanted. His fantasies, their awesome sex, it didn't hold a candle to just being with her. Having her fall asleep on top of him, sharing food with her and being able to laugh about guys who got ginger stuck inside themselves. What Dean wanted, what he'd come here for was Ash, real world Ash.

The thought made him sit bolt upright. What was he doing lying around in bed? He should be up, making breakfast, or coffee, doing something to prove to Ash she could come to him for all her household as well as cuddle and dick related needs. He kissed her on the back of the head. "Be back soon, beautiful."

He tugged on his boxers and made a pit stop in the hideous slime green bathroom. He knew it was ugly last night, but seeing it the bright morning light it was something else. The sink was cracked, the shower was a bathtub/rubber curtain deal and the knobs on the hot and cold taps were lumps of fake crystal. It made the labourer in him want to cry.

He'd always thought Julia was exaggerating about their house being a shitheap, but now that he'd seen it with his own eyes, Dean had to agree. If anything she'd undersold it. It was a hole. Just a big ol' hole full of mission brown tiles and orangey-pink walls, frosted windows and pine floorboards that looked like a bear had been set loose on them. The kitchen was a little better, still ugly and old, but clean. Dean got himself a glass of water from the sink and stared out at the backyard. It was a mini desert wasteland, with weeds and random bits of crap everywhere—sun-bleached Frisbees, a bicycle pump, a garden gnome with its face broken off.

Ash didn't belong in this mausoleum of splintery nightmares. She belonged in a bright white three-bedroom like the one Max owned. Marble kitchen counter, stainless steel dishwasher, backyard with rosebushes and a trampoline. Dean understood she'd inherited the place from her grandma, and it was all she could afford, but how could this be the place where she'd raise her child? Possibly *their* child.

At least she's got a house, a nasty part of his brain reminded him. *What the hell do you have dickhead?*

That was a good point, even if it depressed him. He was subletting off Max, and in no position to judge. The doctor, on the other hand, had offered Ash four hundred thousand bucks. He'd thrown her a life vest, and Dean had slapped it out of Ash's hands with no way to replicate or improve the deal.

"Settle down," he told himself as anxiety built in his chest. "Breakfast first, then figure out what you'll do with the house and kid and everything else."

After a dinner of wine, skittles, and pussy it was hardly surprising he was starving his ass off. He examined the orange cupboards but couldn't see anything worth making into anything else—not bread for toast or eggs for omelettes. There were instant soups, but he kind of doubted Ash wanted to drink powdered laksa for breakfast.

The smart thing to do would be to head out and pick something up, but he wasn't sure the shops in a small country town were open on Sundays. As he stood there, contemplating his next move, he heard a plaintive whine from the kitchen door, which was painted a dull rubbish bin black. Dean opened it to find three dogs blinking up at him.

"Hi!" he said as if they were people arriving unexpectedly on his doorstep.

The dogs examined him politely. There was an ancient Labrador, a Jack Russell with a crooked tail, and a Greyhound. None of them seemed aggressive, so Dean crouched down and let them sniff his hands. The Labrador and the Jack Russell gave him a few snuffles then lost interest and padded off, but the Greyhound stayed, pressing its sleek grey body against Dean's palms, demanding pats.

Dean obliged at once. He'd always loved dogs, but after Earl had died, his dad had never let him get another one. Maybe the Greyhound could sense his need to make up for lost time because it wriggled into his arms and started licking his face.

"Who's a good girl? Or boy? Are you a boy?" Dean paused, then decided against examining the dogs' swimsuit area for answers. He resumed scratching under its chin. "I don't know if you're a boy or a girl, but you're definitely very good."

"Girl," came a soft voice from behind him. "Bongo's a girl. The other two, George and Spanner, are boys."

Dean turned to see Ash looked tousle-haired and gorgeous in a neon green kimono. Dean could hardly believe they'd spent the night making love. "You're up, I was uh, gonna try and make breakfast."

"You don't need to do that. Especially since you're already busy dog-sitting."

Dean rubbed the Greyhounds' silky ears, glad for something to do with his hands. "She's a sweet dog. Are they allowed inside?"

"Not anymore, I stopped once Julia started spending more time at Max's place. She was the one who was obsessed with snuggling a million animals at once. Plus, I thought with a baby…"

Ash blushed like she was also suddenly thinking about him pounding into her bareback, vowing to get her pregnant. *Stop patting the dog and find out, moron.*

Dean gave the Greyhound one last cuddle and nudged her out of the door. "About breakfast, I could head into town and get some food if you want? Or a coffee?"

"You'd do that?" Ash asked, with an endearing amount of skepticism.

"Sure. You look beautiful, by the way."

Ash smiled the paper-thin smile he'd come to associate with her tension. "Thanks, but I feel kind of gross. I'm gonna wash up."

"Oh," he said stupidly.

"I'd offer for you to join me, but it's tiny and I'm pretty sure you'd slip over and die."

Dean's guts turned to ice. "Ash, do you…? Do you want me to leave?"

To his relief, she shook her head. "Sorry if I'm being weird. It just, it's kind of embarrassing to have you in this house…" She gestured around at the cramped room. "It's pretty rank. Nothing like Max's house."

Dean crossed his fingers behind his back. "You live here, so I think it's the best place in the world."

Ash smiled wide enough to expose the gap in her teeth. "You're a liar, Red, but thanks." She moved over to the kettle. "Tea?"

"Sure. You know, if you and Jules hate this house so much, why don't you sell it?"

"We can't. A guy killed his wife in the bathroom. Makes for shitty real estate press. Plus the whole house needs a tonne of work. One real estate agent said we'd be better off burning it down and starting all over again."

"Seems a bit harsh."

"He was right. My grandma, the one who left us the place, was a bit crazy. She's the one who installed everything, painted the walls these batshit colours... Have you seen the scratches on the floorboards?"

Dean nodded.

"It's from a kangaroo. She kept one inside for ages."

"No fucking way!"

Ash laughed. "Way. It was a rescue joey, but she got attached and let it live with her until it was like, five and a half feet tall."

"Holy shit."

"Yeah, the woman had problems." Ash's face softened. "Still, she loved us, me and Julia. And she gave us a place to live when we had nowhere to go. Without her we would have been screwed."

"Yeah, Jules told me your mum was a bit of a wild card."

Ash snorted. "That's putting it lightly. Still, I wasn't much better when I was young."

"I'm sure that's not true."

Ash looked like she was going to argue, then changed her mind. She reached for two mugs on a high shelf. "I guess we should um, talk about you and me?"

Dean nodded, his heart in his throat. He'd been planning this for as long as he'd been planning his visit but that didn't make it any easier. "Can I just say something first?"

"Sure. What?"

He took a deep breath. "I'm in love with you. I know that sounds crazy because we haven't known each other that long, but I am. I look at you, and I feel like we could be good together forever. Kids, house, family trips to theme parks. All that stuff."

He expected resistance, but Ash was still, unmoving, unblinking, coffee mugs dangling loosely from her hands.

Dean crossed his fingers behind his back again. This time for luck. "You don't have to say you love me back, but does that make you feel anything?"

Ash licked her upper lip. "Yeah. I... Do you trust that feeling, Red?"

"I do. I've done a lot of thinking since Wide Open Road and I promise I'm done pissing around. I'm never gonna be a guy you want on your bar trivia team, but I'm gonna do a lot better Ash. I don't know if you remember what I told you last night because I was... You know, making love to you, but I went to my boss and asked if I could get qualified and he said yes."

Ash's sea blue eyes grew wide. "Wow. Um, congratulations Dean."

"Thanks. And it gets even better." He couldn't help grinning like an idiot. "He said I've done such a good job I can stay on full time wages. No dropping down to the apprentice pay rate."

"Double wow."

"I know. And I know it doesn't change everything, but soon I'll be qualified. I sold my sports bike so I've got a decent bit in the bank now. I make good money roofing and I've got at least another season with the Bulls, which means a second income. I'll have enough money for kids, I promise. Enough to support you if things go wrong, too."

"Dean..." Ashley's voice was husky. "I don't want you to kill yourself trying to prove you're ready."

"I'm not doing that." Dean took the coffee mugs from her hands, placed them on the kitchen counter and pulled her into his arms. "I'm doing what I have to do to have a baby with you. Not that we have to have a kid right now—"

"Except we just had unprotected sex?"

"Oh, yeah. Well, we don't have to do it again. If you want time to see how serious I am about changing, we can go back to using condoms and just date for a while."

"Date?" Ash sounded like he'd proposed a trip to the Antarctic.

"Yeah, date. Go to the movies, dinner. Get to know each other."

Ash sucked her cheeks in. "I don't know, Red..."

Dean took her hand and pressed it to his chest. "Babe, I know you have your doubts, but I'm a fuckin' nice guy. I have a job. I can only cook packet stuff right now, but I'm working on it. If you agree to be my girlfriend, I will fuck you every night like it's my second but equally important job. Third job I guess, if you count footy."

"Dean—"

"I can't promise not to be a useless dickhead now and again, that's kinda who I am. I forget stuff, and I'm careless and I'm shit at concentrating, but I will love you and try as hard as I can not to drive you crazy. That is a guarantee."

Ash smirked. "I'm kind of enjoying your new bossy side, Red."

"Then say yes. Say you'll be my girlfriend."

Instead, she tilted her head up and, powerless to do anything else, Dean kissed her. It was a strange kiss, hesitant but eager. He could taste the way she wanted to say yes, sense the fear that had her holding back. He cupped her cheeks and tried to show her, without words, that she had nothing to be afraid of.

"Whew," he said when they broke apart.

"Yeah." Ash rubbed a thumb over her upper lip. "You're scary good at that."

"That was all you, beautiful."

Ash smiled. "You really do like me, don't you?"

"More than I've ever liked anyone."

He was thrilled to see Ash's cheeks go pink. Then she glared at him. "Enough sweet nothings, Red. I'll make you a deal. We can date, but no labels. At least not for a few weeks. We can mess around and see where this takes us. I'm not your girlfriend, and you're not my boyfriend. We're just... Seeing each other. Exclusively. Okay?"

Dean was disappointed, but it was better than eating Ash out in cars and pretending he wasn't in love with her. "Deal."

He had a sudden burst of inspiration. "You know, I've got a footy presentation night coming up next month. How about if you're still into me, we go as a couple? It's at Crown Casino. Should be pretty swanky."

"A Football Presentation night?" Ash repeated. "I don't know, Red…"

"I'm not gonna get drunk and act like a knob," he promised. "I just think it'll be fun, getting all dressed up and going out."

Ash rubbed her palms against her kimono. "Red, about footy clubs… There's something you should know…"

Dean stared at her, sure she was going to refuse to come, but then Ash's face broke into a reluctant smile. "How the fuck can I say no to you when you look that freaking cute?"

"I look cute?"

"Only every day of your life."

Dean grinned. "So that means you'll come as my date to the presentation night, or…?"

Ash shook her head. "Yes, I'll be your date to your bro-down, Red."

Dean punched the air. "Yes."

"You're such a dork."

"No, I'm not." Dean reached down and swept her into her arms. "Wanna go cement our relationship?"

"With you carrying me like a dork?"

"With fucking Ashley, with fucking."

She laughed and reached up to tug his ear. "Dork."

14

As the Uber sped past three-tiered houses and brightly lit restaurants Ash's stomach growled like a bear. She hadn't eaten all day, but the thought of eating made her want to puke. She could barely get coffee down.

Beside her, Dean chatted away with the driver. He looked gorgeous in his Italian suit. Max had picked it out and helped him get it tailored so that it bound to his heavy frame like a dream. His hair was styled, his beard trimmed, and his ragged fingernails filed (by her) into smoothness. He was always a good looking boy, but tonight Ash felt like the groom from her fantasies had stepped into the third dimension. Sure, that imaginary husband had never been ginger, but body and penis-wise it was an almost perfect match. Their driver stopped chatting to take a phone call and Dean squeezed her hand. "Are you okay?"

"Fine," she lied. "I'm excited."

Dean's eyes glowed with boyish enthusiasm. "I can't tell you how happy that makes me. I can't wait to introduce you to the team."

Ash bit her tongue. She wanted to warn him that she'd gone online and discovered she already knew a few members of his team. Knew them in the most intimate sense of the word. In her teens and early twenties, she was what people referred to as a 'footy slut.' That hypocritical label applied to any girl who hooked up with more than two footballers in the space of twenty years, but she'd done a lot more than that.

She hadn't cared at the time, but her reputation as 'that bikini chick who could drink her weight in vodka and suck the leather off a cricket ball' hadn't exactly faded the way she'd hoped. She hadn't dated a footballer in years but clubs were incestuous little paddling pools and she was sure exactly no one had forgotten who she was. Her chances of flying under the radar while also being the date of an unmissable redheaded giant, were miniscule. Life was full of small ironies. Or as Julia said 'munted bullshit.'

Her sister had been texting her a combination of support and excuses all day.

'You don't have to go. You don't have to put up with all that crap, just tell Dean you've got congenital heart failure and you need to stay home and eat Pringles in bed."

As tempting as the idea of bailing was, Ash didn't want to. She was Ash fucking Bennett. She didn't run from anything, not pain, not breach births so painful the mother told her to go fuck herself with a chainsaw, and not her past.

She *was* a footy slut. She was the daughter of a white-trash alcoholic. She did pay for her car and university degree by posing in her underwear for teenage wank mags. She was also an accomplished midwife with amazing hair and a sexy not-boyfriend and everyone at this presentation night was going to know it.

Heartened, Ash pulled out her compact. Her smoky eye was as flawless as it had been in the hotel, every corner perfectly angled, the shades blending effortlessly from kohl black to muted silver. Her lips were plumped with menthol and stained cranberry red. She'd painted close to a dozen thin layers over her skin: primer, concealer, contouring cream, highlighter fluid, foundation and pressed powder. In the dim light of the cab, her skin looked as close to flawless as it ever would.

The look had taken her close to two hours to achieve. She'd stood naked in front of the mirror at the hotel and Dean had sat on the bath and watched. "It's amazing how you know how to do all this," he said.

"Thanks," Ash said, as she teased false lashes over her real ones. "I love makeup."

"Why?"

"It's like you can become a different person when you put it on. Or, like the best version of yourself."

Dean smiled into the mirror. "This is going to sound like a line, but you're more beautiful without it. I mean, you look nice now, but I like seeing you the way you really are."

It was a sweet sentiment, but she hadn't wanted to show who she really was tonight. Her looks, given to her entirely by chance, had always been her ticket into places a dirt-poor bogan would never have been allowed to enter otherwise. Tonight she planned to use them as a weapon and as armour, look so immaculate anyone who looked at her and *dared* to say something about her past would think twice.

For the first time in days, Ash found herself thinking about Nate. He didn't play club football, he probably engaged in recreational water polo or golf or some other sport relevant to his stratum in life. For all his flaws, if they'd gotten together, she'd never be staring down the barrel of this nightmare.

But then you wouldn't have Dean, she reminded herself. *Dean's worth it.*

Is he? A quiet voice in the back of her brain asked. *Is he worth all of this?*

Yes, Ash thought as hard as she could. *Yes, he is.*

For the past month, she and Dean had spent almost every night together. They'd gone to the movies, out for dinner, had coffee after work. Dean visited her in Brenthill, bringing Indian takeaway kept warm in a cloth bag. He patted her dogs, he massaged her feet, he was interested in everything to do with her job. He even, though this might have been due to new relationship blinkers, thought she looked sexy in scrubs.

"A hot nurse," he said as he watched her getting dressed one morning. "I can't believe I'm dating a hot nurse."

There were a lot of things to love about Dean, but there were things that drove her crazy, too.

He giggled incessantly at GIFs of people falling over. His memory had more holes than a sieve. He couldn't name a single political figure, not even the Prime Minister. He thought, for some unknown reason, there were seventy-two weeks in a year. He'd made her a million cups of tea but he could *never* remember how she liked it (Irish breakfast with milk and one sugar). Once he went to the shops to buy her dishwashing liquid, and he returned with flowers, a Boston bun, and a packet of double A batteries. If they were driving anywhere, he broke off mid-conversation to point out interesting-looking dogs. Even at his most mature and self-reliant, he was, at heart, a lostie. When they were together, she tended to find this charming, but when they were apart, it worried her. It worried her enough that she'd drafted a text message in the notes app on her phone: *Dean these past few weeks have been amazing, but I was right the first time. I just don't think we're suited for one another, I'm sorry, Ashley."*

She'd been waiting for a sign, a universal indication that she was on the right path or needed to abandon ship. As of this morning she knew she might just have one. Her period was late. It was only out by a day. but usually she was regular as clockwork. While she and Dean were using condoms, they had gone bare that first time at her house and there had been a couple of nights where, after a couple of glasses of wine, she begged Dean to take her with nothing between them. And if there was one thing about Dean, it was that he always gave her what she wanted.

If she was pregnant, then she and Dean would make a proper go of things. If she wasn't pregnant, then she was in for more nail-biting indecision and possibly a break up. The terrifying thing was, Ash didn't know whether she wanted to be pregnant or not pregnant.

"Hey, beautiful." Dean's voice was husky in her ear. "Are you okay? You look nervous."

She breathed out a thin stream of air, wishing it was cigarette smoke. "I'm fine. Just thinking about what we did in our hotel."

Dean ducked his head. "It was pretty good, huh? You weren't

um..." He bent his head closer to hers. "Embarrassed? By what I wanted?"

Ash smiled, forgetting her worries for the first time since they'd gotten in the car. "It wasn't embarrassing, Red. It was hot."

Last week she'd gotten Dean drunk and convinced him to talk about the kinks she was sure he was dancing around. He'd refused to say anything until finally, under the power of twelve scotches and an unfulfilled blowjob, admitted *The Princess Bride*-inspired stable boy thing.

After that, the sex had been fucking electric. Ash didn't know how she'd ever managed to come without imagining herself using some poor peasant boy for orgasms. The idea just turned her on in ways she'd never thought possible.

If she was going to recap Dean's good points, his being a spectacular lay would be right at the top. After he'd admitted what turned him on, he'd been so worked up from discussing his fantasies that he fucked her three times in five hours. Ash had never known such violent orgasms. They were screaming, clawing black holes of pleasure, closing in on themselves, dragging her into nothingness.

Earlier at the hotel, she'd ordered Dean to use Eric on her. He'd worked the silicone in and out of her pussy, pleading for the right to make her come on him instead. She'd refused until he was practically shaking with need and then she allowed him to slide the toy away and replace it with his cock. He had ruined her coffee maker by pouring boiling water in the hole where the beans were meant to go, but there was no denying the boy could fuck.

"Ashley," Dean whispered in her ear. "I know you're not ready for me to say it again but I... You know. Three words."

Ash's stomach was a whorl of pleasure and guilt. "I, um, thanks."

"I promise I don't want to push you, but I just wanted you to know that I'd never thought I'd ever have a girl like you."

Unsure whether Dean had her or not and unwilling to discuss it either way, Ash reached over and toyed with Dean's perfectly straight collar. "Do you still want me, Red?"

He gave a soft chuckle. "Always."

"Well, maybe I'll let you have me later. Unless I'm too tired to deal with your cock, then you'll just have to go down on me."

He swallowed audibly. "I'll do whatever you want me to do."

"I know you will." There was something forewarning in those words and Ash felt herself withdrawing slightly, staring out of her side window. She could feel Dean on the verge of asking her what was wrong again, but mercifully the car pulled into Crown Casino.

The Crown Complex was such a weird amalgamation of things. Situated right by the Yarra river, it managed to be high class and tacky as hell at the same time. Five-star restaurants lay meters away from rubbery food court dumplings. Five-figure handbags were displayed in front of teenagers getting drunk on goon. Men in bow ties gambled next to haggard women in tracksuit bottoms. Families went to the movies, hipsters ate at the trendy burger joints, and people like her and Dean milled about in formal wear, looking for the location of their wedding or awards ceremony. Everything was both in and out of place.

"Over there." Dean placed a hand on her back and guided her toward a sign marked *'Bundoora Bulls Presentation Night. Palladium room.'*

"Palladium room? Isn't that where they film the Brownlow medal?"

"Yeah, Club President knows a guy who let us have the room at cost."

"Wow." Ash made a mental note to text Julia, then remembered she hated everything to do with football and was on yet another mysterious outing with Max. Lately Connor had become obsessed with elaborate date nights: ice skating, picnics in the botanical gardens, wine tours. Tonight they were having a nine-course dinner in some old heritage mansion. If Ash didn't know better, she'd swear someone was paying him to tick shit off his bucket list.

The Palladium room was guarded by an attendant in a tux. Dean told the guy his name and they were ushered inside. Ash's damp palms didn't get any drier as she stepped inside the ballroom and instantly recognised no less than five people. She felt them staring at her as she and Dean were steered toward their table, right in the middle of the fucking room. Their fellow diners looked up as they arrived.

"Hi," said a thickset guy. "You ginger's new bird?"

On the one hand, at least he didn't already know who she was. On the other hand, *vom*. Ash donned her most polite smile. "Dean and I are seeing each other."

The guy grinned, his eyes dipping to visually weigh her rack. "Nice. And you are?"

"This is Ashley," Dean said in a firm voice. He gestured to the mercifully unfamiliar man beside him. "Ash, this is Broden and his wife, Tania…"

She nodded. "Hey."

"Nice to meet you."

"How's it going?"

Dean pointed to the bored-looking man beside Tania. "This is Jesse and next to him is his girlfriend, Kate."

"I *love* your dress," Kate gushed. She was a tiny Asian woman whose magenta lipstick Ash would certainly be asking about.

She felt her spirits lift ever so slightly. "Thanks."

"You've already met Hector," Dean continued. "And next to him is… I'm sorry I don't know your name."

"Vanessa," Hector shouted. "Works with my mum. Tickets are two hundred bucks, and I didn't want it to go to waste."

Vanessa, a slender Italian-looking girl turned bright red. Ash felt profoundly sorry for her and immediately sat down on her free side. "Hey, I'm Ash. How are you?"

"Good!" Vanessa's relief was obvious. "This is a beautiful room, isn't it?"

"For sure," Ash agreed. "Any idea what we're having for tea?"

"Scallops are first, I think—"

"Seriously, do I know you?" Hector leaned across Vanessa to stare at Ash's boobs, as though trying to forensically identify her from her 36 C's. "You look really fuckin' familiar."

Ash, who was in no mood to discuss her former modelling career, was about to suggest the emergency room when Hector lifted his gaze from her tits to her eyes. "Are you Robbie Hoss's ex?"

Shit. Robbie, one of her teenage sweethearts, was now a Brownlow Medallist and one of the most recognisable faces in the AFL. So much for flying under the radar. "We dated a long time ago," she said, burningly conscious of the way everyone was watching her.

"Yeah, I remember you." Hector snapped his fingers. "You're that model from the country, yeah? You've got the…"

He gestured to his front teeth and Ash knew he meant her other modelling trademark, the tiny gap in her teeth she'd tried and failed to refuse to let anyone photograph.

"Yes, but I'm a nurse these days."

Hector smirked. "A nurse, huh?"

Ash knew he was picturing her in a latex uniform with a red cross on it and cursed herself for not saying 'midwife.' A man conjured no sexy thoughts when you said 'midwife.'

"Which hospital do you work at?" Vanessa asked.

"Southern Star. I help deliver babies."

Vanessa and Kate gave an obligatory 'naww,' but Hector's sleaze bag smile widened. "So you've seen your fair share of pussy, huh?"

Where the fuck was Dean? She was under heavy artillery fire here and she needed backup. Ash glanced in his direction and saw he was deep in conversation with Broden. She was going to have to handle this alone. She gave Hector her sweetest smile. "More pussy than you, I'm sure."

Kate and Jesse laughed and even Vanessa gave a small giggle. Then she and the rest of the women discussed nursing and the grossest childbirth stories they knew. Eventually, Hector, tired of being ignored and grossed out by all the talk of vaginal tearing, joined the boys' discussion about some guy's torn ACL.

One crisis down, Ash thought. *Only a billion to go.*

The presentation night tottered on with all the speed and vibrancy of a wet week. The votes were called out, people cheered and hooted accordingly. The entrées arrived, buttery scallops wrapped in bacon, and bright green asparagus tips dotted with feta.

Ash ate slowly, forcing herself to enjoy the expensive meal. The other girls on the table were nice, but their wine consumption was making it harder and harder to hold an actual conversation. Ash desperately wanted to lose herself in a bottomless glass of chardonnay, especially since she kept catching people pointing at her, but her lack of a period stayed her hand.

Beside her, Dean drank beer and chatted with his teammates. It was strange to see him being so blokey. He grinned like a big-shot, patted men on the back and kept his sentences short and to the point as he talked football, insults, and that eternal man-topic—That Time I Did That Thing That Was So Good.

He kept his hand on her thigh, but she was never invited to join the conversation. Ash felt like the biggest hypocrite in the world, but she missed his attentive goofiness. As she drank Coke and stared down at the tabletop, she began to feel decidedly lonely.

At least no one has shouted anything or pulled Dean aside to ask him if he knew he was dating a skank, she reminded herself. *That's better than having a good time.*

Mains were a choice between steak and salmon. Ash swapped her salmon for Dean's steak, and he was subsequently ribbed by his teammates for fifteen straight minutes.

"Come on, Sherwood, I know she's a new girlfriend, but there's no need to trade in your man-card."

"Are you gonna ditch your wallet for her purse?"

"Would you like a packet of tampons for dessert?"

Dean laughed it all off like a good little soldier, but Ash's mood darkened. As mains were cleared away, the vote count climbed higher. Every ten minutes the overall tallies were shown on a huge screen and, to Ash's surprise, Dean's name had begun to steadily rise in the ranks for Best and Fairest.

"You never told me you were a contender," Ash whispered when she managed to snag his attention. "You could win."

"I won't. Corey's got more than me. He just won this round, see?" He gestured toward a kid with a shaved head, waving his fork in honour of his own victory.

"He looks like he might keel over before they give out the medals."

Dean chuckled softly. "He's just getting warmed up. Just you wait, it'll get worse. Sorry about not being able to hang out with you, by the way. I've forgotten these events are like this."

"It's fine," Ash lied.

"It isn't, but it's kinda hard to talk in a mixed group with these guys. Are the girls nice?"

"Yes," Ash said, neglecting to mention that they were all too sozzled to talk.

"Well, I promise when we get out of here, I'll make it up to you."

"You'll let me eat the complimentary hotel biscuits?"

Dean bent closer to her ear. "I was thinking of a more personal way of making it up to you."

Ash couldn't help but smile. "That sounds excellent, but don't stress. I'm all right."

At least she was until she saw Fran Chalmers. Fran Chalmers once walked in on her and the captain of the Hawks having sex on a Deer Hunter arcade game. Fran was now pointing at Ash from across the room. As each person on her table turned and stared, Ash knew the odds they were talking about her outfit were minimal. "Fucking hell."

"What?" Dean asked.

"I think I'm getting a headache," she lied as Fran said something and her whole table laughed.

It only got worse as the night went on. Men and women stared at her. Some of them smiled when she met their gaze or looked a little awestruck, but most of them sneered like she was carrying an infectious disease. It was like she was standing under a white-hot spotlight, the glare of all that attention melting her mask away. Ash pressed a palm to where her womb lay. If there was another life growing inside her, would it love her in spite of her past? Or would it be embarrassed to be brought into the world by a former party girl and a man who thought 'tangerine' was the Spanish word for orange?

I'll love you so much, Ash thought desperately. *I'll try so hard. I can be a good mum, I promise. I promise times a million million.*

Finally, the night seemed to be drawing to a close. The Club President got up and talked about how the Bulls had all played a great season and had plenty to look forward to for next year. Then the coach, his face red with booze, began to talk. Ash zoned out as he told several rambling jokes and praised the players, the game, the support staff and the sponsors. He was just thanking the wives and girlfriends (couldn't get the grass stains out of your shorts without 'em, could we, boys?) when she felt it. A slickness easing its way out of her labia, thick and heavy. She clenched her fist so hard her nails dug into her palm. *No,* she thought. *No, maybe it's just that weird discharge that looks like Greek yogurt.*

She sat perfectly still, praying what she thought was happening wasn't happening and then her insides began to ache in a way that was painfully familiar and she knew her slightly overdue period had arrived.

Dean's hand brushed her thigh. "Almost done now, babe."

"Red, we need to talk—"

"Time for the best and fairest!" The coach shook out a small piece of paper. "Without further ado, I'd like to announce the winner of the Bundoora Bulls Firsts Football Club Best and Fairest. A man who sums up both of those words and has a bloody great head of hair, Dean Sherwood."

"Ash." Dean gripped her thigh. His mouth was slightly parted, his eyes wide with shock. "I... I won?"

Despite her tangled fears, Ash found herself beaming. "You did! Get up on stage, Red!"

Dean stared at her, his eyes blank. "But I... I don't understand how this happened."

Ash kissed him on his cheek. "You're the best, Dean, that's what happened. Now go get your medal."

The firm command worked as well as they did in bed. Dean stood to tumultuous applause and he wove his way over to the stage, a little unsteady on his feet but beaming from ear-to-ear.

He reached the podium and the president placed a medal around Dean's neck. Ash cheered along with the crowd, her frustrations and fears forgotten. He looked so dazed and happy it made her chest ache. He turned to walk off the stage but the club president gestured to the microphone. Dean flushed and stepped forward towards the podium. "I, uh, won't keep you too long but I can't tell you how much this means to me. I know I'm older than most players here—"

"Damn right, ginger!"

"'Nother few months and you'll be on the pension, ay?"

Ash ignored the hecklers and watched Dean's face. His bright brown eyes were wet with tears. Up on stage, not a trace of his faux-blokiness remained. He looked as vulnerable as he did the morning when he asked her to be his girlfriend. She pressed a hand to her chest, her heart swollen so tight it hurt to breathe.

"Football's been a huge part of my life since I was a kid," Dean said. "It was the only thing me and my old man could ever talk about and being acknowledged like this, especially as a part of a great club like the Bulls, means more than I could ever possibly say. Thank you and uh, have a good night."

He staggered away from the podium amidst more applause, loud cheers and drunken catcalls.

"Was I okay?" he asked in an undertone when he sat back down.

"You were wonderful." Ash kissed his cheek again. "Congratulations, Dean."

"Thanks. I uh, think everyone's gonna give me shit for crying. I don't know what happened, I think I was just too happy or something."

"Fuck what anyone else says. You're the one who won the fucking medal."

Dean beamed at her. "Want to come and meet my coach? I'd love to introduce him to my girlfriend."

Just like that Ash's elation faded. The coach who felt it so appropriate to thank WAGS for their crucial role in washing men's shorts was one of the people she'd caught staring at her like she was a leper. What if he told Dean who and what she was? What if he said something about her past? She felt another flush of blood drip between her legs and leapt to her feet. "Sorry Red. I-I need to go to the bathroom."

Dean gave a good show of concealing his disappointment. "No problem. I should go talk to people. You know, the coach, the rest of the team…"

"That's cool, you go do what you have to. I'll find you later."

Ash grabbed her clutch and strode across the hall to the ladies' toilets, ignoring everyone who looked her way. In the stall, she similarly refused to look at her underwear, to see the blood and think of the baby that did not, and had never existed. Instead, she put in her diva cup, and sent Julia a text.

Hey, buddy, I got my period, people keep giving me 'you're a ho' side-eye, and they don't even have raspberry lemonade. Still, hopefully the worst is over. I hope your night has been way less dramatic than mine. Ash xx

ps. Dean won the Best and Fairest.

Ash knew she should have gone right back to her medal-winning date, but instead she sat on the toilet, trying to steady her breathing. Despite what she'd told Julia, it didn't feel like the worst was over. It kind of felt like the worst was yet to come. She waited for as long as she could possibly stand, then pulled herself together and exited the toilet stall. She was reapplying her lipstick (Yves Saint Laurent, Rouge Flamme) when a girl standing by the paper towel dispenser caught her eye. She was young, twenty-three tops, with big brown eyes, a big smile, and thick caramel hair down to her ass.

"Hi," Ash said. "Having a good night?"

"For sure! I'm Chelsea by the way, Dean's ex."

Ash stared at the girl trying to process her youth, her girly pink dress, her general 'I have a fake ID and I really like guava-flavoured Vodka Cruisers' vibe. "I'm er, Ashley."

"I know!" Chelsea bounced on the balls of her feet, so her boobs shook like fleshy coconuts. "I love your dress! And your hair! You're so beautiful! Which is like, classic Dean, because he has such good taste. Although I would say that because, like, we went out."

Ash stared at her some more. This was Dean's ex? Call her naive, but when she'd pictured his exes she pictured adult humans, not sexy little girl-babies. "Uh... When did you and Dean go out exactly?"

"Last year! My dad's the club treasurer, and I help out by running water and helping to organise the events and stuff. That's how I met Dean." Chelsea's big brown eyes were dreamy. "He is *such* a great guy. So funny and *such* a good mid-fielder. Did you see him go up for his medal? So cute how he cried. I *love* when men do that, like *be* vulnerable and stuff."

"Uh-huh." Ash's insides cramped in a way that had nothing to do with her period. "Do you mind if I ask why you and Dean stopped seeing each other?"

"I went on a trip to Japan! When I got back Dean was seeing Donna Woodrow, which was fine because I know he's a popular guy and heaps of girls want to date him, but I guess you know that, right?"

"Right. Of course. Why wouldn't they?" Ash backed away from the mirror. "I should, uh, get back to my table..."

"Me too!" Chelsea threw her paper towel in the bin. "See you around, Ashley!"

She swanned out, leaving Ash alone to contemplate this fresh hell.

"Jesus Christ," she said to the empty bathroom. "How much worse can this night get?"

The bathroom didn't respond.

15

"Want to get out of here?" Dean muttered the instant she found him again.

"Dear God, yes." For a brief moment Ash felt like the universe might finally be done fucking with her, before she realised just how wrong she was. Dean's goodbye tour of the Palladium room took another hour and a half as hordes of people crowded around to touch his medal, swap stories about his best games, and ramble in a way that only people wankered on free booze could. Ash stood by his side, smiling politely and nodding. No one talked to her but she didn't care, her head was too full of thoughts about her period, and Chelsea, the sexy, sexy baby. The younger woman had come up to Dean shortly after Ash left the bathroom, wrapping her arms around Dean's middle and squealing, *"Ermagerd I'meh sah praaaud of yurrrr!"*

How, she asked herself for the millionth time, *how did he follow that with me? Chelsea doesn't want a baby. Chelsea is a baby. They only broke up because she went to Japan. Is that who a sweet, clueless guy should be with? A sexy baby?*

When they finally managed to slip away, Ash was aching all over and in no mood for the conversation she knew she and Dean would have back at the hotel. Maybe she could convince him, as a part of kinky role play, to stay silent for the rest of the week? Dean suddenly rubbed her shoulder. "Hey beautiful, where's your wrap-scarf thingy?"

Ash groaned. "I left it on my seat."

"No problem, I'll go get it."

Before she could respond he was already jogging away, his beautiful suit all crumpled at the back. While she waited, Ash paced around the hallway, trying to look like she belonged there. *Dear God just let us get out of here before anything else happens.*

"Ash?" A man's voice called from behind her. "Ash Bennett, is that you?"

She whirled around, and her stomach sank like a stone. *I need to stop saying things can't get worse.*

With his thick blue-black hair and razor-blade cheekbones, Mick Malone looked more like a poet than a footballer. Then again, he also looked like he had a soul, which proved looks were deceiving. He and Ash had dated for a hot minute four years ago, and it had been his catastrophically asshole-ish ways that turned her off football players for good.

"It is you." Mick sauntered toward her, hands in his suit pockets. "It's been too fucking long."

"Hi, Mick."

Her ex-boyfriend eyed her up and down and Ash knew he was cataloguing any changes her body might have undergone since he'd last seen it naked. He must have liked what he saw because he grinned. "You look stunning, as usual."

Ash silently prayed Dean would get back to her fast. "Thanks. I didn't know you played for the Bulls?"

"I don't, but a few of the boys told me to join 'em once the boring shit wraps up." Mick's smile now verged on a leer. "You know, I think about you all the time. You were the best girlfriend I ever had."

Ash snorted. Her time with Mick was defined by jealously, increasing paranoia and arguments about whether he was at his mates place like he claimed, or at a club getting his cock jerked by some impressionable young woman (always the latter). "I won't say you were *the* worst boyfriend I ever had, but you're a top five contender."

Mick only smiled wider. Being turned down had always been his aphrodisiac of choice. He lived for the chase. Ash was surprised it took a whole fortnight for him to start cheating on her. "Bit harsh."

"The truth hurts."

"We had fun together, you have to admit that."

"It's been years, man. Get over it."

"There's no getting over a body like yours. Wouldn't mind getting under it again, though."

Ash rolled her eyes. "Yeah, excellent wordplay. Very classy. Now, run along and pester someone who'll actually fuck you."

"I dunno, you still might. You single?"

Ash gestured down at her dress. "Obviously I came here with someone, dickhead."

"Who?" Mick's navy blue eyes were full of the kind of base jealousy that used to thrill Ash to bits. At least, before she knew a man treating you like a bone he needed to defend from other dogs was a warning, not a gift. "Dean Sherwood."

Mick laughed, causing a wave of whiskey fumes to wash over her face. "That silly bloodnut? How'd he manage that?"

Ash put a finger to Mick's chin and gently pushed him backward. "Well, he's big and nice and awesome in the sack, and he just won Best and Fairest."

"Yeah, yeah." Mick looked sulky. "You know Grant's here tonight, too? Maybe we could have a little reunion?"

Ash had once spent an evening crammed into a cheap hotel room with Mick in her mouth and Grant Fallon taking her from behind. It had been a thrilling, brain-twisting experience, but like all the sex she'd had with Mick, she'd been too focused on how she looked to come. Too busy being his trophy girlfriend to enjoy herself. She'd also been pissed off with his constant requests to record the action on his phone. "Yeah... I don't think so."

"Sherwood's welcome to join in. He can hold the camera?"

Ash's patience, already on tenterhooks, officially wore thin. "Just bugger off, Mick. Please?"

"Come on, Ashy, ginger can't complain, he's got his own little sex tape out there."

Ash's cheeks suddenly felt like thick rubber sheets. "What are you talking about?"

"Ginger's video. You've gotta know he was taped snowboarding with his dick out in Kiwiland, yeah?"

It wasn't relief, but it was a close cousin. Shoving aside that Dean's snowboarding incident had been recorded, Ash sneered at Mick. "That's not a sex tape, dickhead, that's just snowboarding with your cock out."

"You obviously haven't seen it, then. Here."

Mick pulled out his phone and pressed the screen. Ash knew she should have walked away, that her ex-boyfriend was an asshole with nothing but bad intentions, but she couldn't move. Mick held up his phone and obligingly she watched. It was unmistakably Dean, stark naked and sliding toward the camera on a black and blue snowboard. His dark red hair was stark against his pale skin and the even paler snow. The camera quality was so good, Ash could see the freckles on his chest, the alcohol glaze in his eyes, the heavy weight of his cock swaying as he pulled up at the foot of the slope. An unknown number of people cheered and a girl ran out to greet him, a tall brunette adorned in one of those fake Native American headdresses you weren't allowed to wear at festivals anymore.

Ash watched, her throat tight, as the girl threw her arms around Dean's neck and kissed him. Considering her would-be lover's feet were trapped in a snowboard, it was unsurprising she and Dean fell backwards into the snow. Whoever was holding the camera whooped as Dean continued sucking the girl's face as though nothing had happened, his pale hips grinding into her clothed ones.

"See?" Mick's face was alight with smugness. "Sex tape."

Ash watched, numb from head to foot as someone called out *"Fuck, it's the cops! Oi, Deano, it's the cops!"* The camera went shaky and then the video ended.

Ash turned away, her fancy dinner churning in her guts. She didn't want to cry in front of Mick, or at all, but it was coming, rising up inside her like vomit. There were too many things to feel without crying. She blinked hard trying to stave off the urge.

"What's going on here?" Dean had returned. Ash looked up to see him glaring at Mick, her silver scarf in his big worn hands. "Is everything okay?"

Mick made a show of tucking away his phone, like an adulterer tucking away his cock. "Nothing much, mate. Congratulations, by the way. Not every day you win Best and Fairest."

He extended a hand, and Dean shook it warily. Ash watched them without seeing. The man who could have been the father of her baby was naked on internet. He was snow humping a woman in a racially insensitive headdress *on the internet*.

As Mick wished them a good night and left, Dean steered her through the lustrous red carpeted hallway towards the escalators. Ash found herself reliving flashbulb images of the past few hours. Chelsea's boobs, the bloodstain in her underwear, Dean naked and on top of another woman, Fran Chalmers pointing and laughing. Dimly, Ash tried to tell herself she had no right to be jealous, but the turmoil building inside her wasn't jealousy, it was wrongness overload. The weight of all this shit bearing down on her was reaching an unbearable mass.

"How do you know Malone?" Dean asked.

"We used to date." Ash caught a muscle twitching in Dean's jaw and some stab of vindictiveness made her say, "If you don't like that, you especially won't like the fact that I once had a three-way with him and Grant Fallon."

Dean stopped dead. "Okay, Ash what's wrong? Are you upset with me because I couldn't talk to you all night? I'm sorry about that, I forgot how full-on these things can be—"

"It's not that. It's more than that."

"Then tell me what it is. Tell me what's wrong, and I'll make it right the way I promised I would."

Ash laughed, a whispery, pathetic sound. "Okay, I'm gonna say what's bothering me, in order, and when I'm done, we'll see what you can do to fix it. Okay?"

Dean nodded.

Ash held up a finger. "Problem one, when I was a model I went through a slutty phase and I banged a lot of footballers. Like *a lot*. And while you were talking to your boys tonight, I was getting pointed at and giggled over because footy clubs are incestuous pits of hell. You won a Best and Fairest, and you know what most people are going to remember? That you rocked up with a slutty blonde slut. I've made it my life's purpose to not be around people who look at and talk about me like that anymore, but you being a part of this club means that'll happen over and over again. And you're a nice guy, so I know you'll say you're not embarrassed by me but we both know you will be once the honeymoon glow wears off."

"Ash..."

"Lemme finish, Red. Problem two. I got my period tonight."

Dean stepped forward, his arms extended. "Baby, I'm so sorry. Come here."

But Ash couldn't go to him, no matter how much she wanted to. "Please just *listen to me*, Dean. I know it's dumb to think you'll get pregnant after a few weeks, but the scary thing is I'm not sure if I'm disappointed or relieved."

Dean went pale. He opened his mouth, but Ash held up a finger. "Problem three. I ran into Chelsea, your bouncy fun-times ex in the bathroom."

Dean flinched, but he didn't say anything.

"She informed me that you only broke up because she went to Japan, and do you know what my first thought was? If she'd stayed here, she'd still be with you. She's perfect for you, all cute and giggly and years away from wanting a baby or a house or stability. Why are you with me when you could be with her, Dean? Why are we trying to make it work between us?"

"Ashley—"

"Problem four," she said, loudly. "Mick just showed me your video. I didn't know that there *was* a video of you snowboarding with your penis out, or that it finished with you snow-humping some idiot woman in a racist hat, but since there is, I'm pretty pissed off about it. Especially because you didn't tell me about it."

"I thought you'd be mad." Dean's brown eyes were feverish again, his brow sweaty. "I thought you'd think it meant I wasn't ready to be a father."

"Yeah, well, I am, and I do." Ash wiped a hand across her own damp forehead, smudging her thin, perfect layers of makeup. "So, Red, you've heard my complaints. How exactly are you going to fix this?"

Dean shoved his hands into his suit pockets and looked at the ground. "I... I don't know. I can't."

"Okay, I thought as much. And I'm going to go down to the food court to be alone for a while. I'm not sure how long I'll be."

Before he could say anything, she turned her back and walked away. The tears were coming and she wanted to be alone when they arrived. She wandered down to the food court in a zombie-like state and bought herself a rainbow ice-cream from the Gelateria. She sat down at one of the dirty marble benches and gnawed at it. A few minutes into her dessert her phone began to buzz. She ignored it, convinced it was Dean, but after the sixth round of vibrations she pulled it out to find Julia's name flashing on the screen. She answered it at once. "Jules? Is everything okay?"

"Ash?" Her sister's voice was watery. "I don't... I can't..."

"Julesie?" Ash's mouth went dry despite the ice cream. "What's wrong?"

"Max... He just... He just *proposed*."

Ash spat out a wad of multi-coloured ice cream. "*What?*"

"He proposed! He gave me a ring, and it's an emerald the size of a fucking chicken nugget, and oh my God, oh my God, everything is so fucked up."

"Everything's okay, Jules," Ash lied. "Now, when Connor proposed did you say yes?"

"Yes!" Julia's crying intensified. "No. I don't know."

Ash's pulse was thrashing in her ears and neck. "How do you not know?"

"I don't remember. We were there, then we were somewhere else, then I just kind of ran away, and now I'm in a KFC, and they're out of original fillets, and I don't know what to do."

Ash didn't know what to do, either. She felt like an over-inflated balloon, her rubber stretched so thin all the colours were bleeding into white.

"I shouldn't have given him an answer," Julia sobbed, oblivious to Ash's near-explosion. "I love him but we've only been together for eighteen months, and I'm not sure Max is ready, he's been engaged twice before me."

"Jules… Wait, he was engaged *twice before you*?"

"Yes, to Bonnie but also to some chick at uni. He never even told me about it until tonight when I said 'maybe you shouldn't propose two times before you're thirty-six.' And he went kind of purple and said 'three times.'"

Ash's vision went hazy. That was enough. Enough, enough, enough. "You know what, Jules? Fuck this. We're leaving."

Her sister gasped. "You mean go to the caravan?"

"Yes. I've had enough of this shit. We're going to the caravan and we're staying there until everything stops being such complete fucking garbage. Okay?"

"But—"

"Julia," Ash snapped. "Do you want to go back to Coburg and talk to your three-times engaged fiancé and his idiot naked snowboarding housemate who I just dumped at Crown Casino?"

There was a short pause then, "Where should we meet?"

16

Ash stared at her sister in bleary disgust. "So, let me get this straight: my choices are Hitler, Pauline Hanson, and the guy we saw eat his own snot on the train?"

"Yep."

"Suicide."

Julia tutted. "You can't pick suicide."

"You can always pick suicide."

"The game is called *'Fuck, Marry, Kill.'*"

"And I'm killing myself." Ash downed her shot of Absolut, then refilled from the almost empty bottle. "We need more—"

Julia slammed a fresh vodka onto the small card table. "Out of all the things Mum gave us, what do you think is the best: the hair, the legs, or the insane vodka tolerance of twenty-eight generations of Russian peasants?"

"The legs. The bitch might be mental, but her legs are fucking mint, and on that note…"

She pulled out the one packet of menthols she'd bought at the Brenthill petrol station and lit up.

Jules watched her, her usually full lips thin. "You're gonna quit again, right?"

"Sure. This isn't me smoking again. It's just a... Calculated pause in my overall quit plan."

"Uh huh."

"Oh, come on." Ash blew smoke out of the corner of her mouth. "We're at the caravan. You know the rules."

Julia rolled her eyes. "I do."

The caravan belonged to their dad. Well, Ash's dad. A large green box with broken wheels, it sat on a scrap of land beside the Goulburn River, two hours from Brenthill. Ash wasn't sure who owned the property, only that the caravan was allowed to remain there, week after week, year after year, slowly bleaching in the sun. It was a shithole, but it was also their safe place. Their retreat. She and Jules had come here three times before. The first when they were still teenagers and their mum was trying to take Julia to Queensland with her. The second when Grandma Bennett died. The third when their mum returned from Queensland and, knowing it was only a matter of time before she showed up at their place demanding money, booze, and a place to stay, they'd gone bush. If sitting in an aluminium box binge-watching *The OC* for hours was 'going bush.'

The rules for the caravan were simple. You could drink or smoke at any time of the day and eat whatever you wanted. You never had to clean up or do anything domestic. Contact with the external world was not allowed, and as long as they were both in agreement, she and Jules could stay as long as they wanted. So far their record was four weeks.

All day Ash had sat by the window, smoking and listening to Fleetwood Mac while Julia tooled around on the internet via her hotspot. They'd eaten an entire block of cheddar cheese and drank their way through a box of wine before hitting the Absolut. She hadn't talked about Dean, and Julia refused to discuss Max. All things considered, Ash was starting to get a bit antsy about that. She wasn't sure if her sister wanted to get married, but if she did, Ash needed to shotgun being the Maid of Honour.

Julia pounded back another shot of vodka. "So, guess I should think up three new people for Fuck, Marry, Kill?"

"That would be the game."

"I know, it's just hard to go anywhere after Hitler…"

"I'll make you a deal. You can skip your turn if you talk to me about Max?"

Julia tensed all over. "No."

"Come on!"

"No. Why don't *you* talk about *Dean*?"

"Because Dean didn't propose to me! That's the bigger news here, Jules. And don't even try and act like you didn't bring the ring, I've seen you staring at it when you think I'm not looking. All hunched over like that creepy grey thing from those movies—"

"Gollum," Julia snapped. "And I'm not like Gollum. If someone gave you a…" she mumbled an indecipherable word "… You'd look at it all the time, too."

"I'm sorry, what was that?"

Her sister tugged her Hawk Girl blanket higher over her shoulders. "Nothing."

Ash threw her hands in the air. "Fine, well, try and think of three more terrible people, then. And I pre-veto Donald Trump."

"You can't do that."

As Julia concentrated on her task, Ash stared out into the semi-darkness. The Goulburn River gleamed blackly beside them, the lean silhouettes of gum trees stretching toward the impossibly starry sky. She'd always thought gum trees were ugly, all gray and mottled, extending in all directions. She liked British trees, pines and apples, all uniform and velvety green. But gum trees were what Australia had; they gave her people wood, eucalyptus, koalas. Maybe wishing they were pine trees was as stupid as—

Wishing a nice redhead boy was an accountant who didn't have his dick swinging on the internet for all of the foreseeable future?

And there they were again. Back on Dean. Ash butted out her cigarette and turned to Julia, who was mouthing, "'Ted Bundy? John Howard?'"

Ash smiled, admiring the swell of Julia's lips and her delicate freckly skin. Her sister was so beautiful. So smart and funny and successful. Almost entirely undamaged, despite all that had been done to her. "Jules?"

"Yah?"

"I love you. So much."

Julia looked mildly taken aback. "I love you too, man. Always. But I'm still not letting you have the horse guy from *Game of Thrones*."

Ash laughed as she poured herself another shot. "What about Bert from *Mary Poppins*?"

"No, and for the millionth time, your crush on him is creepy as fuck."

"Right. Well, I leave my Fuck, Marry, Kill in your hands, then." Ash downed her shot and resumed looking out the window. She wanted another cigarette, but knew she couldn't have one. She only got one pack, they needed to last.

"Ash?" Julia's voice was barely above a whisper.

"Yeah?"

"He took me to Botticelli on Lygon Street. Max did. Because our first real date was there."

Ash didn't move or look at her sister. "You mean last night?"

"Yeah. He was sweating bullets all through dinner. I was half-convinced he was going to tell me he'd been sent to an operation in Perth and I'd have to lie and say he'd died in a fire so he could resurface as a super-hot meth dealer and I could visit him, and we could have sex on top of a bunch of drug money."

"But... It wasn't that, right?"

"No." Julia sighed, apparently disappointed. "After dinner Max wanted to walk through the Fitzroy Gardens, which is so not like him because he always thinks someone is gonna jump out at us from behind a bush if we walk through the city at night, but I was too full of gnocchi to notice. Anyway, Max said we should go look at the fountain, and we did, and it was nice, there was a full moon, and the roses smelled nice, and I was just trying to guess how much change was in the basin when..."

"He proposed?"

"Yeah. He got on one knee and everything."

"And you said...?"

"I dunno." Julia began tracing patterns onto the linoleum table with her fingertip. "I just... I dunno."

Ash was at her wits' end. *"Julia Catherine Bennett.* What did you say? Did you accept? Did you tell him to fuck off? What the fuck happened?"

Her sister looked up, her hazel eyes full of tears. "I said yes. I don't know why. Even at the time, I was like, 'What the fuck Connor? Why are you doing this, you weirdo?' but I dunno, there was the ring and the moon and the way he was looking at me, and I felt like my heart exploded."

Ash pictured Dean standing on stage, giving his speech as he fought back tears, then swiftly kicked the memory aside. "So, Max gave you the ring after that?"

"Yeah. It fits perfectly. He must have measured me in my sleep or something."

"And can I...? Y'know, look at it?"

She hadn't viewed this alleged mega-rock yet, and Christ, she wanted to. If Julia said no she was only a few drinks away from instigating a physical takeover.

Mercifully, Julia reached into her flannel pocket and pulled out the ring. "Here. Look to your heart's content."

Ash's mouth fell the fuck open. The ring was fucking *gorgeous*— an emerald, green as a slab of Irish countryside, set in a halo of tiny diamonds. It was classy, sexy, and a little bit retro. It suited her sister to a T. Ash took the ring and held it up to Julia's face, confirming the gemstone exactly matched the green in her sister's hazel eyes. "God, this is, like, the nicest ring ever."

Julia blew a raspberry. "Urgh, don't even. I don't wanna know how much it costs. I think it's from Tiffany's. I *know* the band's platinum."

Ash didn't say anything. She had to give the narc credit; if someone thrust that rock in her face, she'd say yes on pure reflex.

Julia cleared her throat. "So after we got... I mean, after the ring was on my hand, I said we should go get a coffee, so we went to Brunettis, and I got a cannoli and Max got a custard tart, and he looked all excited and wouldn't stop talking…" She chewed her bloodless lips.

"And?"

"And I just kind of checked out. I looked at the ring on my finger, and it was like I'd never seen it before. I couldn't believe I'd done something so dumb. I couldn't believe I'd gotten engaged without even *talking* to you."

"Hey, I don't need to be talked to," Ash said, alarmed. "It's your decision, Jules!"

"But I'm only twenty-six! And Max's already *been* married, and it was a shit-show. Everyone's marriage is a shit-show, our mum and dad, Tiff's mum and dad, Dean's mum and dad. Oh my god, what have I done—"

"Jules! Calm the fuck down, everything's fine."

Julia burst into tears. "No, it isn't. Max and I were so happy. Why did he have to drop a fucking emerald on my head? Why couldn't he just let things be?"

"Because he loves you and he wants to be married to you?"

"Then why has he proposed to two other girls?"

"I don't know. That is a bit weird, but hey, everyone's fucked up somewhere along the line, right? Remember when you had those frosted foils?"

"Eww yes." Julia gave a loud sniff. "But what if Max is some kind of King Henry VIII serial monogamist and I'm just the third in a long line of chicks who are gonna get their heads cut off?"

"Jules, I hate to come to Max's defence, but I don't think he's going to cut your head off. I think he just wants to marry you because he's a big fucking square. The real question here is, do you want to marry him back?"

"Can you believe he proposed to a girl at uni?" Julia said, ignoring her question. "He did it at a fun park. He just pulled out a pawnshop ring and proposed right next to the go-karts."

Jesus. "Well, uh, how long was he with the chick?"

Julia snorted. "Like, three months. Apparently, Dean came past and saw what Max was doing, and he stole the ring and chucked it into the waterslide. Max couldn't find it, so he never got his money back."

Hearing Dean's name—especially in relation to another one of his fuck-ups—hurt like hell, but Ash ignored the sensation. "So, it didn't work out, but Max was just a kid. People do stupid shit when they're young. They can't take it back just because they eventually get older and wiser. Believe me, I know."

Julia's brows drew together. "We can talk about Dean and the party if you want—"

"No." Ash held up the ring, the metal now as warm from her skin. "Do you want to get married to Max?"

Julia stared at the ring as though hypnotised. "I don't know, maybe."

"Yes, you do! You know how I know? You said yes. In the moment, you wanted to marry that big, boring, black-haired, super bossy son of a bitch. So do it. Marry the narc and no one will think less of you."

A tear dripped from Julia's cheek onto her flannel. "Don't call Max a narc."

"See, you do love him." Ash placed the ring on the table in front of Julia. "Just marry him. It'll be fun. Fuck knows you can always get divorced."

Julia's lip trembled, her big eyes full of what, by now, had to be mostly vodka tears. "I... What if I'm not ready to leave?"

"Leave what? Max isn't gonna make you quit your job. I'm pretty sure that's illegal now."

Julia shook her head. "I don't want to leave you."

"Leave me?" Ash laughed. "Girl, you *can't* get rid of me. I'm gonna be your Maid of Honour. Speaking of which, how do you feel about photo booths? Some people think they're lame, but Monica had one at her wedding last year, and it was fun—"

"Ash! You're not listening! If Max and I get married, even if I don't change my name, and even if we're still close, I'll be... Leaving you. Forever."

Ash stared at her sister. "What do you mean?"

"I mean it won't be *us* forever. Living in Brenthill, having a million dogs and ordering pineapple pizza without anyone judging us. It was meant to be me and you, taking care of each other, having each other's backs forever. If I move out and marry Max then it feels like I'm... betraying you."

It was snug in the tiny caravan, but Ash was suddenly cold all over. "Jules, you can't think like that, okay? We'll always be together. We'll always be sisters."

"But not the way we are now! This is all wrong. It's all out of order. I thought Max and I could wait until you had a baby, that way you'd have something bigger than me in your life, but now I'm engaged and—"

"Don't be stupid! No matter what happens, whether I have a baby or not you'll always be the most important person in the world to —*shit*." She felt her sinuses burn as tears brewed behind her eyes. "You're making me cry. You know I hate crying."

"I'm sorry," Julia said, sobbing harder.

For a few minutes they just sat there, shoulders shaking, tears dripping onto the table, and Ash thought about why they'd retreated to the caravan. They hadn't come when Max told Julia she was too young for him, though she'd been devastated. They hadn't come when Ash's relationship with Zach blew up in her face. The caravan was for sister problems, family problems, for grief and pain and solace. And though the catalyst for this visit had been man troubles, it wasn't why they were really there. They were there because this was the end of something and the beginning of something else.

"Things have changed," she whispered, as much to herself as Julia. "You can't stop it by not getting married and I can't stop it by... Doing whatever I do. We need to embrace the change Jules. We can't keep holding everyone else at arm's length forever."

"You mean like Dean?"

Ash's stomach cramped. "No, I mean like you and Captain Narc."

"You mean Dean, I know you do—"

"Dean is a whole separate matter. We're talking about you getting married and here is my final fucking say, you don't have to say yes, but if you think saying yes means you're abandoning me, don't. You will never be able to get rid of me. Even if I die I will follow you around as a ghost, closing my eyes whenever you have sex."

The corners of Julia's mouth lifted. "Promise?"

"Promise." Ash rocked her head from side to side, trying to ease the tension in her neck. "But we can't live in a wooden shack in Brenthill forever."

"That house is a piece of shit," Julia agreed.

"Yes it is, and it's full of bad memories and super far from work and smack bang in the middle of the world's most boring, shitty town. I kind of hate it. I didn't realise that until—"

She stopped, on the verge of mentioning Dean and how the house always seemed danker when his vibrant, ginger ass was inside it.

"Yes?" Julia asked, one eyebrow raised.

"I just think we should try and sell it again," Ash blustered. "Even if we have to put a decent amount of money into making it less shit, I don't want to own that place. We need to move on."

"I know we do." Julia picked up her ring and slipped it on the third finger of her left hand. "It... It looks good, doesn't it?"

"It does. It looks perfect."

They drank a little more, listened to Triple J, talked about work and their mutual friends. At three in the morning they decided to go to bed, climbing into the same bunk the way they had when they were kids. It was tricky, what with Julia being five foot ten, but neither of them suggested giving up.

"She's not my mum," Jules whispered, right when Ash was nodding off.

"Mmph?"

"Our mum. She's not really my mum," Jules repeated. "*You're* my mum. That's how I know you'll be a great mum. Because you're already my mum."

Ash kissed the back of her sister's head. "Thanks, Jules. Or should I say Mrs. Narc?"

Julia groaned. "I'm going to sleep."

"Good." Ash was just drifting off into the starry hammock of dreamland when Julia spoke again. "If shit gets bad, we can always come here, can't we? To the caravan? No matter what happens with Max or Dean or a baby or anything. We can come here?"

"Yes. Always. Now please, shh."

"Okay. Love you."

"Love you, too. Shh."

17

Though she desperately wanted to sleep, Ash woke up early. She couldn't help it; the sunlight streaming in through the caravan windows was like bleach on her eyelids. She stared up at the water-stained roof and realised, without any dramatic overtones, that she missed Dean. Missed him in a way she'd only ever missed Julia before.

Unable to lie still, she gently rolled a mumbling Julia out of the way and tugged on her gumboots. Amidst the debris of the night before, she found her disappointingly light packet of smokes, collected a can of beer from the esky, and headed outside. The morning air was damp, so was the yellowish grass. She lit up the third last cigarette in her pack and stared out at the river. She would miss cigarettes when they were gone, but the way she missed modelling, or dating multiple men, or being so involved in the club scene you were almost a minor celebrity. It was fun, but there were better things to have and be.

Ash had a feeling once Julia woke up and had breakfast, they'd leave the caravan. Her sister had slept with her engagement ring on, both hands tucked into her chest as though protecting it. She'd want to see Max again. Leaving today would mean it was the shortest retreat to the caravan they'd ever made. That seemed appropriate.

She sat on a tattered deck chair and breathed in the eucalyptus and warm dirt smell of the bush. "When I get home," she told a nearby gum tree. "I'm going to clean out the kitchen, re-paint the walls, do up the garden, buy some new fucking taps, and fix the floor. Then I'm going to sell that fugly piece of shit house and move somewhere else."

The tree swayed gently in the morning breeze, saying nothing.

"I don't know about Dean," Ash continued. "I think I've fallen in love with him, but he's so silly. Whenever I pictured myself trusting and loving someone as much as Julia, it wasn't someone silly. What do you think?"

The tree didn't reply.

Ash took a long drag on her menthol. "Well, I guess bees have sex in your flowers so you can have kids. This isn't your area of expertise."

She stood up, stretching her arms over her head. "Fuck!"

She'd just spotted a familiar black four wheel drive on the horizon and unless she was mistaken, she knew exactly who it was who'd come to find them. Ash squinted, trying to read the number plate and saw she was right. "Fuck. Fuckity, fuck, fuck."

She dropped her cigarette butt into her beer and sprinted toward the caravan.

"Jules, he's here! Or they're both here, but yours is *definitely* here." She swung open the caravan door. "You need to get up, right now."

The pile of blankets that was Julia moaned. "Whhhut? Who's here?"

"Your fiancé."

There was a small yelp as Julia pulled the covers even higher over her head. "I can't see him. No way. Not right now. I'm not ready. Don't make me go out there. I can't go out there. Get him to go away."

Ash glared at the blanket mound. "Jules, we're supposed to be strong independent women."

"You are! And I am too, but not right now. Please just make Max go away? For old times' sake?"

Ash blew out an angry breath. "How the fuck does he even know where we are? Did you tell him?"

"No!" Julia sounded horrified. "I've never told anyone where this place is. He must have used cop powers."

"So this is happening then, is it? I'm going to go confront your fiancé for you?"

"Yes, please," Julia said in a feeble voice. "Love you."

Ash closed the caravan door behind herself, pulled the deck chair over, and sat. "I have officially formed a barricade between you and your future husband."

"Cool." Considering there were aluminium walls and at least ten layers of blankets between them, Ash was amazed she could hear Julia talk.

Max's Ford Ranger slowly turned, its tinted windows concealing whoever lay within. Ash's throat and fingers hummed with nerves. Had Dean come? Even after everything she'd said and done, was he here to declare his feelings for her once again? He wouldn't be angry, Ash knew he wouldn't. He just wasn't that kind of guy. Julia's boyfriend, on the other hand...

The driver side door click-swooshed open, and Max Connor stepped into the morning air. Ash wasn't remotely attracted to him, but she had to admit he cut a nice figure, stomping toward her all angry-like, his black hair gleaming in the sun.

"Well, well, well," she called. "If it isn't the boy who cried marriage."

Max's already sinister expression grew murderous. "Where's Julia?"

"How'd you find us?"

He shot her a withering look. "I'm a cop."

"So?"

"So I have the means to find people who don't want to be found."

Ash raised an eyebrow at him. "Isn't that illegal? You knew Julia wasn't missing because she texted you. And you responded by what? Tracking her phone, I'm guessing?"

"Your sister knows I can track people's phones. If she didn't want me to find her, she'd have pulled her battery out."

Ash snorted. "That's some extremely dubious logic there, stalker."

Max ignored her, his gaze fixed on the caravan. "Julia's in there, isn't she?"

It wasn't a real question, so Ash didn't feel all that inclined to answer. She pulled out her cigarettes and placed a fresh one between her teeth.

Max glared at her. "Smoking again, are you?"

"It's been a stressful weekend." She lit up, her eyes on Max's car. Dean wasn't here. He'd never travel hours to see her, only to try and make her feel guilty by staying away. Her heart sank down to her gumboots.

Max took a step forward. "Ash, can you get out of the way?"

"No." She held her smoke alight, daring him to come closer.

Max pressed both palms to the back of his head and turned away from her, exhaling hard. Ash watching him closely. He was big, angry and fast enough to try to break through her human barrier.

He turned back around. "Look, I just need to talk to Julia."

"Well, that's too fucking bad, she didn't ask you to come here. This is a place we come to when we want to get *away* from our problems."

Max's nostrils flared. "This isn't like when I came to your house before. Julia's my... Well, she's *at least* my girlfriend now."

"She was my sister first."

Max moved closer still, his face taut as though he did intend to tear her away from the door by force. Ash held up her cigarette. "Take one more step, and I'll singe the fuck out of you."

"Ashley—"

"Julia doesn't want to see you, Connor. You have to respect that and not be a creepy, phone tracking piece of shit."

Max's angry-cop glare vanished, and pain swallowed up his sharp features. "She... She really doesn't want to see me?"

It was then Ash noticed how crappy Max looked. He had shadows under his eyes and patches of stubble where he'd missed bits shaving. His usually perfect hair was sticking up at the back and there was what looked like a marmalade stain on the front of his t-shirt. He'd been suffering, that much was plain, and Ash felt her resolve weaken slightly. "Connor, Jules does want to see you, but you can't just show up here out of the blue and expect it's not going to freak her out."

Max rubbed his eyes with the backs of his hands. "Okay. Okay, I get that. I just... What do I do? I can't fucking think, I can barely breathe, I'm so scared she's gonna leave me 'cos I fucked everything up and if she leaves me I won't be able to live anymore, so what the hell do I do, Ash? Go on. Tell me, because I don't fucking know."

There was a loud banging on the caravan wall.

"Jules?" She and Max asked at the same time.

"Um, yeah it's me."

Max's face went slack. "Gorgeous, please just let me talk to you. I promise we don't have to get married—"

Ash kicked him in the legs. "Shut up, Connor." She raised her voice. "What do you want, Jules? You want him to leave?"

"Um, no. Can you, maybe let him in?"

"Are you sure?" Ash asked. "You know you don't have to see him just because he's here, right?"

"I think so." Julia's voice was muffled again and Ash was sure she'd dived back under the blankets.

"So..." Max shifted from foot to foot, clearly trying to tamp down his elation. "Can I go in now?"

Ash pointed her cigarette at his face. "You'll be calm and listen to my sister when she talks to you."

"Whatever you want... I'll do whatever you want. Please just let me see Jules?"

Ash took a deep drag on her cigarette then stood up and moved away from the door. "Mess up and you're dead, copper."

Max was inside the caravan faster than any human should have been able to move.

"Julia," he said, in a voice that implied he'd just returned from a six month stint on some war-torn battlefield. "Baby, I missed you so much. Wait, you're there, right? Under the blankets?"

"Yes," came her sisters muffled reply.

Ash slapped the side of the caravan. "Oi, I'll be right out here monitoring this situation so no fucking funny business, Connor. You too, Julia."

"Okay," both of them shouted back, but she could tell they weren't paying attention.

Ash wandered around the caravan for close to an hour, trying not to listen to what Julia and Max were saying while monitoring the overall tone. It became pretty clear pretty fast they weren't fighting. Both their voices were thrumming with the low, blissed out frequency Ash knew well from the delivery room at the hospital. When new mums and dads crowded around the life they'd created, awestruck, and/or tripped out on drugs. And much like when a newborn was nestled in their parents' arms for the first time, Ash could hear a lot of crying, but that wasn't surprising either. When you were overwhelmed, what else was there to do but cry?

For the hundred thousandth time she thought about Dean accepting his Best and Fairest medal. The way he'd beamed out at her as though she was the only other person in the world and she'd wanted to cry, too, because he was so happy. Then, like a garish red FOR SALE sticker slapped on a DVD, she saw Dean naked and drunk, dry humping a Caucasian woman in a Native American headdress.

"Ashley!"

She turned to see Max coming down the caravan steps. His awkward stance and the ruffled hair said the talking part of the make-up session was over.

"What, Connor?"

Max shifted his weight awkwardly from foot to foot.

"Oh, Christ... Let me guess, you and Jules want me to take a walk?"

Max went red, opening and closing his mouth like a dying fish.

"Okay, I'm gone, but you better not make a mess, and you better fucking open a window when you're done. That's when you're DONE, not before, not during, *done*. I've already had a bad enough weekend without hearing that."

Max held up a hand. "It's not that. Well, it is that, but also, I've got something for you."

"Eww."

Max's cheeks and forehead managed to go even redder. "No, I uh... Not that I, uh..."

"What, narc? Spit it out."

The insult seemed to kick Max back into gear. "I've got a letter for you. From Dean."

Ash's insides squirmed. "Oh. Cool."

"Do you want it?"

"Yes! I mean..." she looked up at the sky. "That'd be great."

Max, obviously scared of ruining his chances of boning her sister in their caravan, didn't tease her or smirk or say anything at all. Instead, he dug in his jean pocket and held out a chunky rectangle of paper. For a moment Ash considered saying no, but then the paper was in her palm, and she was opening it. It was covered in large loopy writing and jagged on one side as though it had been torn from an exercise book. *Of course not a card huh, Red?* Ash thought. *That would require actual planning.*

"Thanks," she told Max.

"Not a problem." Max turned to leave, then faced her once again, deep furrows creasing his forehead. "I know it's none of my business, and I know what a pain in the hole Dean can be, but for what it's worth, I think you'd be good together."

Ash let out a small laugh. "You mean you think I'd be good for him? Straighten him out. Teach him how to be an adult at the age of thirty-five?"

"No. I think he'd be good for you." It was Max's turn to laugh. "I get what you're thinking, and it *would* be great for Dean to have someone as tough and loyal as you on his team. He's had a hard life. I know it doesn't seem like it, because he's such a sweet guy, but he has."

"What do you—"

"You'll have to ask him yourself," Max said bluntly. "But take it from someone who's also a little controlling and uptight, Dean has something people like us need. Something that's rare as fucking diamonds."

"What?"

"He's kind. Right to the bottom of his heart. Makes you feel better just being near him."

Ash swallowed, trying to keep down the lump in her throat. "I know he's a nice guy."

"He's the *nicest* guy," Max corrected. "I know he's not perfect, he's forgotten my birthday every single year since we were thirteen, but when my ex cheated on me and my whole life came crashing down around my ears, he sat with me every day for a fortnight. Told me everything was going to be okay, brought me food. It was mostly Kit Kats but still, he never asked for anything in return, he just wanted me to be okay."

Ash felt her eyes prickle. "That uh, sounds like Dean."

"Read his letter." Max tapped the paper in her hands. "Maybe he'll surprise you. He fucking surprises me."

"Sure."

Max began to walk away then paused, his cheeks and forehead red once more. "You know I thought about asking your permission, to uh, marry Julia. I just couldn't find the right time."

"Oh…" Ash felt both uncomfortable and weirdly flattered. "I um, don't know what I would have said."

"Right."

"But uh, I can tell you now that you guys make a pretty nice couple and uh, if you want to get married you should."

Max smiled. "Cool. Well, thanks Ash, and I guess I'll talk to you later."

"One hour, narc. That's all you get."

Max turned and headed for the caravan, shaking his head.

"And I was serious about that fucking window, Connor! Don't make me threaten to kill you again."

She didn't mind that Max flipped her off, after all, he was her future brother-in-law.

Her letter in hand, Ash walked along the river until she found a nice sitting place then settled in the shade of a willow tree, pulling out the boxy piece of paper Max had given her. Dean's writing was clumsy, the markings of someone who rarely put pen to paper after high school. Her heart in her mouth, she began to read.

Dear Ash,
The other night I told you I couldn't fix your problems. I was wrong. I can totally fix them, I promise. Look.
Problem One: you think the people I know are judging you for your past. Solution: They can go fuck themselves. You're the hottest chick in the world, of course, you hooked up with loads of people when you were younger. That's what hot people do. Anyway, you're with me now, and that's all that matters. Besides, do you know how many people came up to me after you left and said we made an awesome couple? Heaps. Maybe they were just staring and not coming over to talk to you because you're intimidating. Not in a bad way, in like a Queen Cersei way. Or maybe people were staring because you're crazy hot. Either way, it doesn't matter to me, and it shouldn't matter to you.

Ash stared up at the willow tree and smiled like a dickhead. God, she fucking liked this human. When she finally contained herself, she kept reading.

Problem Two: you got your period.
Oh, babe, I'm so sorry. I know how much you want to be pregnant and I'm not gonna lie, I wanted that, too.

Ash pressed a palm against her empty belly and felt sadness stab her like a frozen blade.

Solution: I keep fucking you until you're pregnant. I've been googling heaps of stuff about babies and the chances I'd bun your oven the first time around were pretty small. Still, from what I'm reading (I googled 'how soon can you get pregnant once you start trying') seventy out of a hundred couples

conceive within six months, so if you're still keen, we've got an excellent shot.
Problem Three: Chelsea.
She asked me out last year, and I said yes because her dad's in the club and she was nice. About fifteen minutes into our first date I wanted to run away. It was like going out with Dora the Explorer.

Ash laughed, then pressed her hand into her mouth, feeling guilty.

We were so fucking awkward together, I have no idea why she wanted to go out with me...

"Because you're gorgeous you stupid, great ginger knob."

... But the only reason we went on more than one date is that I didn't want to hurt her feelings, and I knew she was going to Japan so I thought it would be better if I just waited until she left. We never slept together, we only kissed once. If I had a choice between being her boyfriend and being the guy you called to fix your washing machine, I'd be at your house with a socket wrench every night. You're my dream girl, Ash. No one even comes close.
Solution: We forget I ever went on some dates with Chelsea and be boyfriend and girlfriend.

Ash pressed the letter to her chest, overwhelmed with stupid spiralling heart-feels. Then she yanked the paper away, embarrassed by her own soppiness.

Problem Four. The video of me snowboarding with my cock out.
I should have told you about the video, it was stupid to think no one would say anything or show it to you and it wasn't fair that your ex was the one who did it. I should have owned up when I had the chance. I was drunk and being an idiot, and someone I didn't know was filming and put it on

Facebook. I wish it hadn't happened, but it did, and there's nothing I can do about it, except say I'm sorry and I'll never do anything that dumb again. Solution: I know the video existing isn't the whole problem. I know it upset you because it's more proof that I'm not responsible. So when you get back to your grandma's house, I hope you'll find something that proves that I am responsible. Don't worry, I haven't set the place on fire or anything. I'm sure you'll like it. Maybe I shouldn't have even mentioned setting the house on fire. I'm sorry and please don't think I would do that. I told you from the start I think you and me have something special. I didn't think I would ever have someone special, Ash. I didn't grow up thinking love or marriage were something I could have. I didn't think anyone would ever be able to put up with me that long. I lived with Max, I played football, I did whatever job I did and I never made any plans because I didn't want to hope too much and end up on my own.

If I'd known you were coming, I would have lived differently. I would have made sure I had something to show for myself when you got there, but I didn't and I can't go back. All I can promise is that going forward I'll be better and I'll never stop trying to be the man you deserve. I love you, Ash, and I'll be waiting. Take all the time you need.

Dean

Ps. Sorry about my shitty handwriting.

Ash sat under the tree, reading and rereading the letter. She laughed and eventually, once she was sure no one but the magpies would see, she cried.

18

Between checking an expectant opera singer's' charts and reassuring her nervy conductor husband that she was okay, Ash consulted, for what felt like the millionth time, her fitness tracker watch. Below her heart rate (seventy-eight beats per minute, she seriously needed to get back into yoga) the little pixels said she had half an hour left on the ward.

She inhaled deeply, relieved. The overnight shift was usually more relaxed than the day, but this particular night had been full of inexplicable crazy: a newborn with a caul, an unexpected breach birth, a husband puking right on the linoleum floor. The tension in the air was palpable making patients tense and doctors snappy. The only way Ash had been able to stay sane as she rushed from crisis to crisis, had been by planning exactly what she'd do when she knocked off.

First, she'd swing by the good café and get a massive coffee and a bacon and egg roll. She'd consume them while driving home and listening to The Beauty Brains podcast. Then she'd get into the bath and stay there, reading the latest Robert Galbraith novel until every trace of this never-ending shift washed away. Then and only then would she craft the perfect text message to Dean and ask him to come over tonight. She'd make Thai green curry with coconut rice, open a thirty-dollar bottle of wine, and wait for him.

It had been five days since she'd returned from the caravan and she and Dean still hadn't met up. The afternoon she and Julia returned home, she'd gotten a call begging her to come into work. Six nurses at Southern Star had contracted mumps and Ash had been working double shifts ever since.

Then Julia and Max's engagement, which they'd been planning on keeping to themselves for a few months, had exploded into the local, then national, then international news.

Tiff, Julia's business partner, had tweeted a photo of Jules holding a Scarlet Woman action figure. A fan, spotting the enormous fuck-off emerald on her finger, correctly guessed Julia was engaged and sent the nerdverse spinning into chaos. No one was entirely sure why the news took off the way it did. Jules was a hot feminist gamer with an impressive job and Max was undeniably buff, but neither of them were celebrities. Maybe it had just been a slow news day. Either way, within eighteen hours, pictures of Jules and her narc fiancé were everywhere; Facebook, Buzzfeed, Mamamia, Instagram. Jules got requests to confirm her engagement from *Vogue, The Herald Sun* and *The Daily Mail*. Pictures of her and Max were stripped from their private social media accounts and splashed all over the Internet. And then came the trolls.

Trolls were already big anti-fans of Julia, what with her being a successful game designer who had a twat, but the engagement coverage sent them into a quivering frenzy.

Death and rape threats started rolling in and someone leaked Max's address so that hate mail arrived directly on his doorstep— decapitated dolls' heads, dead flowers and cum-stained letters accusing Julia of ruining mankind, stealing testicles, making the letter-writers wife leave him, etcetera.

Despite there being a zero percent chance any of these keyboard warriors would actually show up at the house, Max insisted Julia stay at a hotel until the heat died down. Despite Ash's requests, he and Dean refused to go anywhere.

"If any of them show up," Dean texted Ash, *"Max and I are going to give them an incredibly shit time."*

Considering his size and Max's access to firearms, that wasn't just macho posturing, but it didn't stop Ash from worrying about him. They'd texted a lot over the last few days, but not about anything serious. Both of them seemed to feel they needed a proper face-to-face chat before they made things official. Mostly they just did small talk, though Dean had texted her a few pictures that made her insides melt. He wasn't above sending her pictures of his cock now, and her life was so much better for it.

An unexpected hand descended on Ash's shoulder almost giving her a heart attack.

"Sorry, Ash!" Maggie, the student on placement, pulled away, looking guilty. "I thought you could hear me coming!"

"It's cool." Ash smoothed a hand through her ponytail and tried to steady her breathing. "I shouldn't be standing around staring into space, anyway."

Maggie beamed at her. She was a cute kid, nineteen and a little in awe of everything. "You're almost done for the morning, aren't you?"

"Yeah. I can't fucking wait."

"Do you have any plans?"

Ash's brain instantly went to Dean, his fresh pepper and clove scent, his bright brown eyes. "Um, I might be meeting up with someone. A guy."

"Oh my God! I heard you were seeing Doctor Huxley, is it him?"

Ash fought to keep herself from snorting. Huxley had been nothing but pissy toward her since she turned down his invitation to 'park her car in his building.' "No. The guy I'm seeing is a roofer."

"Wow, like one of those super-rich tradies who owns their own homes and a big car and stuff?"

"No, he's poor and he lives with his mate in Coburg."

Maggie's expression didn't dim in the slightest. "Is he hot?"

"So hot. He's tall and buff and a redhead, but not a carrot redhead, an auburn redhead."

The younger woman smiled happily. "That's so cute. Wait, does he want kids? Like right away? Are you not thinking about a donor anymore?"

Ash had forgotten her barren womb was such a hot topic around the hospital. A lie was on the tip of her tongue and then she just thought 'fuck it.' "Dean wants kids. Depending on how tonight goes, we might start trying right away."

Maggie squealed. "That's amazing! How did you know he was like, the right guy?"

Ash looked around for eavesdroppers and finding none, whispered. "I went away for a day with my sister, and when I got back, I saw he'd redone my entire front yard."

Maggie, who'd clearly been expecting something a little more Harlequin, looked confused. "You mean he, like, fixed up your garden?"

"Yeah. But you have no idea how big of a deal that is. It was a feral fucking mess. Dean put in a new fence and dug up the side-beds and hired a skip so that he could throw out all the hard rubbish. It was a massive job and he did it all by himself."

When she'd read his letter, Ash had assumed Dean had left flowers or fed her dogs or something. The reality of coming home to a picture-perfect front yard had blown her mind.

Maggie gave her a weak smile. "I um, I guess that's romantic."

"Trust me, it was. You want to see a picture of my boy?"

Maggie brightened up at once. "Oh my God, *yes!*"

"Topless or not topless?"

"Topless! Duh!"

Ash pulled out her phone and was scrolling for a shirtless but non-explicit image of Dean when a loud *beep-beep-beep* rang through the hospital's PA system. Both she and Maggie froze.

"Is that...?" Maggie asked.

Ash shushed her. The announcement came loud through the speakers. *'Attention all personnel, we have a code blue in the ER. I repeat, we have a code blue in the ER.'*

"Oh God!" Maggie danced on the spot, her purple tipped ponytail bouncing. "Is that someone with a gun? Or is that black? Should I go? I can't go. I'm not qualified! Should I go?"

"No!" Ash shoved her phone back into her pocket. "I'll head to ER. If I don't come back in ten, tell Katie and the other supervisors where I am."

"Okay! Good luck!"

Ash ran, grateful for her trainers, ungrateful for her lack of a sports bra. Emergency codes this serious were rare, and she knew that if she was the first nurse to get to the ER, she could kiss her lazy morning and rendezvous with Dean goodbye. "Let it be some idiot motorcyclist with superficial skin shit. Come on, it's only a couple of hours left until sunrise. No more weird shit universe, please?"

But as in the bathroom at Crown Casino, she had a sense that her wish was going to go unfulfilled. Sure enough, when she burst into ER, the air was swampy with panic and the tang of blood.

"Ashley!" Gerard, a thickset ER nurse, gripped her arm. "Thank God you're here, we were just about to page someone from prenatal. We've got a woman here, she's pregnant and it looks... It looks bad."

He directed her towards a gurney where a tiny Sri Lankan woman lay. Her face was drawn, her dark hair plastered to her scalp. "Mage daruvā," she moaned. "Mage daruvā."

At first, Ash stupidly thought the plum coloured stains on her sari were part of the pattern, but then she saw it was blood, so much blood it didn't seem possible the woman could still be alive. It was clear even through her flowing clothes that she was at least eight months pregnant. Ash's heart gave a sharp squeeze.

"Would you mind if I put my hands on you?" she asked the woman.

A man at her side cleared his throat. He wore a black turban and looked as terrified as a person could look without screaming. "My wife doesn't speak much English. Please examine her. Please help her."

Ash pressed along the woman's belly and found it was rock hard, a bad sign. She attempted to palpate her abdomen and the tiny woman went rigid, her small face twisting in agony. Ash stopped at once. "When did your wife start bleeding?" she asked the husband.

"Thirty minutes ago, but she was in pain yesterday. I offered to bring her in, but she said she was fine, she said she could manage..." The husband broke off with a loud racking sob.

"It's okay," Ash assured him. "I promise a lot of mothers say that."

She attempted to palpate the woman's womb again, trying to block out the screams of pain and the pounding of her own terrified heart, but it was no good.

"Please," the husband said. "Please, tell me she will be fine?"

Ash could do no such thing. She was almost sure his wife's placenta had detached from the walls of her uterus. If she was right and it was placental abruption, then she and her unborn baby were in very real danger.

Ash turned to Gerard. "She needs to deliver now. We need to get her into theatre for an emergency ceaser. Who's on staff? Are any surgeons on hand?"

"I'll check he said, moving away at once.

As Ash tried to set up a CTC to trace the baby's heartbeat, the woman let out a sharp scream. It was more fury than pain, as though she was protesting the forces who had done this to her.

The husband hovered by her side, his hands rising and falling uselessly by his sides. "Please, what's wrong with her?"

Ash placed a hand on his shoulder. "We don't know yet, but it's likely your wife is having prenatal complications. She's in a lot of pain."

"Can you give her anything? Pills? An epidural?"

"Not at this point, not without knowing what's happening to the baby."

The woman let out another sharp scream. Ash ghosted a hand over the woman's arm. "I know this sucks but stay strong and try to stay conscious. A surgeon is coming, I promise."

The woman couldn't have possibly understood her but she gave Ash a sharp nod, her dark eyes glittering with an almost violent determination. Ash's heart pulsed again like someone had reached inside her chest and crushed the organ like a sponge.

"What's your wife's name?" she asked the husband.

"Shashi. I'm Kusal. Please tell me she will be fine?"

Ash ignored his question. "What is Shashi's EDD?"

"I-I... Pardon?"

"Sorry, when is your wife's estimated due date? When is the baby meant to come?"

"Three... Three weeks from now," Kusal said. "It's a little girl. We're going to call her Elizabeth. Shashi, she picked the name. She loves Elizabeth Taylor."

Please shut up, Ash thought, *please don't tell me things I won't be able to forget.* "How old is your wife?"

"Twenty-nine, she will be thirty in July."

Ash's heart clenched harder than ever. She and Shashi were the same age, their birthday was in the same month. "Is this her first child?"

"Yes." Kusal's face contorted in pain. "I went to work yesterday even though she was cramping, I should have brought her in, I should have known she was lying about how much it hurt. She's so strong, she's always so strong... So fierce. I know she doesn't look it, but she's my rock, my everything..."

Ash could hear the panic rising in the man's voice, knew he was seconds away from a breakdown. "Please, Kusal, sit down. Hold your wife's hand. You need to be strong for her and your baby."

Kusal obliged as Ash busied herself with the heart rate chart, trying not to think about everything she knew about placental abruption—clotting, haemorrhaging, organ damage, twelve percent foetal mortality rate...

A scorching hot hand closed over her own. Shashi's skin was rose-petal soft, but Ash barely had time to register it before the woman squeezed so hard her joints cracked.

"Mage daruvā bērā ganna," Shashi said and this time it was Ash who knew exactly what she meant "*Save my baby. I don't care if I die, save my baby.*"

Kusal began to protest, no doubt telling his wife in their language that she and the baby would be fine, but Shashi continued to stare at Ash, as though begging her to understand, and she did. For some fucked up, insanely unfair reason, Shashi's body had failed and death was coming, death with all its endless questions and complete lack of answers, but the woman in front of her wasn't afraid. All she wanted was for Elizabeth to survive.

"I know," Ash told her. "I know you want us to make your baby the priority. I promise I'll tell the doctors."

Shashi nodded and relaxed slightly into her gurney.

"No!" Kusal was weeping openly now. "No, she doesn't know what she's saying. Save her then save the baby. Or just save her. I need her! I need her! I can't live without her! Shashi, listen to me..." he began speaking to her rapidly in the fluid language they shared.

Snapping leather footsteps announced the arrival of a surgeon and because Murphy's Law was Murphy's Law it was Doctor Nathanial Huxley II. A thirty-second examination and he was demanding Gerard wheel Shashi to the theatre.

"Ash," Nate said as he strode out of the room. "You're assisting. Come on."

Ash hurried in his wake, dizzy with dread.

"It's my second last day," Nate said as she fell into step beside him. "Great going away present, isn't it?"

Gerard made sympathetic noises but Ash refused. Kusal's cries were ringing in her ears. One moment he and his wife were poised on the edge of parenthood, now death was rising up in front of them like a tsunami, arching over their heads in a wet invincible wall.

"We'll have to calm the husband down," Nate said. "He's next of kin and judging from the bleeding, we'll have to make a call between mother and child."

"The mother's already said she wants us to save the baby," Ash said.

Nate smirked. "You speak Sinhala, do you?"

"The husband confirmed it. Get a translator in if you have to. That's what she wants."

"Fine," Nate said coolly as they approached the door to the theatre. "We'll try and calm the husband down, anyway. Make sure you scrub in properly."

Ash barely heard him. From her place on the gurney, Shashi had met her gaze once more. She was pale and seemed to have shrunk since Ash had first seen her, but her eyes were still hot with purpose. "Elizabeth," she said.

Though Ash was sure she could feel no more than she already did, her heart gave an almighty wrench. "I know. I promise we'll save Elizabeth."

Shashi smiled. "Elizabeth," she agreed, then fainted.

19

The staff kitchen was full of familiar sounds. Rubber shoes squeaking down the hall, laughing visitors trying to get the shitty TVs to work, lost people harassing less-lost people for directions.

Sexy doctor shows talked about hospitals in a lot of fancy ways. They used flowery metaphors and compared the buildings to wheels of life and death, but that had never been Ash's experience. There *was* life and death in a hospital, but it was more often drudgery, paperwork, and routine. It was old people with the flu, jocks with toe infections, kids who swallowed weird shit, and couples who refused to go to the breastfeeding short course. Ash had been a nurse for years, but she'd only ever assisted in delivering a stillborn, and she'd never seen a mother die. Until today. Today she had seen death with her own eyes; she had helped Nate pull a healthy pink and brown baby from a corpse.

When she closed her eyes, Ash could still picture little Elizabeth screaming, screaming with that half triumphant, half incredibly pissed-off tone of the newborn. Everyone in the theatre had sighed to see such a beautiful, healthy baby but all Ash could see was Shashi lying on the table. No one had yet called the time of death, but her skin was brown and blue and her eyes were blank as a horrible doll's. As Elizabeth wailed louder, Ash willed Shashi to wake up, to hear her daughter's cry and come back to the world where she was so desperately needed. But she just stayed horribly, painfully dead.

A nurse had taken Elizabeth into her arms, rocking her the way Ash had seen a hundred mothers rock their babies, crooning, "It's okay, little girl your daddy will be here soon."

But her mother, the woman who had housed her for eight months then given her life to save her, would never be there. Elizabeth would never know her.

Ash stared down at the kitchen table. She wanted to cry, but it hurt too much. It was too real and fresh. She wanted to talk to someone, but she didn't have the words to explain any of it. To do it justice. So she was sitting in the staff kitchen eating salt and vinegar chips and drinking Diet Vanilla Coke. Alone, alone, alone.

"There you are," said a familiar voice. "I was looking for you."

Ash turned and saw Nate. He'd changed into a new shirt and his hair was perfectly mussed in that surfer boy way that made him look a decade younger than he was. "Hi Nate, how's it going?"

"Good." Nate sat down across from her. "First death up close?"

"Pretty much."

"Ah well, the first one's always the hardest."

Ash had heard that bullshit before, but right now it meant even less than it usually did. "Sure."

"I know you don't believe me, but it does get easier. First time I saw a man die, a cement truck had rolled over him. It was ten times more gruesome than what we had today and I was shook up at the time, but two weeks later they brought in a motorcyclist with half his back flayed off and I didn't flinch."

Because I'm a big-shot fucking doctor, in case you didn't know, Ash thought. "Yeah, sure."

"Thinking about what you could have done differently?" Nate asked, with something bordering on actual empathy.

Ash shook her head. "I just can't believe it's over. I knew it was bad when I felt her stomach, but a part of me didn't think she could actually die."

Nate helped himself to some of her chips. "Happens every day."

"I've helped hundreds of women give birth," Ash couldn't help but shoot back. "I've never seen one die before."

"Well, they do. You've just been lucky."

Ash felt her temper flare. She knew she was being an idiot, that some doctors just couldn't help acting like they were the unequivocal masters of death, but she couldn't stop talking. "It just doesn't seem right. Shashi was so healthy, her bloodwork was perfect. She was young, fit and strong right up until she…"

Ash pictured the body lying, stiff and alone on the operating table. "I-I just don't *understand*."

"Hate to say it, Ash, but that's life. None of us know what's going to happen in the end."

Suddenly Ash found that she hated Nate. Hated his stupid eye wrinkles. Hated his perfect hair. Hated his smug, plummy, rich boy voice. "I know that. I'm just saying it sucks."

"At least she got what she wanted. The kid survived."

Yeah, Shashi got what she wanted. She died before she ever saw her baby's face. What a happy fucking ending.

Ash took a big swallow of Diet Vanilla Coke, willing it to scald her insides so she could feel something that wasn't misery and rage. She wanted to go and pay her respects to Kusal, to see Elizabeth again, but she didn't think she should. The other nurses said the family of two was holed up in a maternity room with Kusal and Shashi's relatives and she was sure he wouldn't appreciate some random nurse stopping by to say she had felt a genuine connection with his dying wife.

I did, though, Ash thought fiercely. *I did feel connected to her. We understood each other, and now she's gone.*

Her breath caught in her throat, harsh as a ball of sandpaper.

"Hey." Nate patted her hand. "Are you okay?"

Ash pulled away from him. "No! I am not okay! I'm fucked up and confused and pissed off and sad. What about you, Nate? You watched a woman die today, too. You saw her baby screaming for a mum who will never, *ever* come for her. Are *you* okay?"

For a moment Nathanial Huxley II's handsome face seemed to crack. He suddenly looked as lost as a little boy, tired and heartbreakingly vulnerable. Then he blinked and the Master of Death mask fell firmly back in place. "Yes, I'm fine. It's always a little jarring when someone dies, but like I said, you can't always predict the outcome in those situations, although you can…"

Ash zoned out. It was either that or punch him in the groin.

She listened without hearing as Nate droned on about best practices and maternal mortality and the importance of early intervention. Then something strange happened—she started to hear the tremor in his voice, see the pallor in his cheeks, the way he kept shoving chips in his mouth, barely chewing before he swallowed and crammed more in.

He *was* upset about Shashi. But instead of admitting it, he'd chosen to come here and give her the big *'that's life, sweet-cheeks'* spiel. They could have been comforting each other, bonding over their shared pain, but instead, he was sitting in front of her pretending nothing was wrong and that she was irrational for being upset.

And as he talked, without so much as taking a breath, Ash imagined they'd had a baby together, a son called Nathaniel Huxley, like his father and his grandfather. What would Nate Huxley III have grown up thinking about disappointment, guilt, and sadness? What would his father have told him if he was crying? Ash guessed he'd offer his son an ice cream or a trip to the park. "Chin up, mate! It'll all be okay! Big boys don't cry! Not even when it hurts!"

She thought of Dean, tearing up as he got his Best and Fairest award. The way he was never embarrassed to say exactly how he felt, to show his fear and excitement. She imagined Dean pulling their crying son into his lap and holding him, perhaps even crying himself if there was nothing else he could do. He was a man who was as soft inside as he was big outside, who was gentle even when it was to his detriment. Who had never lost that boyish way of letting every emotion radiate out of him, as though he had nothing to hide. Ash stood, cutting Nate off mid-sentence. "I'm sorry, but I have to go."

"Where?"

Ash gathered up her phone, Diet Coke, and handbag. "I need to see someone. Thanks for checking on me, and if I don't work with you before you leave for the Royal Melbourne, good luck."

"Sure." Nate stood up. "You know I'm sorry we never worked out the whole baby thing. I, uh, thought you understood where I was coming from."

"I do," Ash agreed. "Take care, Nate, I hope you find someone you can be a father with."

"Sure." Nate shoved his hands back in his pockets. "Goodbye."

As soon as she was in the hospital car park, she called Dean. He didn't pick up right away, and with every flat 'brrr' of the dial tone, Ash grew more convinced he'd changed his mind, met someone else, decided she was too much work. Finally, the line went silent and then, "Hey beautiful girl, what's going on?"

How someone managed to inject so much love into one sentence, Ash had no idea. She began to cry, not silent tears but big ugly sobs, like when you were a kid and you didn't know you could feel so much pain. "Dean." Her voice was pitiful even to her own ears. "*Dean.*"

"Ash, sweetheart, what's wrong?"

"I lost a patient," she sobbed. "A mother. She died giving birth. I wanted to help her but I couldn't, and now her baby's going to grow up without a mum and I don't know what to do."

"Are you at the hospital?" Dean asked, his voice low and calm.

"Yes. In the car park."

"Stay right where you are. I'm coming to get you. I'm leaving right now. Don't go anywhere."

So she didn't. She waited for him near the hospital entrance, her hands fisting the sleeves of her flannel shirt so it looked like she didn't have hands. When she saw Dean's car pull into the parking lot, she grew almost frantically needy for his touch. Dean parked so fast it seemed it had barely stopped before he was there, hugging her. Ash felt like a magnet, snapping together with its opposite. Click, and they were together, warm and safe and whole.

"I'm so sorry," she said into his shirt.

Dean smoothed a palm over her head. "You have nothing to be sorry for."

"I think I love you, Red. I'm sorry I waited so long to see it."

"You waited as long as you needed to." Dean's breath was warm and sweet in her ear. "I love you too, Ash."

They got into the back seat of his car, and Dean held her as she cried and cried and cried, not caring how ugly she looked, or how terrible she sounded or what anyone who saw them thought. She told him about Shashi, and Elizabeth the baby, and Kusal and Nate telling her it was all part of life, and Dean listened and held her and kissed her cheeks and forehead. When she was done, when she knew she couldn't possibly say anymore, she asked him if he could take her somewhere nice. Somewhere where people were happy.

Dean didn't even hesitate. "Of course. I'm gonna take you to my favourite place in the world."

Ash went to say something light-hearted, but as she opened her mouth, thoughts of the hospital, the baby, the world, and all her worries rose up inside her again. "Dean, before you do that, can you tell me that everything's going to be okay?"

He kissed her forehead lightly. "Everything *is* okay, Ash. I promise."

20

School kids tore through the dinosaur exhibit like a living wave of red, white, and grey. They couldn't have been older than eight or nine, talking non-stop and clearly pumped to be out of their classrooms for a day. It amazed Dean how different they were—grubby kids with chocolate on their hands, clean kids whose trainers matched their backpacks. Skinny kids whose legs were so twiggy they looked like they shouldn't have been able to support their weight and fat kids with round red cheeks. As the kids ran around the exhibition, one thing he noticed was the same: they all looked up at the model dinosaurs with delight bordering on hysteria.

"They're so happy to be here," Ash whispered. She seemed steadier than she was in the hospital car park, but her eyes were still red-rimmed and she hadn't touched her iced coffee.

Dean took her hand. "All kids love dinosaurs. They're so huge, like monsters or aliens."

"The last time I came to the Melbourne Museum, I was their age. I don't even remember the dinosaurs. All I remember is being jealous because my friend Ruby's mum got to be a parent helper. That and the butterfly display."

"You liked butterflies?"

The corners of Ash's mouth quirked. "I was a little girl, Red. Of course I liked butterflies."

"Well, they're still here, would you like to go see them?"

"Not yet." Ash looked up at the huge model T-Rex. "So this is your favourite place in the world, huh?"

Dean nodded. "I used to ask my mum to bring me here like, every weekend. In a good year I'd come at least once a month."

"What about now you have a car? Are you here every day?"

He grinned. "Only if I can get someone to go with me. I worry that I look like a bit of a pedo if I go on my own."

Ash giggled. Only a little bit, but it seemed to Dean that it was a start. They sat and watched the kids for a while, screaming and chatting and touching things they weren't meant to touch and pretending to be dinosaurs.

"What kind of kid were you?" Ash moved her palm in an arc across the room. "Out of all of them, who were you like?"

Dean already knew. He'd spotted the kid as soon as he wandered in, but he decided to make it a bit of a game. "Guess?"

"Okay, but you have to guess for me first."

"Easy." He pointed out a Pakistani girl herding her friends from display to display like a sheepdog. "Her."

Ash started to laugh. "You're right. I was such a little dictator."

"I was thinking more a natural leader," Dean protested. "Plus she's really cute! Look at her little tiger hair-clip!"

"You're sweet, but trust me, Red, I was a nightmare. I was so used to looking after Julia, I couldn't help trying to browbeat everyone else into doing what I wanted as well."

Dean squeezed her hand. "I'm sure you were a great kid."

"Maybe when I was asleep. What about the boy over there, is that you?"

Dean followed her pointed finger to a mischievous-looking Asian kid who, along with his mates, was trying to climb one of the glass panels separating man from fake brontosaurus bones. "Not a chance."

"Oh, but he's all big and silly! Who then?"

Dean rubbed the back of his neck, feeling slightly nauseous.

"You don't have to," Ash said at once. "Don't worry about it, Red."

Dean was instantly ashamed. Less than an hour ago Ash had been spilling her heart to him and he couldn't point out a kid who looked like the kid he'd once been? He took a deep breath and pointed at the boy standing under the pterodactyl. He was short with curly blond hair, a bit grubby and overweight in the way kids who get fed from cardboard boxes instead of plates were overweight. He was staring, open-mouthed, up at the pterodactyl, oblivious to everything around him.

"I-I didn't even see him," Ash whispered. "You were like that?"

"Oh yeah. One hundred percent. I was tiny and chunky. Kids used to call me 'pink marshmallow.' You know, because of my hair?"

"Kids are the worst." Ash scanned him up and down. "You can't be serious, though! You're so tall and jacked!"

"This was before football. When all I used to like doing was drawing pictures of horses and eating Rainbow Paddle Pops. I was the chubbiest little ginger you ever saw."

"I bet you were so fucking cute, Red."

The look of almost furious adoration on Ash's face made him smile. "I don't know about that, but I wasn't little forever. I hit a massive growth spurt when I was fourteen. It was just a shame it didn't make a difference."

Ash frowned. "Didn't make a difference to what?"

Shit. Dean looked away. "Hey, they've busted our friend."

A teacher had come along and grabbed the little blond boy by the arm. "There you are, Gavin! I thought we'd lost you."

"I'm fine!" The boy had a high, whistling voice. "Miss Mahony, can we take a picture of the flying dinosaur? It's my favourite. If we take a picture, then I can show my dad. Then it'll be like he came with me!"

But the teacher either didn't hear or ignored him. She looked around for the rest of the group and steered Gavin toward them. "Come on mate, you need to keep up. You don't want to get lost, do you?"

"He does." Tears were welling up in Ash's eyes again. "He wants to get lost and stay here forever."

Dean wrapped his arm around her. "Babe, are you okay?"

"Yeah, just… Why was it too late by the time you were big?"

Dean felt his body spike with adrenaline. "I, um, it's not a nice story, and after the day you've had—"

"I want to know," Ash interrupted. "If you want to tell me, I want to know."

"Okay, but you need to move closer to me first."

Ash snuggled into his side, her face pressed against his chest. "Like this?"

Dean, in spite of his nerves, felt a little better. "Yeah, that'll do it."

"Whenever you're ready. I promise."

Dean inhaled, trying to fill his shrivelled lungs. "My dad didn't like me very much when I was a kid."

He noticed his voice was weirdly steady, as though this was a practiced speech. He swallowed a couple of times, trying to calm down and Ashley waited, her body still pressed against his.

Dean kissed the top of her head, drawing strength from the smell of her fruity shampoo. "I just wasn't what my dad wanted. He's a man's man, you know? He used to be a great football player, he runs a chain of auto-shops, and I was his firstborn and I was a fat little redhead who liked horses and couldn't remember shit and cried all the time. I… Embarrassed him."

Ash lifted her face from his chest. "What did you cry about?"

"Movies. Stuff I didn't understand. When I found out what dying was, that freaked me out."

Ash's arms squeezed him tight. "Death is a pretty scary thing, Red."

"I know, but you couldn't tell my dad that. He thought I was, and I'm quoting here, 'a little poofter.' I used to hear him and Mum arguing about it. He thought it was her fault. My uncle, the one who runs the riding ranch is gay, and he's, uh, he's a redhead, too. Dad thought I got it from her side of the family."

"Yeah, because gayness is *soo* genetic. And so related to having red hair."

The venom in Ash's voice made him smile. "It's fine. It was only bad until I started football."

"Football?"

"Yeah, my old man dragged me to the under twelves one weekend because he was so pissed at me for playing mums and dads with girls at school. I thought I'd hate it, but I was a natural."

"And things were better after that, right?"

Dean didn't have the heart to lie, but he couldn't bring himself to tell the truth. "They didn't get worse."

"Oh." Ash's face fell. "You said it was too late by the time you got big, didn't you? Too late for what?"

"Too late for me to forget…" Dean cleared his throat, unable to get the fucking words out. But he didn't need to because Ash said, "He hit you, didn't he? Your dad? Until you got big enough to stop him?"

"Not when I was really little."

Dean winced, amazed how even after all this time, the excuses came so easily. "Yeah, he hit me. Not all the time, but enough that I had to lie about it."

"And your mum?"

"She knew. She never stopped him. I think a part of her hoped it'd straighten me out. Make me grow up." Dean bowed his head, glad it was so noisy, glad none of the visitors were looking at him. Ash pressed herself so close to him he could feel her breathe. So close it hurt a little. "I'm so sorry, Red."

"It's okay." Dean ducked his head, pressing his jaw along her hair. "I had Max and his family. And I got away when I was eighteen. I think I'm pretty intact."

"You're better than intact, you're perfect." Ash looked up at him. "Not like, 'you never do anything wrong' perfect, but you're like, the most kind human I know. I'm so glad your parents didn't ruin that about you."

The back of Dean's neck grew hot. "Thanks."

"Is that why you don't have any pictures of your family in your room? I noticed when I was in there for... You know."

"When you snuck into my bed to seduce me?"

Ash laughed. "I snuck in there to smell your pillow and touch all your things. I didn't know you'd be home, remember?"

"You tell it your way, I'll tell it mine. And you're right. I, um, didn't plan on telling you this until later on, but I don't see them. My family that is. My dad is still a huge jerk, my brother and I never got along, and my mum only calls when she needs money or a favour."

"That sucks."

"I know, but trust me when I say I'm used to it and that I'm done trying to make them like me by bailing them out of whatever shit they get into."

A week ago his mother had called to tell him she'd left rehab prematurely and needed two thousand bucks to go to Perth. Dean had refused, telling her he was trying to save for a deposit on a house. She'd screamed and cried and said he was just like his dad, then hung up. He hadn't heard from her since. He didn't want to hear from her. That was his past, Ashley and everything they would have together was his future.

Ash kissed his chest. "I'm sorry that your parents are shit, Red."

"It's okay. I don't mind anymore. I promise."

"Glad to hear it." Ash was smiling, but Dean could tell she had something on her mind. "What are you thinking?"

"That I just don't understand," she said quietly. "My parents and your parents were such buttholes but they got to have kids and live long enough to ruin their lives. Shashi wanted a baby so badly, I could tell, and she died before she ever got to meet her. It just doesn't make any sense."

"I know it doesn't, gorgeous." Dean hugged her close. "You know why this is my favourite place in the world?"

"Why?"

"Because sometimes life seems fast and hard and shitty and like nothing ever changes, but then you come here, and you see all these beautiful, amazing things, and you realise how big and old the world is." He gestured up at the T-Rex. "I don't mean to talk down to you or say you shouldn't be sad, but there used to be monsters all over the earth, *real monsters,* and now you and I can walk in a big air conditioned room and look at statues of them. I know that doesn't sound like much, but when I was a kid and I was hurting all over, it always made me feel better."

Ash smiled up at him. "You know you're kinda smart, Red."

"A stopped clock is right twice a day."

"That's not what I meant."

"I know." Dean kissed her forehead. "You make me feel the same way as museums."

"Better?"

"Better and happy."

"So being with me *in* a museum must be something, huh?"

"It's pretty great."

"Then what if I tell you that you're my official, one and only boyfriend?"

Dean started to laugh. "Then I'd say thank you, and uh, I'm happy to be here, and you won't regret this."

She smiled wide. "Glad to hear it."

Dean tapped Ash's upper lip with his thumb. "I like when you can see the gap between your teeth."

Ash's smile dimmed. "I hate it. I always wanted to get them fixed but we couldn't afford braces when I was a kid."

"I'm glad." Dean bent down and pecked her on the mouth. "And don't say you hate stuff about yourself that I love, Nurse Ashley."

"Don't tell me what to do, pink marshmallow." Ash grabbed the back of his shirt and kissed him. Dean spent one second worrying about the few kids still milling around, then figured there was no tongue, so it was fine. And it was, it was perfect.

"You know what I think is funny?" Ash said when they broke apart.

"What?"

"The idea of you playing mums and dads at school."

Dean felt himself blush. "Don't tell Julia."

"I can't promise that. Did you practice kissing? Is that why you're so good at it?"

Dean pointed to one of the remaining teachers, an exhausted looking woman in her fifties. "See her? I'm going to tell on you if you're not careful."

"Do it, you big pussy."

Dean cupped his hands around his mouth. "Excuse me, miss, this blonde girl is bullying me—"

Ash shoved him in the chest. "Okay, we're leaving, before you get us both in trouble."

"And where are we going?" Dean asked innocently.

"To the butterfly section. Then to my place for dinner and you know..." Ash looked around, presumably for stray kids. "Sex stuff."

Dean grinned. "I'm at your service."

"I know. Let's go, big guy."

He and Ash were walking hand-in-hand to the butterfly section when Dean had a thought. "I know you've had a big day, so I just want you to know that there's no pressure on the whole baby thing. I've bought so many condoms. They're in my car, my bed, my football bag, the bathroom, the garage, although I don't know why we'd ever have sex in the garage but still, easy access—"

Ash pressed a finger to his mouth. "That's enough rambling, ginger."

Dean bit her gently, worrying the digit between his teeth like a puppy and Ash laughed. "Do you want the good news or not?"

"I do."

Ash's smile was as wicked as an evil queens. "Unless you've changed your mind about becoming a daddy, Red, you're not wearing a condom inside me ever again."

Jesus Christ, Dean thought. *The Melbourne Museum really is the best place in the world.*

EPILOGUE

"You guys aren't going to be canoodling all through the ceremony, are you?" Julia asked as Ash applied pearly green-grey shadow to her eyelid. "It's gross and it bums single people out."

Ash put down her brush. "Dean and I don't *canoodle*."

"You do! You're always rubbing your hands over him like he's a Golden Retriever and he's always kissing your nose and cheeks like you're some kind of..." Julia rolled her eyes back, clearly struggling to find an appropriately cutesy-gross thing to compare them to. "I don't know, but it's fuckin' uncivilised."

"Well, we're in love, so get over it," Ash picked up her eyeliner pen. "Stop talking, or you'll wind up with a black eye."

Julia ignored her request on both fronts. "You and Dean have been in love for ages. I don't see why you're still all over each other."

"We're not!"

Tiff, who was curling her electric blue hair on the other side of the room, laughed. "I kind of agree. There is a lot of heavy petting happening. '*Snuzzling*' I think the kids are calling it these days."

Ash glared at Julia's business partner. "We're. In. Love."

"And I get that!" Tiff held up her heavily tattooed arms. "But since you guys live together now, I think Jules expected the PDA would calm down a bit."

"It's nice to have our own house," Ash said, tracing a thick black line onto Julia's right eyelid. "But that doesn't mean me and Dean have to act like business partners in public."

"I don't think anyone would confuse you for business partners," Julia grumbled. "Unless your business was humping each other with your eyes."

"Maybe it is."

Tiff giggled. "I do think it's nice you're still so hot for each other despite your, erm, condition."

"Thanks. I swear my pussy is way more sensitive—"

Julia made a loud gagging noise. "Please don't make me spew on myself on my wedding day."

Ash tugged the end of her sister's French braid. "I won't if you hurry up and do your hair. You're due to walk down the aisle in…" She checked her fitness watch. "Jesus, two hours!"

Julia yawned. "Relax. This is the beauty of getting ready in the attic above where your ceremony's being held. We've got heaps of time."

"Max's sisters will be here soon, and you're still wearing a Xena dressing gown."

"Oh yeah." Julia sat bolt upright. "Let's get cracking."

None of them talked for the next thirty minutes as Tiff and Ash curled Julia's hair and helped her into her white silk and lace jumpsuit.

"You look beautiful," Ash said, fighting back tears.

"Weird but sexy," Tiff agreed. "It's very you."

"Thanks," Julia turned around to admire her butt. "Can you tell I'm not wearing underwear?"

"Yes."

"Great. I intend to be mega laid tonight. This jumpsuit will be destroyed."

Ash groaned. "Now who's being gross?"

"It's my wedding. I'm allowed. Oh, by the way, have the pinball machines arrived yet?"

Ash rolled her eyes. "Yes, and the PlayStation. Though why you'd want people playing *Legends of Zelda* at your wedding, I have no idea."

"Trust me, it'll be fun."

Her sister and Max had decided to go against a lot of wedding conventions. This was partly because Max hadn't wanted a repeat of the wedding that came before he met the love of his life, but mostly because Julia was a freaky nerd and Max would do anything short of committing murder to make her happy. The wedding entrée was toasted cheese sandwiches, the official drink was black cherry sangria, and the ceremony and reception were being held in an old bowling alley in Brunswick. Even without Mason jars, it was set to be the most hipster thing in existence. Not that Julia wasn't aware of that. While they were inspecting the bowling alley, Ash had pointed out it was as hipster as a building could be without actually being made of beards.

"If being a hipster means I have a wedding I like, then fine, I'm a fucking hipster." Julia pounded a fist into her chest. "Hipster! Hipster! Hipster!"

After that, Ash stopped mentioning the twee factor of the corkboard photo collages and the chalkboard signs and let Julia do whatever she wanted. Having a wedding in a bowling alley wasn't as low budget as Ash and Jules had hoped, but last year they had finally, miraculously sold their grandma's house. Most of the credit went to Dean, who'd put hours of labour into making it look nice and not somewhere a kangaroo had once used as a toilet. They hadn't made heaps off the sale but enough to fund part of Julia's wedding and honeymoon to Japan and enough for Ash to put a deposit on a three-bedroom house in Reservoir, just fifteen minutes away from Max and Jules.

"Where are the boys?" Tiff asked as she examined her eyelashes in a compact. "You'd think they'd want to get ready here, too."

"The groom can't see the Jules before the wedding," Ash said firmly. "They're getting ready at my place. Although they're not 'getting ready' so much as 'chucking on suits then drinking an entire bottle of whiskey.'"

Jules fiddled with her fringe in the mirror. "Hey, you know Max. He's going to take longer to get ready than me, guaranteed. What we need to worry about is Dean losing the rings."

Ash smiled at her sister. "No need to worry about that."

"But—"

"But nothing. I sewed them to his jacket and told all the other groomsmen where they are, and he's been texting me pictures of them every fifteen minutes for the last five hours."

"Wow." Tiff's eyebrows vanished into her blue hair. "You really get him, don't you?"

Ash thought of all the hours Dean had spent holding her, stroking her hair and skin, and promising that everything was okay. "We kind of get each other."

There were a series of loud, echoing steps as Max's sisters ascended the stairs waving bottles of champagne and Chambord. Over the next hour she, Julia, Tiff, and the Connors drank, listened to music, took selfies, and laughed themselves stupid. When there were only fifteen minutes until the wedding, Raff and Lisa began assuring a nervous Julia that she was the perfect woman for their brother. "And we would know," Raff said. "We watched the idiot do all of this before. Trust me, you're the right one."

Julia burst into grateful tears and Ash had to chivvy Max's siblings away before they ruined her sister's eyeliner. She, Tiff, and Jules waited nervously in the attic until they heard Lior begin to play and knew it was time for them to descend. Tiff went first, walking slowly and steadily down the stairs, her bouquet of daisies clutched to her chest.

"Ash," Julia whispered. "Holy shit." She was shaking violently from top to toe.

"Are you okay? You're not like, having second thoughts, are you?"

"No." Julia's eyes glowed as bright as the emerald on her finger. "It's just... This is happening. Like, I thought it was just some ordinary day in a bowling alley, but I'm going to be *married*. I'm going to be Max's wife."

"Yes, you are."

Julia blew out a nervous breath. "Shit, well, I'm glad you're here for this. Both of you."

"Trust me, so are we."

The second chorus to *This Old Love* started playing and Ash felt all the butterflies in her stomach take off. "That's our cue. Shall we go?"

Julia flashed her a terrified smile. "What if I fall down the stairs and die?"

"You won't."

"But what if I do?"

Ash grabbed her sister's hand and pressed it to her belly, where deep inside her another Bennett girl was growing. "Feel that?"

"Oh my God. She's so *alive*. And kicky."

"She is, and she thinks you should stop being such a Max Connor and make your move already because her mum spent the last six months helping this event take place, and she's incredibly hot and sweaty."

Julia's eyes filled with more tears. "Oh, Ash... I can't believe all of this."

"No crying! I fucking mean it!"

"Okay." Julia tilted her head back as though trying to get the liquid to return to her eyes. "Let's fucking do this. Me, you, and future Elizabeth."

They'd taken a few steps when Jules began to giggle. "I still can't believe you're going with Elizabeth."

Ash scowled. "You know why we chose that name! And it's a great name!"

"I'm not saying it's not a great name, I'm just saying people, are going to lol."

"They can lol all they fucking want," Ash snapped. "Elizabeth Bennett is going to be too amazing to give a single fuck."

She rubbed her belly. "Isn't that right, Libby? You're not going to give a fuck. Are you?"

Julia snorted. "You're not trying to shed our bogan image anymore, are you?"

"Nah." Ash squeezed her sister's arm. "Now, let's go get you married, scrag."

Together they walked toward the stairs, perfectly in time with the music.

As they descended into the bowling alley turned chapel, Ash knew she should have been looking at Max. He was the star of the show, all handsome and eager in his suit. But her attention was entirely on the man beside him. The man whose hair gleamed like fire and whose eyes, as he stared at her, were already wet with tears. When their gaze met he opened his jacket slightly, revealing the silver wedding bands.

"Nice work!" Ash mouthed.

He gave her a thumbs up.

As it turned out, fairy-tale fantasies weren't real, but love, actual and real love was. Even for skanky ex-models from terrible country towns. Turned out if you were smart enough to set aside your dumb expectations about what a boyfriend should be, you could find something even better than what you thought you wanted. One day when Libby was old enough to be a flower girl, she and Dean would get married. They talked about it all the time. It turned out they did ceremonies at the Melbourne Museum, and Ash couldn't think of anything better than marrying Dean among the dinosaurs.

When they reached the balloon arch where her sister would be married, Ash kissed Jules on the cheek and stepped aside, taking her place on Tiff's right-hand side. She was crying a little bit, but not enough to fuck up her eyeliner. She wasn't an idiot. As Max and Julia gave each other giddy, breathless smiles and the celebrant began reciting the vows, Dean's gaze found hers again.

"Love you," he mouthed, then he looked pointedly down at her stomach. "Love you, too."

And Ash pressed her hand to the place where their daughter lived. "There's your daddy," she whispered to the girl dreaming inside her womb. "There he is."

The End

ACKNOWLEDGMENTS

Thank you to Julia Ferguson who gave me midwifery tips. Any errors in hospital or nursing procedure are entirely down to me being a noob who was too distracted by chocolate coffee to take notes good. Thank you to Ansley for editing the first round of this book and Kole who took over the second. Both of you were so reassuring and kind. Also, Kole was the first person to identify Dean as 'ditzy' which I love because he so fucking is. Thank you's as always to Claire and Peasy who stand by my side as sentries of love and support no matter what batshit thing I do. Extra special thanks go to my boy who first taught me love doesn't always look the way you thought it would, and whose silly moments I stole and gave to Dean. I know you know sugar comes from sugar cane now. I love you, please don't throw my phone in the toilet.

ABOUT THE AUTHOR

Eve Dangerfield's novels have been described as 'genre-defying,' 'insanely hot' and 'the defibrillator contemporary romance needs right now' and not just by those who might need bone marrow one day... OTHER PEOPLE! She lives in Melbourne with her beautiful family and can generally be found making a mess.

ALSO BY EVE DANGERFIELD

The Daddy Dearest series

Act Your Age

Not Your Shoe Size

The Playing For Love series

Begin Again Again

Return All

First and Forever

Back Into It

The Silver Daughters Ink Series

So Wild

So Steady

So Hectic

The Snow White Series

Velvet Cruelty

Silk Malice

Lace Vengeance

Bound to Sin (3x1)

The Beyond Bondage Series

Degrees of Control

James and the Giant Dilemma

Taunt (A Why Choose Romance)

Captivated (with NYT Bestseller Tessa Bailey)

The Bennett Sisters series

Locked Box

Open Hearts

Paying For It

Baby Talk

The She's on Top Series

Something Borrowed

Something Else

Dysfunctional

Sweeter

Printed in Great Britain
by Amazon